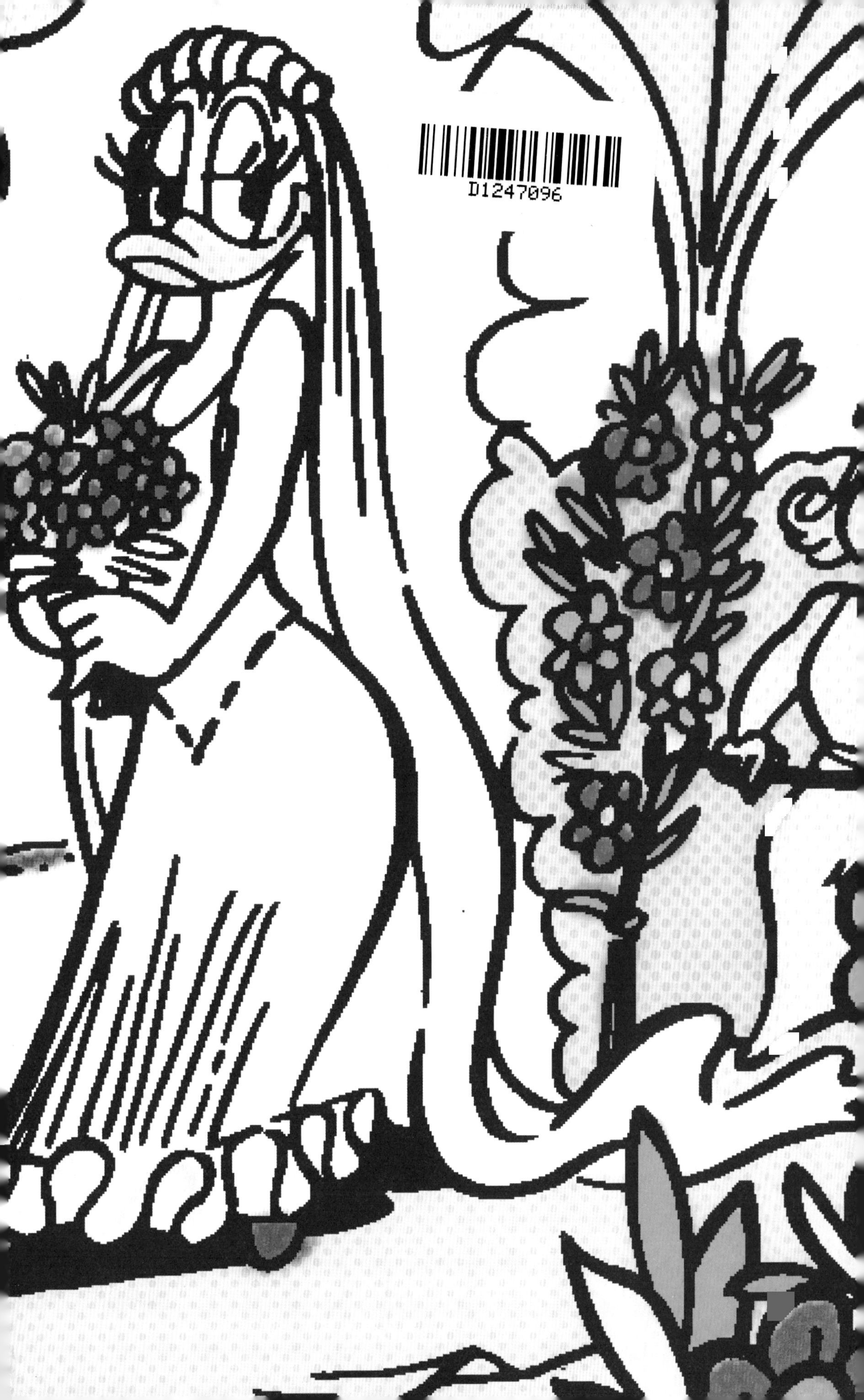

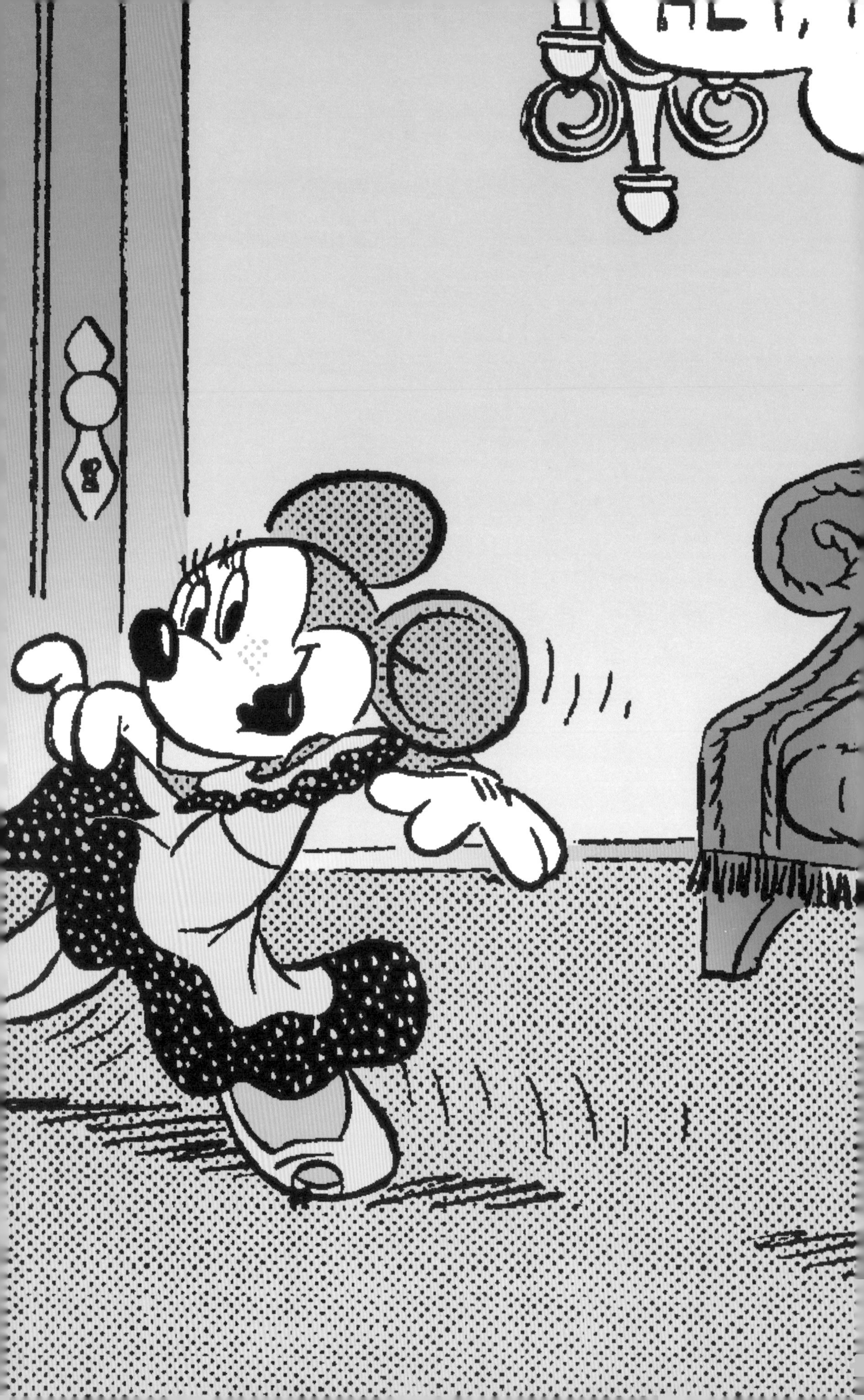

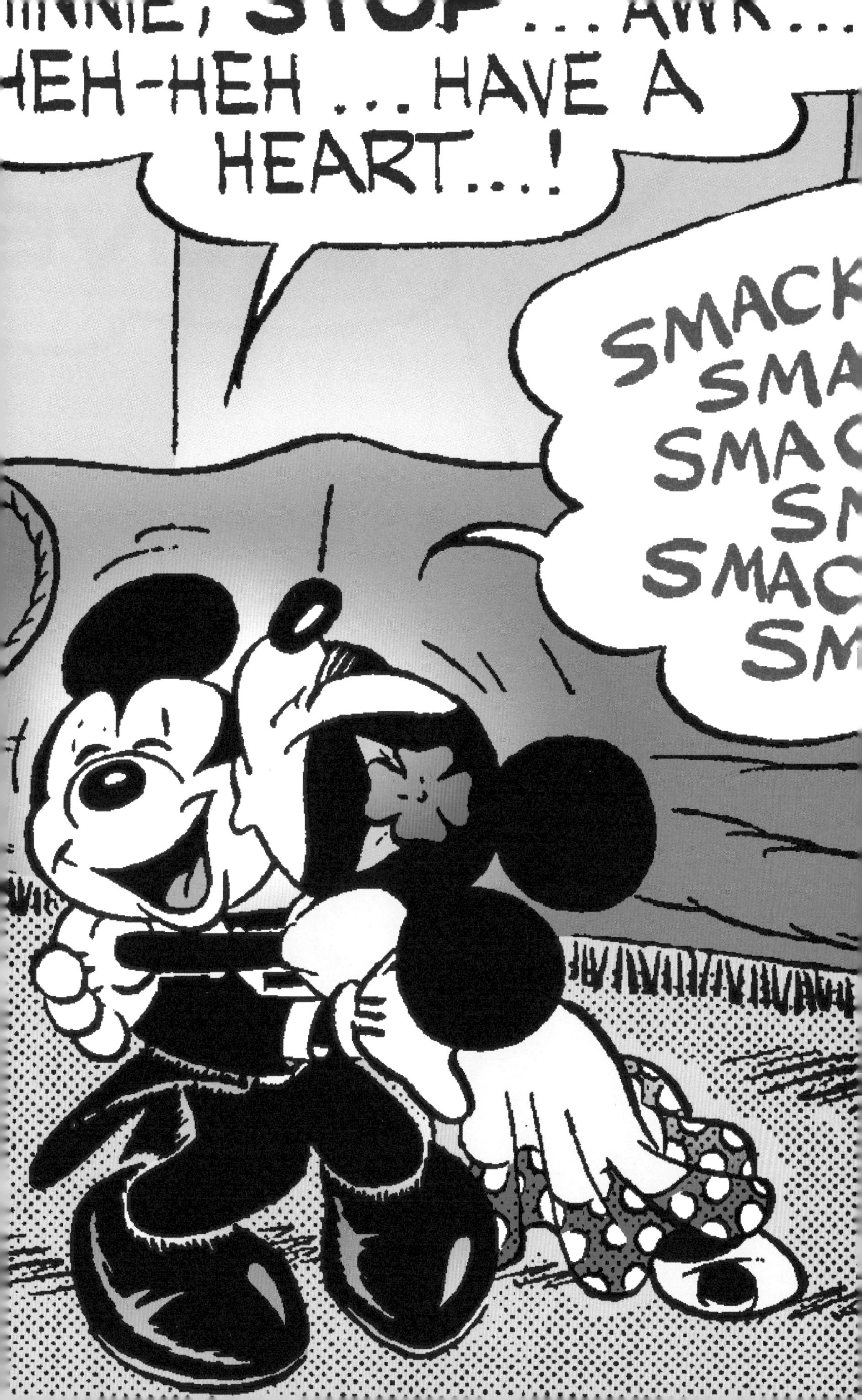
INNIE, STOP ... AWK ...
EH-HEH ... HAVE A HEART...!
SMACK
SMA
SMA
SM
SMAC
SM

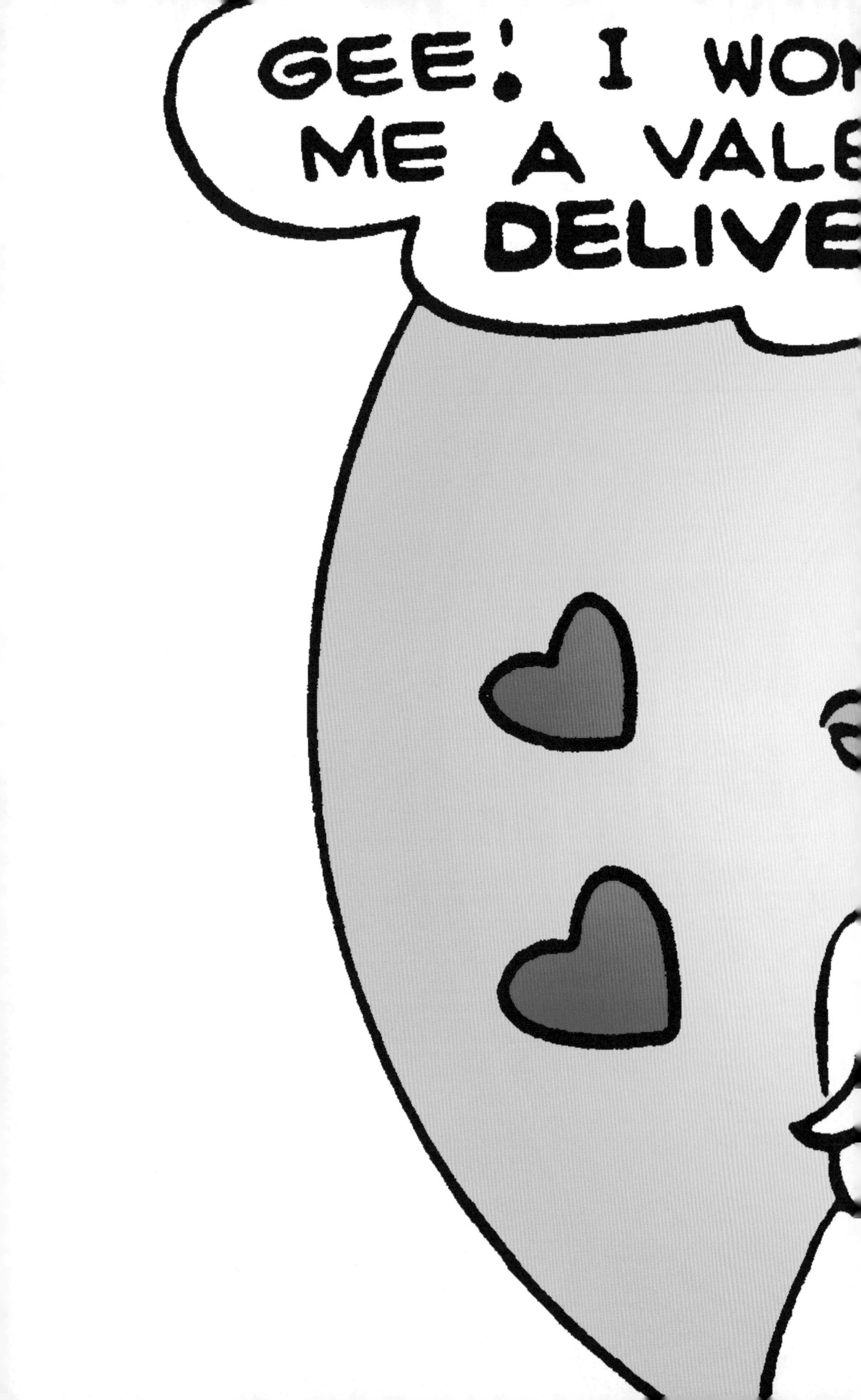
GEE! I WO
ME A VALE
DELIVE

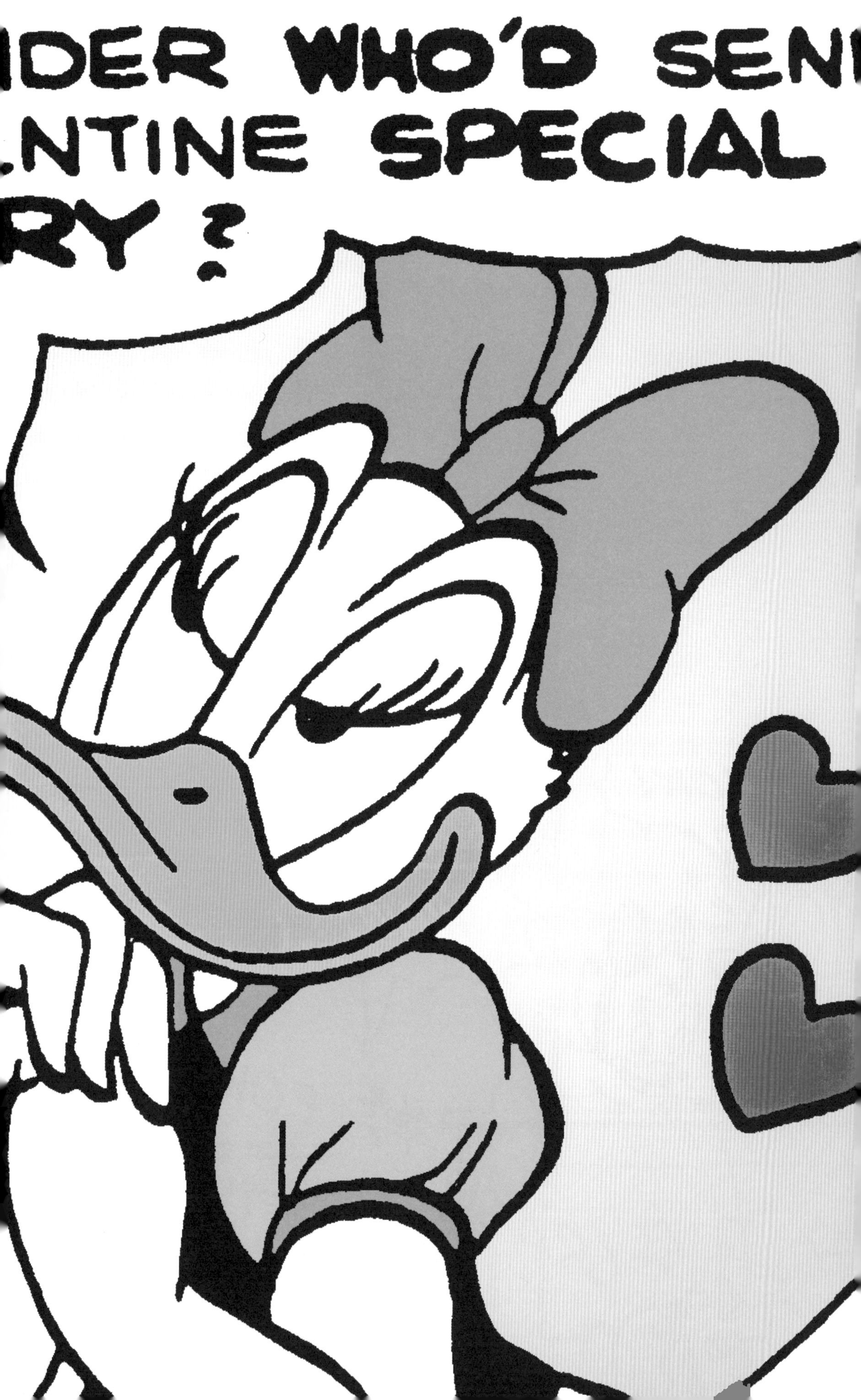
IDER WHO'D SEND
NTINE SPECIAL
RY?

ROSS RICHIE
chief executive officer

ANDREW COSBY
chief creative officer

MARK WAID
editor-in-chief

ADAM FORTIER
vice president,
publishing

CHIP MOSHER
marketing director

MATT GAGNON
managing editor

FIRST EDITION: FEBRUARY 2010

10 9 8 7 6 5 4 3 2 1

PRINTED IN KOREA

Office of publication: 6310 San Vicente Blvd Ste 404, Los Angeles, CA 90048.

A catalog record for this book is available from the Library of Congress and on our website at www.boom-studios.com on the Librarian Resource Page.

Walt Disney's

Valentine's Classics

COVER PENCILS - Cèsar Ferioli Pelaez
COVER COLOR & INKS - Egmont

EDITOR - Aaron Sparrow
ASSISTANT EDITOR - Christopher Burns
DESIGNER - Erika Terriquez

HOO-HAH!
RIP

Contents

Raven Mad (1972)

Story & Art - Daan Jippes
Translation - Byron Erickson
Letters - Bill Spicer
Colors - Magic Eye Studios

Love's a Gas (1961)

Story - Bob Karp
Art & Letters- Al Taliaferro
Colors - Magic Eye Studios

Marriage of the Century (1988)

Plot - Izomar C. Guilherme
Script - Júlio de Andrade
Translation - David Gerstein & Jonathan Gray
Lettered - Deron Bennett
Pencils - Euclides K. Miyaura and Irineu Soares Rodrigues
Colors - Disney Italia

Special Thanks To:
Jesse Post, Lauren Kressel,
and David Gerstein

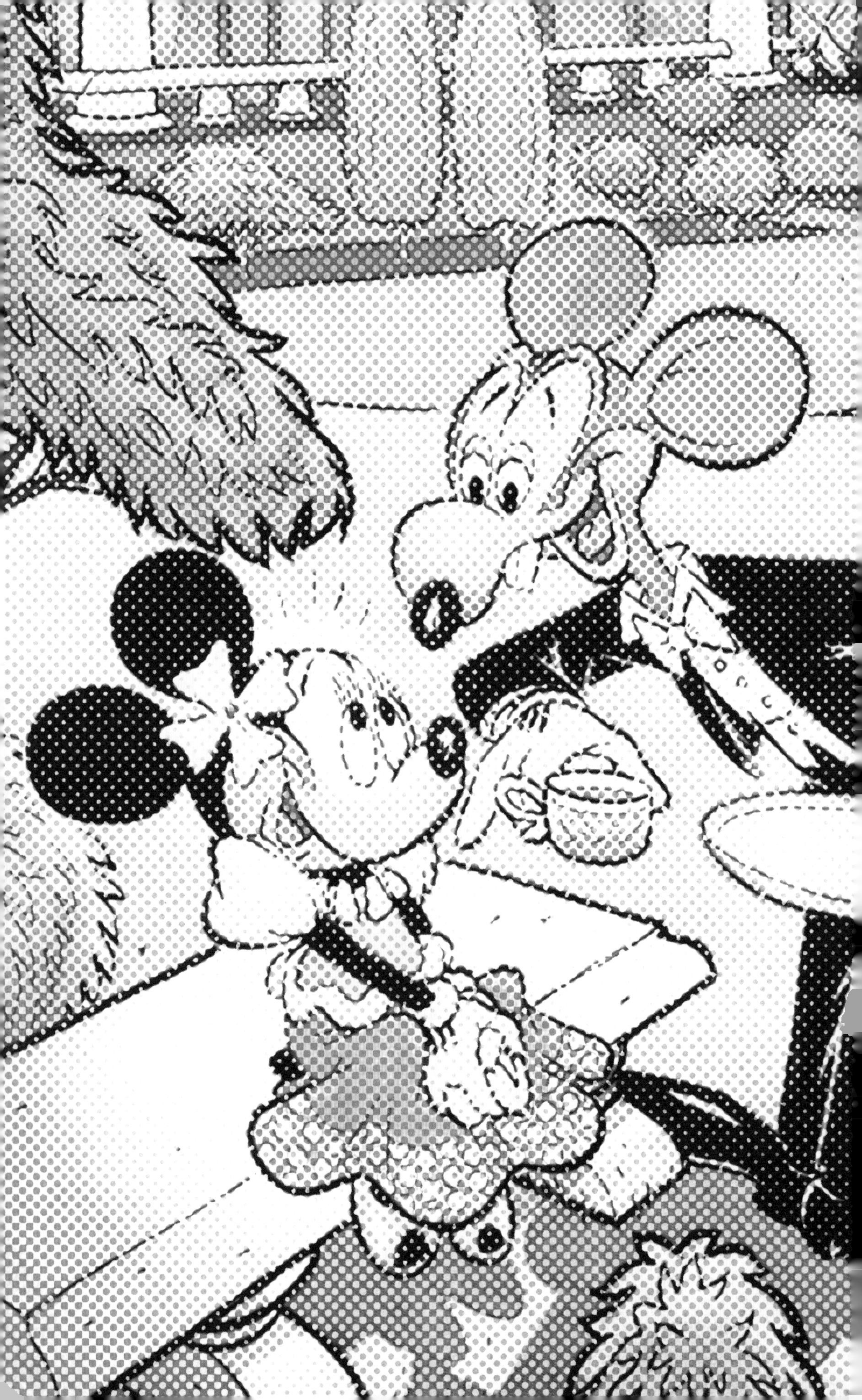

Walt Disney's Mickey Mouse in love trouble

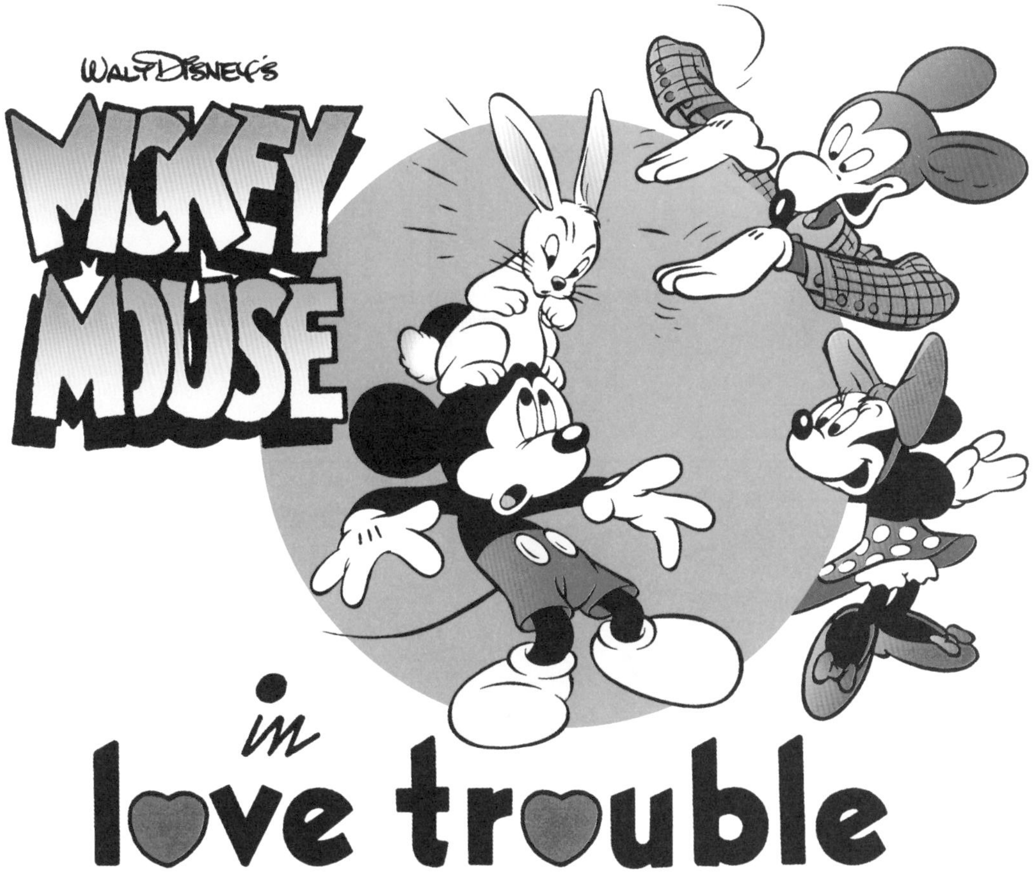

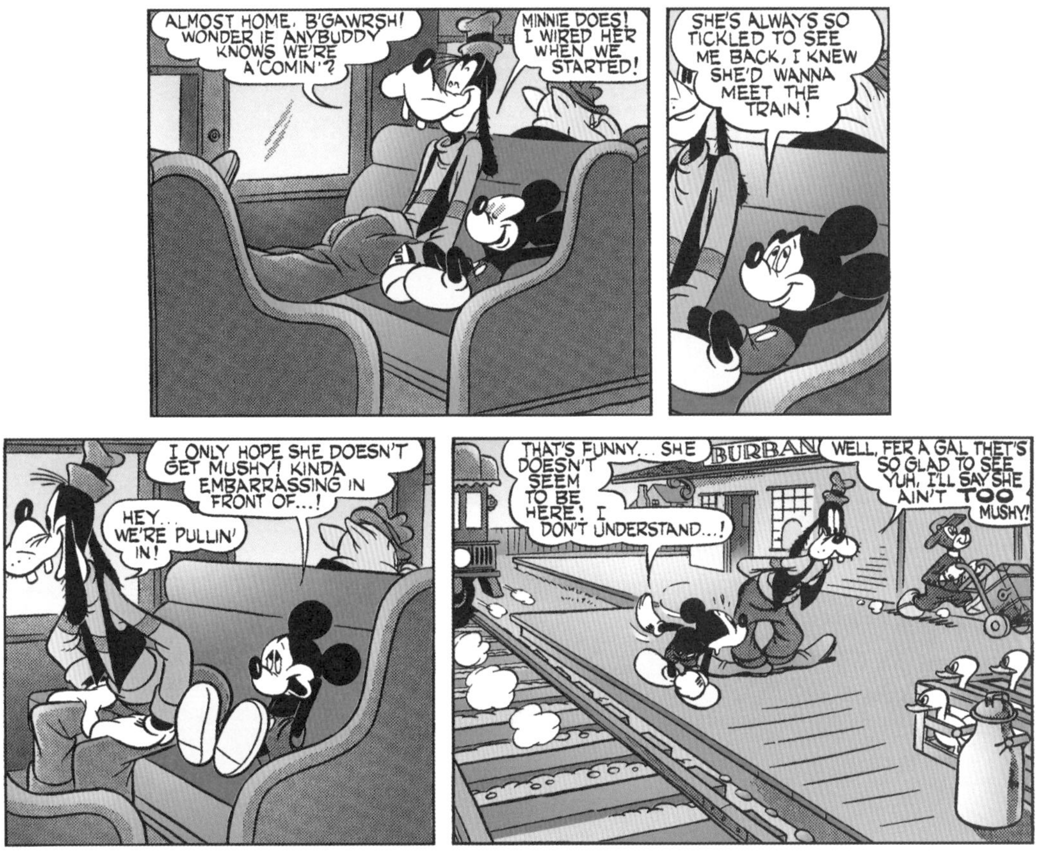

ALMOST HOME, B'GAWRSH! WONDER IF ANYBUDDY KNOWS WE'RE A'COMIN'?
MINNIE DOES! I WIRED HER WHEN WE STARTED!
SHE'S ALWAYS SO TICKLED TO SEE ME BACK, I KNEW SHE'D WANNA MEET THE TRAIN!
I ONLY HOPE SHE DOESN'T GET MUSHY! KINDA EMBARRASSING IN FRONT OF...!
HEY... WE'RE PULLIN' IN!
THAT'S FUNNY... SHE DOESN'T SEEM TO BE HERE! I DON'T UNDERSTAND...!
BURBAN
WELL, FER A GAL THET'S SO GLAD TO SEE YUH, I'LL SAY SHE AIN'T TOO MUSHY!

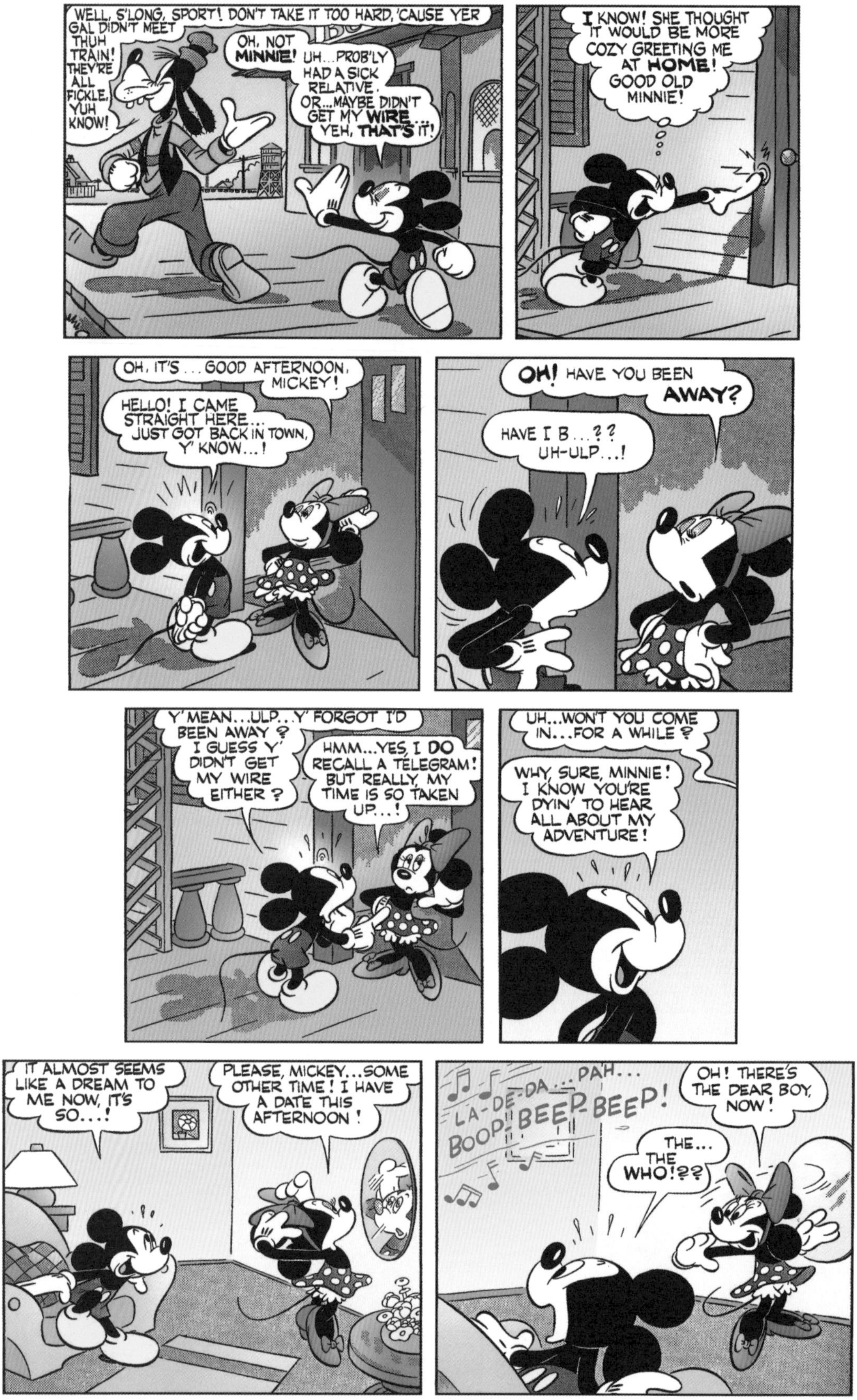
WELL, S'LONG, SPORT! DON'T TAKE IT TOO HARD, 'CAUSE YER GAL DIDN'T MEET THUH TRAIN! THEY'RE ALL FICKLE, YUH KNOW!
OH, NOT MINNIE!
UH...PROB'LY HAD A SICK RELATIVE. OR...MAYBE DIDN'T GET MY WIRE... YEH, THAT'S IT!
I KNOW! SHE THOUGHT IT WOULD BE MORE COZY GREETING ME AT HOME! GOOD OLD MINNIE!
HELLO! I CAME STRAIGHT HERE... JUST GOT BACK IN TOWN, Y' KNOW...!
OH, IT'S . . . GOOD AFTERNOON, MICKEY!
OH! HAVE YOU BEEN AWAY?
HAVE I B . . . ? ? UH-ULP . . . !
Y' MEAN . . . ULP . . . Y' FORGOT I'D BEEN AWAY ? I GUESS Y' DIDN'T GET MY WIRE EITHER ?
HMM...YES, I DO RECALL A TELEGRAM! BUT REALLY, MY TIME IS SO TAKEN UP...!
UH...WON'T YOU COME IN...FOR A WHILE ?
WHY, SURE, MINNIE! I KNOW YOU'RE DYIN' TO HEAR ALL ABOUT MY ADVENTURE!
IT ALMOST SEEMS LIKE A DREAM TO ME NOW, IT'S SO...!
PLEASE, MICKEY...SOME OTHER TIME! I HAVE A DATE THIS AFTERNOON!
LA-DE-DA...PAH...
BOOP! BEEP-BEEP!
OH! THERE'S THE DEAR BOY, NOW!
THE... THE WHO!??

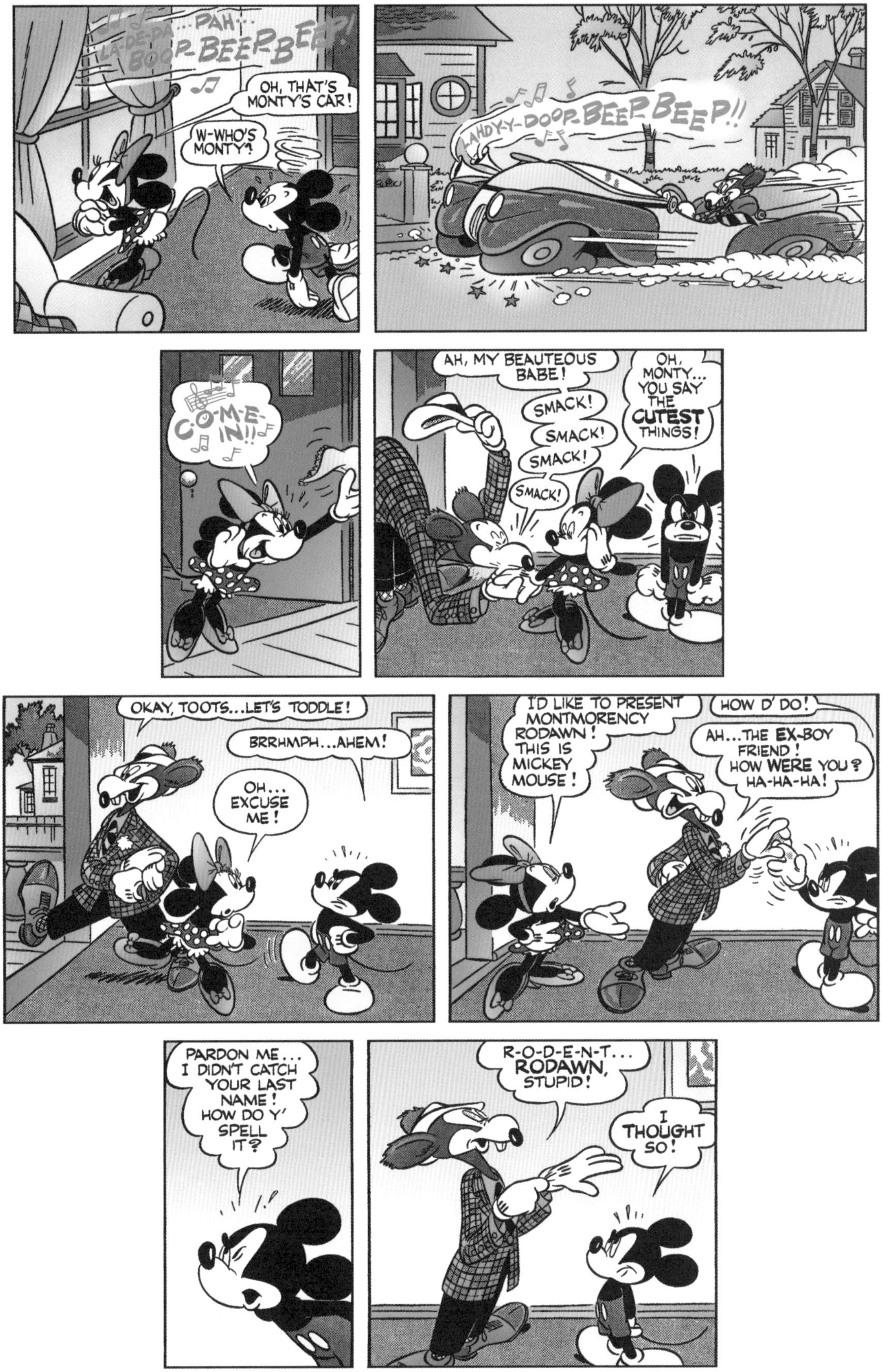
LA-DE-DA...PAH...
LA-DE-DA...BOOP-BEEP-BEEP!
OH, THAT'S MONTY'S CAR!
W-WHO'S MONTY?
LAHDY-Y-DOOP-BEEP-BEEP!!
C-O-M-E-IN!!
AH, MY BEAUTEOUS BABE!
SMACK!
SMACK!
SMACK!
SMACK!
OH, MONTY... YOU SAY THE CUTEST THINGS!
OKAY, TOOTS...LET'S TODDLE!
BRRHMPH...AHEM!
OH... EXCUSE ME!
I'D LIKE TO PRESENT MONTMORENCY RODAWN! THIS IS MICKEY MOUSE!
HOW D' DO!
AH...THE EX-BOY FRIEND! HOW WERE YOU? HA-HA-HA!
PARDON ME... I DIDN'T CATCH YOUR LAST NAME! HOW DO Y' SPELL IT?
R-O-D-E-N-T... RODAWN, STUPID!
I THOUGHT SO!

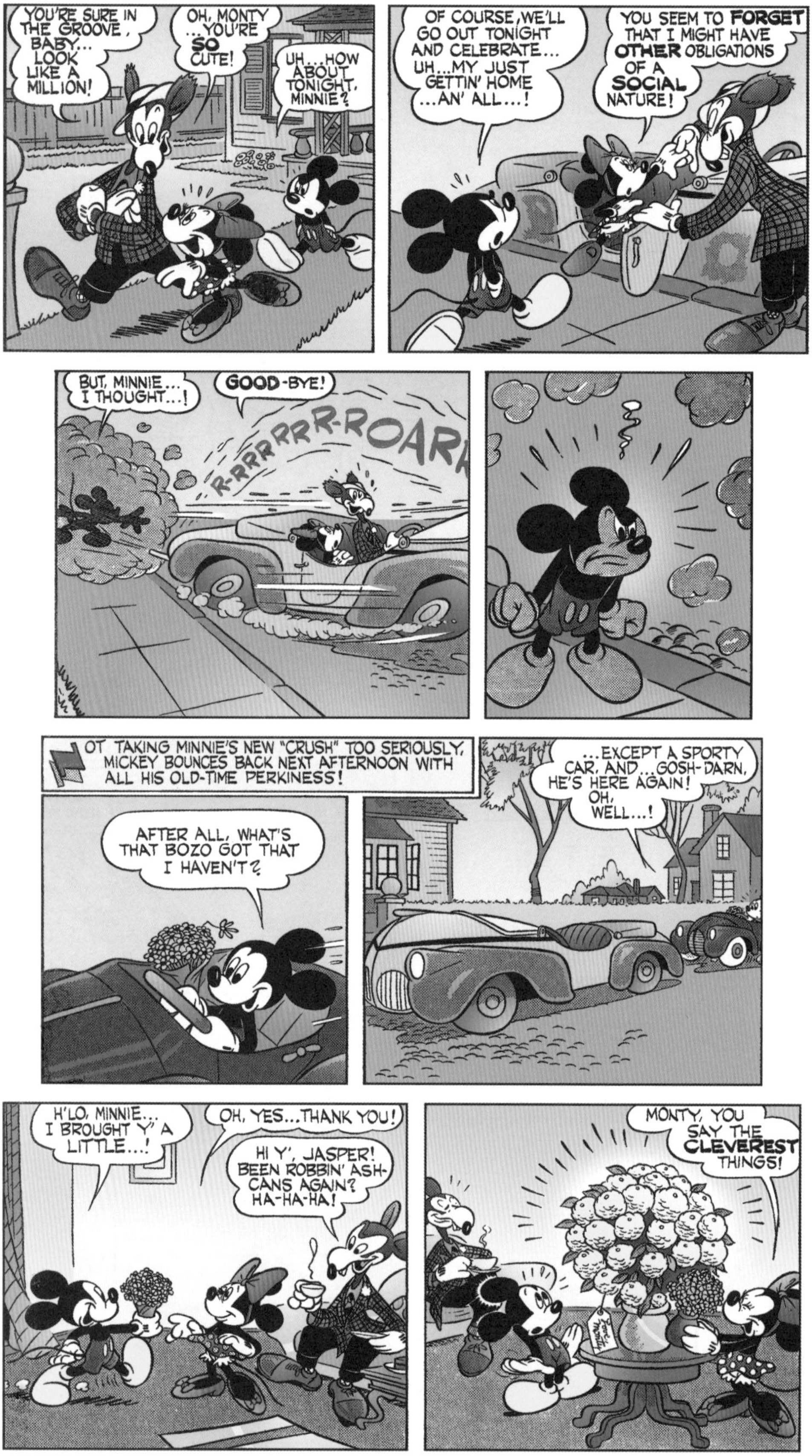
YOU'RE SURE IN THE GROOVE, BABY... LOOK LIKE A MILLION!
OH, MONTY ...YOU'RE SO CUTE!
UH...HOW ABOUT TONIGHT, MINNIE?
OF COURSE, WE'LL GO OUT TONIGHT AND CELEBRATE... UH...MY JUST GETTIN' HOME ...AN' ALL...!
YOU SEEM TO FORGET THAT I MIGHT HAVE OTHER OBLIGATIONS OF A SOCIAL NATURE!
BUT, MINNIE... I THOUGHT...!
GOOD-BYE!
R-RRRRRR-ROAR
NOT TAKING MINNIE'S NEW "CRUSH" TOO SERIOUSLY, MICKEY BOUNCES BACK NEXT AFTERNOON WITH ALL HIS OLD-TIME PERKINESS!
AFTER ALL, WHAT'S THAT BOZO GOT THAT I HAVEN'T?
...EXCEPT A SPORTY CAR, AND...GOSH-DARN, HE'S HERE AGAIN! OH, WELL...!
H'LO, MINNIE... I BROUGHT Y' A LITTLE...!
OH, YES...THANK YOU!
HI Y', JASPER! BEEN ROBBIN' ASH-CANS AGAIN? HA-HA-HA!
MONTY, YOU SAY THE CLEVEREST THINGS!

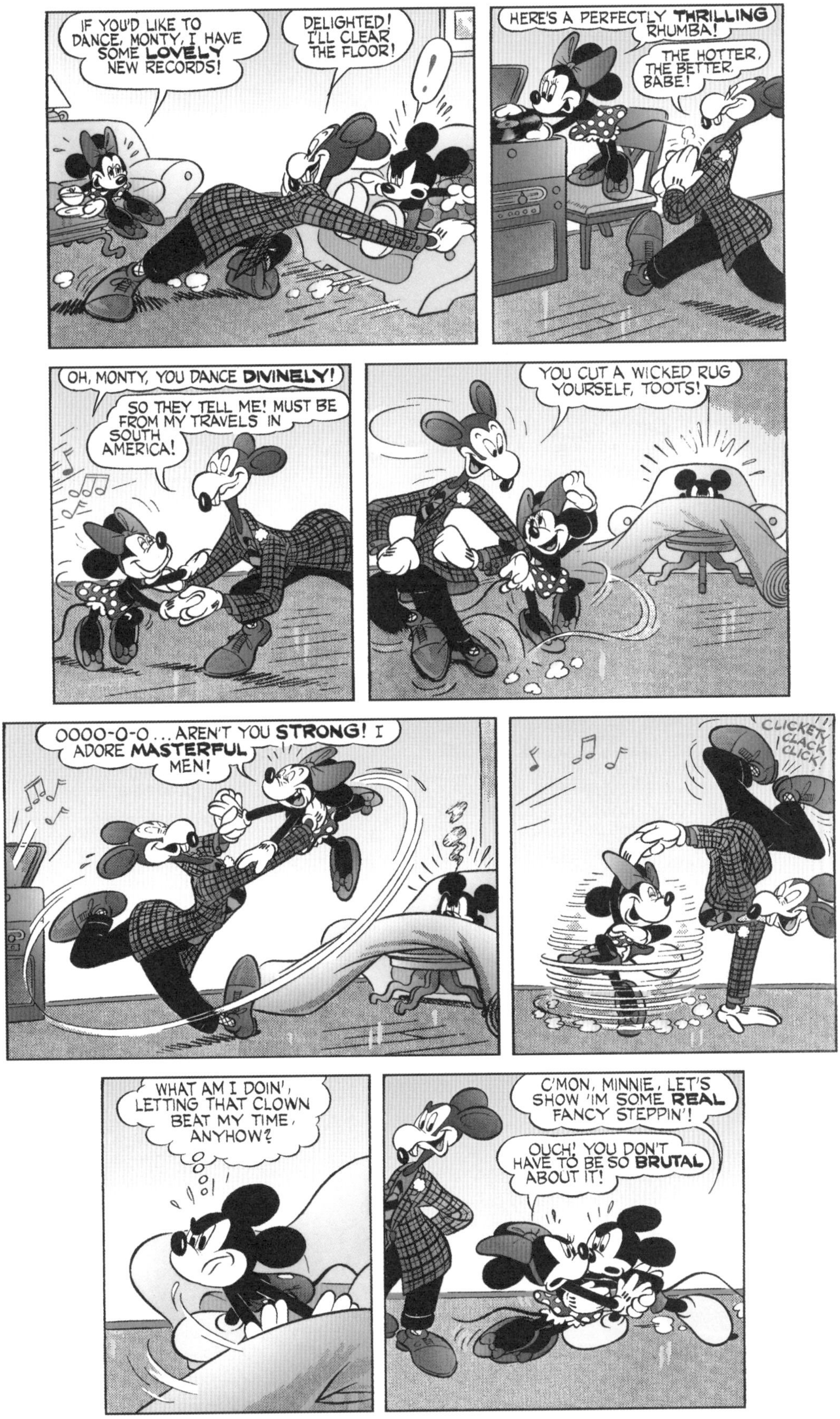
IF YOU'D LIKE TO DANCE, MONTY, I HAVE SOME **LOVELY** NEW RECORDS!
DELIGHTED! I'LL CLEAR THE FLOOR!
!
HERE'S A PERFECTLY **THRILLING** RHUMBA!
THE HOTTER, THE BETTER, BABE!
OH, MONTY, YOU DANCE **DIVINELY**!
SO THEY TELL ME! MUST BE FROM MY TRAVELS IN SOUTH AMERICA!
YOU CUT A WICKED RUG YOURSELF, TOOTS!
OOOO-O-O... AREN'T YOU **STRONG**! I ADORE **MASTERFUL** MEN!
CLICKETY CLACK CLICK!
WHAT AM I DOIN', LETTING THAT CLOWN BEAT MY TIME, ANYHOW?
C'MON, MINNIE, LET'S SHOW 'IM SOME **REAL** FANCY STEPPIN'!
OUCH! YOU DON'T HAVE TO BE SO **BRUTAL** ABOUT IT!

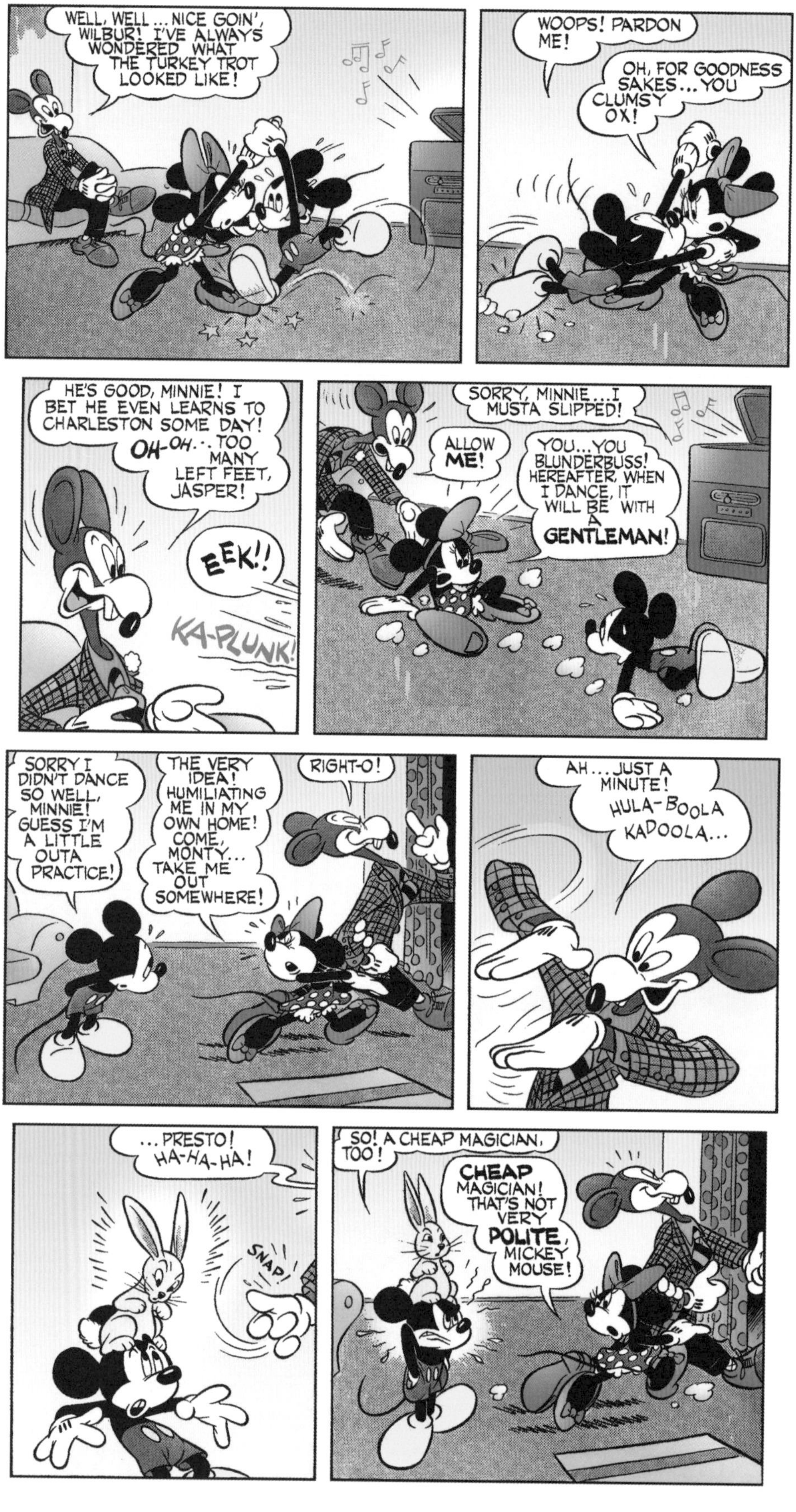

WELL, WELL ... NICE GOIN', WILBUR! I'VE ALWAYS WONDERED WHAT THE TURKEY TROT LOOKED LIKE!
WOOPS! PARDON ME!
OH, FOR GOODNESS SAKES ... YOU CLUMSY OX!
HE'S GOOD, MINNIE! I BET HE EVEN LEARNS TO CHARLESTON SOME DAY!
OH-OH... TOO MANY LEFT FEET, JASPER!
EEK!!
KA-PLUNK!
SORRY, MINNIE ... I MUSTA SLIPPED!
ALLOW ME!
YOU ... YOU BLUNDERBUSS! HEREAFTER, WHEN I DANCE, IT WILL BE WITH A GENTLEMAN!
SORRY I DIDN'T DANCE SO WELL, MINNIE! GUESS I'M A LITTLE OUTA PRACTICE!
THE VERY IDEA! HUMILIATING ME IN MY OWN HOME! COME, MONTY ... TAKE ME OUT SOMEWHERE!
RIGHT-O!
AH ... JUST A MINUTE!
HULA-BOOLA KADOOLA ...
... PRESTO! HA-HA-HA!
SNAP!
SO! A CHEAP MAGICIAN, TOO!
CHEAP MAGICIAN! THAT'S NOT VERY POLITE, MICKEY MOUSE!

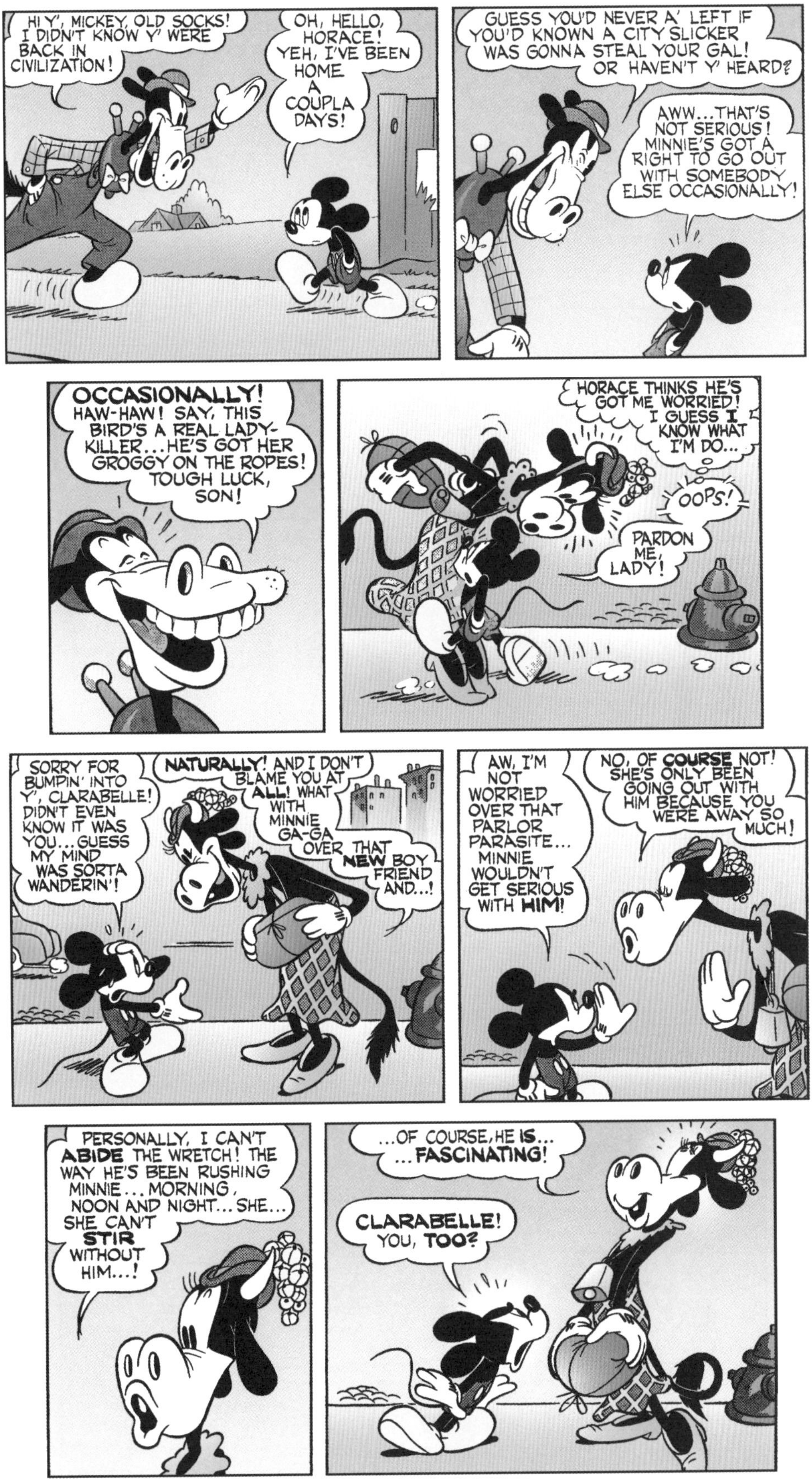
HI Y', MICKEY, OLD SOCKS! I DIDN'T KNOW Y' WERE BACK IN CIVILIZATION!
OH, HELLO, HORACE! YEH, I'VE BEEN HOME A COUPLA DAYS!
GUESS YOU'D NEVER A' LEFT IF YOU'D KNOWN A CITY SLICKER WAS GONNA STEAL YOUR GAL! OR HAVEN'T Y' HEARD?
AWW...THAT'S NOT SERIOUS! MINNIE'S GOT A RIGHT TO GO OUT WITH SOMEBODY ELSE OCCASIONALLY!
OCCASIONALLY! HAW-HAW! SAY, THIS BIRD'S A REAL LADY-KILLER...HE'S GOT HER GROGGY ON THE ROPES! TOUGH LUCK, SON!
HORACE THINKS HE'S GOT ME WORRIED! I GUESS I KNOW WHAT I'M DO...
OOPS!
PARDON ME, LADY!
SORRY FOR BUMPIN' INTO Y', CLARABELLE! DIDN'T EVEN KNOW IT WAS YOU...GUESS MY MIND WAS SORTA WANDERIN'!
NATURALLY! AND I DON'T BLAME YOU AT ALL! WHAT WITH MINNIE GA-GA OVER THAT NEW BOY FRIEND AND...!
AW, I'M NOT WORRIED OVER THAT PARLOR PARASITE... MINNIE WOULDN'T GET SERIOUS WITH HIM!
NO, OF COURSE NOT! SHE'S ONLY BEEN GOING OUT WITH HIM BECAUSE YOU WERE AWAY SO MUCH!
PERSONALLY, I CAN'T ABIDE THE WRETCH! THE WAY HE'S BEEN RUSHING MINNIE... MORNING, NOON AND NIGHT... SHE... SHE CAN'T STIR WITHOUT HIM...!
...OF COURSE, HE IS... ...FASCINATING!
CLARABELLE! YOU, TOO?

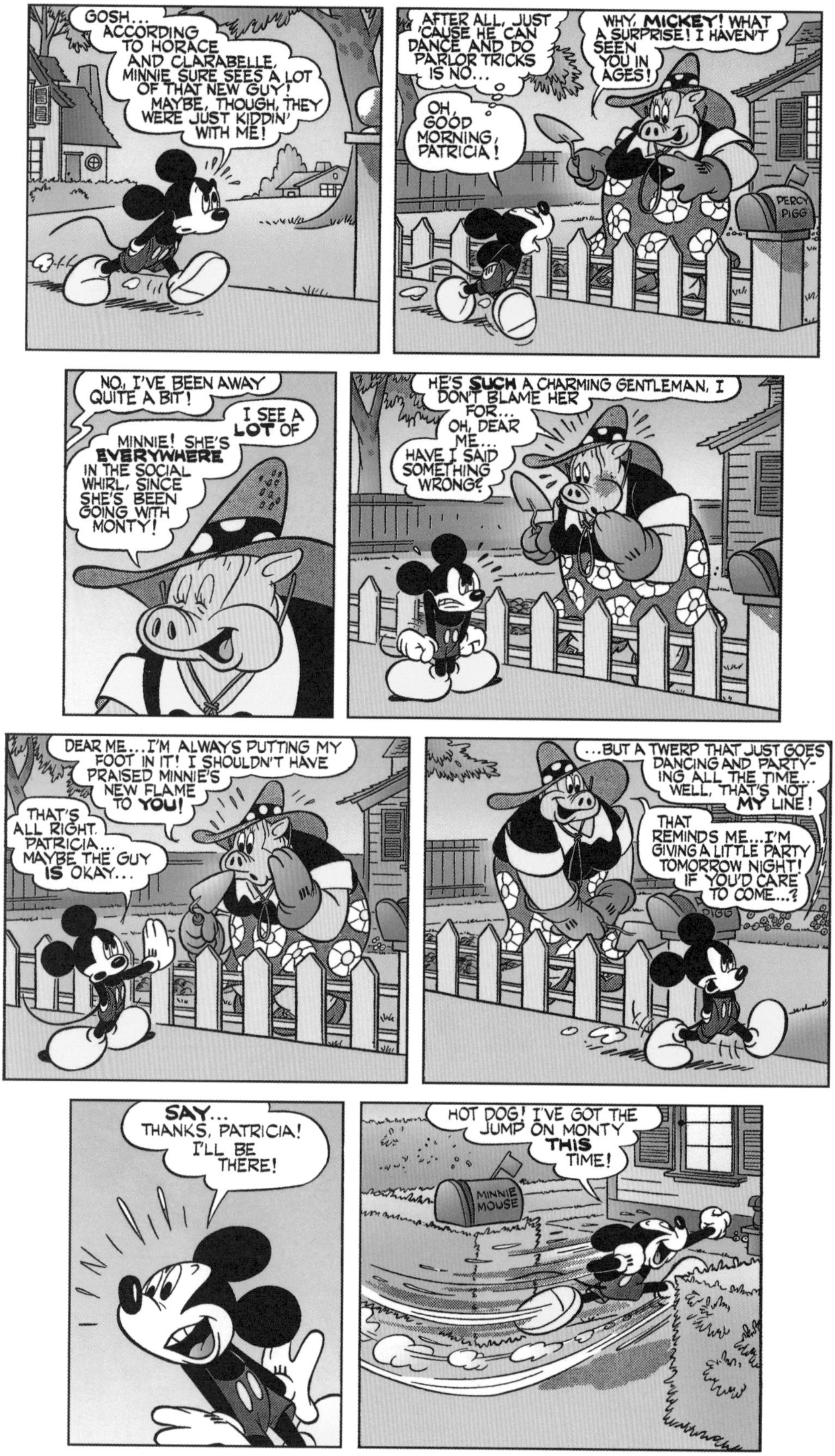
GOSH... ACCORDING TO HORACE AND CLARABELLE, MINNIE SURE SEES A LOT OF THAT NEW GUY! MAYBE, THOUGH, THEY WERE JUST KIDDIN' WITH ME!
AFTER ALL, JUST 'CAUSE HE CAN DANCE AND DO PARLOR TRICKS IS NO...
WHY, MICKEY! WHAT A SURPRISE! I HAVEN'T SEEN YOU IN AGES!
OH, GOOD MORNING, PATRICIA!
PERCY PIGG
NO, I'VE BEEN AWAY QUITE A BIT!
I SEE A LOT OF MINNIE! SHE'S EVERYWHERE IN THE SOCIAL WHIRL, SINCE SHE'S BEEN GOING WITH MONTY!
HE'S SUCH A CHARMING GENTLEMAN, I DON'T BLAME HER FOR...
OH, DEAR ME... HAVE I SAID SOMETHING WRONG?
DEAR ME... I'M ALWAYS PUTTING MY FOOT IN IT! I SHOULDN'T HAVE PRAISED MINNIE'S NEW FLAME TO YOU!
THAT'S ALL RIGHT, PATRICIA... MAYBE THE GUY IS OKAY...
...BUT A TWERP THAT JUST GOES DANCING AND PARTY-ING ALL THE TIME... WELL, THAT'S NOT MY LINE!
THAT REMINDS ME... I'M GIVING A LITTLE PARTY TOMORROW NIGHT! IF YOU'D CARE TO COME...?
PIGG
SAY... THANKS, PATRICIA! I'LL BE THERE!
HOT DOG! I'VE GOT THE JUMP ON MONTY THIS TIME!
MINNIE MOUSE

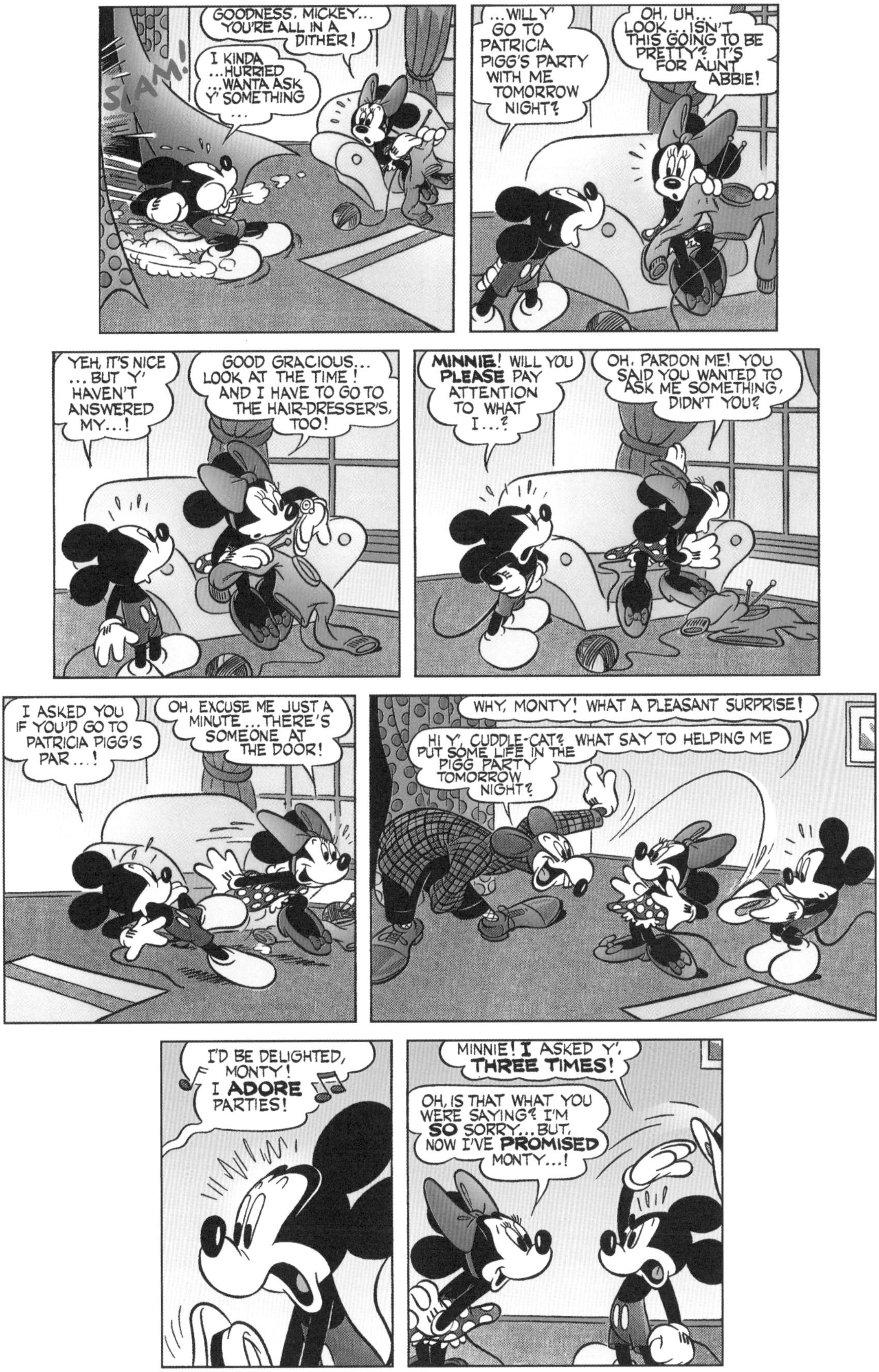
SLAM!
GOODNESS, MICKEY... YOU'RE ALL IN A DITHER!
I KINDA ...HURRIED ...WANTA ASK Y' SOMETHING ...
...WILL Y' GO TO PATRICIA PIGG'S PARTY WITH ME TOMORROW NIGHT?
OH, UH... LOOK... ISN'T THIS GOING TO BE PRETTY? IT'S FOR AUNT ABBIE!
YEH, IT'S NICE ... BUT Y' HAVEN'T ANSWERED MY...!
GOOD GRACIOUS... LOOK AT THE TIME! AND I HAVE TO GO TO THE HAIR-DRESSER'S, TOO!
MINNIE! WILL YOU PLEASE PAY ATTENTION TO WHAT I...?
OH, PARDON ME! YOU SAID YOU WANTED TO ASK ME SOMETHING, DIDN'T YOU?
I ASKED YOU IF YOU'D GO TO PATRICIA PIGG'S PAR...!
OH, EXCUSE ME JUST A MINUTE... THERE'S SOMEONE AT THE DOOR!
WHY, MONTY! WHAT A PLEASANT SURPRISE!
HI Y', CUDDLE-CAT? WHAT SAY TO HELPING ME PUT SOME LIFE IN THE PIGG PARTY TOMORROW NIGHT?
I'D BE DELIGHTED, MONTY! I ADORE PARTIES!
MINNIE! I ASKED Y', THREE TIMES!
OH, IS THAT WHAT YOU WERE SAYING? I'M SO SORRY... BUT, NOW I'VE PROMISED MONTY...!

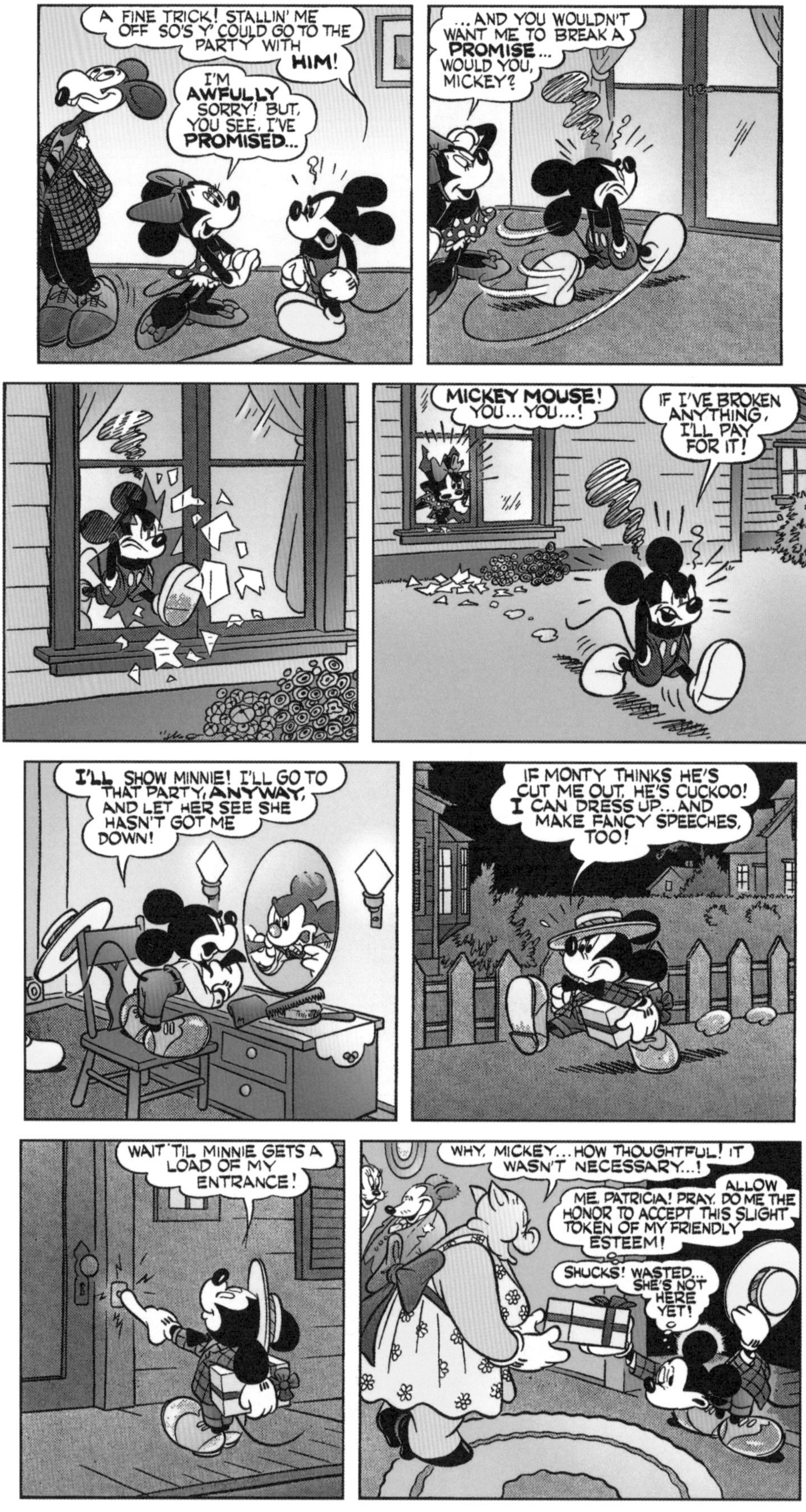
A FINE TRICK! STALLIN' ME OFF SO'S Y' COULD GO TO THE PARTY WITH HIM!
I'M AWFULLY SORRY! BUT, YOU SEE, I'VE PROMISED...
...AND YOU WOULDN'T WANT ME TO BREAK A PROMISE... WOULD YOU, MICKEY?
MICKEY MOUSE! YOU...YOU...!
IF I'VE BROKEN ANYTHING, I'LL PAY FOR IT!
I'LL SHOW MINNIE! I'LL GO TO THAT PARTY, ANYWAY, AND LET HER SEE SHE HASN'T GOT ME DOWN!
IF MONTY THINKS HE'S CUT ME OUT, HE'S CUCKOO! I CAN DRESS UP...AND MAKE FANCY SPEECHES, TOO!
WAIT 'TIL MINNIE GETS A LOAD OF MY ENTRANCE!
WHY, MICKEY...HOW THOUGHTFUL! IT WASN'T NECESSARY...!
ALLOW ME, PATRICIA! PRAY, DO ME THE HONOR TO ACCEPT THIS SLIGHT TOKEN OF MY FRIENDLY ESTEEM!
SHUCKS! WASTED... SHE'S NOT HERE YET!

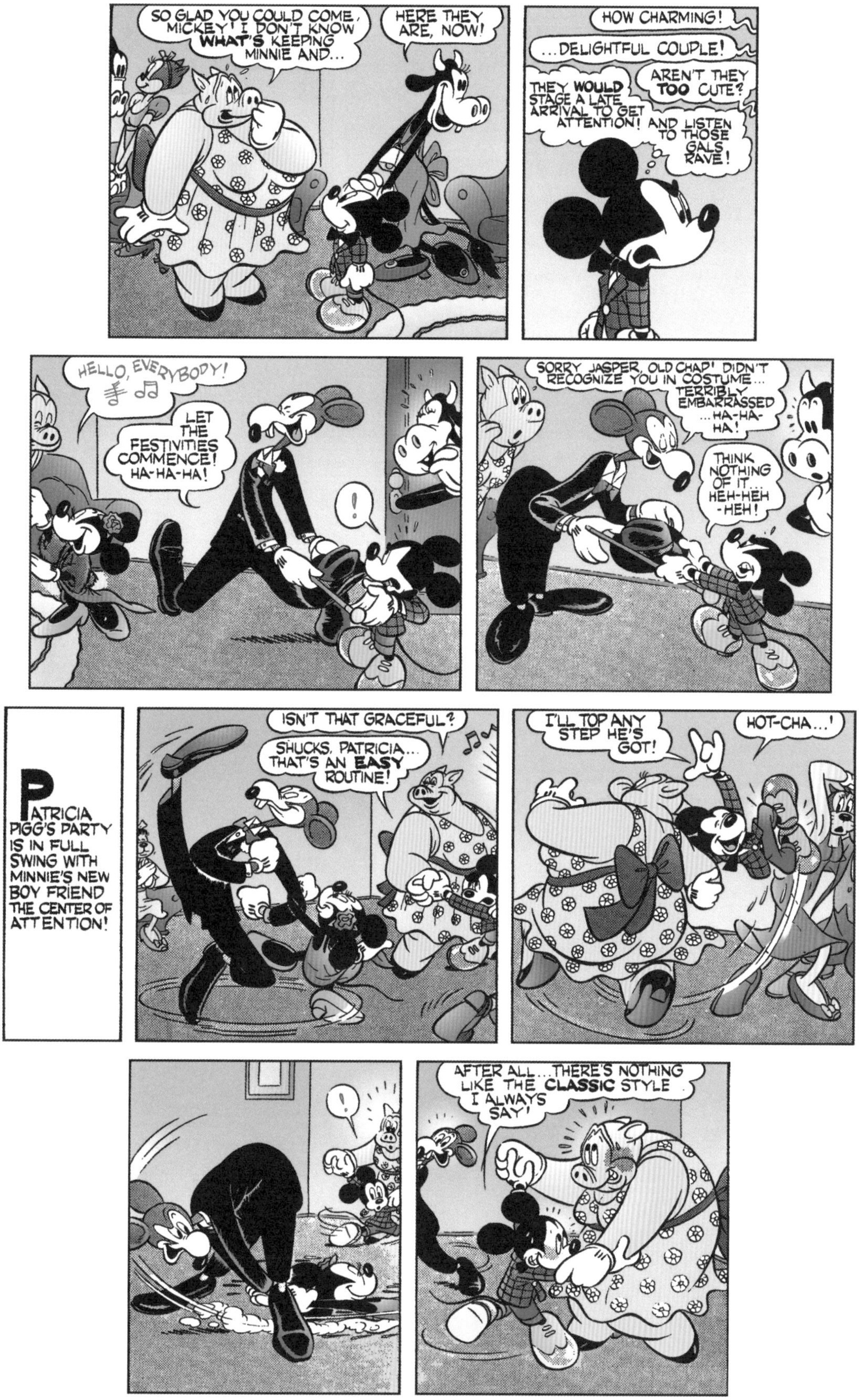

SO GLAD YOU COULD COME, MICKEY! I DON'T KNOW WHAT'S KEEPING MINNIE AND...
HERE THEY ARE, NOW!
HOW CHARMING!
...DELIGHTFUL COUPLE!
AREN'T THEY TOO CUTE?
THEY WOULD STAGE A LATE ARRIVAL TO GET ATTENTION! AND LISTEN TO THOSE GALS RAVE!
HELLO, EVERYBODY!
LET THE FESTIVITIES COMMENCE! HA-HA-HA!
!
SORRY JASPER, OLD CHAP! DIDN'T RECOGNIZE YOU IN COSTUME... TERRIBLY EMBARRASSED ...HA-HA-HA!
THINK NOTHING OF IT... HEH-HEH -HEH!
PATRICIA PIGG'S PARTY IS IN FULL SWING WITH MINNIE'S NEW BOY FRIEND THE CENTER OF ATTENTION!
ISN'T THAT GRACEFUL?
SHUCKS, PATRICIA... THAT'S AN EASY ROUTINE!
I'LL TOP ANY STEP HE'S GOT!
HOT-CHA...!
!
AFTER ALL...THERE'S NOTHING LIKE THE CLASSIC STYLE I ALWAYS SAY!

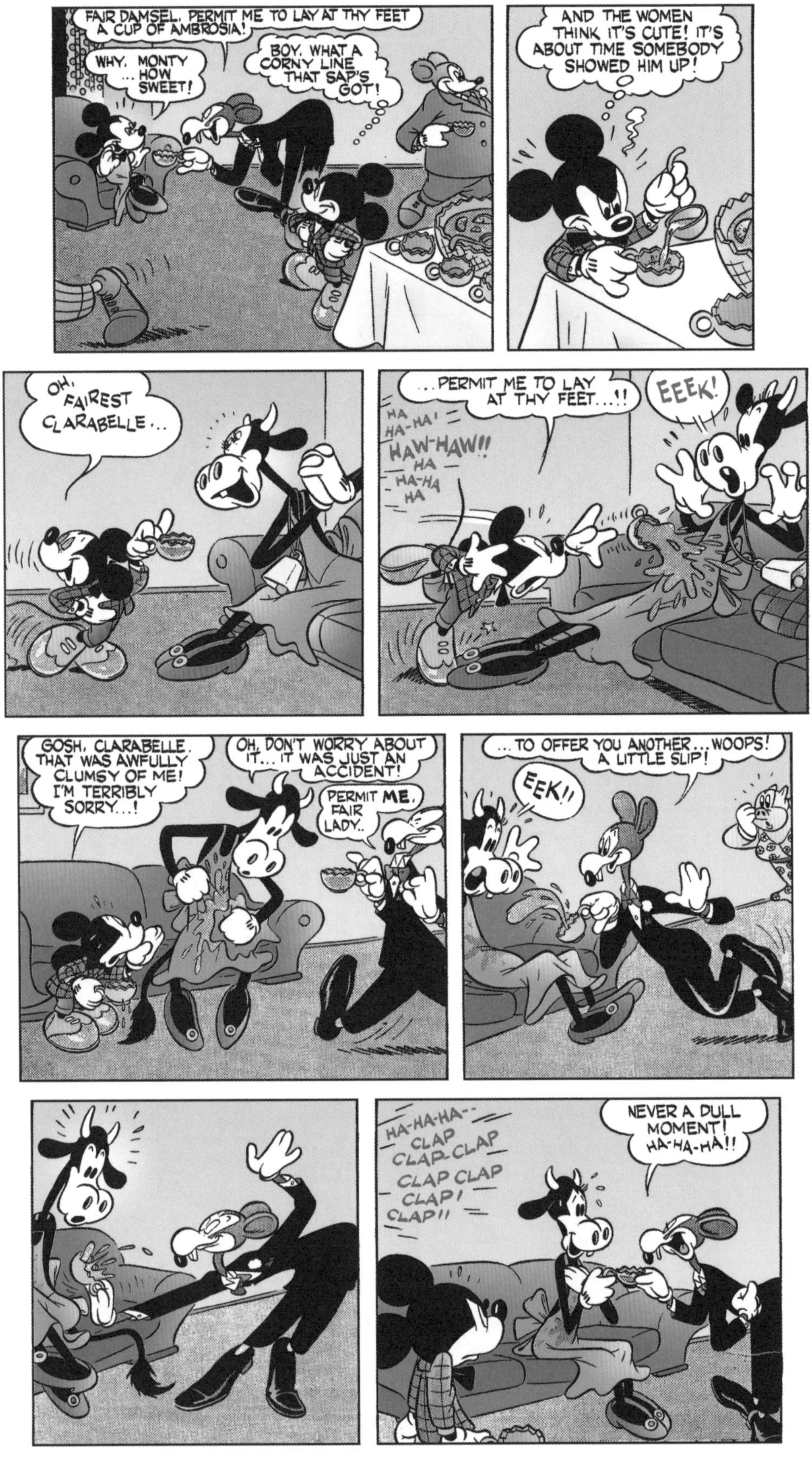
FAIR DAMSEL, PERMIT ME TO LAY AT THY FEET A CUP OF AMBROSIA!
WHY, MONTY ... HOW SWEET!
BOY, WHAT A CORNY LINE THAT SAP'S GOT!
AND THE WOMEN THINK IT'S CUTE! IT'S ABOUT TIME SOMEBODY SHOWED HIM UP!
OH, FAIREST CLARABELLE...
...PERMIT ME TO LAY AT THY FEET...!!
EEEK!
HA HA-HA! HAW-HAW!! HA HA-HA HA
GOSH, CLARABELLE, THAT WAS AWFULLY CLUMSY OF ME! I'M TERRIBLY SORRY...!
OH, DON'T WORRY ABOUT IT... IT WAS JUST AN ACCIDENT!
PERMIT ME, FAIR LADY..
...TO OFFER YOU ANOTHER... WOOPS! A LITTLE SLIP!
EEK!!
HA-HA-HA-- CLAP CLAP-CLAP CLAP CLAP CLAP! CLAP!!
NEVER A DULL MOMENT! HA-HA-HA!!

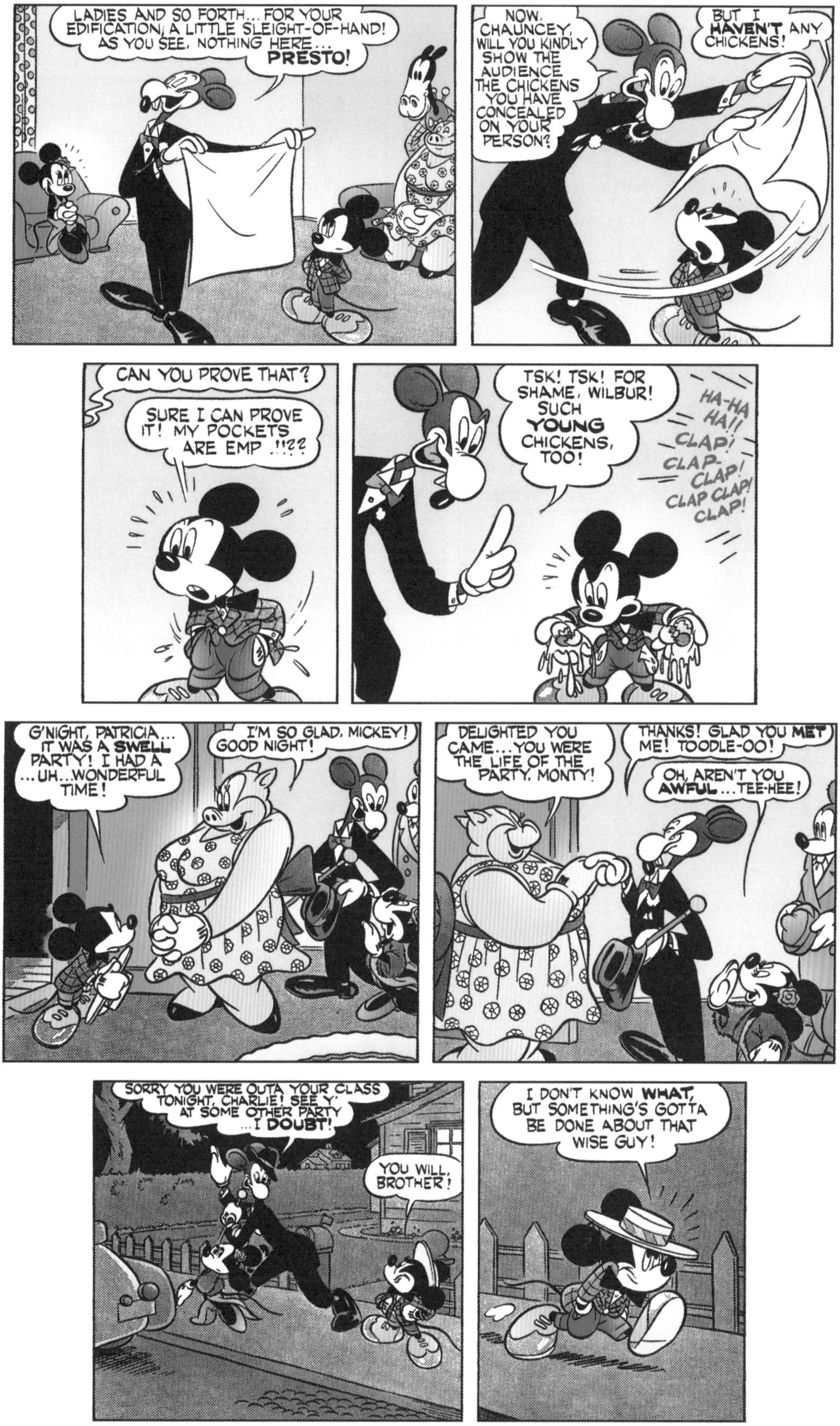
LADIES AND SO FORTH... FOR YOUR EDIFICATION, A LITTLE SLEIGHT-OF-HAND! AS YOU SEE, NOTHING HERE... PRESTO!
NOW, CHAUNCEY, WILL YOU KINDLY SHOW THE AUDIENCE THE CHICKENS YOU HAVE CONCEALED ON YOUR PERSON?
BUT I HAVEN'T ANY CHICKENS!
CAN YOU PROVE THAT?
SURE I CAN PROVE IT! MY POCKETS ARE EMP !!??
TSK! TSK! FOR SHAME, WILBUR! SUCH YOUNG CHICKENS, TOO!
HA-HA HA!! CLAP! CLAP-CLAP! CLAP CLAP! CLAP!
G'NIGHT, PATRICIA... IT WAS A SWELL PARTY! I HAD A ...UH...WONDERFUL TIME!
I'M SO GLAD, MICKEY! GOOD NIGHT!
DELIGHTED YOU CAME... YOU WERE THE LIFE OF THE PARTY, MONTY!
THANKS! GLAD YOU MET ME! TOODLE-OO!
OH, AREN'T YOU AWFUL... TEE-HEE!
SORRY YOU WERE OUTA YOUR CLASS TONIGHT, CHARLIE! SEE Y' AT SOME OTHER PARTY ...I DOUBT!
YOU WILL, BROTHER!
I DON'T KNOW WHAT, BUT SOMETHING'S GOTTA BE DONE ABOUT THAT WISE GUY!

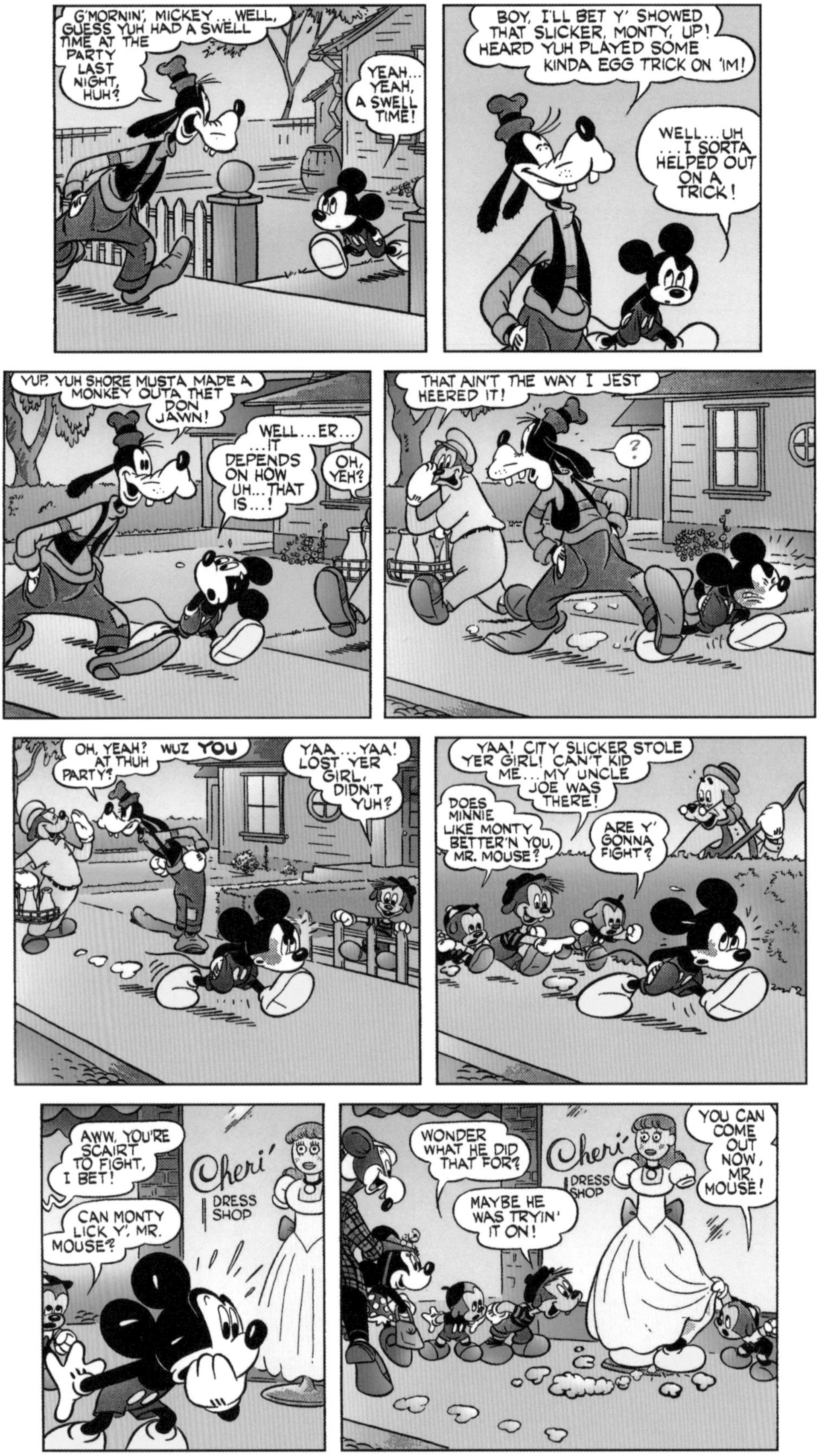
G'MORNIN', MICKEY... WELL, GUESS YUH HAD A SWELL TIME AT THE PARTY LAST NIGHT, HUH?
YEAH... YEAH, A SWELL TIME!
BOY, I'LL BET Y' SHOWED THAT SLICKER, MONTY, UP! HEARD YUH PLAYED SOME KINDA EGG TRICK ON 'IM!
WELL... UH ... I SORTA HELPED OUT ON A TRICK!
YUP, YUH SHORE MUSTA MADE A MONKEY OUTA THET DON JAWN!
WELL... ER... ...IT DEPENDS ON HOW UH... THAT IS...!
OH, YEH?
THAT AIN'T THE WAY I JEST HEERED IT!
?
OH, YEAH? WUZ YOU AT THUH PARTY?
YAA... YAA! LOST YER GIRL, DIDN'T YUH?
YAA! CITY SLICKER STOLE YER GIRL! CAN'T KID ME... MY UNCLE JOE WAS THERE!
DOES MINNIE LIKE MONTY BETTER'N YOU, MR. MOUSE?
ARE Y' GONNA FIGHT?
AWW, YOU'RE SCAIRT TO FIGHT, I BET!
CAN MONTY LICK Y', MR. MOUSE?
Cheri' DRESS SHOP
WONDER WHAT HE DID THAT FOR?
MAYBE HE WAS TRYIN' IT ON!
Cheri' DRESS SHOP
YOU CAN COME OUT NOW, MR. MOUSE!

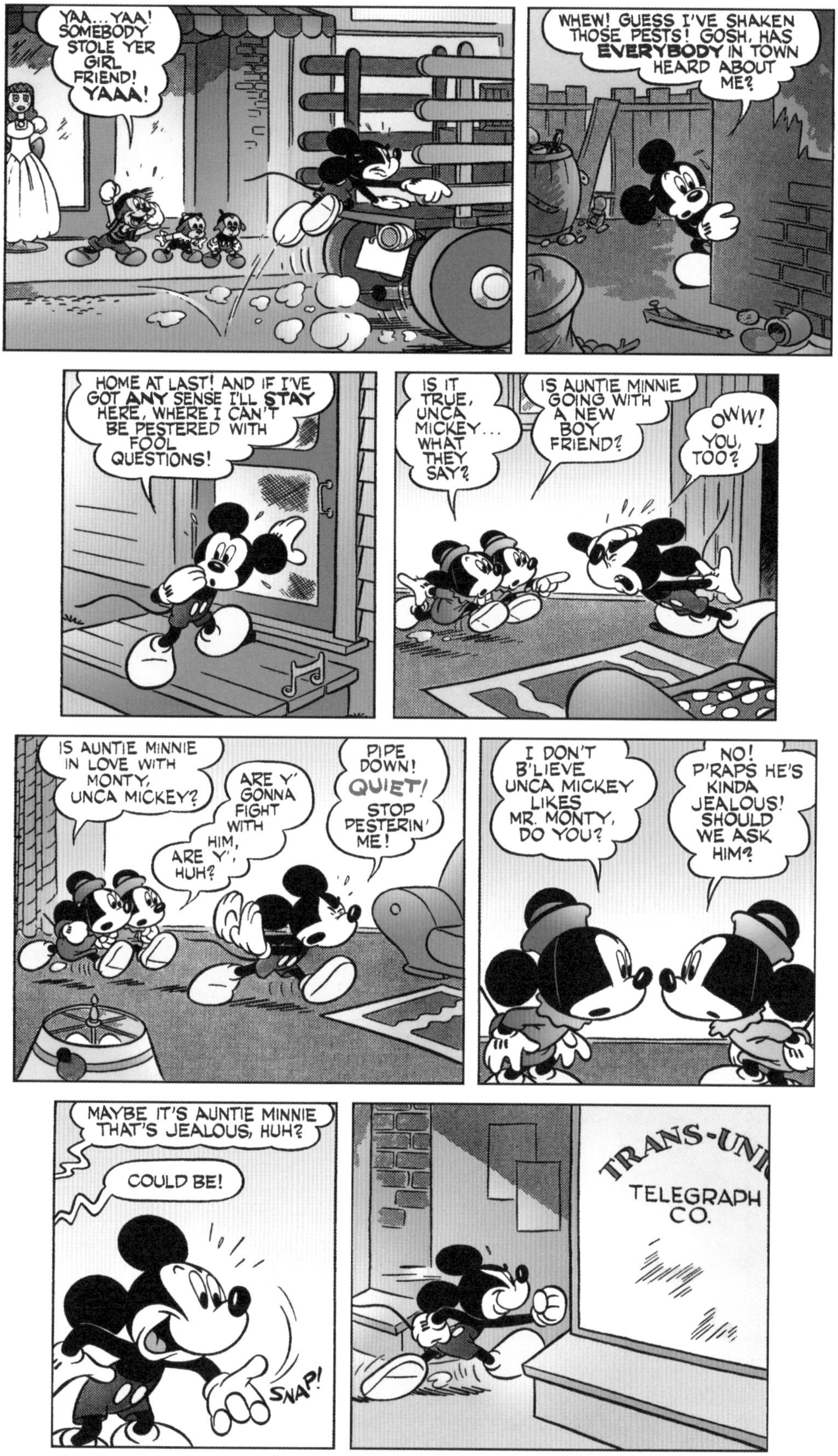
YAA...YAA! SOMEBODY STOLE YER GIRL FRIEND! YAAA!
WHEW! GUESS I'VE SHAKEN THOSE PESTS! GOSH, HAS EVERYBODY IN TOWN HEARD ABOUT ME?
HOME AT LAST! AND IF I'VE GOT ANY SENSE I'LL STAY HERE, WHERE I CAN'T BE PESTERED WITH FOOL QUESTIONS!
IS IT TRUE, UNCA MICKEY... WHAT THEY SAY?
IS AUNTIE MINNIE GOING WITH A NEW BOY FRIEND?
OWW! YOU, TOO?
IS AUNTIE MINNIE IN LOVE WITH MONTY, UNCA MICKEY?
ARE Y' GONNA FIGHT WITH HIM, ARE Y', HUH?
PIPE DOWN! QUIET! STOP PESTERIN' ME!
I DON'T B'LIEVE UNCA MICKEY LIKES MR. MONTY, DO YOU?
NO! P'RAPS HE'S KINDA JEALOUS! SHOULD WE ASK HIM?
MAYBE IT'S AUNTIE MINNIE THAT'S JEALOUS, HUH?
COULD BE!
SNAP!
TRANS-UNI
TELEGRAPH CO.

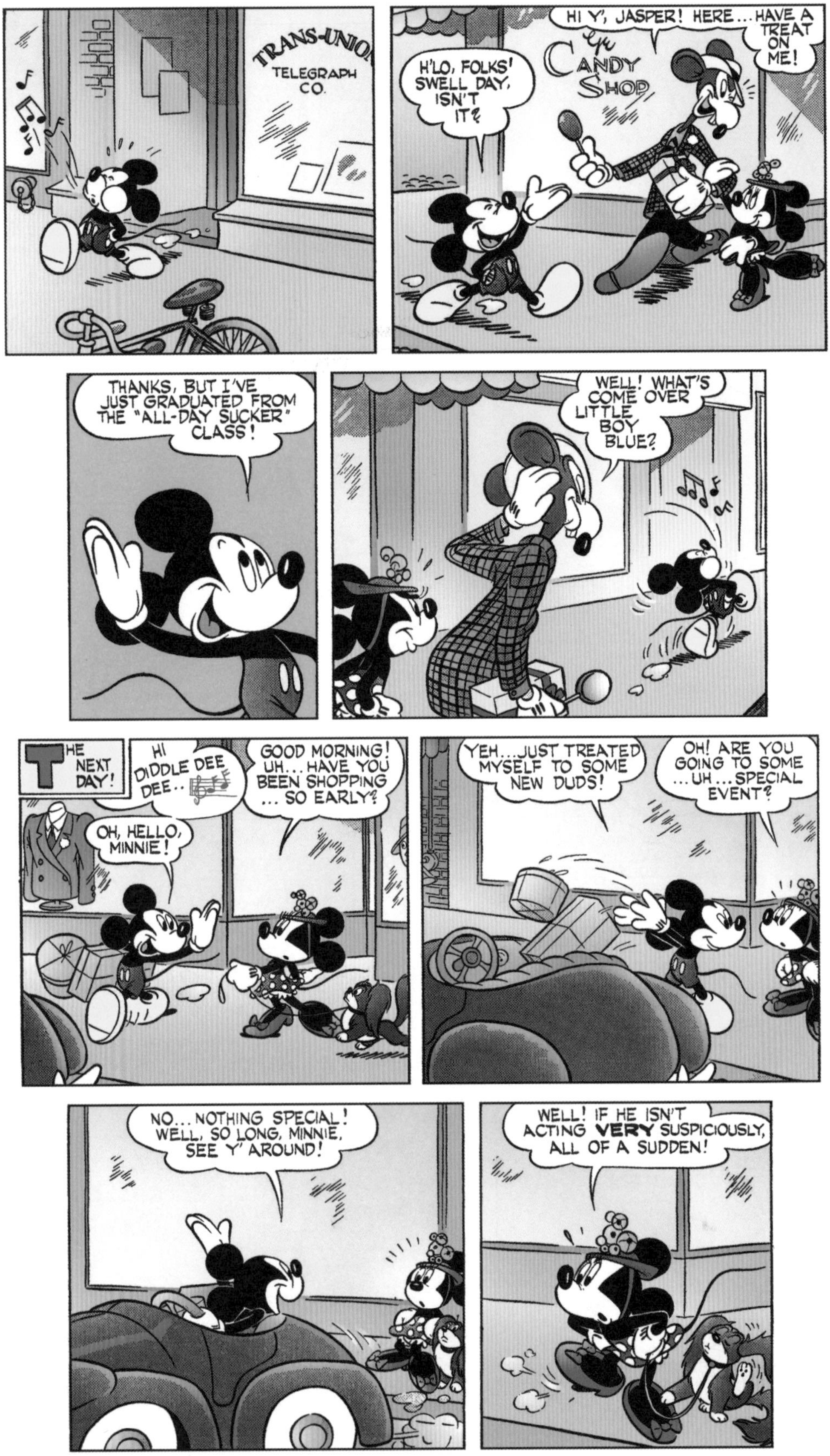
TRANS-UNION
TELEGRAPH CO.
H'LO, FOLKS! SWELL DAY, ISN'T IT?
Ye CANDY SHOP
HI Y', JASPER! HERE... HAVE A TREAT ON ME!
THANKS, BUT I'VE JUST GRADUATED FROM THE "ALL-DAY SUCKER" CLASS!
WELL! WHAT'S COME OVER LITTLE BOY BLUE?
THE NEXT DAY!
HI DIDDLE DEE DEE..
OH, HELLO, MINNIE!
GOOD MORNING! UH... HAVE YOU BEEN SHOPPING ... SO EARLY?
YEH... JUST TREATED MYSELF TO SOME NEW DUDS!
OH! ARE YOU GOING TO SOME ...UH... SPECIAL EVENT?
NO... NOTHING SPECIAL! WELL, SO LONG, MINNIE, SEE Y' AROUND!
WELL! IF HE ISN'T ACTING **VERY** SUSPICIOUSLY, ALL OF A SUDDEN!

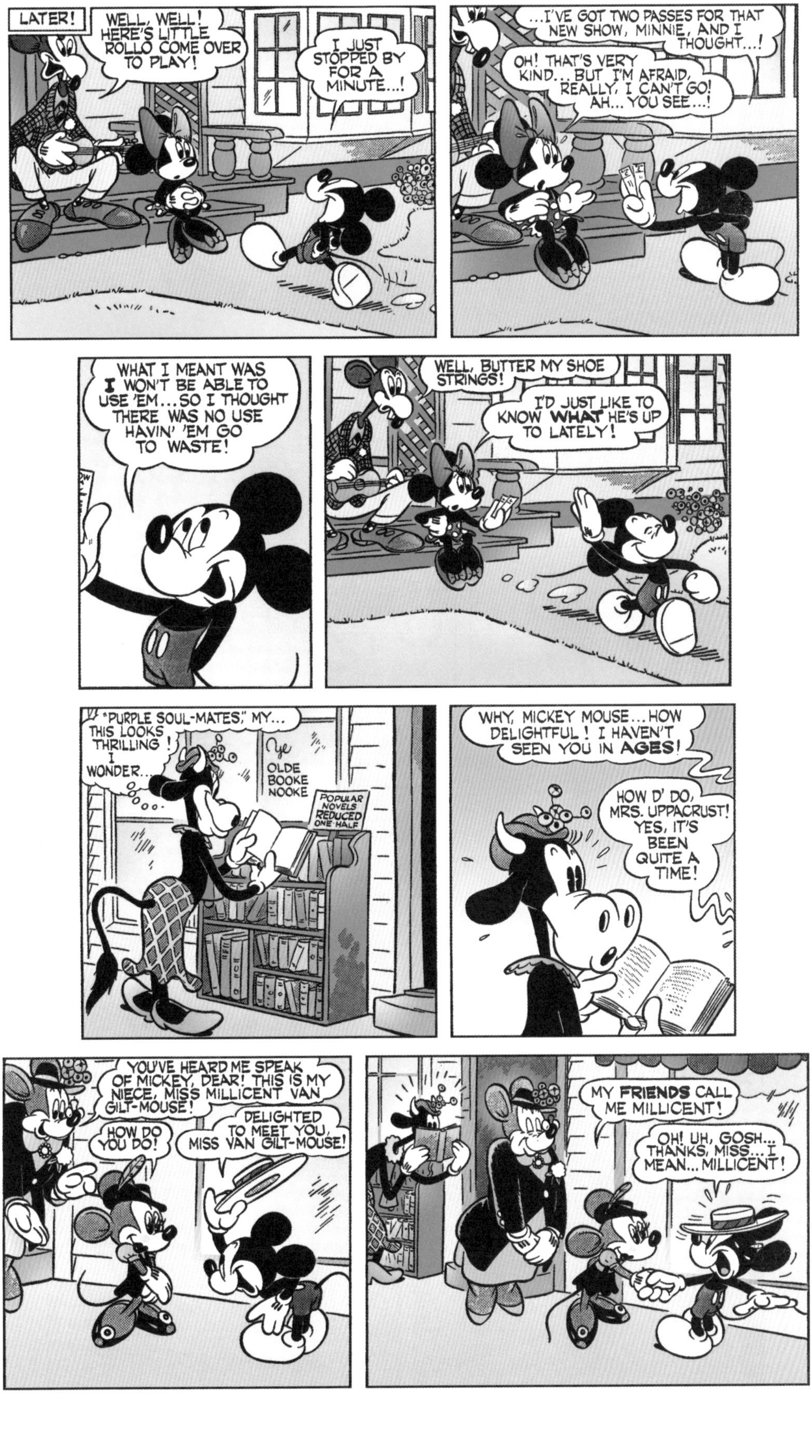

LATER!
WELL, WELL! HERE'S LITTLE ROLLO COME OVER TO PLAY!
I JUST STOPPED BY FOR A MINUTE...!
...I'VE GOT TWO PASSES FOR THAT NEW SHOW, MINNIE, AND I THOUGHT...!
OH! THAT'S VERY KIND... BUT I'M AFRAID, REALLY, I CAN'T GO! AH... YOU SEE...!
WHAT I MEANT WAS I WON'T BE ABLE TO USE 'EM...SO I THOUGHT THERE WAS NO USE HAVIN' 'EM GO TO WASTE!
WELL, BUTTER MY SHOE STRINGS!
I'D JUST LIKE TO KNOW WHAT HE'S UP TO LATELY!
"PURPLE SOUL-MATES," MY... THIS LOOKS THRILLING! I WONDER...
Ye OLDE BOOKE NOOKE
POPULAR NOVELS REDUCED ONE HALF
WHY, MICKEY MOUSE...HOW DELIGHTFUL! I HAVEN'T SEEN YOU IN AGES!
HOW D' DO, MRS. UPPACRUST! YES, IT'S BEEN QUITE A TIME!
YOU'VE HEARD ME SPEAK OF MICKEY, DEAR! THIS IS MY NIECE, MISS MILLICENT VAN GILT-MOUSE!
HOW DO YOU DO!
DELIGHTED TO MEET YOU, MISS VAN GILT-MOUSE!
MY FRIENDS CALL ME MILLICENT!
OH! UH, GOSH... THANKS, MISS... I MEAN... MILLICENT!

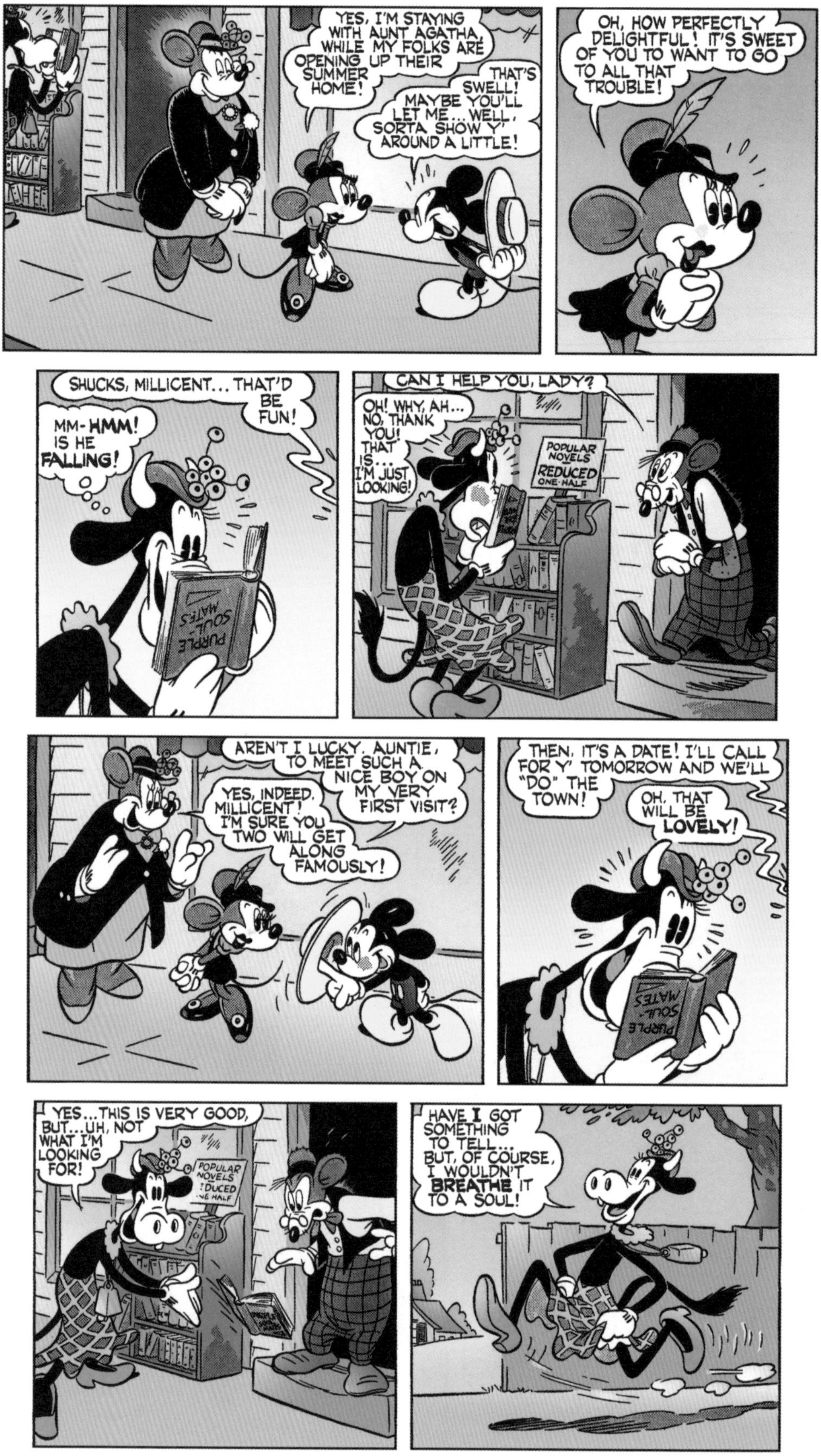

YES, I'M STAYING WITH AUNT AGATHA, WHILE MY FOLKS ARE OPENING UP THEIR SUMMER HOME!
THAT'S SWELL! MAYBE YOU'LL LET ME... WELL, SORTA SHOW Y' AROUND A LITTLE!
OH, HOW PERFECTLY DELIGHTFUL! IT'S SWEET OF YOU TO WANT TO GO TO ALL THAT TROUBLE!
SHUCKS, MILLICENT... THAT'D BE FUN!
MM-HMM! IS HE FALLING!
PURPLE SOUL-MATES
CAN I HELP YOU, LADY?
OH! WHY, AH... NO, THANK YOU! THAT IS... I'M JUST LOOKING!
POPULAR NOVELS REDUCED ONE-HALF
ARE'N'T I LUCKY, AUNTIE, TO MEET SUCH A NICE BOY ON MY VERY FIRST VISIT?
YES, INDEED, MILLICENT! I'M SURE YOU TWO WILL GET ALONG FAMOUSLY!
THEN, IT'S A DATE! I'LL CALL FOR Y' TOMORROW AND WE'LL "DO" THE TOWN!
OH, THAT WILL BE LOVELY!
PURPLE SOUL-MATES
YES... THIS IS VERY GOOD, BUT... UH, NOT WHAT I'M LOOKING FOR!
HAVE I GOT SOMETHING TO TELL... BUT, OF COURSE, I WOULDN'T BREATHE IT TO A SOUL!

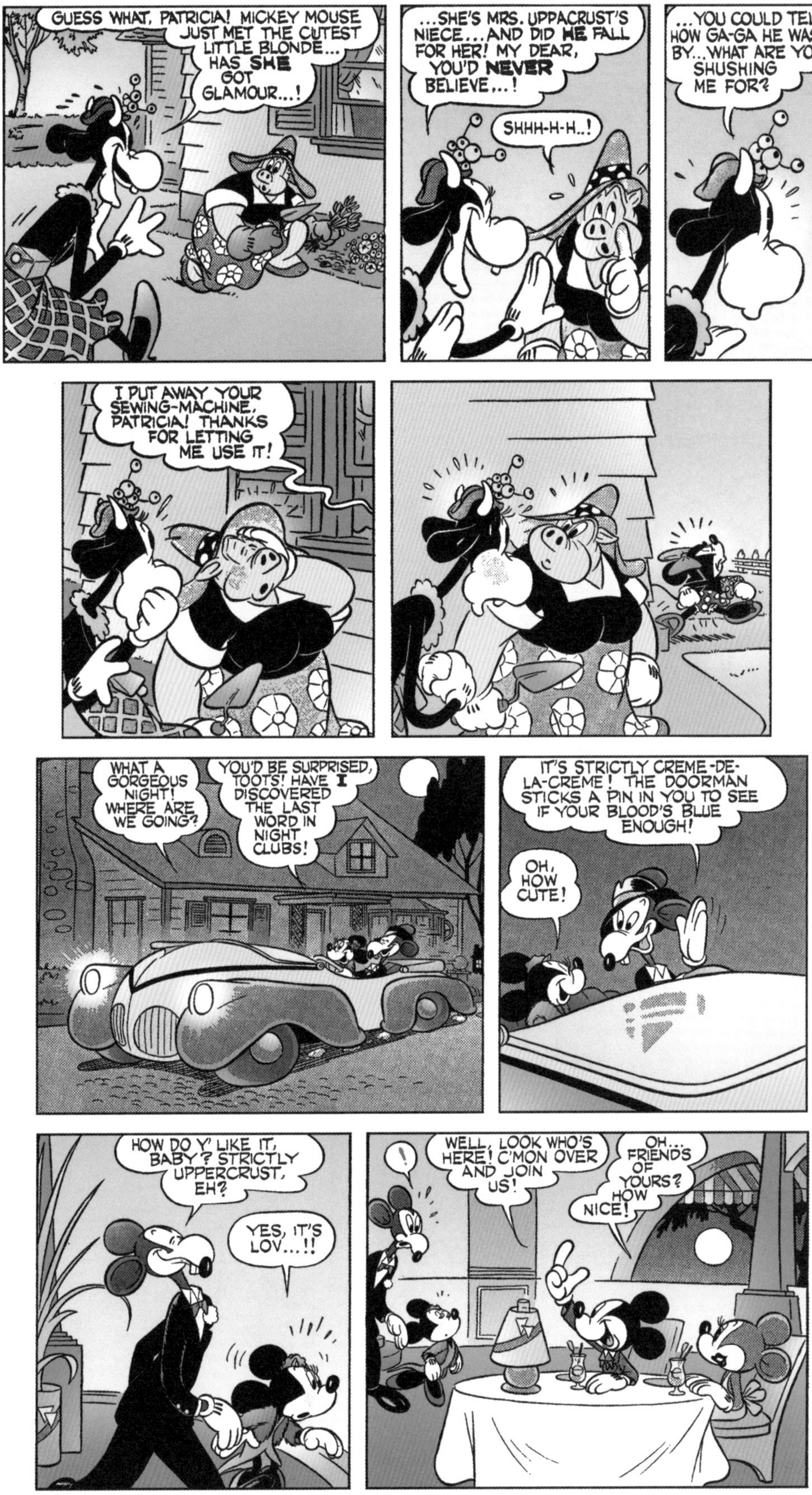
GUESS WHAT, PATRICIA! MICKEY MOUSE JUST MET THE CUTEST LITTLE BLONDE... HAS SHE GOT GLAMOUR...!
...SHE'S MRS. UPPACRUST'S NIECE...AND DID HE FALL FOR HER! MY DEAR, YOU'D NEVER BELIEVE...!
SHHH-H-H..!
...YOU COULD TELL HOW GA-GA HE WAS BY...WHAT ARE YOU SHUSHING ME FOR?
I PUT AWAY YOUR SEWING-MACHINE, PATRICIA! THANKS FOR LETTING ME USE IT!
WHAT A GORGEOUS NIGHT! WHERE ARE WE GOING?
YOU'D BE SURPRISED, TOOTS! HAVE I DISCOVERED THE LAST WORD IN NIGHT CLUBS!
IT'S STRICTLY CREME-DE-LA-CREME! THE DOORMAN STICKS A PIN IN YOU TO SEE IF YOUR BLOOD'S BLUE ENOUGH!
OH, HOW CUTE!
HOW DO Y' LIKE IT, BABY? STRICTLY UPPERCRUST, EH?
YES, IT'S LOV...!!
!
WELL, LOOK WHO'S HERE! C'MON OVER AND JOIN US!
OH... FRIENDS OF YOURS? HOW NICE!

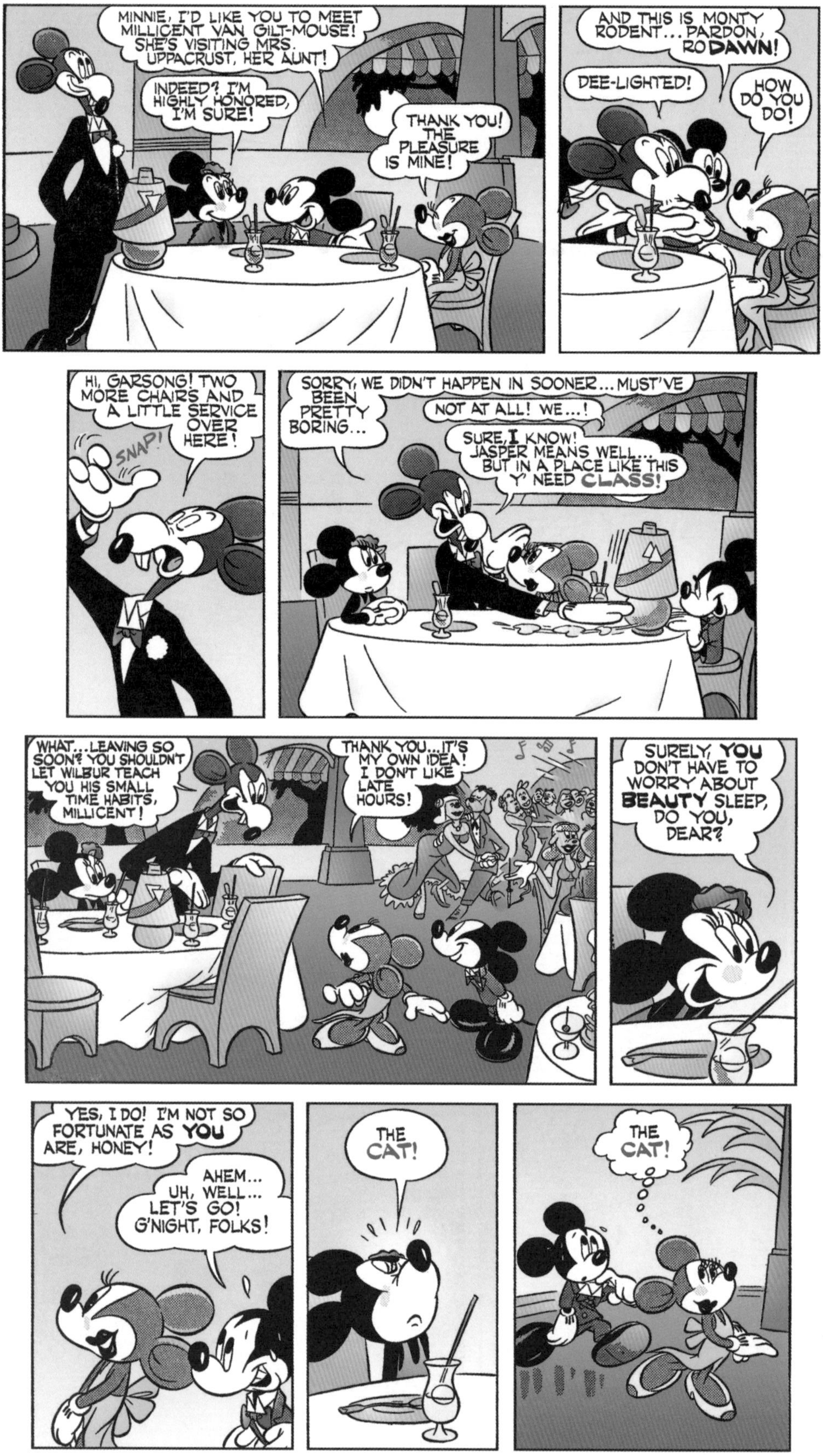
MINNIE, I'D LIKE YOU TO MEET MILLICENT VAN GILT-MOUSE! SHE'S VISITING MRS. UPPACRUST, HER AUNT!
INDEED? I'M HIGHLY HONORED, I'M SURE!
THANK YOU! THE PLEASURE IS MINE!
AND THIS IS MONTY RODENT... PARDON, RODAWN!
DEE-LIGHTED!
HOW DO YOU DO!
HI, GARSONG! TWO MORE CHAIRS AND A LITTLE SERVICE OVER HERE!
SNAP!
SORRY, WE DIDN'T HAPPEN IN SOONER... MUST'VE BEEN PRETTY BORING...
NOT AT ALL! WE...!
SURE, I KNOW! JASPER MEANS WELL... BUT IN A PLACE LIKE THIS Y' NEED CLASS!
WHAT... LEAVING SO SOON? YOU SHOULDN'T LET WILBUR TEACH YOU HIS SMALL TIME HABITS, MILLICENT!
THANK YOU... IT'S MY OWN IDEA! I DON'T LIKE LATE HOURS!
SURELY, YOU DON'T HAVE TO WORRY ABOUT BEAUTY SLEEP, DO YOU, DEAR?
YES, I DO! I'M NOT SO FORTUNATE AS YOU ARE, HONEY!
AHEM... UH, WELL... LET'S GO! G'NIGHT, FOLKS!
THE CAT!
THE CAT!

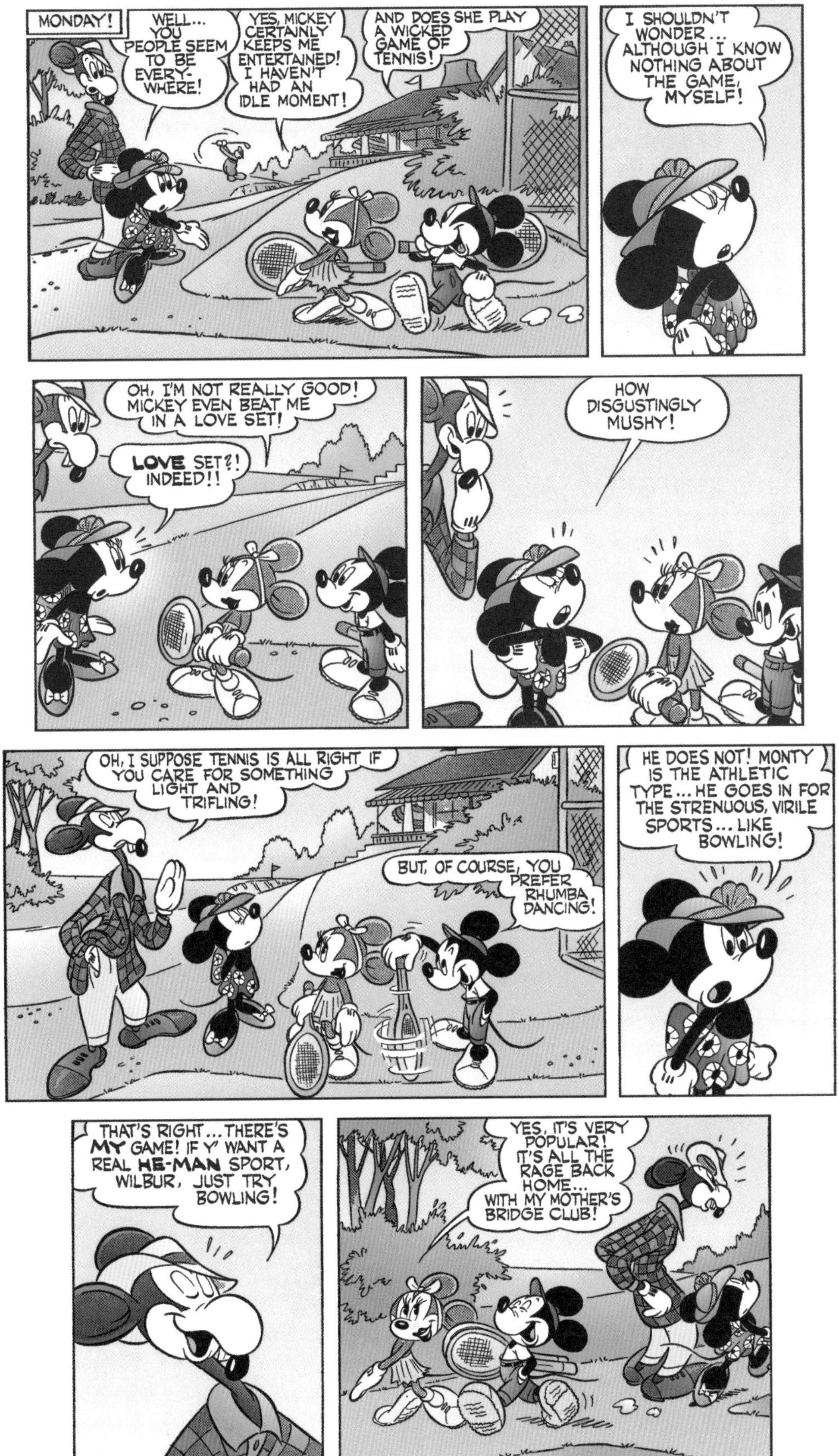
MONDAY!
WELL... YOU PEOPLE SEEM TO BE EVERY-WHERE!
YES, MICKEY CERTAINLY KEEPS ME ENTERTAINED! I HAVEN'T HAD AN IDLE MOMENT!
AND DOES SHE PLAY A WICKED GAME OF TENNIS!
I SHOULDN'T WONDER... ALTHOUGH I KNOW NOTHING ABOUT THE GAME, MYSELF!
OH, I'M NOT REALLY GOOD! MICKEY EVEN BEAT ME IN A LOVE SET!
LOVE SET?! INDEED!!
HOW DISGUSTINGLY MUSHY!
OH, I SUPPOSE TENNIS IS ALL RIGHT IF YOU CARE FOR SOMETHING LIGHT AND TRIFLING!
BUT, OF COURSE, YOU PREFER RHUMBA DANCING!
HE DOES NOT! MONTY IS THE ATHLETIC TYPE... HE GOES IN FOR THE STRENUOUS, VIRILE SPORTS... LIKE BOWLING!
THAT'S RIGHT... THERE'S MY GAME! IF Y' WANT A REAL HE-MAN SPORT, WILBUR, JUST TRY BOWLING!
YES, IT'S VERY POPULAR! IT'S ALL THE RAGE BACK HOME... WITH MY MOTHER'S BRIDGE CLUB!

TUESDAY!

YOU KNOW WHAT I'D LIKE, MONTY? LET'S RENT SOME HORSES AND GO FOR A CANTER THROUGH THE PARK!

GREAT IDEA, TOOTS! SOUNDS KEEN!

BRIDLE PATH CROSSING

I JUST ADORE HORSES!!

YIPPEE! HI Y', FOLKS!

HELLO, THERE!

I WOULDN'T GO **RIDING** IF THERE WAS NOTHING ELSE TO DO **ON EARTH!**

WEDNESDAY!

Chic CHAPEAU SHOP.

WHAT A HEAVENLY NEW STYLE! I **MUST** HAVE IT TO WEAR TO THE BAZAAR TOMORROW!

HI, MINNIE!

OH...GOOD MORNING! DON'T TELL ME YOU'RE SUDDENLY INTERESTED IN WOMEN'S HATS!

Chic CHAP SHOP.

NOPE! JUST PICKIN' UP A LID THAT MILLICENT BOUGHT YESTERDAY... IT'S LIKE THAT ONE THERE!

Chic CHAPEAU SHOP.

THAT LITTLE COUNTRY MODEL?

HOW QUAINT!

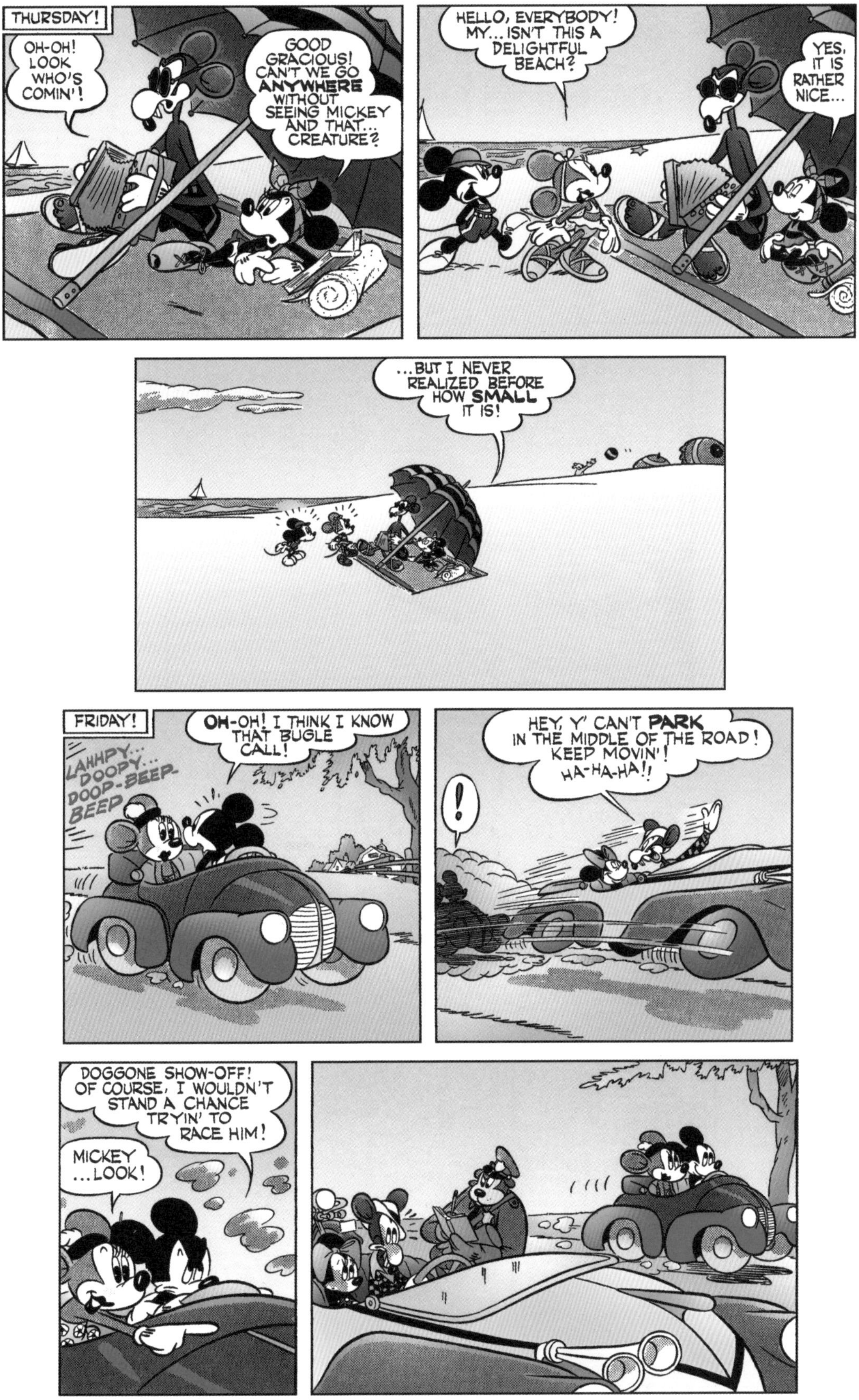
THURSDAY!
OH-OH! LOOK WHO'S COMIN'!
GOOD GRACIOUS! CAN'T WE GO ANYWHERE WITHOUT SEEING MICKEY AND THAT... CREATURE?
HELLO, EVERYBODY! MY... ISN'T THIS A DELIGHTFUL BEACH?
YES, IT IS RATHER NICE...
...BUT I NEVER REALIZED BEFORE HOW SMALL IT IS!
FRIDAY!
LAHHPY... DOOPY... DOOP-BEEP-BEEP
OH-OH! I THINK I KNOW THAT BUGLE CALL!
!
HEY, Y' CAN'T PARK IN THE MIDDLE OF THE ROAD! KEEP MOVIN'! HA-HA-HA!!
DOGGONE SHOW-OFF! OF COURSE, I WOULDN'T STAND A CHANCE TRYIN' TO RACE HIM!
MICKEY ...LOOK!

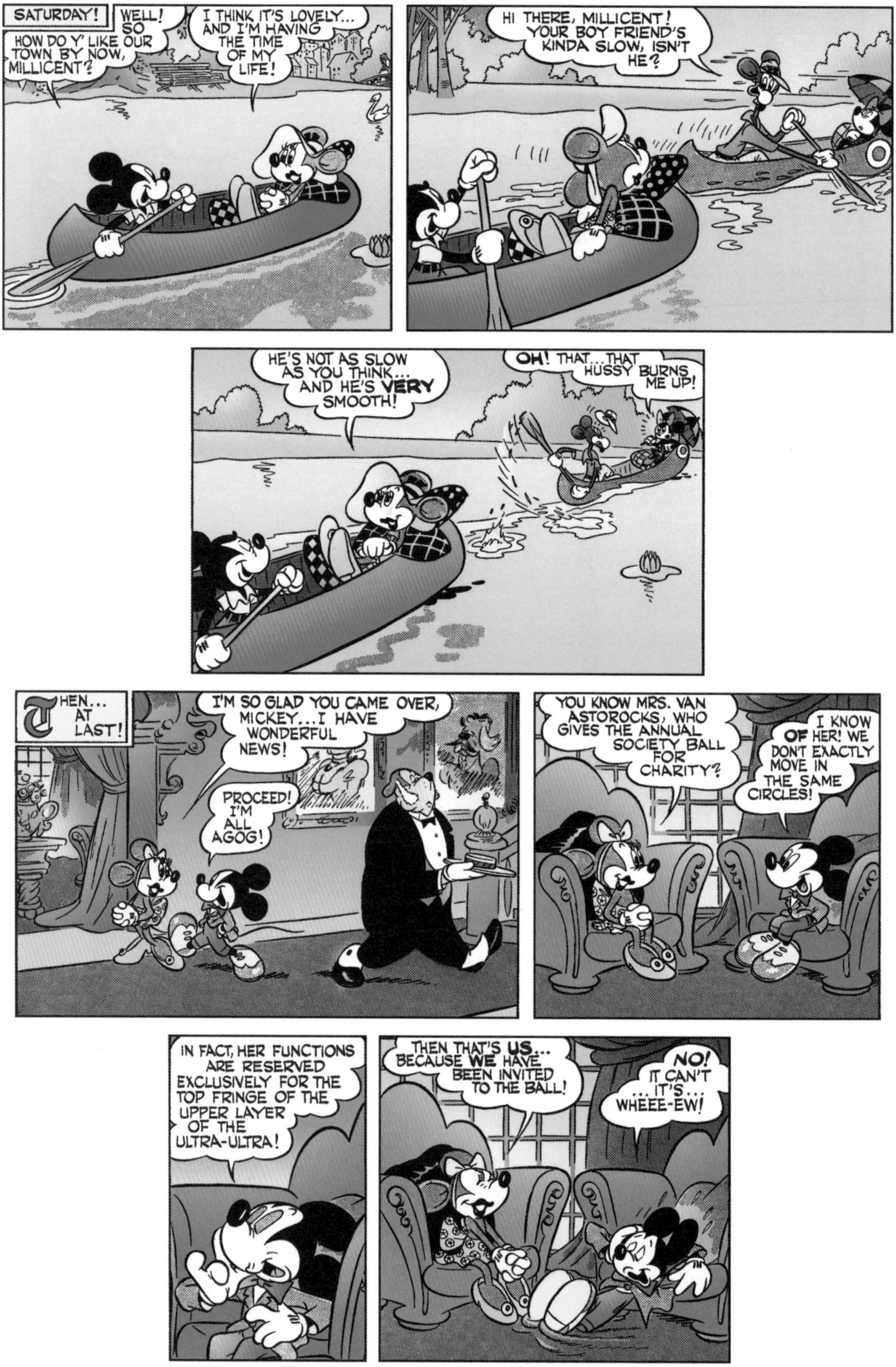
SATURDAY!
HOW DO Y' LIKE OUR TOWN BY NOW, MILLICENT?
WELL! SO
I THINK IT'S LOVELY... AND I'M HAVING THE TIME OF MY LIFE!
HI THERE, MILLICENT! YOUR BOY FRIEND'S KINDA SLOW, ISN'T HE?
HE'S NOT AS SLOW AS YOU THINK... AND HE'S VERY SMOOTH!
OH! THAT...THAT HUSSY BURNS ME UP!
THEN... AT LAST!
I'M SO GLAD YOU CAME OVER, MICKEY...I HAVE WONDERFUL NEWS!
PROCEED! I'M ALL AGOG!
YOU KNOW MRS. VAN ASTOROCKS, WHO GIVES THE ANNUAL SOCIETY BALL FOR CHARITY?
I KNOW OF HER! WE DON'T EXACTLY MOVE IN THE SAME CIRCLES!
IN FACT, HER FUNCTIONS ARE RESERVED EXCLUSIVELY FOR THE TOP FRINGE OF THE UPPER LAYER OF THE ULTRA-ULTRA!
THEN THAT'S US... BECAUSE WE HAVE BEEN INVITED TO THE BALL!
NO! IT CAN'T ... IT'S... WHEEE-EW!

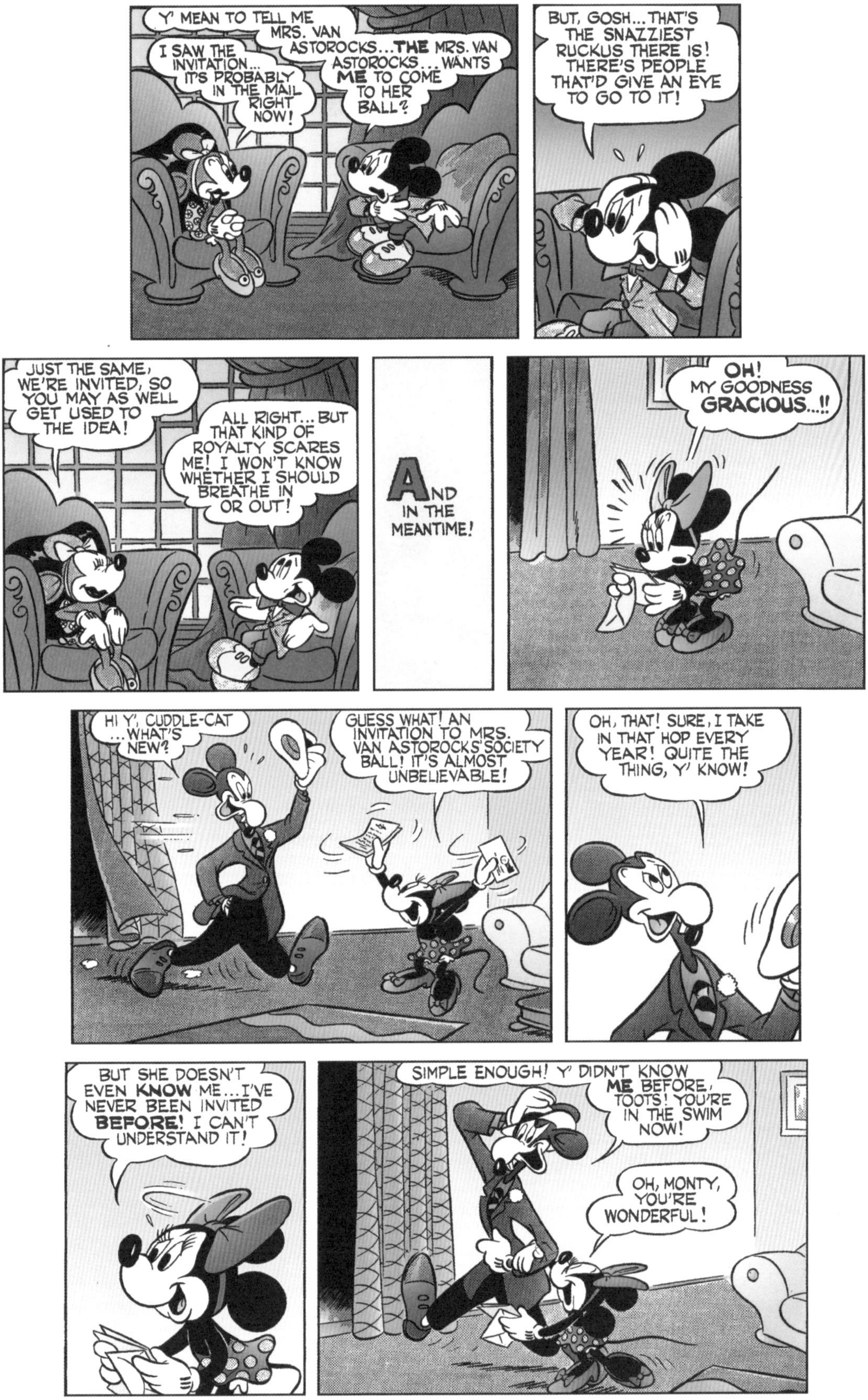

Y' MEAN TO TELL ME MRS. VAN ASTOROCKS... THE MRS. VAN ASTOROCKS... WANTS ME TO COME TO HER BALL?
I SAW THE INVITATION... IT'S PROBABLY IN THE MAIL RIGHT NOW!
BUT, GOSH... THAT'S THE SNAZZIEST RUCKUS THERE IS! THERE'S PEOPLE THAT'D GIVE AN EYE TO GO TO IT!
JUST THE SAME, WE'RE INVITED, SO YOU MAY AS WELL GET USED TO THE IDEA!
ALL RIGHT... BUT THAT KIND OF ROYALTY SCARES ME! I WON'T KNOW WHETHER I SHOULD BREATHE IN OR OUT!
AND IN THE MEANTIME!
OH! MY GOODNESS GRACIOUS...!!
HI Y', CUDDLE-CAT ...WHAT'S NEW?
GUESS WHAT! AN INVITATION TO MRS. VAN ASTOROCKS' SOCIETY BALL! IT'S ALMOST UNBELIEVABLE!
OH, THAT! SURE, I TAKE IN THAT HOP EVERY YEAR! QUITE THE THING, Y' KNOW!
BUT SHE DOESN'T EVEN KNOW ME... I'VE NEVER BEEN INVITED BEFORE! I CAN'T UNDERSTAND IT!
SIMPLE ENOUGH! Y' DIDN'T KNOW ME BEFORE, TOOTS! YOU'RE IN THE SWIM NOW!
OH, MONTY, YOU'RE WONDERFUL!

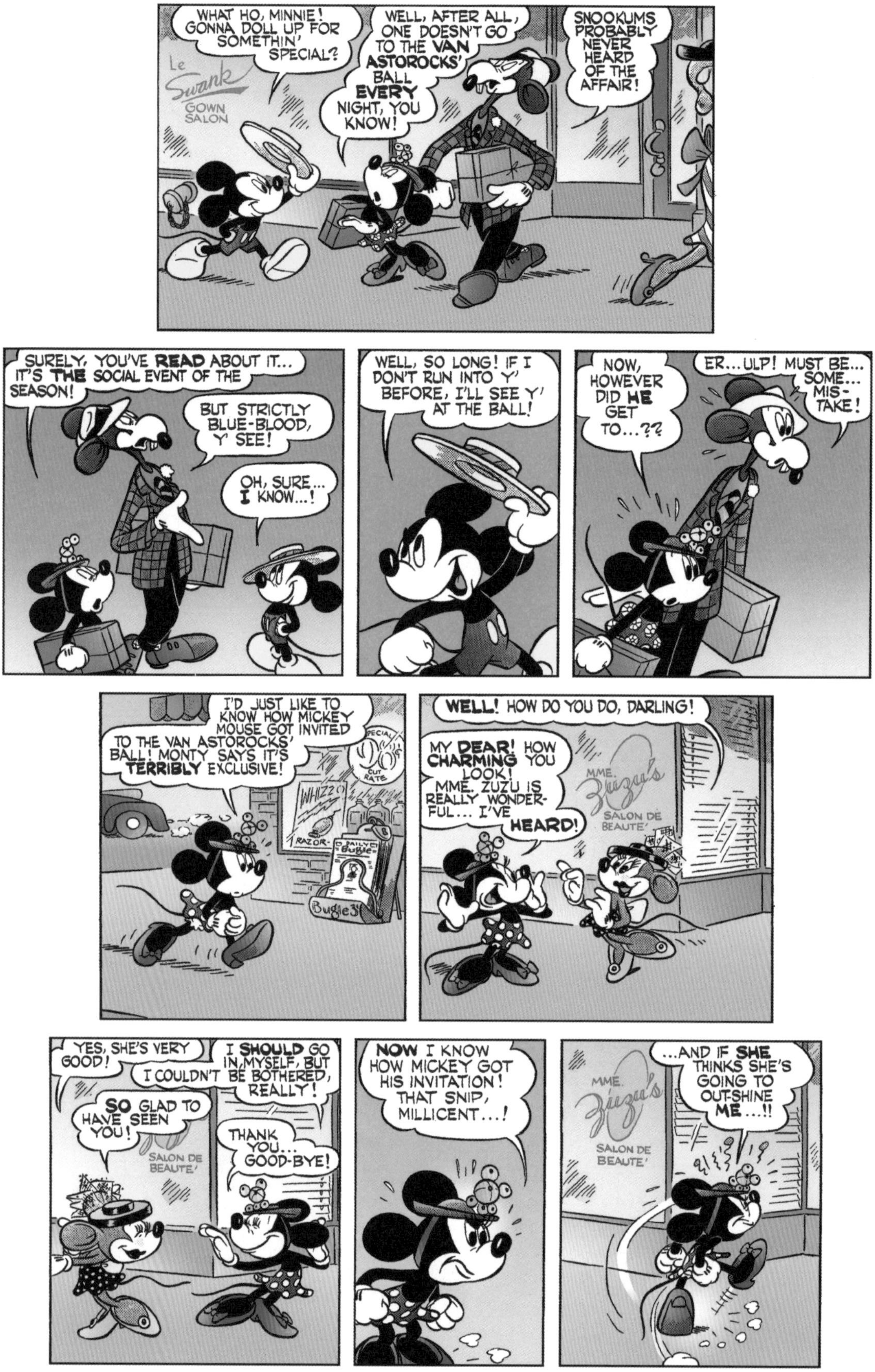

Le Swank GOWN SALON
WHAT HO, MINNIE! GONNA DOLL UP FOR SOMETHIN' SPECIAL?
WELL, AFTER ALL, ONE DOESN'T GO TO THE VAN ASTOROCKS' BALL EVERY NIGHT, YOU KNOW!
SNOOKUMS PROBABLY NEVER HEARD OF THE AFFAIR!
SURELY, YOU'VE READ ABOUT IT... IT'S THE SOCIAL EVENT OF THE SEASON!
BUT STRICTLY BLUE-BLOOD, Y' SEE!
OH, SURE... I KNOW...!
WELL, SO LONG! IF I DON'T RUN INTO Y' BEFORE, I'LL SEE Y' AT THE BALL!
NOW, HOWEVER DID HE GET TO...??
ER...ULP! MUST BE... SOME... MIS-TAKE!
I'D JUST LIKE TO KNOW HOW MICKEY MOUSE GOT INVITED TO THE VAN ASTOROCKS' BALL! MONTY SAYS IT'S TERRIBLY EXCLUSIVE!
PECIAL CUT RATE
WHIZZ RAZOR
DAILY Bugle
Bugle 3¢
WELL! HOW DO YOU DO, DARLING!
MY DEAR! HOW CHARMING YOU LOOK! MME. ZUZU IS REALLY WONDERFUL... I'VE HEARD!
MME. Zuzu's SALON DE BEAUTE'
YES, SHE'S VERY GOOD!
I SHOULD GO IN MYSELF, BUT I COULDN'T BE BOTHERED, REALLY!
SO GLAD TO HAVE SEEN YOU!
SALON DE BEAUTE'
THANK YOU... GOOD-BYE!
NOW I KNOW HOW MICKEY GOT HIS INVITATION! THAT SNIP, MILLICENT...!
MME. Zuzu's SALON DE BEAUTE'
...AND IF SHE THINKS SHE'S GOING TO OUT-SHINE ME...!!

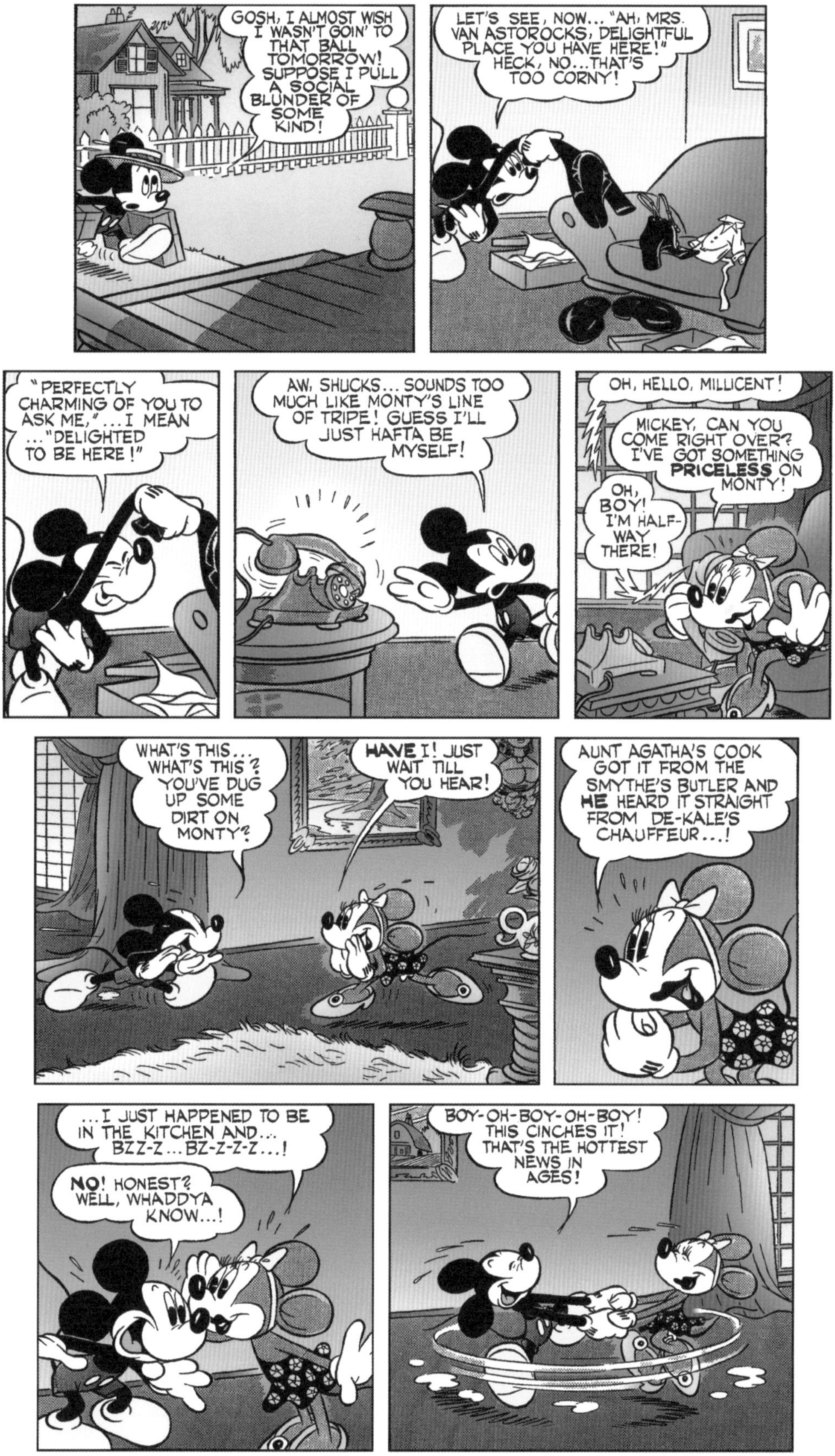
GOSH, I ALMOST WISH I WASN'T GOIN' TO THAT BALL TOMORROW! SUPPOSE I PULL A SOCIAL BLUNDER OF SOME KIND!
LET'S SEE, NOW... "AH, MRS. VAN ASTOROCKS, DELIGHTFUL PLACE YOU HAVE HERE!" HECK, NO...THAT'S TOO CORNY!
"PERFECTLY CHARMING OF YOU TO ASK ME," ... I MEAN ... "DELIGHTED TO BE HERE!"
AW, SHUCKS... SOUNDS TOO MUCH LIKE MONTY'S LINE OF TRIPE! GUESS I'LL JUST HAFTA BE MYSELF!
OH, HELLO, MILLICENT!
MICKEY, CAN YOU COME RIGHT OVER? I'VE GOT SOMETHING **PRICELESS** ON MONTY!
OH, BOY! I'M HALF-WAY THERE!
WHAT'S THIS... WHAT'S THIS? YOU'VE DUG UP SOME DIRT ON MONTY?
HAVE I! JUST WAIT TILL YOU HEAR!
AUNT AGATHA'S COOK GOT IT FROM THE SMYTHE'S BUTLER AND **HE** HEARD IT STRAIGHT FROM DE-KALE'S CHAUFFEUR...!
...I JUST HAPPENED TO BE IN THE KITCHEN AND... BZZ-Z... BZ-Z-Z-Z...!
NO! HONEST? WELL, WHADDYA KNOW...!
BOY-OH-BOY-OH-BOY! THIS CINCHES IT! THAT'S THE HOTTEST NEWS IN AGES!

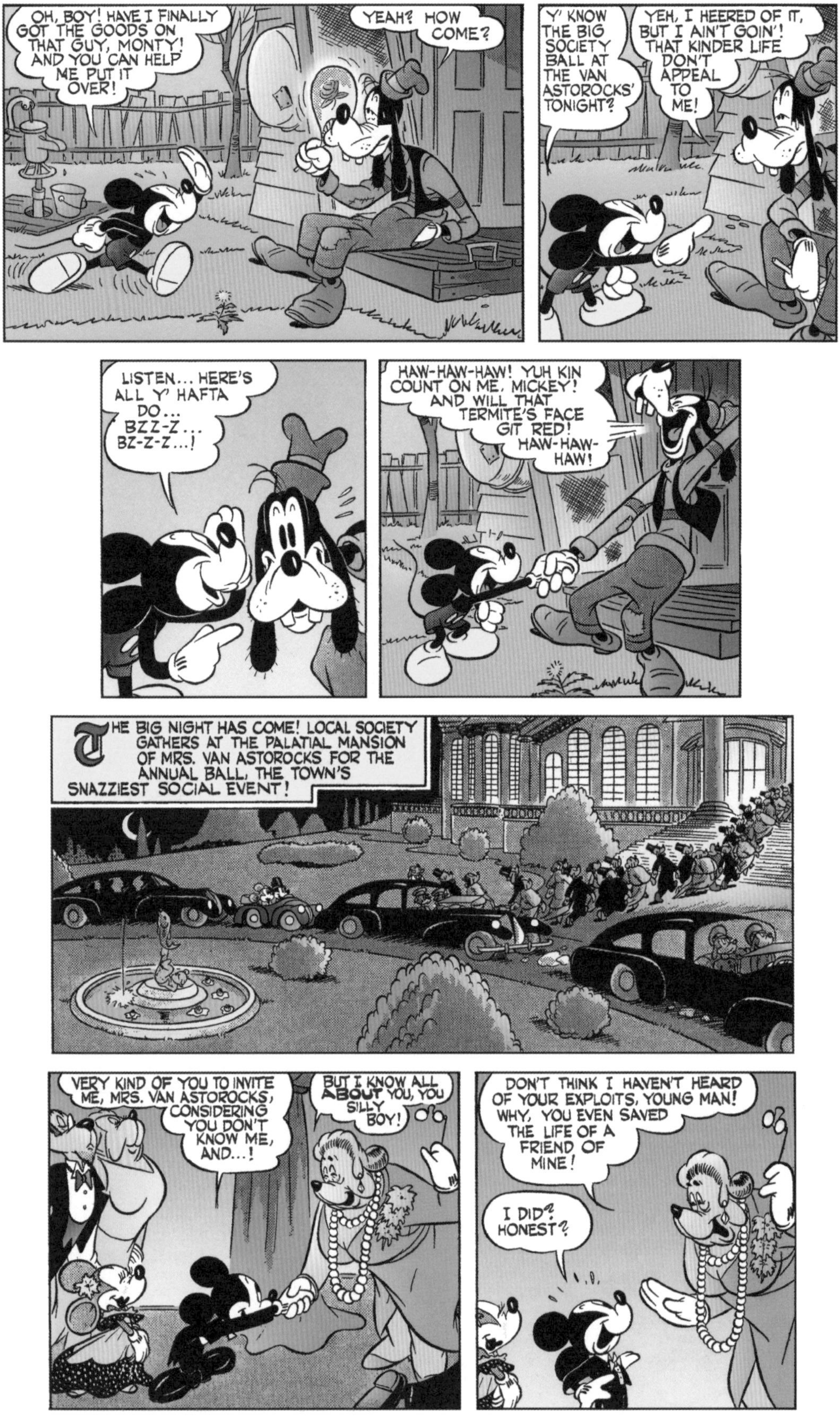
OH, BOY! HAVE I FINALLY GOT THE GOODS ON THAT GUY, MONTY! AND YOU CAN HELP ME PUT IT OVER!
YEAH? HOW COME?
Y' KNOW THE BIG SOCIETY BALL AT THE VAN ASTOROCKS' TONIGHT?
YEH, I HEERED OF IT, BUT I AIN'T GOIN'! THAT KINDER LIFE DON'T APPEAL TO ME!
LISTEN... HERE'S ALL Y' HAFTA DO... BZZ-Z... BZ-Z-Z...!
HAW-HAW-HAW! YUH KIN COUNT ON ME, MICKEY! AND WILL THAT TERMITE'S FACE GIT RED! HAW-HAW-HAW!
THE BIG NIGHT HAS COME! LOCAL SOCIETY GATHERS AT THE PALATIAL MANSION OF MRS. VAN ASTOROCKS FOR THE ANNUAL BALL, THE TOWN'S SNAZZIEST SOCIAL EVENT!
VERY KIND OF YOU TO INVITE ME, MRS. VAN ASTOROCKS, CONSIDERING YOU DON'T KNOW ME, AND...!
BUT I KNOW ALL ABOUT YOU, YOU SILLY BOY!
DON'T THINK I HAVEN'T HEARD OF YOUR EXPLOITS, YOUNG MAN! WHY, YOU EVEN SAVED THE LIFE OF A FRIEND OF MINE!
I DID? HONEST?

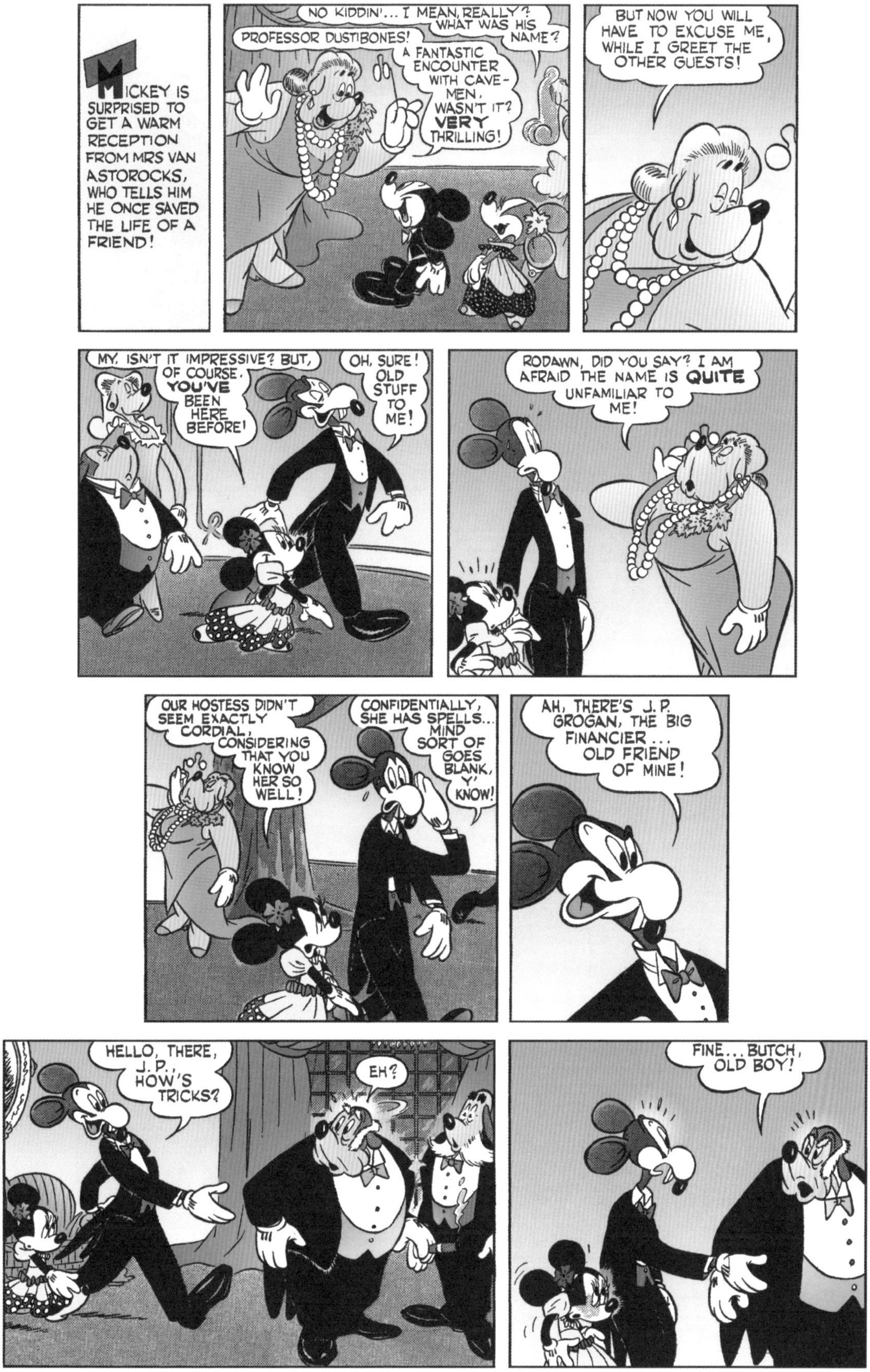
MICKEY IS SURPRISED TO GET A WARM RECEPTION FROM MRS VAN ASTOROCKS, WHO TELLS HIM HE ONCE SAVED THE LIFE OF A FRIEND!
PROFESSOR DUSTIBONES!
NO KIDDIN'... I MEAN, REALLY? WHAT WAS HIS NAME?
A FANTASTIC ENCOUNTER WITH CAVE-MEN, WASN'T IT? VERY THRILLING!
BUT NOW YOU WILL HAVE TO EXCUSE ME, WHILE I GREET THE OTHER GUESTS!
MY, ISN'T IT IMPRESSIVE? BUT, OF COURSE, YOU'VE BEEN HERE BEFORE!
OH, SURE! OLD STUFF TO ME!
RODAWN, DID YOU SAY? I AM AFRAID THE NAME IS QUITE UNFAMILIAR TO ME!
OUR HOSTESS DIDN'T SEEM EXACTLY CORDIAL, CONSIDERING THAT YOU KNOW HER SO WELL!
CONFIDENTIALLY, SHE HAS SPELLS... MIND SORT OF GOES BLANK, Y' KNOW!
AH, THERE'S J. P. GROGAN, THE BIG FINANCIER... OLD FRIEND OF MINE!
HELLO, THERE, J. P., HOW'S TRICKS?
EH?
FINE... BUTCH, OLD BOY!

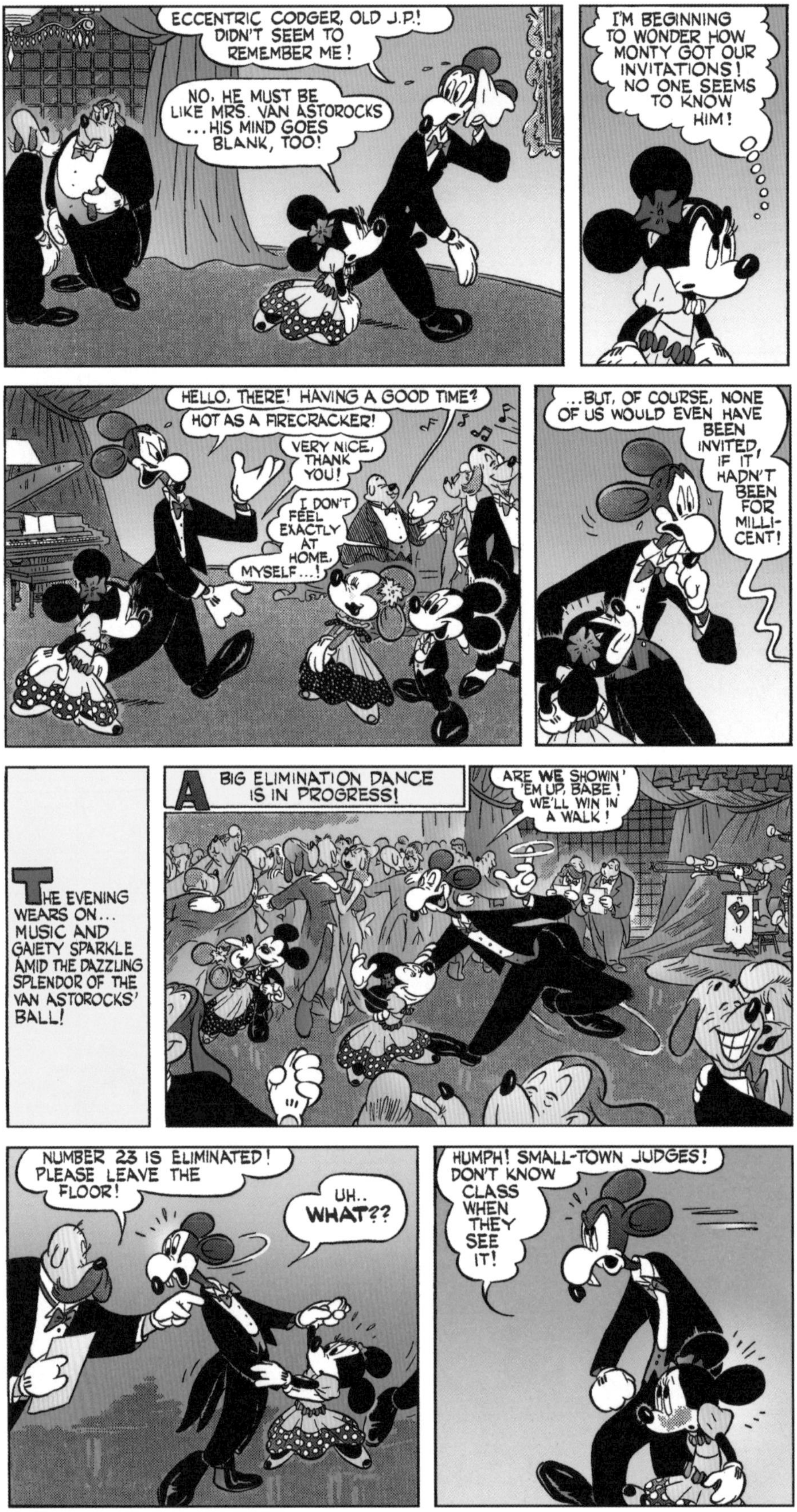

ECCENTRIC CODGER, OLD J.P.! DIDN'T SEEM TO REMEMBER ME!
NO, HE MUST BE LIKE MRS. VAN ASTOROCKS ...HIS MIND GOES BLANK, TOO!
I'M BEGINNING TO WONDER HOW MONTY GOT OUR INVITATIONS! NO ONE SEEMS TO KNOW HIM!
HELLO, THERE! HAVING A GOOD TIME?
HOT AS A FIRECRACKER!
VERY NICE, THANK YOU!
I DON'T FEEL EXACTLY AT HOME, MYSELF...!
...BUT, OF COURSE, NONE OF US WOULD EVEN HAVE BEEN INVITED, IF IT HADN'T BEEN FOR MILLICENT!
THE EVENING WEARS ON... MUSIC AND GAIETY SPARKLE AMID THE DAZZLING SPLENDOR OF THE VAN ASTOROCKS' BALL!
A BIG ELIMINATION DANCE IS IN PROGRESS!
ARE WE SHOWIN' 'EM UP, BABE! WE'LL WIN IN A WALK!
NUMBER 23 IS ELIMINATED! PLEASE LEAVE THE FLOOR!
UH.. WHAT??
HUMPH! SMALL-TOWN JUDGES! DON'T KNOW CLASS WHEN THEY SEE IT!

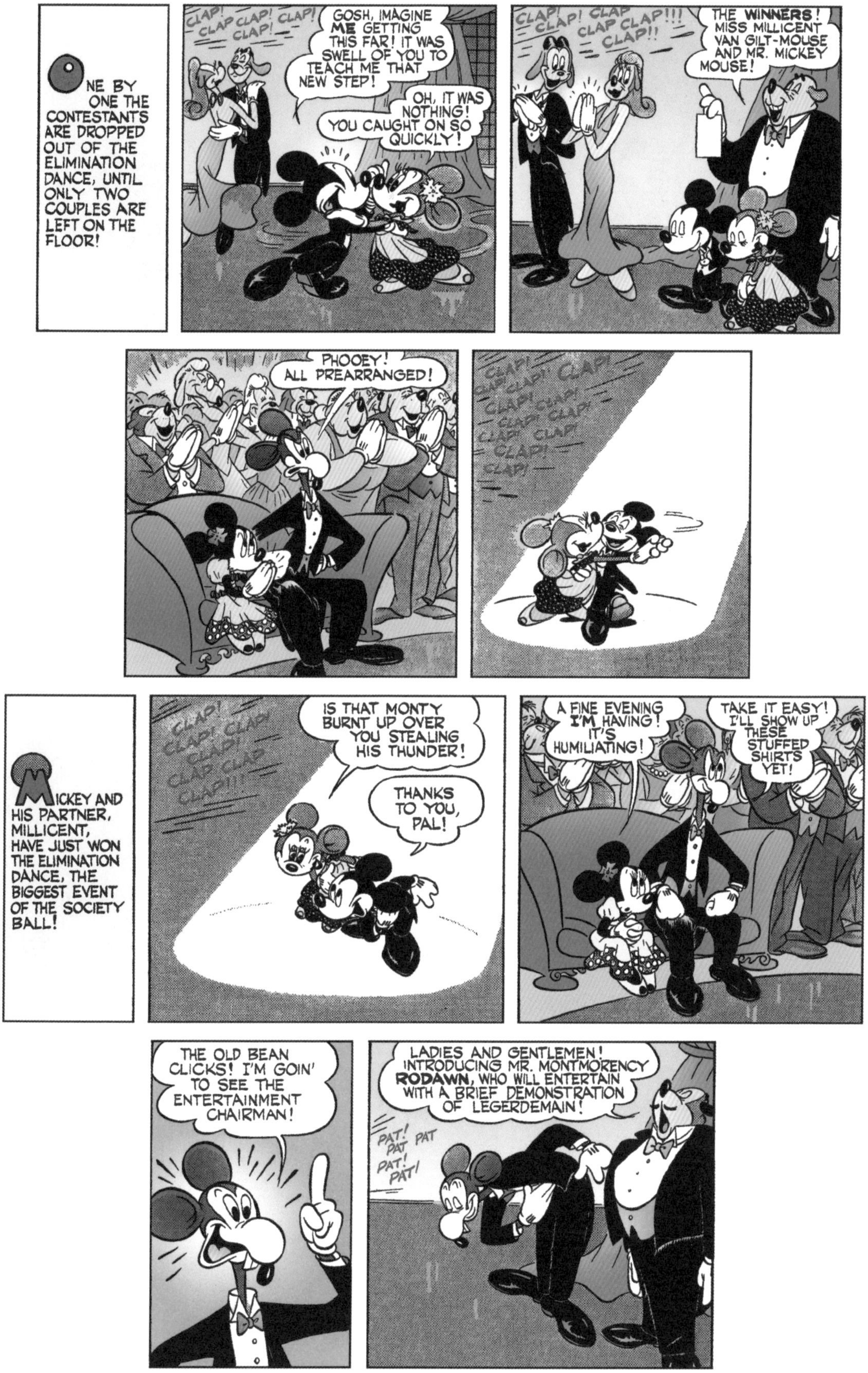
ONE BY ONE THE CONTESTANTS ARE DROPPED OUT OF THE ELIMINATION DANCE, UNTIL ONLY TWO COUPLES ARE LEFT ON THE FLOOR!
CLAP! CLAP CLAP! CLAP! CLAP!
GOSH, IMAGINE ME GETTING THIS FAR! IT WAS SWELL OF YOU TO TEACH ME THAT NEW STEP!
OH, IT WAS NOTHING! YOU CAUGHT ON SO QUICKLY!
CLAP! CLAP! CLAP CLAP CLAP!!! CLAP!!
THE WINNERS! MISS MILLICENT VAN GILT-MOUSE AND MR. MICKEY MOUSE!
PHOOEY! ALL PREARRANGED!
CLAP! CLAP! CLAP! CLAP! CLAP! CLAP! CLAP! CLAP! CLAP! CLAP! CLAP! CLAP!
MICKEY AND HIS PARTNER, MILLICENT, HAVE JUST WON THE ELIMINATION DANCE, THE BIGGEST EVENT OF THE SOCIETY BALL!
CLAP! CLAP! CLAP! CLAP! CLAP CLAP! CLAP!!!
IS THAT MONTY BURNT UP OVER YOU STEALING HIS THUNDER!
THANKS TO YOU, PAL!
A FINE EVENING I'M HAVING! IT'S HUMILIATING!
TAKE IT EASY! I'LL SHOW UP THESE STUFFED SHIRTS YET!
THE OLD BEAN CLICKS! I'M GOIN' TO SEE THE ENTERTAINMENT CHAIRMAN!
LADIES AND GENTLEMEN! INTRODUCING MR. MONTMORENCY RODAWN, WHO WILL ENTERTAIN WITH A BRIEF DEMONSTRATION OF LEGERDEMAIN!
PAT! PAT PAT PAT! PAT!

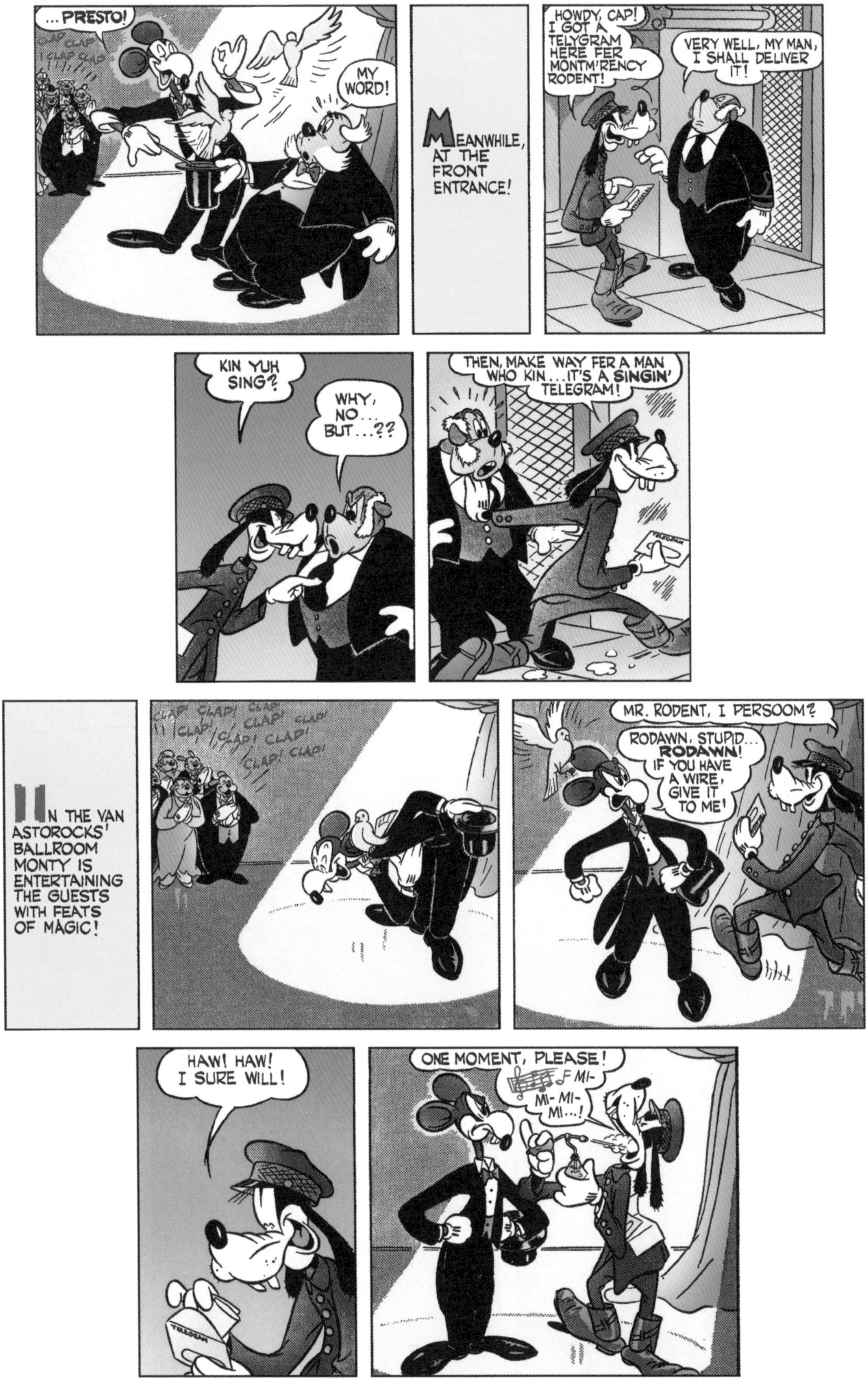
...PRESTO!
CLAP CLAP CLAP CLAP
MY WORD!
MEANWHILE, AT THE FRONT ENTRANCE!
HOWDY, CAP! I GOT A TELYGRAM HERE FER MONTM'RENCY RODENT!
VERY WELL, MY MAN, I SHALL DELIVER IT!
KIN YUH SING?
WHY, NO... BUT...??
THEN, MAKE WAY FER A MAN WHO KIN... IT'S A SINGIN' TELEGRAM!
TELEGRAM
IN THE VAN ASTOROCKS' BALLROOM MONTY IS ENTERTAINING THE GUESTS WITH FEATS OF MAGIC!
CLAP! CLAP! CLAP! CLAP! CLAP! CLAP! CLAP! CLAP! CLAP! CLAP!
MR. RODENT, I PERSOOM?
RODAWN, STUPID... RODAWN! IF YOU HAVE A WIRE, GIVE IT TO ME!
HAW! HAW! I SURE WILL!
TELEGRAM
ONE MOMENT, PLEASE!
MI- MI- MI- MI...!

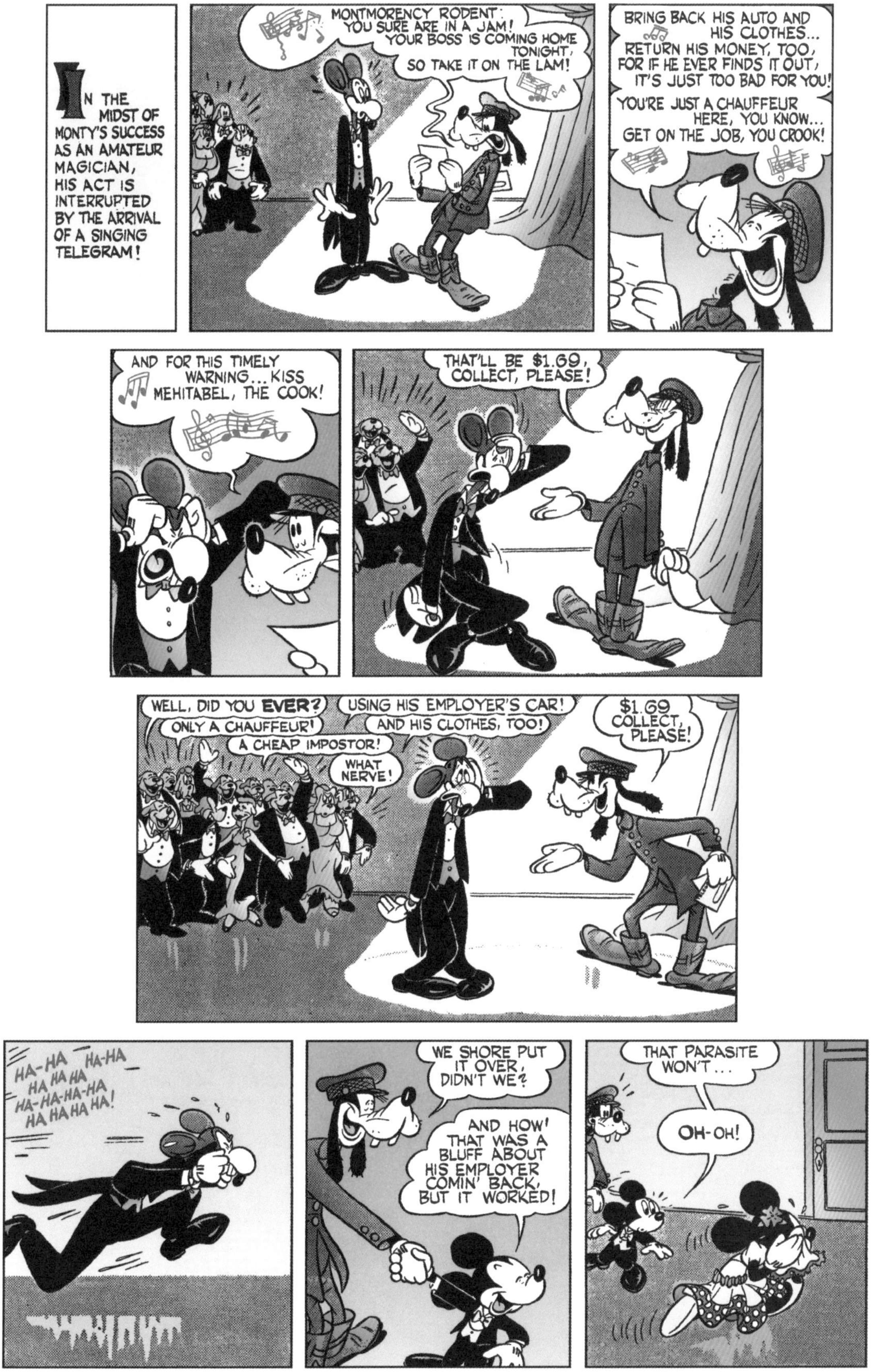

IN THE MIDST OF MONTY'S SUCCESS AS AN AMATEUR MAGICIAN, HIS ACT IS INTERRUPTED BY THE ARRIVAL OF A SINGING TELEGRAM!
MONTMORENCY RODENT: YOU SURE ARE IN A JAM! YOUR BOSS IS COMING HOME TONIGHT, SO TAKE IT ON THE LAM!
BRING BACK HIS AUTO AND HIS CLOTHES... RETURN HIS MONEY, TOO, FOR IF HE EVER FINDS IT OUT, IT'S JUST TOO BAD FOR YOU!
YOU'RE JUST A CHAUFFEUR HERE, YOU KNOW... GET ON THE JOB, YOU CROOK!
AND FOR THIS TIMELY WARNING... KISS MEHITABEL, THE COOK!
THAT'LL BE $1.69, COLLECT, PLEASE!
WELL, DID YOU EVER?
USING HIS EMPLOYER'S CAR!
ONLY A CHAUFFEUR!
AND HIS CLOTHES, TOO!
A CHEAP IMPOSTOR!
WHAT NERVE!
$1.69 COLLECT, PLEASE!
HA-HA HA-HA HA HA HA HA-HA-HA-HA HA HA HA HA!
WE SHORE PUT IT OVER, DIDN'T WE?
AND HOW! THAT WAS A BLUFF ABOUT HIS EMPLOYER COMIN' BACK, BUT IT WORKED!
THAT PARASITE WON'T...
OH-OH!

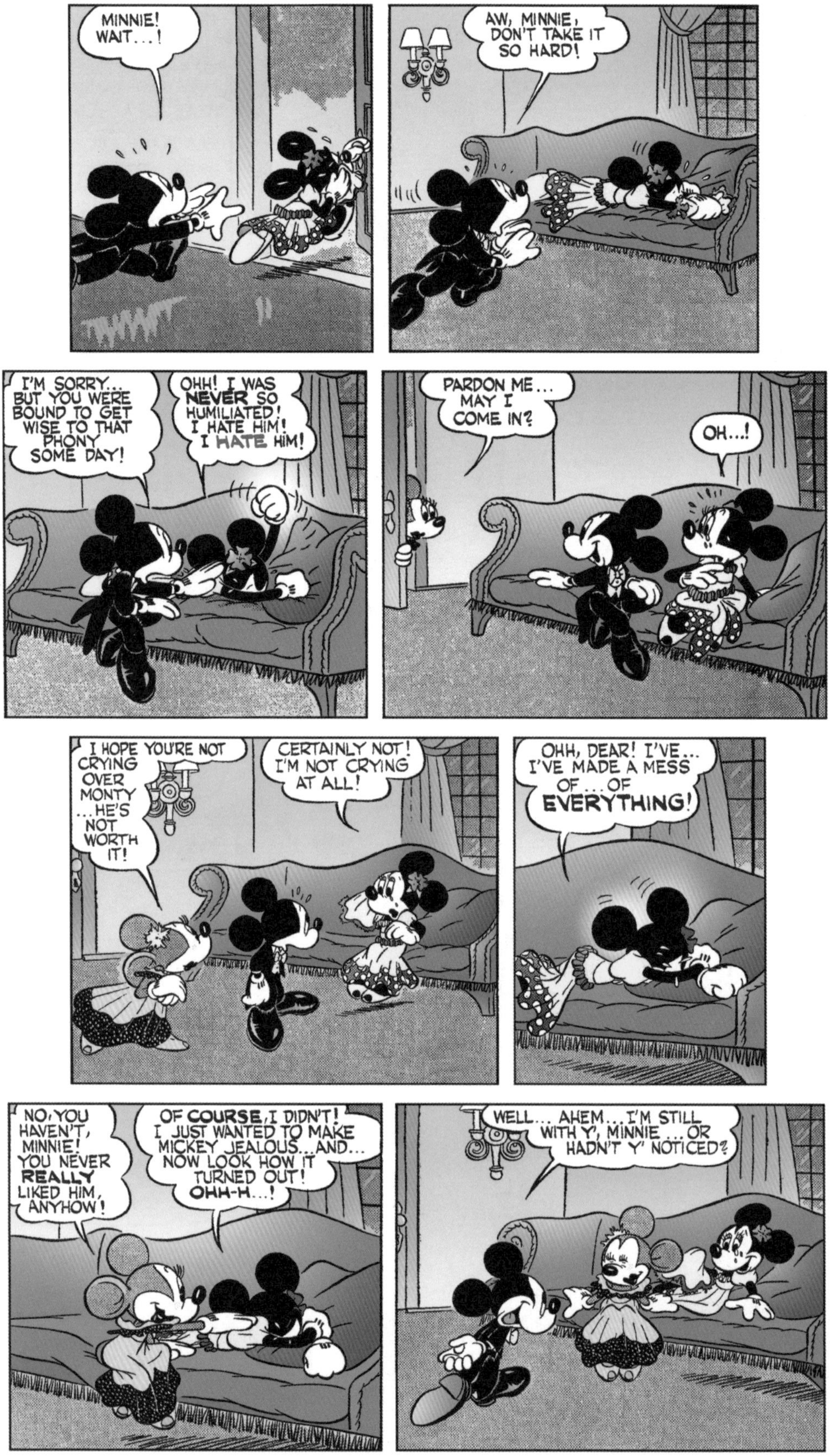
MINNIE! WAIT...!
AW, MINNIE, DON'T TAKE IT SO HARD!
I'M SORRY... BUT YOU WERE BOUND TO GET WISE TO THAT PHONY SOME DAY!
OHH! I WAS NEVER SO HUMILIATED! I HATE HIM! I HATE HIM!
PARDON ME... MAY I COME IN?
OH...!
I HOPE YOU'RE NOT CRYING OVER MONTY ...HE'S NOT WORTH IT!
CERTAINLY NOT! I'M NOT CRYING AT ALL!
OHH, DEAR! I'VE... I'VE MADE A MESS OF... OF EVERYTHING!
NO, YOU HAVEN'T, MINNIE! YOU NEVER REALLY LIKED HIM, ANYHOW!
OF COURSE, I DIDN'T! I JUST WANTED TO MAKE MICKEY JEALOUS...AND... NOW LOOK HOW IT TURNED OUT! OHH-H...!
WELL... AHEM... I'M STILL WITH Y', MINNIE ... OR HADN'T Y' NOTICED?

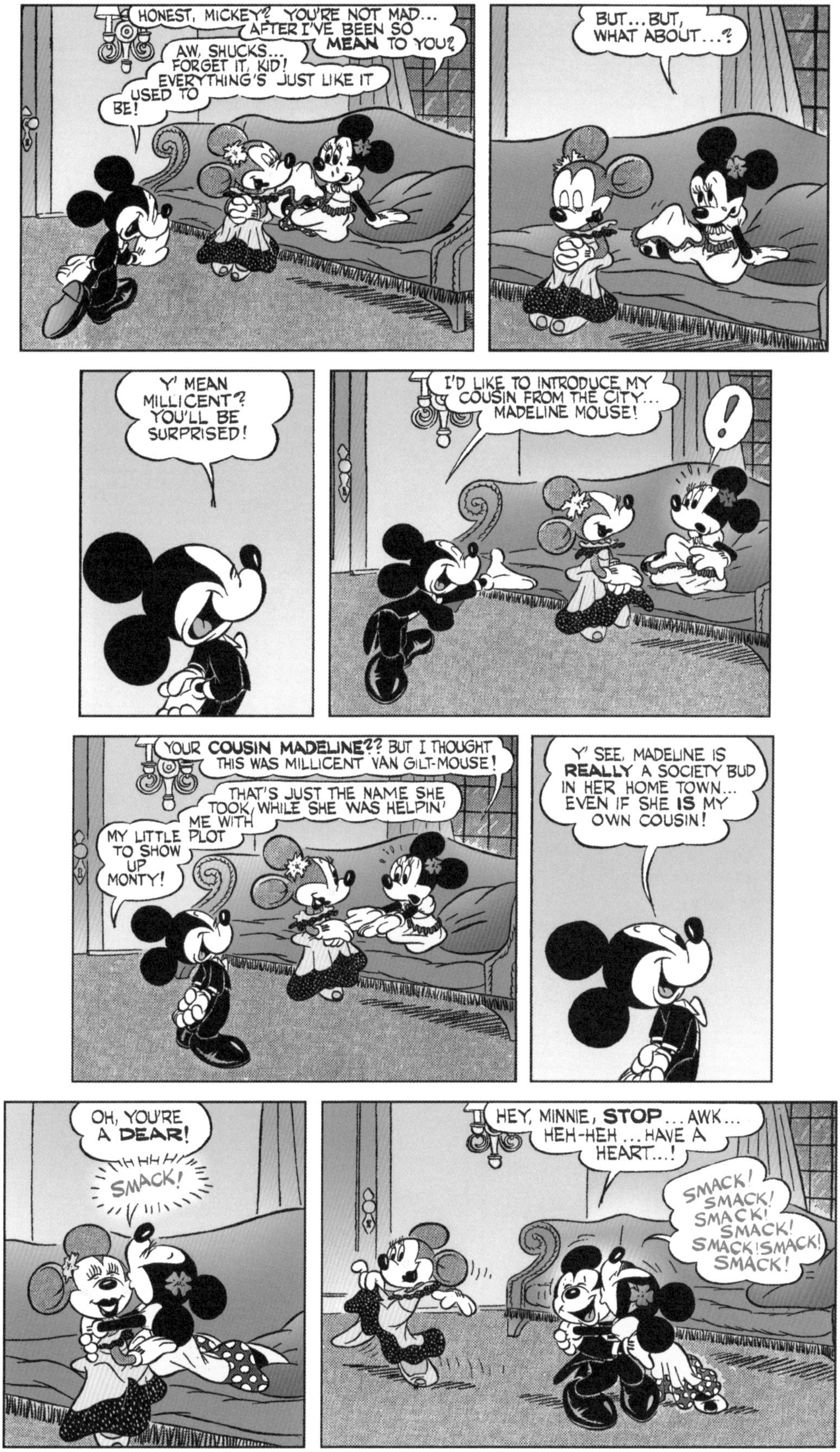
HONEST, MICKEY?? YOU'RE NOT MAD... AFTER I'VE BEEN SO **MEAN** TO YOU?
AW, SHUCKS... FORGET IT, KID! EVERYTHING'S JUST LIKE IT USED TO BE!
BUT... BUT, WHAT ABOUT...?
Y' MEAN MILLICENT? YOU'LL BE SURPRISED!
I'D LIKE TO INTRODUCE MY COUSIN FROM THE CITY... MADELINE MOUSE!
!
YOUR **COUSIN MADELINE??** BUT I THOUGHT THIS WAS MILLICENT VAN GILT-MOUSE!
THAT'S JUST THE NAME SHE TOOK WHILE SHE WAS HELPIN' ME WITH MY LITTLE PLOT TO SHOW UP MONTY!
Y' SEE, MADELINE IS **REALLY** A SOCIETY BUD IN HER HOME TOWN... EVEN IF SHE **IS** MY OWN COUSIN!
OH, YOU'RE A **DEAR**!
SMACK!
HEY, MINNIE, **STOP**... AWK... HEH-HEH... HAVE A HEART...!
SMACK! SMACK! SMACK! SMACK! SMACK! SMACK! SMACK!

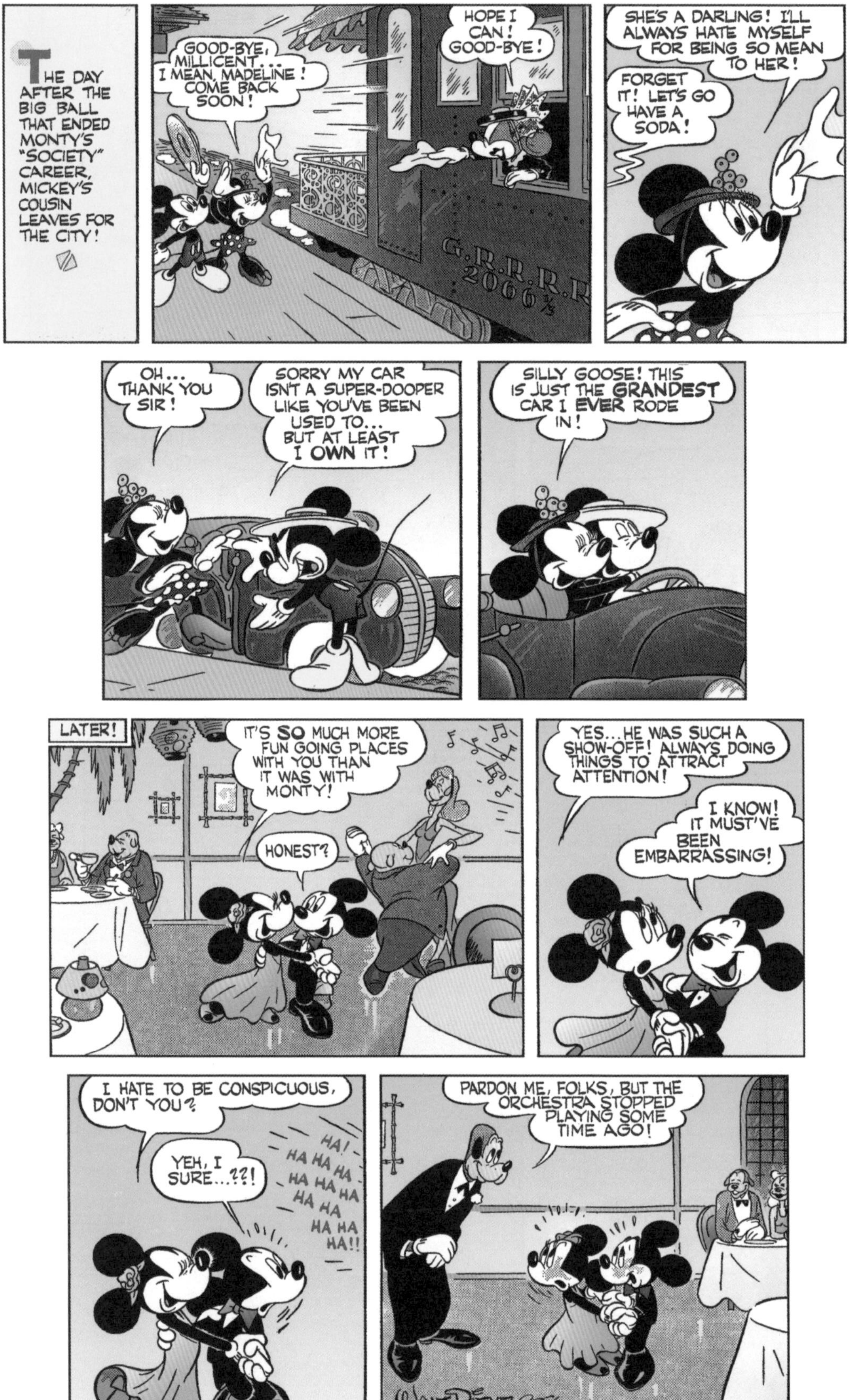
THE DAY AFTER THE BIG BALL THAT ENDED MONTY'S "SOCIETY" CAREER, MICKEY'S COUSIN LEAVES FOR THE CITY!
GOOD-BYE, MILLICENT... I MEAN, MADELINE! COME BACK SOON!
HOPE I CAN! GOOD-BYE!
G.R.R.R.R.R. 2066 1/3
SHE'S A DARLING! I'LL ALWAYS HATE MYSELF FOR BEING SO MEAN TO HER!
FORGET IT! LET'S GO HAVE A SODA!
OH... THANK YOU SIR!
SORRY MY CAR ISN'T A SUPER-DOOPER LIKE YOU'VE BEEN USED TO... BUT AT LEAST I OWN IT!
SILLY GOOSE! THIS IS JUST THE GRANDEST CAR I EVER RODE IN!
LATER!
IT'S SO MUCH MORE FUN GOING PLACES WITH YOU THAN IT WAS WITH MONTY!
HONEST?
YES... HE WAS SUCH A SHOW-OFF! ALWAYS DOING THINGS TO ATTRACT ATTENTION!
I KNOW! IT MUST'VE BEEN EMBARRASSING!
I HATE TO BE CONSPICUOUS, DON'T YOU?
YEH, I SURE...??!
HA! HA HA HA HA HA HA HA HA HA HA HA HA!!
PARDON ME, FOLKS, BUT THE ORCHESTRA STOPPED PLAYING SOME TIME AGO!
WALT DISNEY

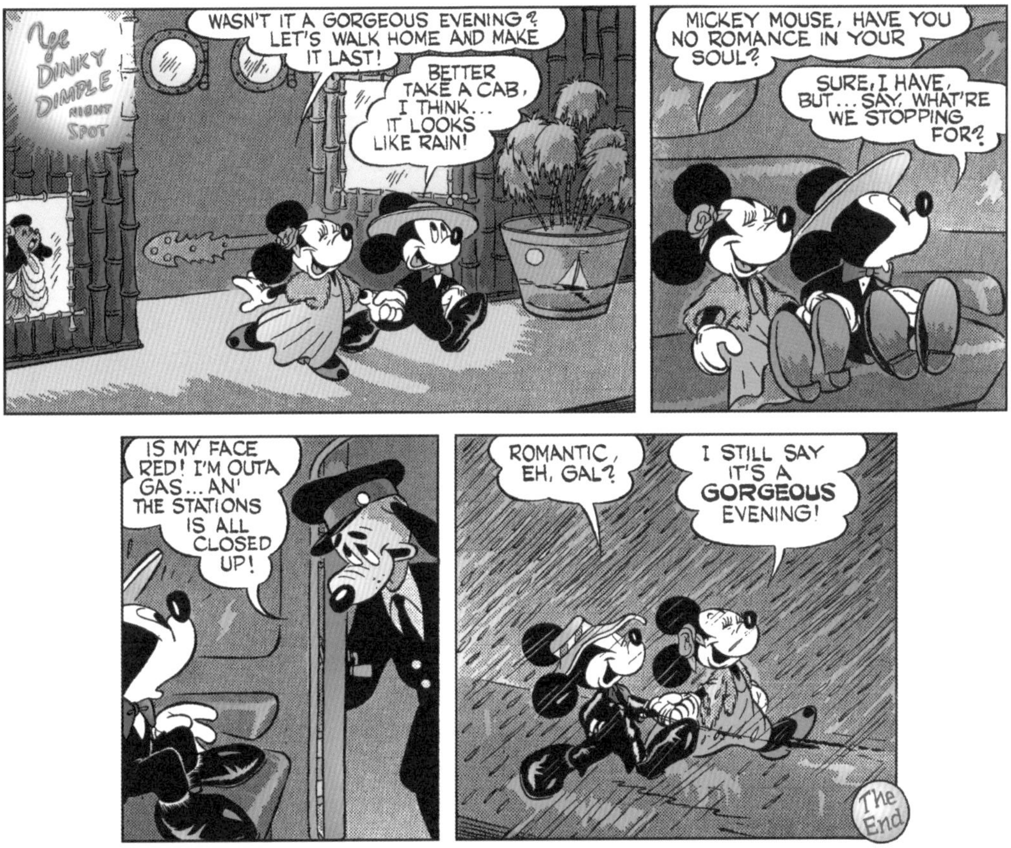
Ye DINKY DIMPLE NIGHT SPOT
WASN'T IT A GORGEOUS EVENING? LET'S WALK HOME AND MAKE IT LAST!
BETTER TAKE A CAB, I THINK... IT LOOKS LIKE RAIN!
MICKEY MOUSE, HAVE YOU NO ROMANCE IN YOUR SOUL?
SURE, I HAVE, BUT... SAY, WHAT'RE WE STOPPING FOR?
IS MY FACE RED! I'M OUTA GAS... AN' THE STATIONS IS ALL CLOSED UP!
ROMANTIC, EH, GAL?
I STILL SAY IT'S A **GORGEOUS** EVENING!
The End

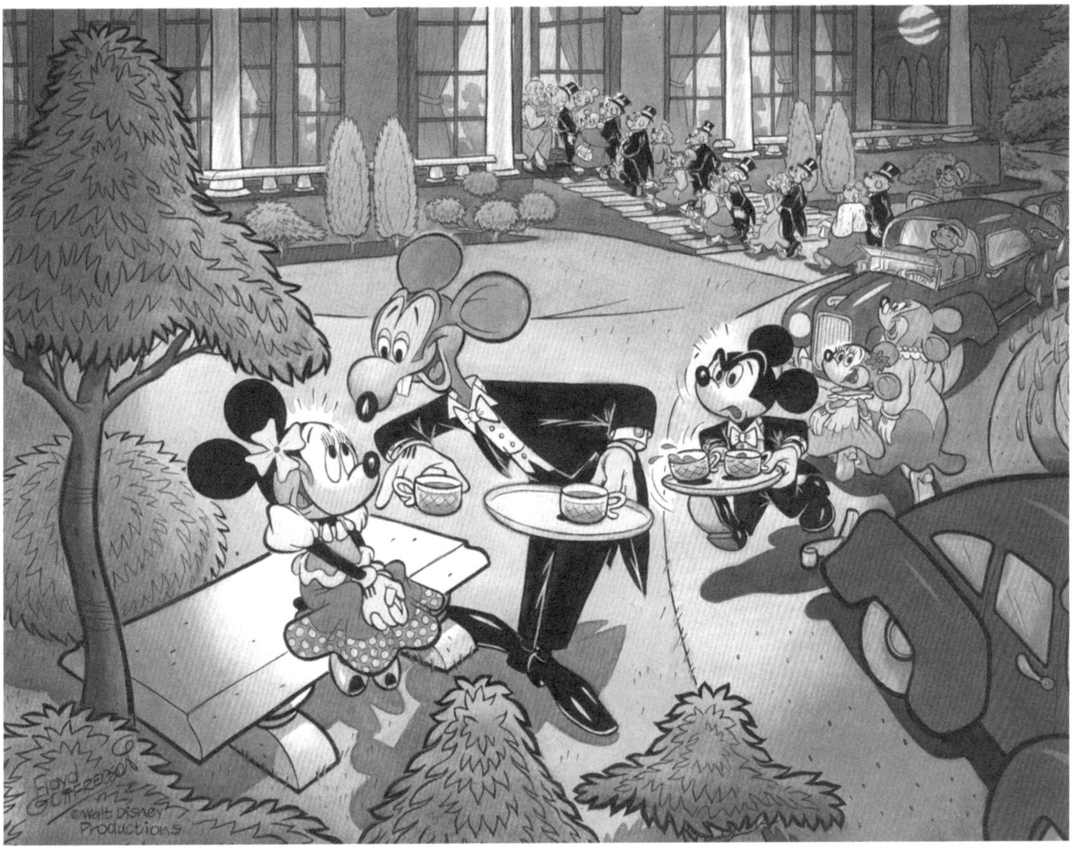
Floyd Gottfredson
©Walt Disney Productions

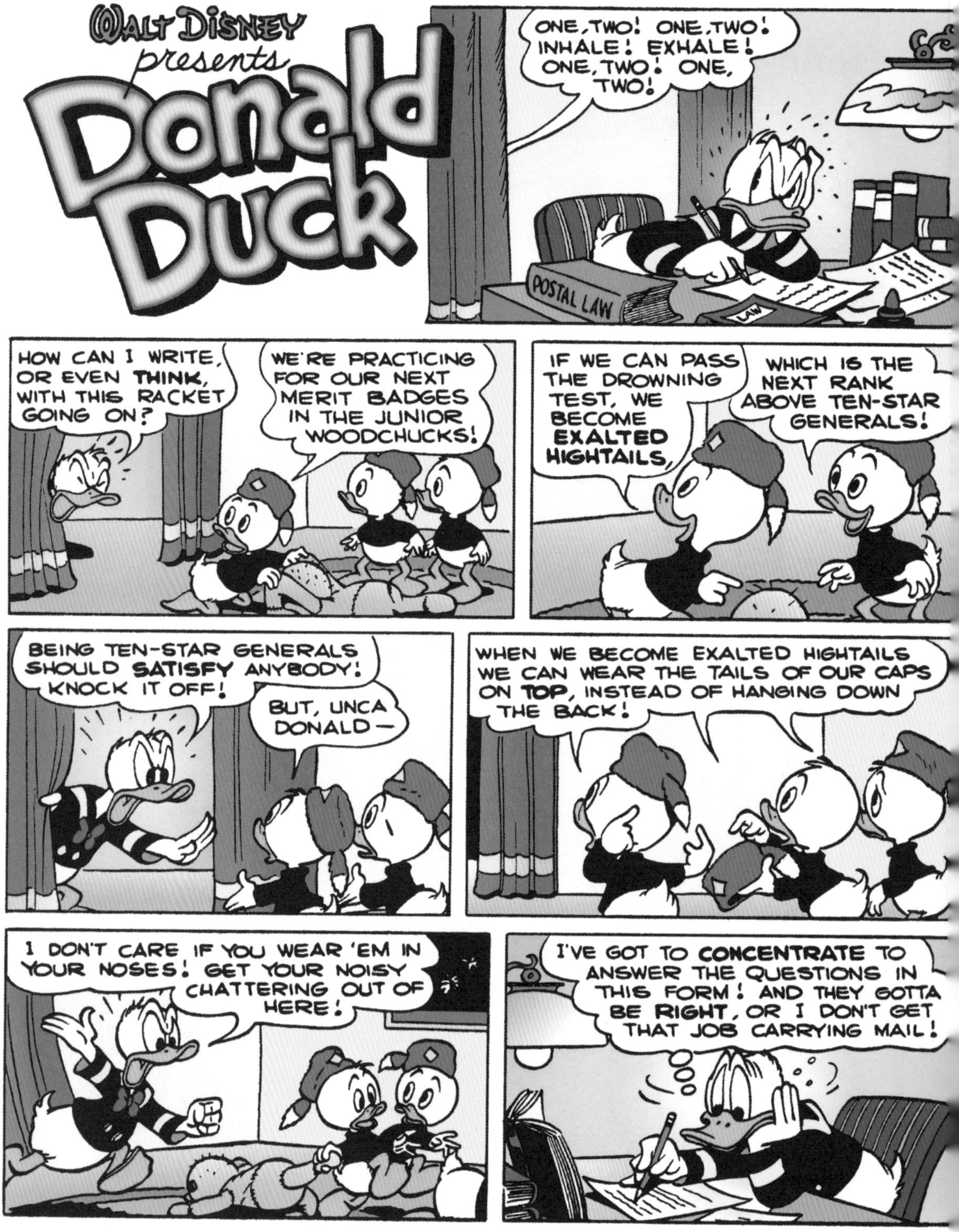
Walt Disney presents Donald Duck
ONE, TWO! ONE, TWO! INHALE! EXHALE! ONE, TWO! ONE, TWO!
POSTAL LAW
LAW
HOW CAN I WRITE, OR EVEN THINK, WITH THIS RACKET GOING ON?
WE'RE PRACTICING FOR OUR NEXT MERIT BADGES IN THE JUNIOR WOODCHUCKS!
IF WE CAN PASS THE DROWNING TEST, WE BECOME EXALTED HIGHTAILS,
WHICH IS THE NEXT RANK ABOVE TEN-STAR GENERALS!
BEING TEN-STAR GENERALS SHOULD SATISFY ANYBODY! KNOCK IT OFF!
BUT, UNCA DONALD—
WHEN WE BECOME EXALTED HIGHTAILS WE CAN WEAR THE TAILS OF OUR CAPS ON TOP, INSTEAD OF HANGING DOWN THE BACK!
I DON'T CARE IF YOU WEAR 'EM IN YOUR NOSES! GET YOUR NOISY CHATTERING OUT OF HERE!
I'VE GOT TO CONCENTRATE TO ANSWER THE QUESTIONS IN THIS FORM! AND THEY GOTTA BE RIGHT, OR I DON'T GET THAT JOB CARRYING MAIL!

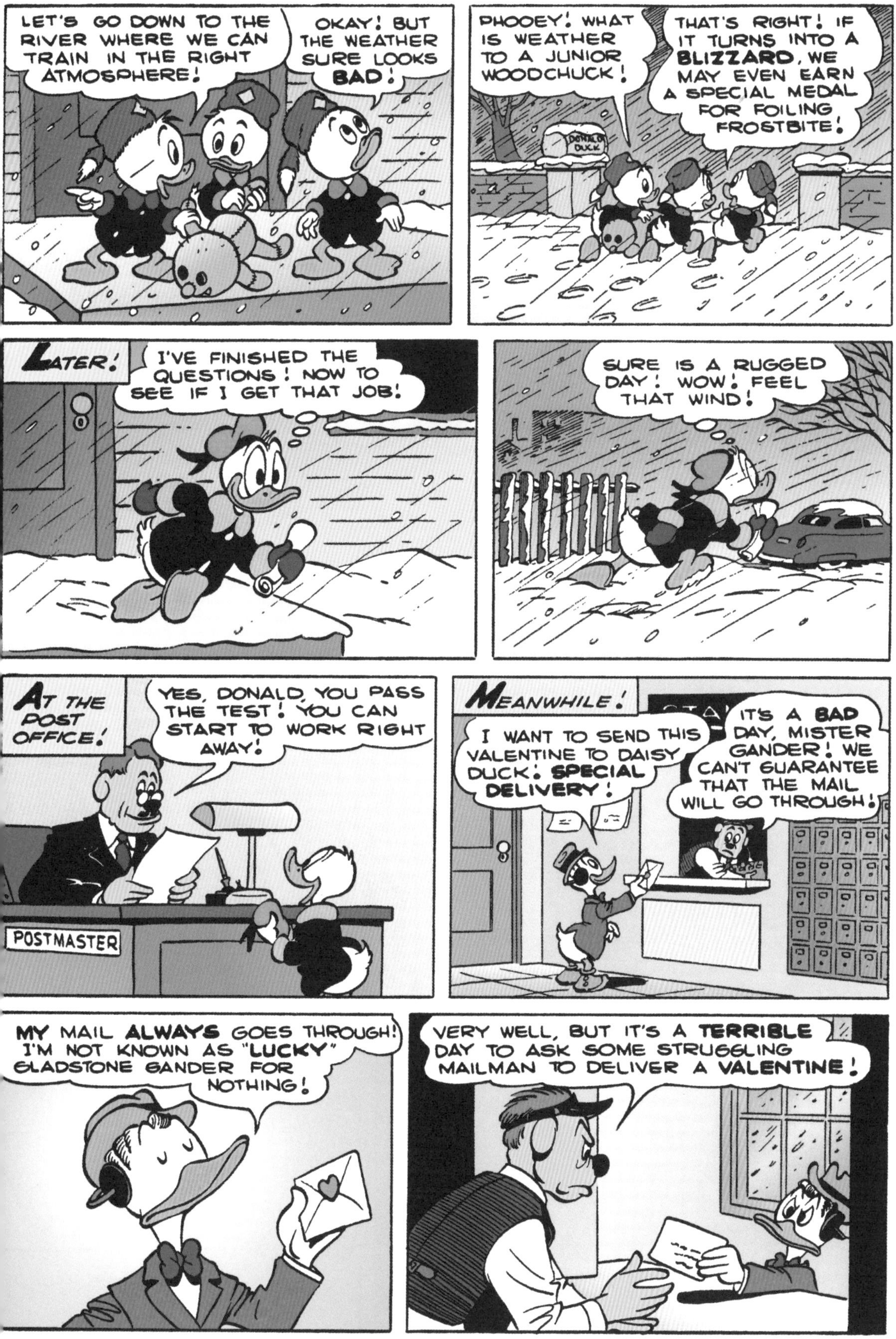
LET'S GO DOWN TO THE RIVER WHERE WE CAN TRAIN IN THE RIGHT ATMOSPHERE!
OKAY! BUT THE WEATHER SURE LOOKS BAD!
PHOOEY! WHAT IS WEATHER TO A JUNIOR WOODCHUCK!
THAT'S RIGHT! IF IT TURNS INTO A BLIZZARD, WE MAY EVEN EARN A SPECIAL MEDAL FOR FOILING FROSTBITE!
DONALD DUCK
LATER!
I'VE FINISHED THE QUESTIONS! NOW TO SEE IF I GET THAT JOB!
SURE IS A RUGGED DAY! WOW! FEEL THAT WIND!
AT THE POST OFFICE!
YES, DONALD, YOU PASS THE TEST! YOU CAN START TO WORK RIGHT AWAY!
POSTMASTER
MEANWHILE!
I WANT TO SEND THIS VALENTINE TO DAISY DUCK! SPECIAL DELIVERY!
IT'S A BAD DAY, MISTER GANDER! WE CAN'T GUARANTEE THAT THE MAIL WILL GO THROUGH!
MY MAIL ALWAYS GOES THROUGH! I'M NOT KNOWN AS "LUCKY" GLADSTONE GANDER FOR NOTHING!
VERY WELL, BUT IT'S A TERRIBLE DAY TO ASK SOME STRUGGLING MAILMAN TO DELIVER A VALENTINE!

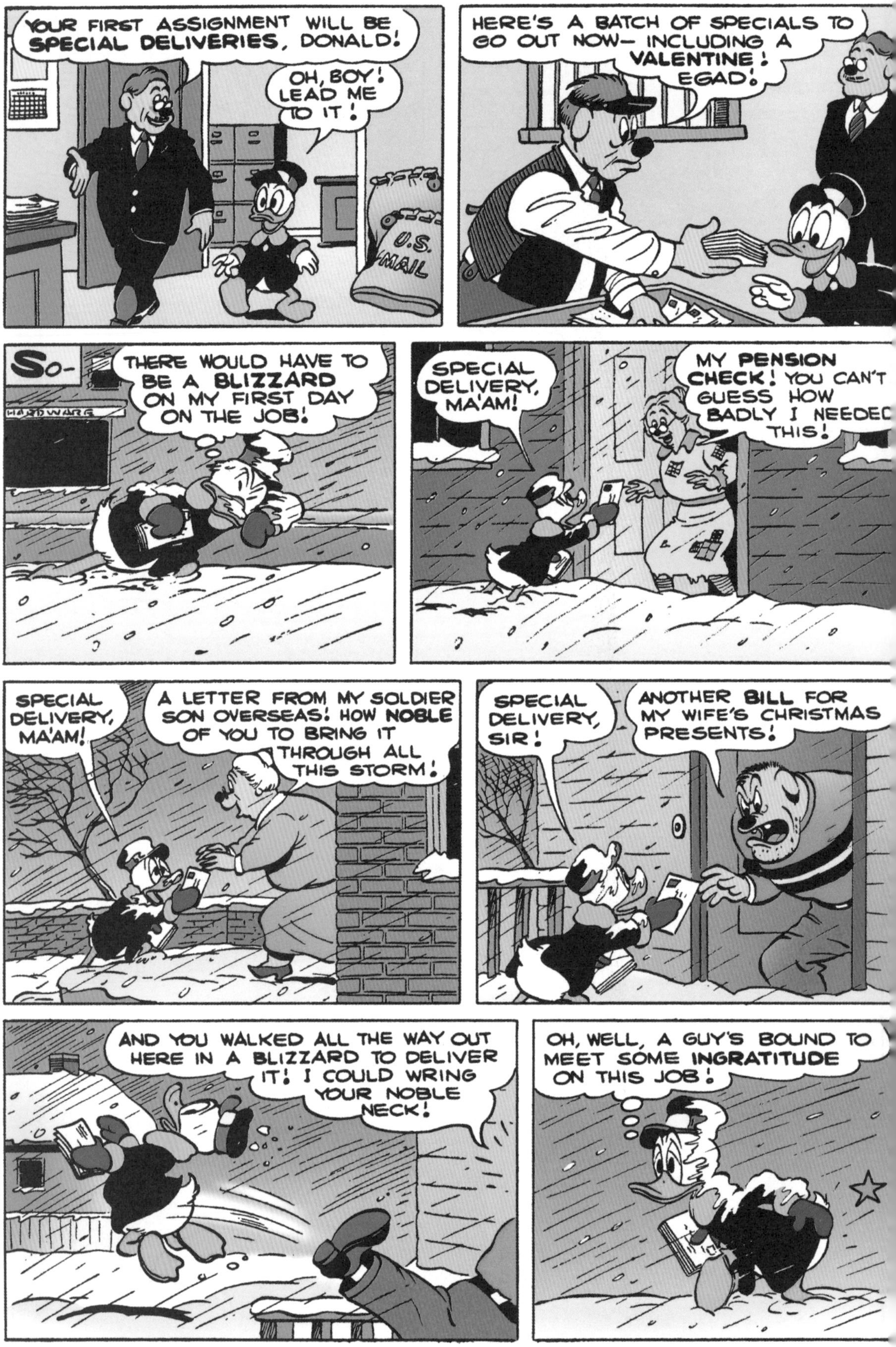
YOUR FIRST ASSIGNMENT WILL BE SPECIAL DELIVERIES, DONALD!
OH, BOY! LEAD ME TO IT!
U.S. MAIL
HERE'S A BATCH OF SPECIALS TO GO OUT NOW— INCLUDING A VALENTINE! EGAD!
SO-
THERE WOULD HAVE TO BE A BLIZZARD ON MY FIRST DAY ON THE JOB!
SPECIAL DELIVERY, MA'AM!
MY PENSION CHECK! YOU CAN'T GUESS HOW BADLY I NEEDED THIS!
SPECIAL DELIVERY, MA'AM!
A LETTER FROM MY SOLDIER SON OVERSEAS! HOW NOBLE OF YOU TO BRING IT THROUGH ALL THIS STORM!
SPECIAL DELIVERY, SIR!
ANOTHER BILL FOR MY WIFE'S CHRISTMAS PRESENTS!
AND YOU WALKED ALL THE WAY OUT HERE IN A BLIZZARD TO DELIVER IT! I COULD WRING YOUR NOBLE NECK!
OH, WELL, A GUY'S BOUND TO MEET SOME INGRATITUDE ON THIS JOB!

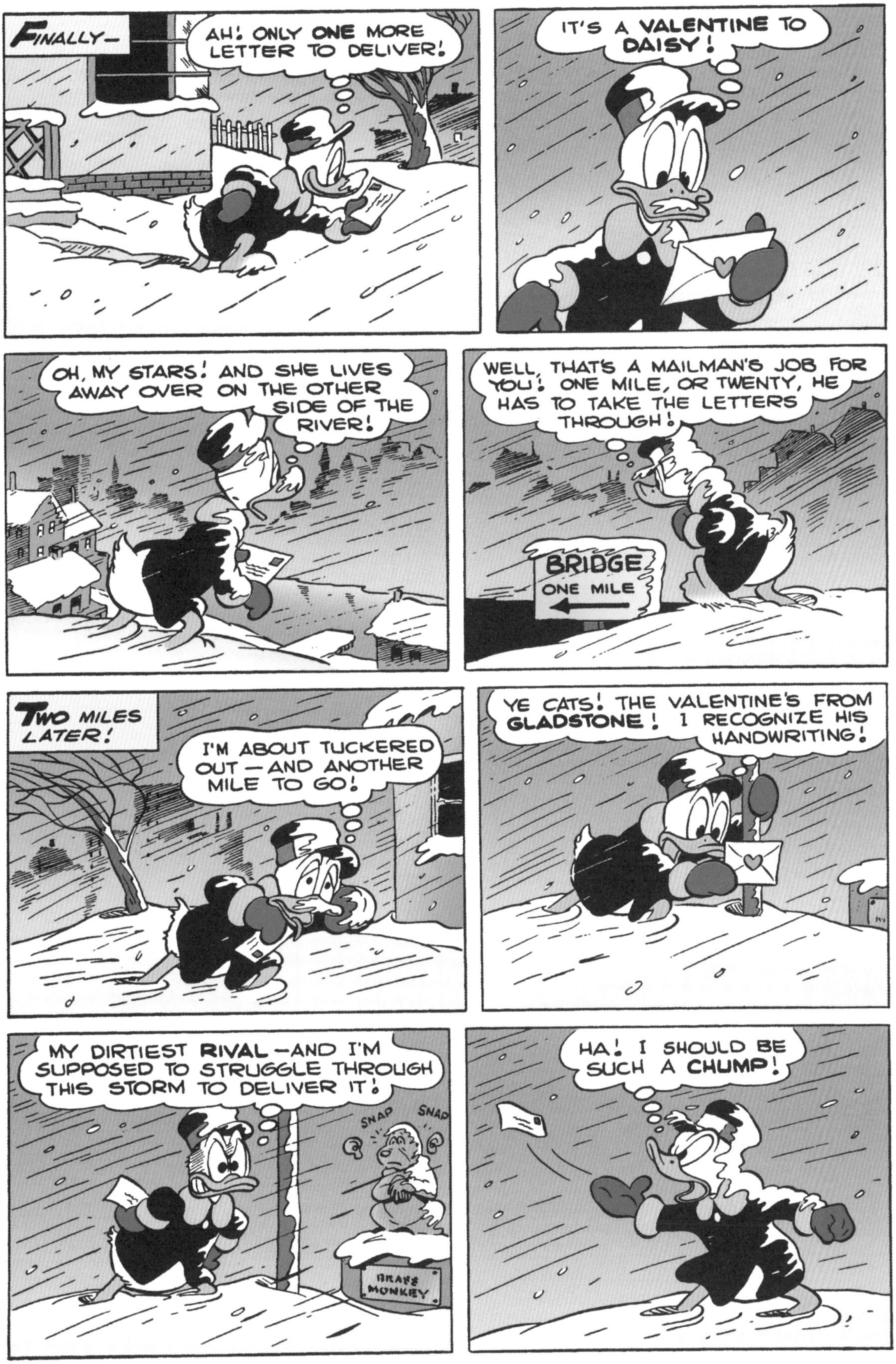
FINALLY—
AH! ONLY ONE MORE LETTER TO DELIVER!
IT'S A VALENTINE TO DAISY!
OH, MY STARS! AND SHE LIVES AWAY OVER ON THE OTHER SIDE OF THE RIVER!
WELL, THAT'S A MAILMAN'S JOB FOR YOU! ONE MILE, OR TWENTY, HE HAS TO TAKE THE LETTERS THROUGH!
BRIDGE
ONE MILE
TWO MILES LATER!
I'M ABOUT TUCKERED OUT—AND ANOTHER MILE TO GO!
YE CATS! THE VALENTINE'S FROM GLADSTONE! I RECOGNIZE HIS HANDWRITING!
MY DIRTIEST RIVAL—AND I'M SUPPOSED TO STRUGGLE THROUGH THIS STORM TO DELIVER IT!
SNAP
SNAP
BRASS MONKEY
HA! I SHOULD BE SUCH A CHUMP!

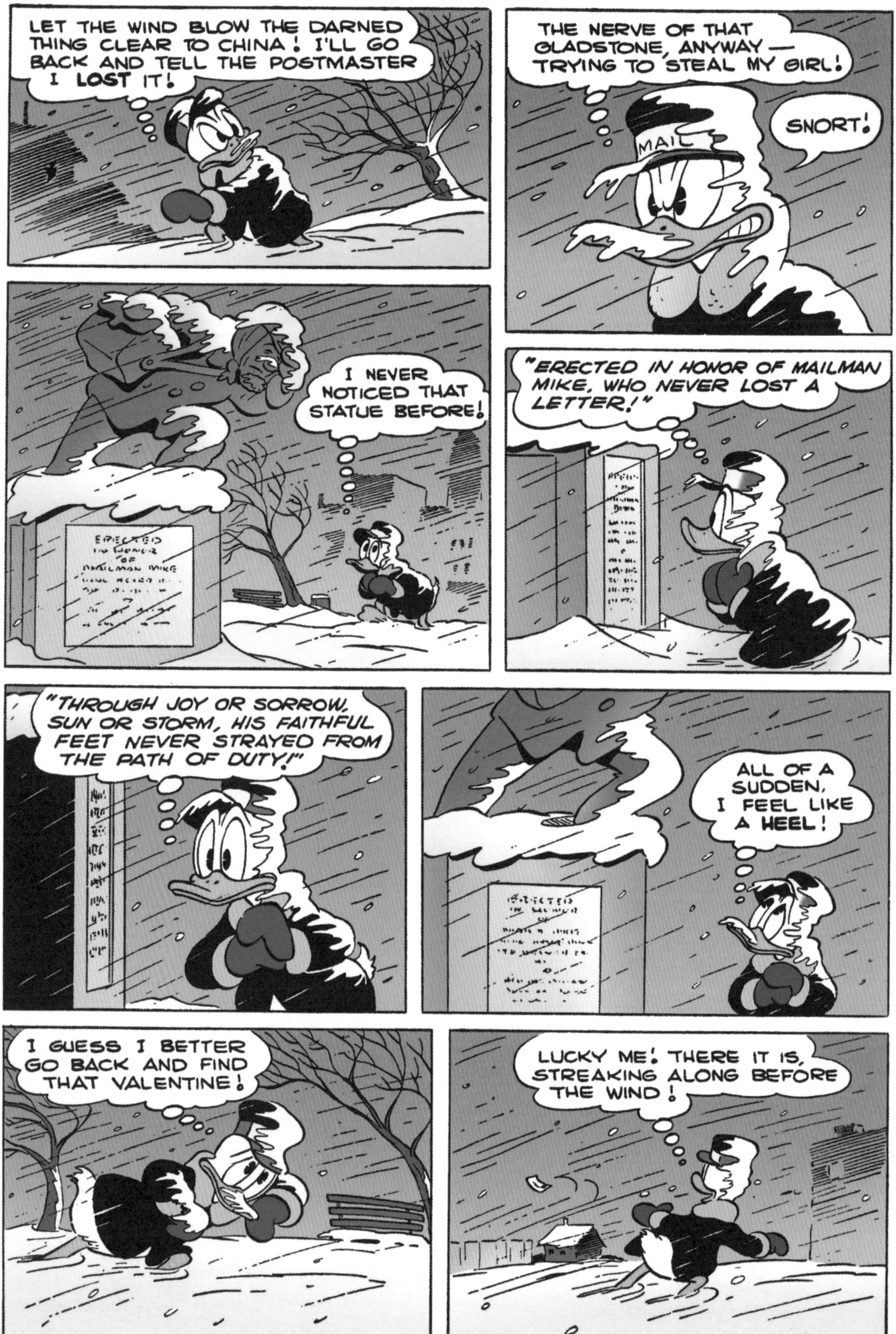
LET THE WIND BLOW THE DARNED THING CLEAR TO CHINA! I'LL GO BACK AND TELL THE POSTMASTER I **LOST** IT!
THE NERVE OF THAT GLADSTONE, ANYWAY — TRYING TO STEAL MY GIRL!
MAIL
SNORT!
I NEVER NOTICED THAT STATUE BEFORE!
"ERECTED IN HONOR OF MAILMAN MIKE, WHO NEVER LOST A LETTER!"
"THROUGH JOY OR SORROW, SUN OR STORM, HIS FAITHFUL FEET NEVER STRAYED FROM THE PATH OF DUTY!"
ALL OF A SUDDEN, I FEEL LIKE A **HEEL**!
I GUESS I BETTER GO BACK AND FIND THAT VALENTINE!
LUCKY ME! THERE IT IS, STREAKING ALONG BEFORE THE WIND!

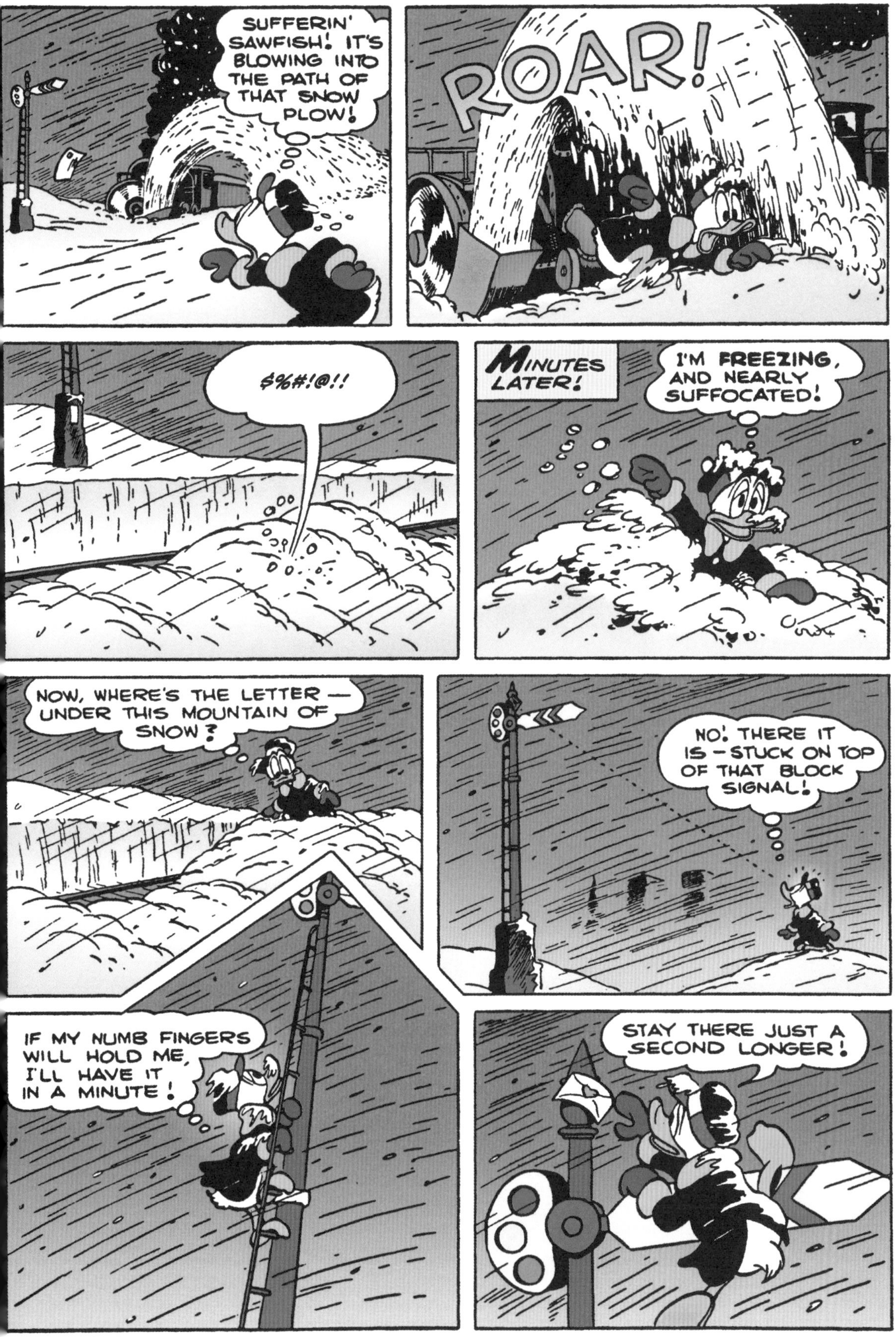
SUFFERIN' SAWFISH! IT'S BLOWING INTO THE PATH OF THAT SNOW PLOW!
ROAR!
$%#!@!!
MINUTES LATER!
I'M FREEZING, AND NEARLY SUFFOCATED!
NOW, WHERE'S THE LETTER — UNDER THIS MOUNTAIN OF SNOW?
NO! THERE IT IS — STUCK ON TOP OF THAT BLOCK SIGNAL!
IF MY NUMB FINGERS WILL HOLD ME, I'LL HAVE IT IN A MINUTE!
STAY THERE JUST A SECOND LONGER!

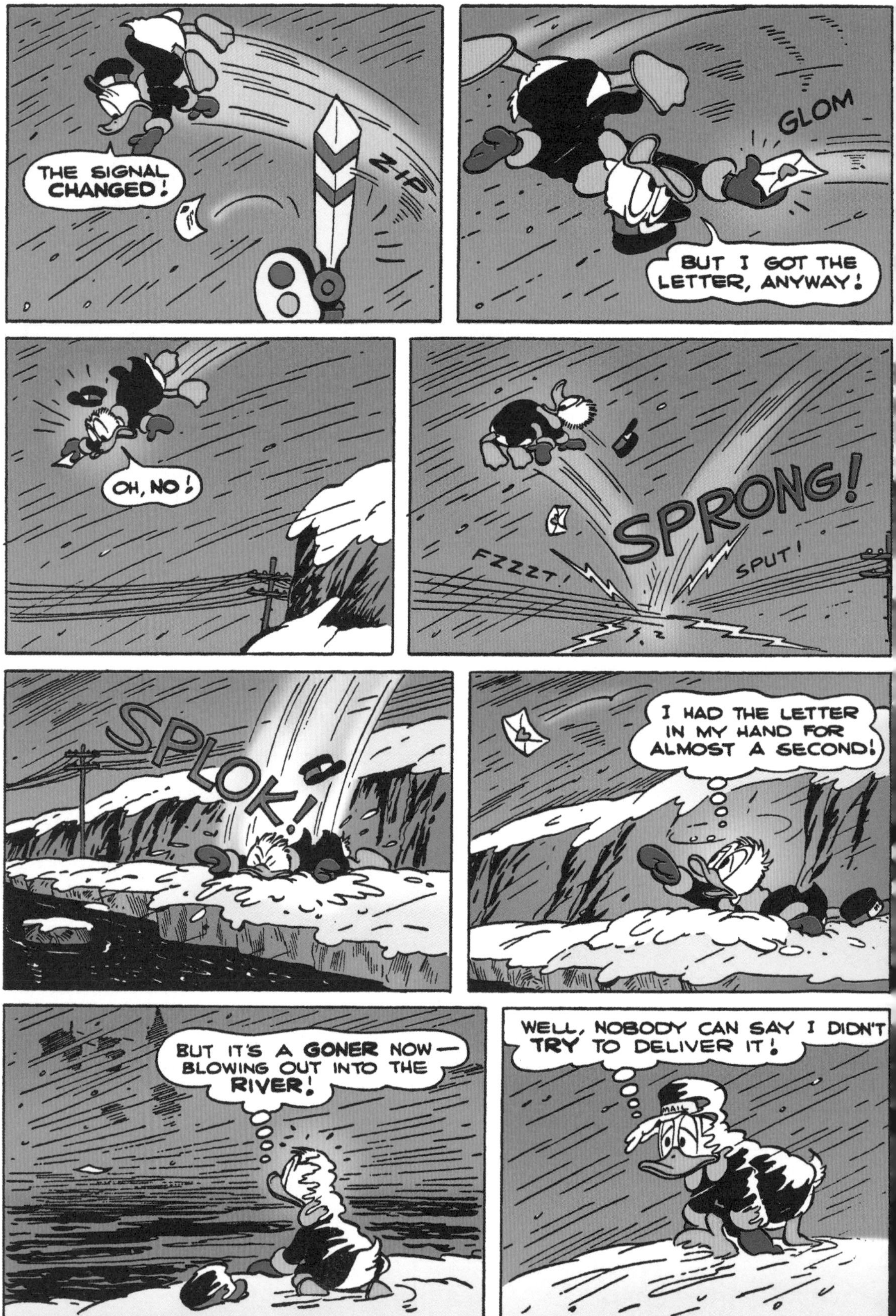
THE SIGNAL CHANGED!
ZIP
GLOM
BUT I GOT THE LETTER, ANYWAY!
OH, NO!
SPRONG!
FZZZZT!
SPUT!
SPLOK!
I HAD THE LETTER IN MY HAND FOR ALMOST A SECOND!
BUT IT'S A GONER NOW— BLOWING OUT INTO THE RIVER!
WELL, NOBODY CAN SAY I DIDN'T TRY TO DELIVER IT!
MAIL

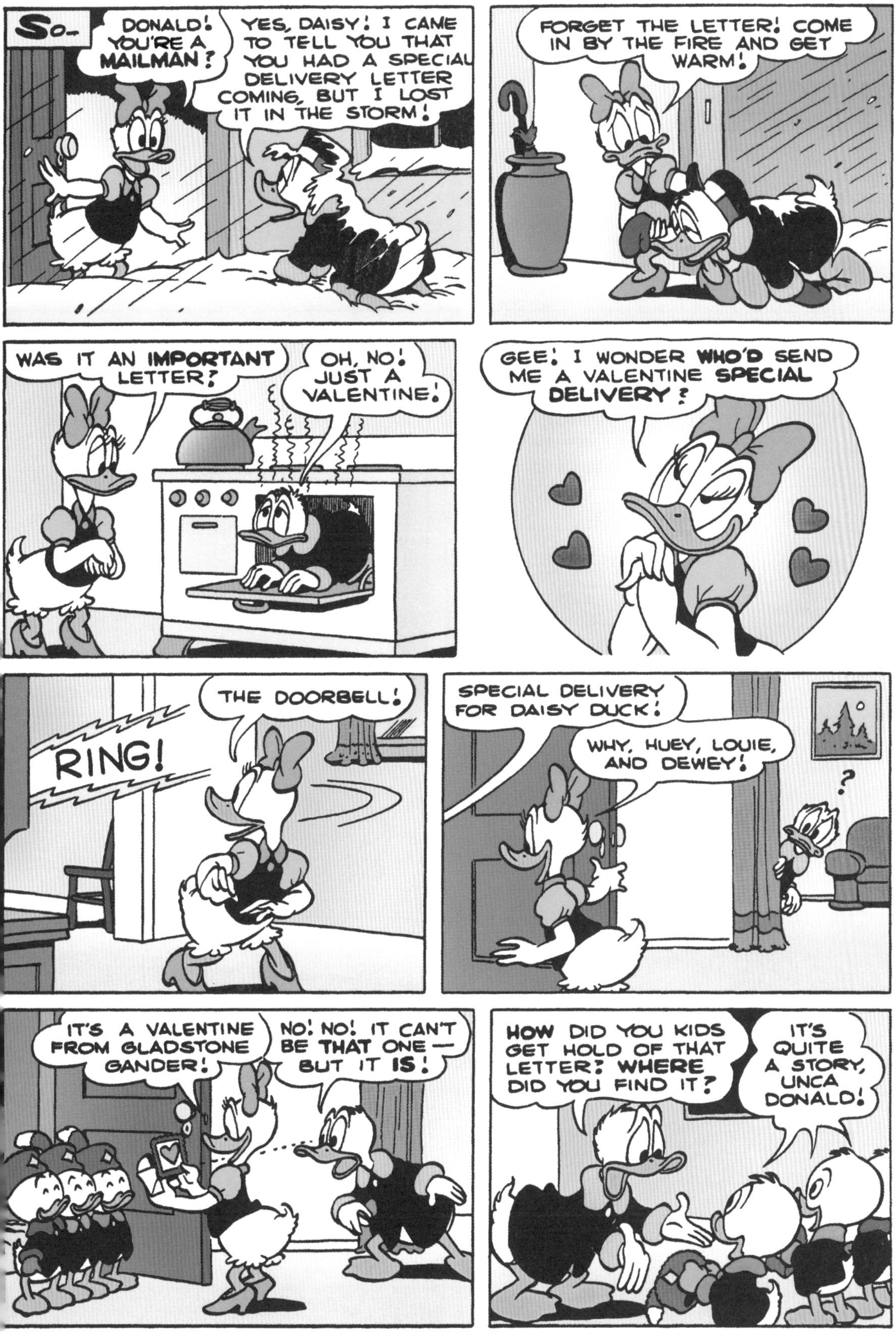
SO—
DONALD! YOU'RE A **MAILMAN**?
YES, DAISY! I CAME TO TELL YOU THAT YOU HAD A SPECIAL DELIVERY LETTER COMING, BUT I LOST IT IN THE STORM!
FORGET THE LETTER! COME IN BY THE FIRE AND GET WARM!
WAS IT AN **IMPORTANT** LETTER?
OH, NO! JUST A VALENTINE!
GEE! I WONDER **WHO'D** SEND ME A VALENTINE **SPECIAL DELIVERY**?
RING!
THE DOORBELL!
SPECIAL DELIVERY FOR DAISY DUCK!
WHY, HUEY, LOUIE, AND DEWEY!
?
IT'S A VALENTINE FROM GLADSTONE GANDER!
NO! NO! IT CAN'T BE **THAT** ONE— BUT IT **IS**!
HOW DID YOU KIDS GET HOLD OF THAT LETTER? **WHERE** DID YOU FIND IT?
IT'S QUITE A STORY, UNCA DONALD!

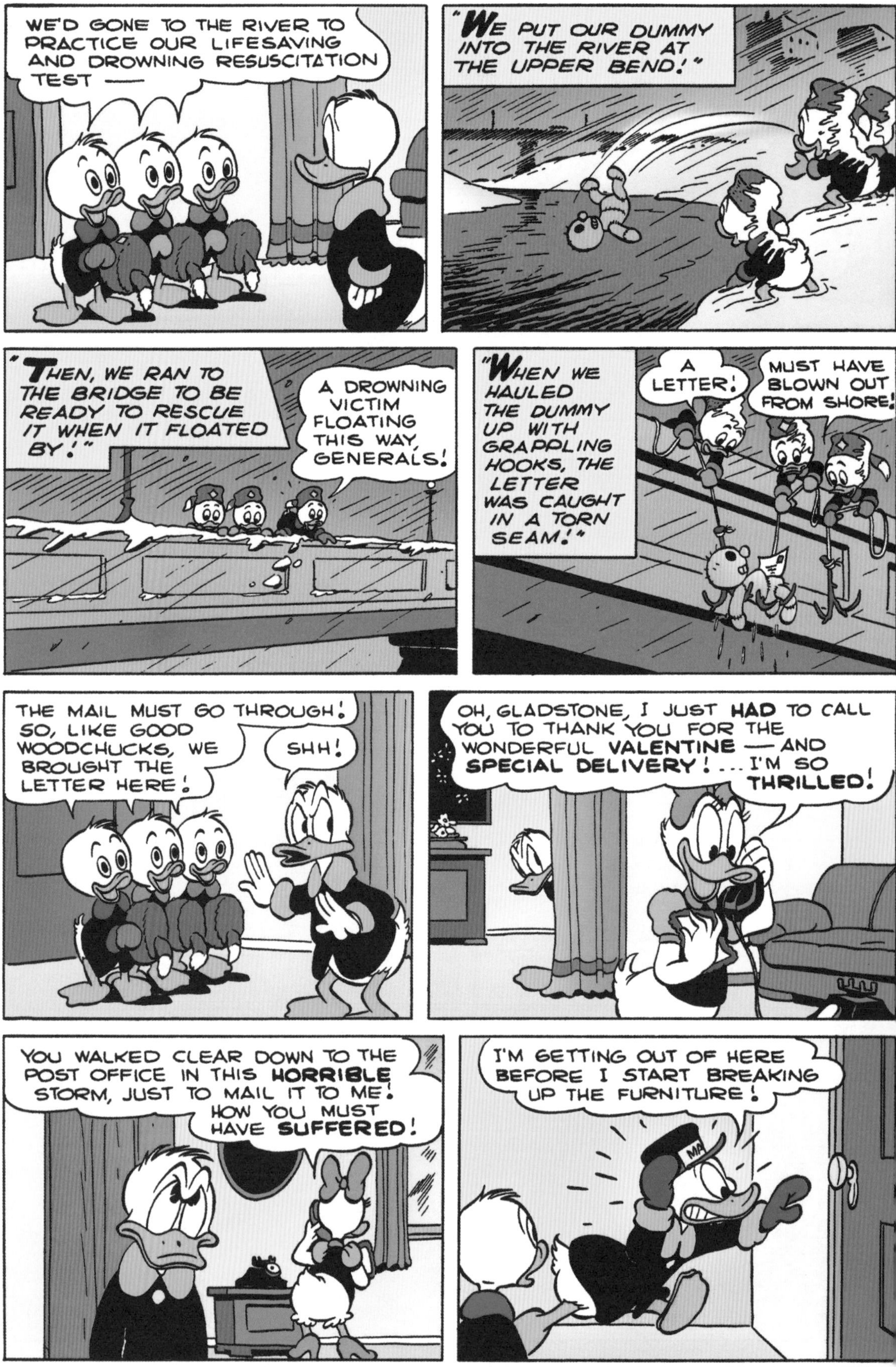
WE'D GONE TO THE RIVER TO PRACTICE OUR LIFESAVING AND DROWNING RESUSCITATION TEST —
"WE PUT OUR DUMMY INTO THE RIVER AT THE UPPER BEND!"
"THEN, WE RAN TO THE BRIDGE TO BE READY TO RESCUE IT WHEN IT FLOATED BY!"
A DROWNING VICTIM FLOATING THIS WAY, GENERALS!
"WHEN WE HAULED THE DUMMY UP WITH GRAPPLING HOOKS, THE LETTER WAS CAUGHT IN A TORN SEAM!"
A LETTER!
MUST HAVE BLOWN OUT FROM SHORE!
THE MAIL MUST GO THROUGH! SO, LIKE GOOD WOODCHUCKS, WE BROUGHT THE LETTER HERE!
SHH!
OH, GLADSTONE, I JUST **HAD** TO CALL YOU TO THANK YOU FOR THE WONDERFUL **VALENTINE** — AND **SPECIAL DELIVERY**! ... I'M SO **THRILLED**!
YOU WALKED CLEAR DOWN TO THE POST OFFICE IN THIS **HORRIBLE** STORM, JUST TO MAIL IT TO ME! HOW YOU MUST HAVE **SUFFERED**!
I'M GETTING OUT OF HERE BEFORE I START BREAKING UP THE FURNITURE!

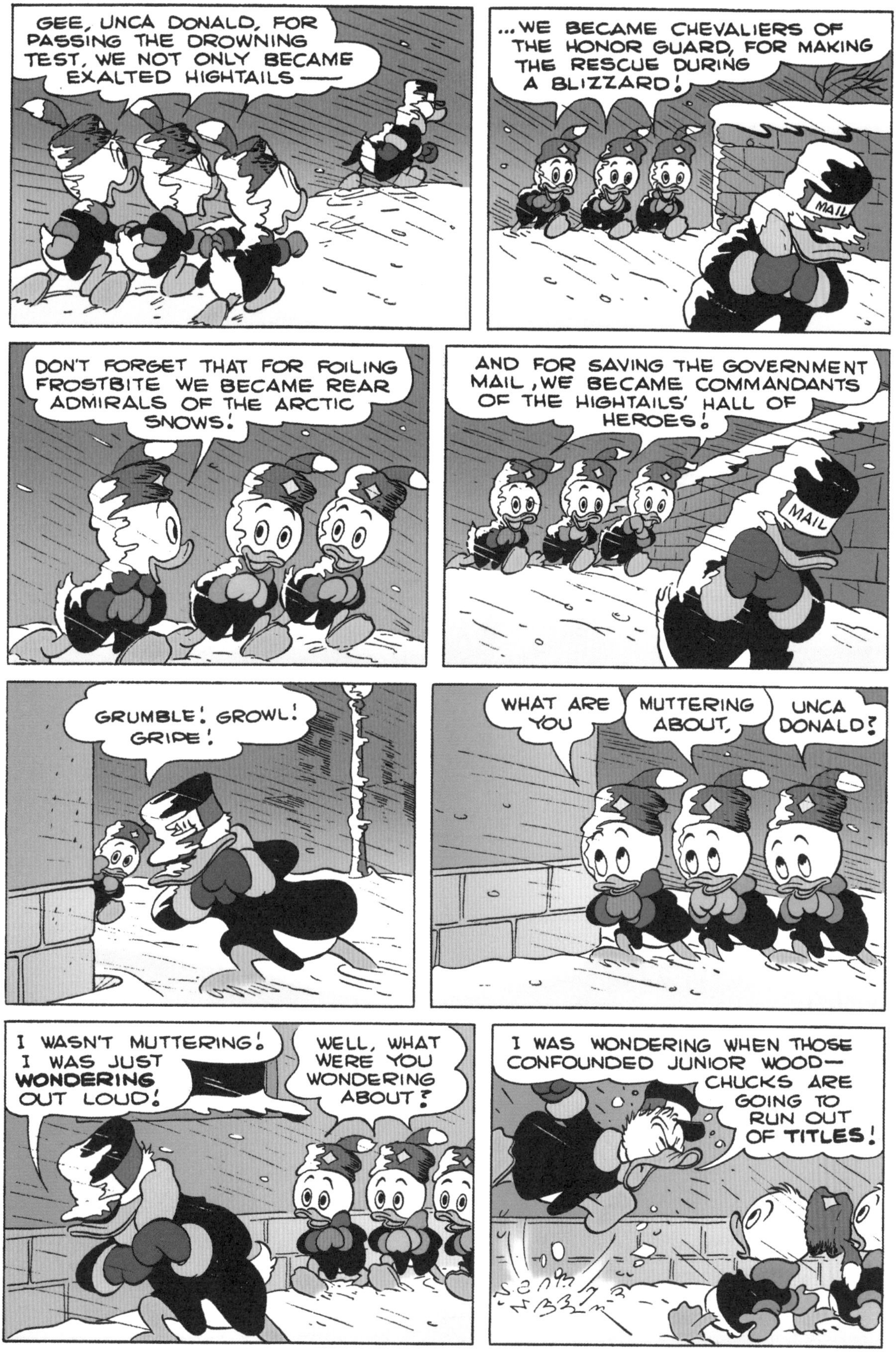
GEE, UNCA DONALD, FOR PASSING THE DROWNING TEST, WE NOT ONLY BECAME EXALTED HIGHTAILS——
...WE BECAME CHEVALIERS OF THE HONOR GUARD, FOR MAKING THE RESCUE DURING A BLIZZARD!
MAIL
DON'T FORGET THAT FOR FOILING FROSTBITE WE BECAME REAR ADMIRALS OF THE ARCTIC SNOWS!
AND FOR SAVING THE GOVERNMENT MAIL, WE BECAME COMMANDANTS OF THE HIGHTAILS' HALL OF HEROES!
MAIL
GRUMBLE! GROWL! GRIPE!
WHAT ARE YOU
MUTTERING ABOUT,
UNCA DONALD?
I WASN'T MUTTERING! I WAS JUST **WONDERING** OUT LOUD!
WELL, WHAT WERE YOU WONDERING ABOUT?
I WAS WONDERING WHEN THOSE CONFOUNDED JUNIOR WOOD-CHUCKS ARE GOING TO RUN OUT OF **TITLES**!

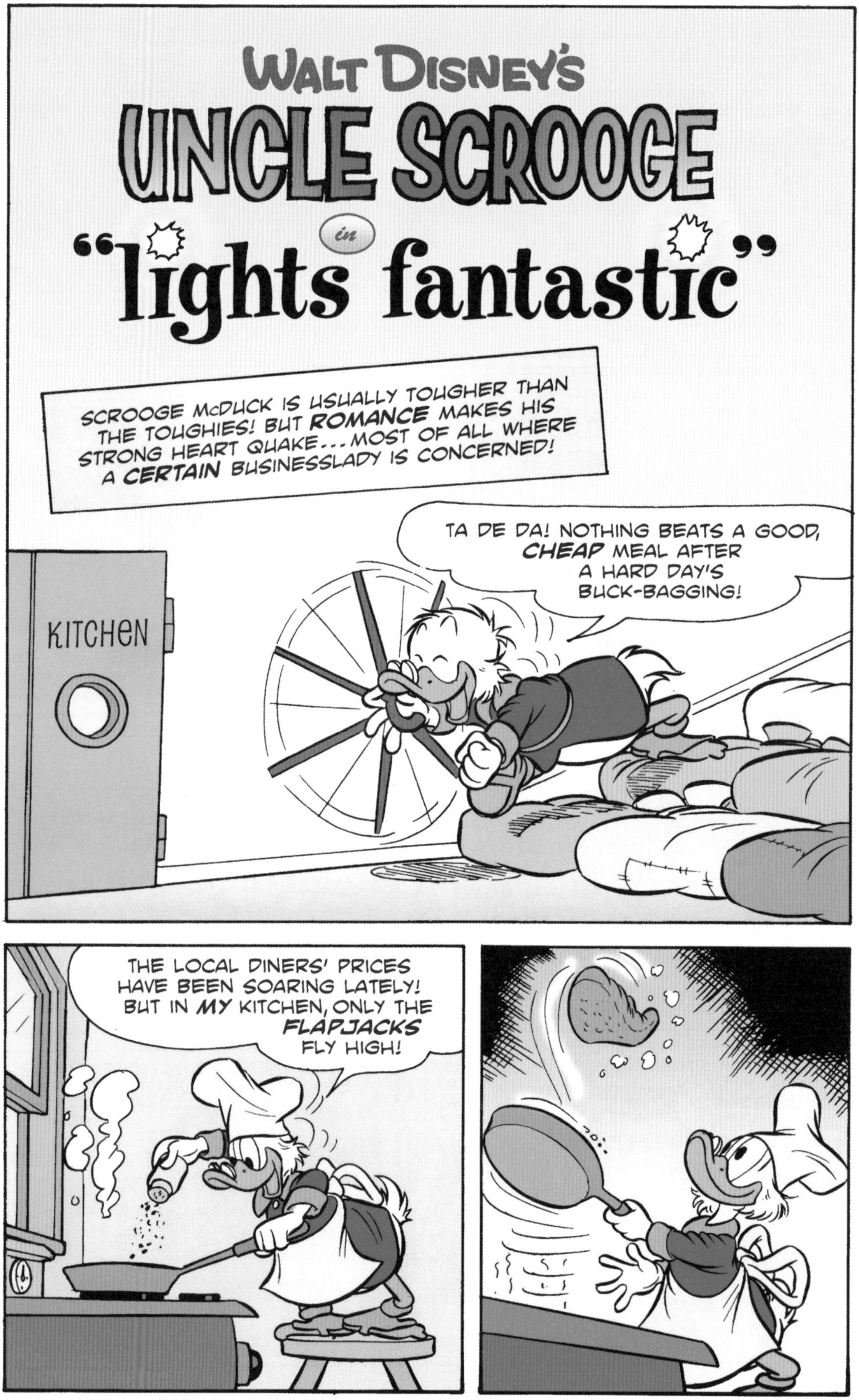
WALT DISNEY'S
UNCLE SCROOGE
in
"lights fantastic"
SCROOGE McDUCK IS USUALLY TOUGHER THAN THE TOUGHIES! BUT ROMANCE MAKES HIS STRONG HEART QUAKE... MOST OF ALL WHERE A CERTAIN BUSINESSLADY IS CONCERNED!
TA DE DA! NOTHING BEATS A GOOD, CHEAP MEAL AFTER A HARD DAY'S BUCK-BAGGING!
KITCHEN
THE LOCAL DINERS' PRICES HAVE BEEN SOARING LATELY! BUT IN MY KITCHEN, ONLY THE FLAPJACKS FLY HIGH!

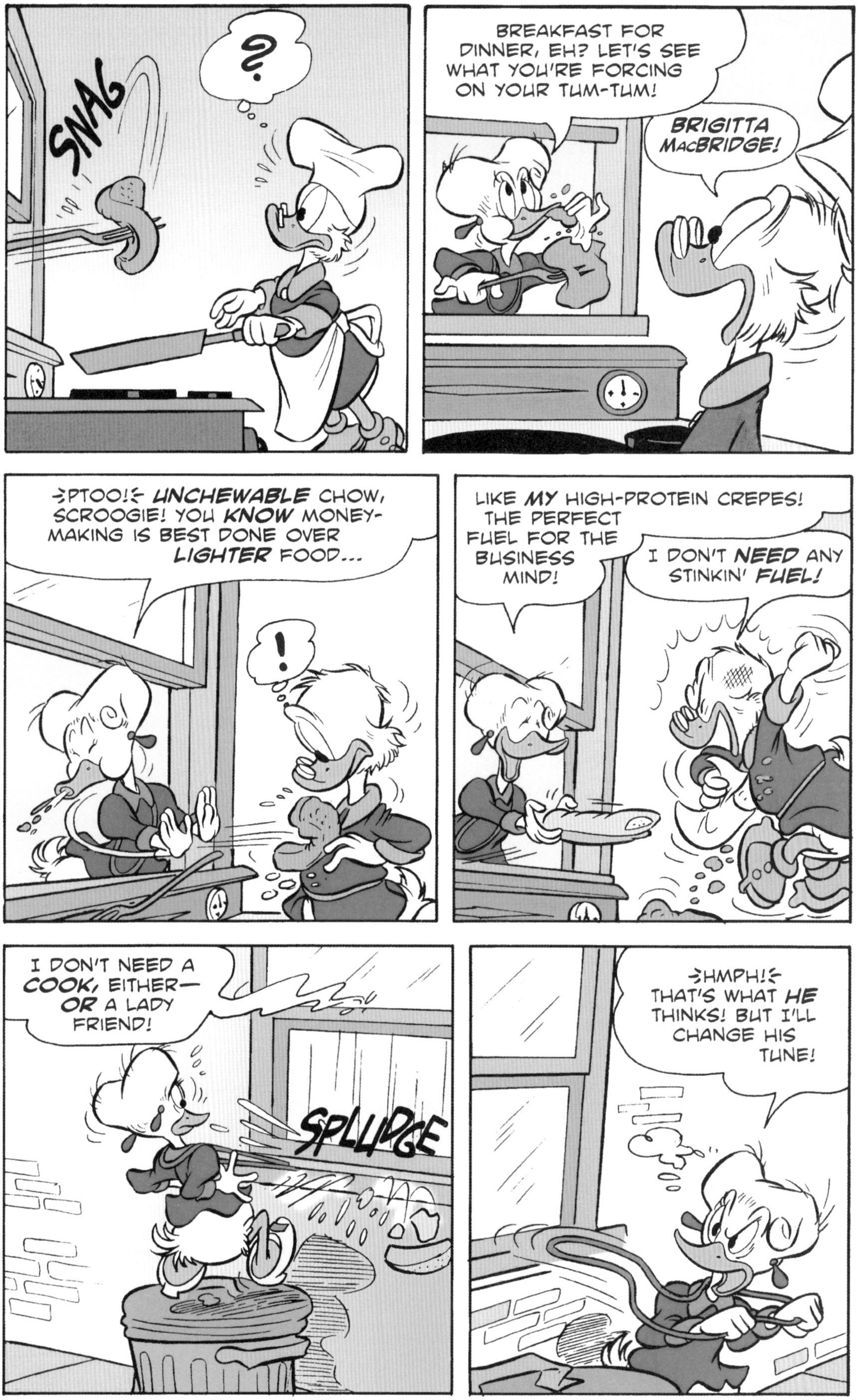
SNAG
?
BREAKFAST FOR DINNER, EH? LET'S SEE WHAT YOU'RE FORCING ON YOUR TUM-TUM!
BRIGITTA MacBRIDGE!
PTOO! UNCHEWABLE CHOW, SCROOGIE! YOU KNOW MONEY-MAKING IS BEST DONE OVER LIGHTER FOOD...
!
LIKE MY HIGH-PROTEIN CREPES! THE PERFECT FUEL FOR THE BUSINESS MIND!
I DON'T NEED ANY STINKIN' FUEL!
I DON'T NEED A COOK, EITHER— OR A LADY FRIEND!
SPLUDGE
HMPH! THAT'S WHAT HE THINKS! BUT I'LL CHANGE HIS TUNE!

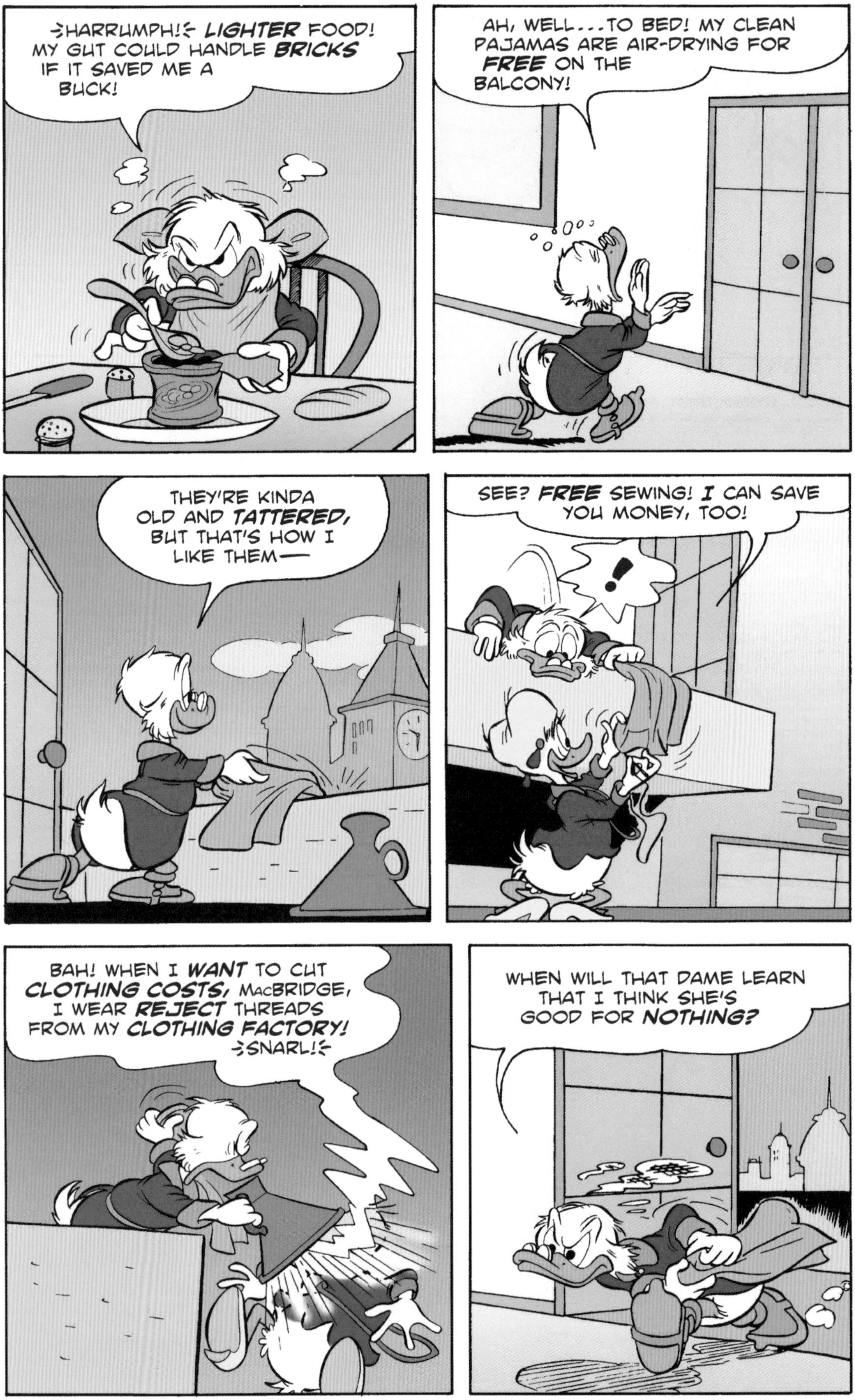

≈HARRUMPH!≈ LIGHTER FOOD! MY GUT COULD HANDLE BRICKS IF IT SAVED ME A BUCK!
AH, WELL...TO BED! MY CLEAN PAJAMAS ARE AIR-DRYING FOR FREE ON THE BALCONY!
THEY'RE KINDA OLD AND TATTERED, BUT THAT'S HOW I LIKE THEM—
SEE? FREE SEWING! I CAN SAVE YOU MONEY, TOO!
!
BAH! WHEN I WANT TO CUT CLOTHING COSTS, MacBRIDGE, I WEAR REJECT THREADS FROM MY CLOTHING FACTORY!
≈SNARL!≈
WHEN WILL THAT DAME LEARN THAT I THINK SHE'S GOOD FOR NOTHING?

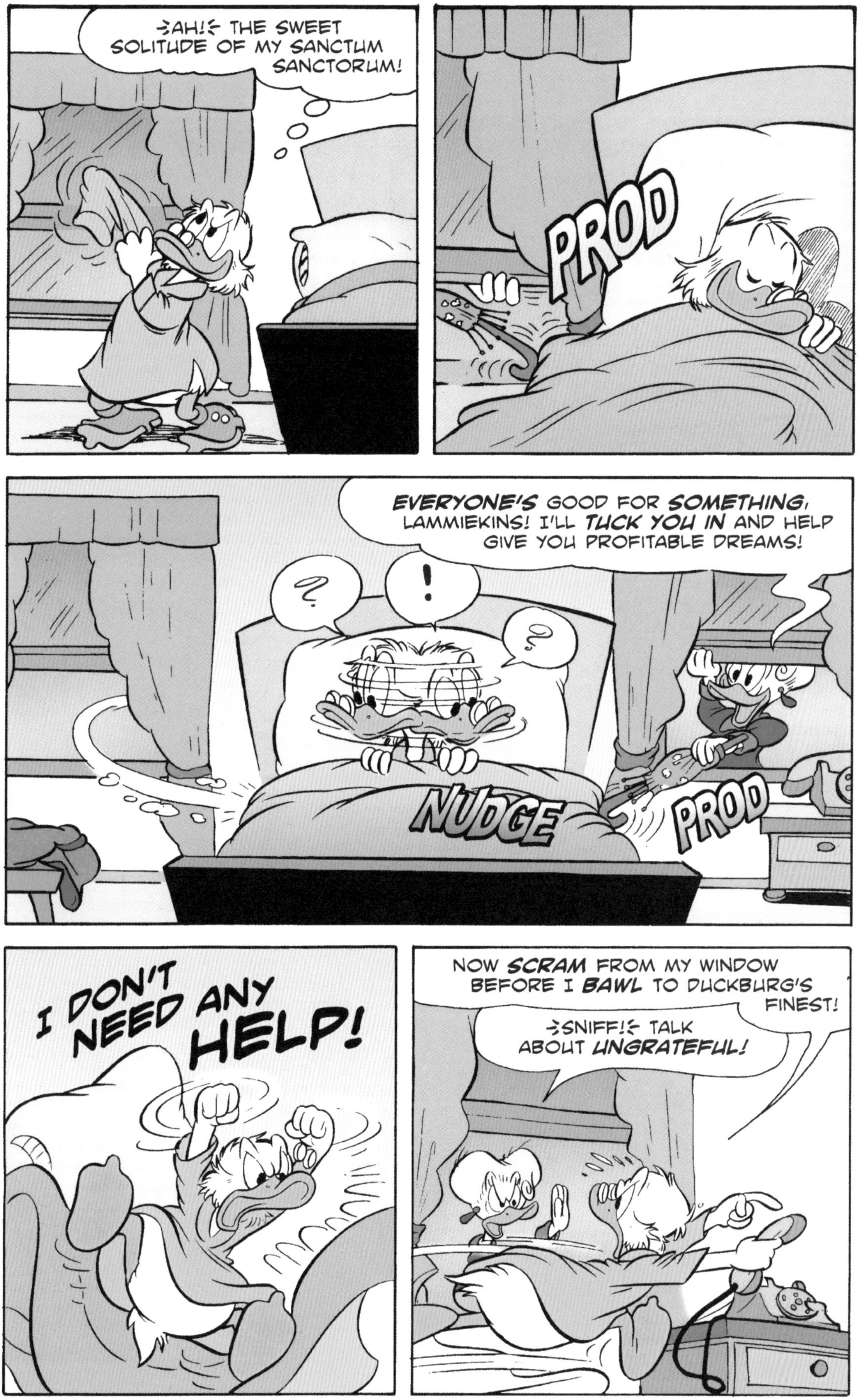
AH! THE SWEET SOLITUDE OF MY SANCTUM SANCTORUM!
PROD
EVERYONE'S GOOD FOR SOMETHING, LAMMIEKINS! I'LL TUCK YOU IN AND HELP GIVE YOU PROFITABLE DREAMS!
?
!
?
NUDGE
PROD
I DON'T NEED ANY HELP!
NOW SCRAM FROM MY WINDOW BEFORE I BAWL TO DUCKBURG'S FINEST!
SNIFF! TALK ABOUT UNGRATEFUL!

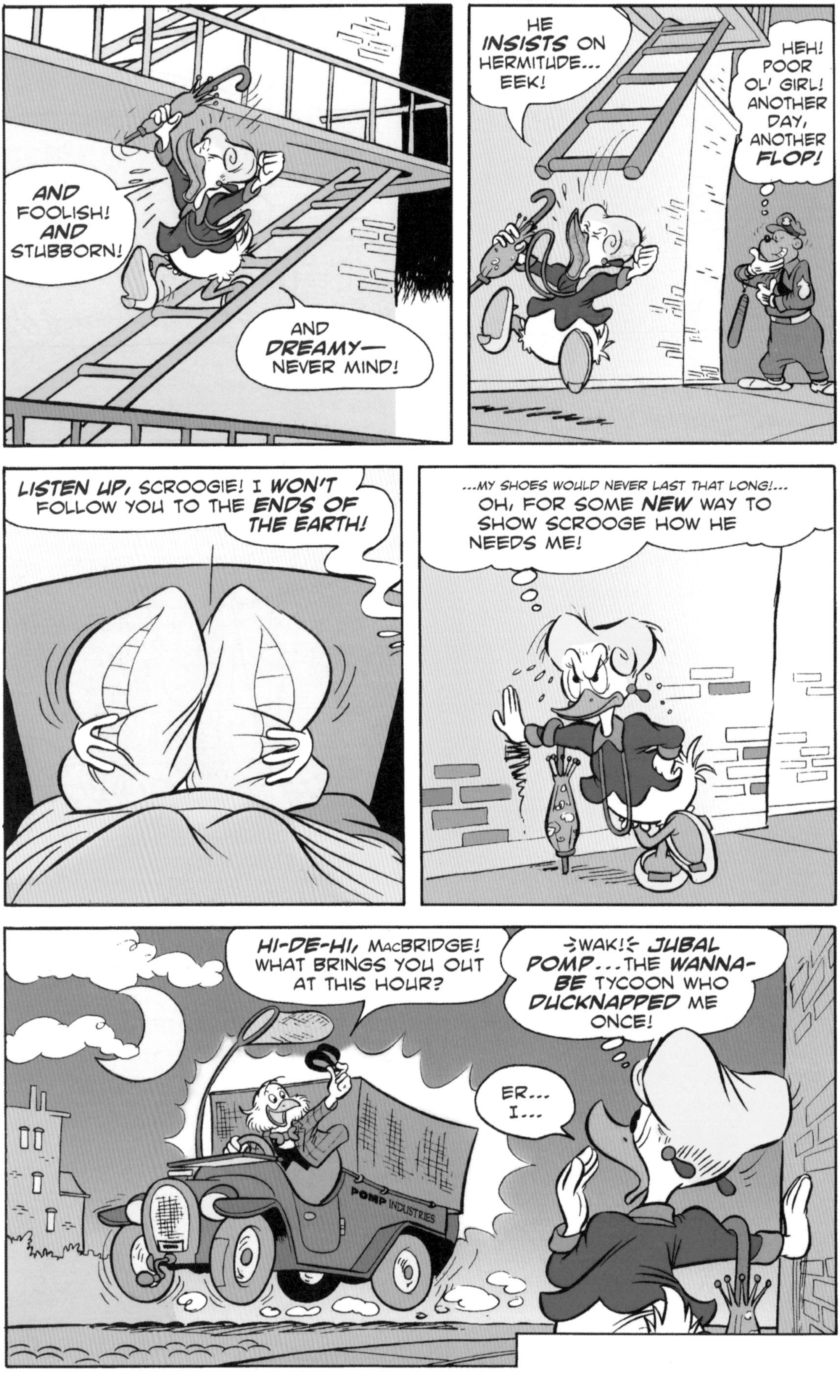
AND FOOLISH! AND STUBBORN!
AND DREAMY— NEVER MIND!
HE INSISTS ON HERMITUDE... EEK!
HEH! POOR OL' GIRL! ANOTHER DAY, ANOTHER FLOP!
LISTEN UP, SCROOGIE! I WON'T FOLLOW YOU TO THE ENDS OF THE EARTH!
...MY SHOES WOULD NEVER LAST THAT LONG!...
OH, FOR SOME NEW WAY TO SHOW SCROOGE HOW HE NEEDS ME!
HI-DE-HI, MacBRIDGE! WHAT BRINGS YOU OUT AT THIS HOUR?
WAK! JUBAL POMP... THE WANNA-BE TYCOON WHO DUCKNAPPED ME ONCE!
ER... I...
POMP INDUSTRIES

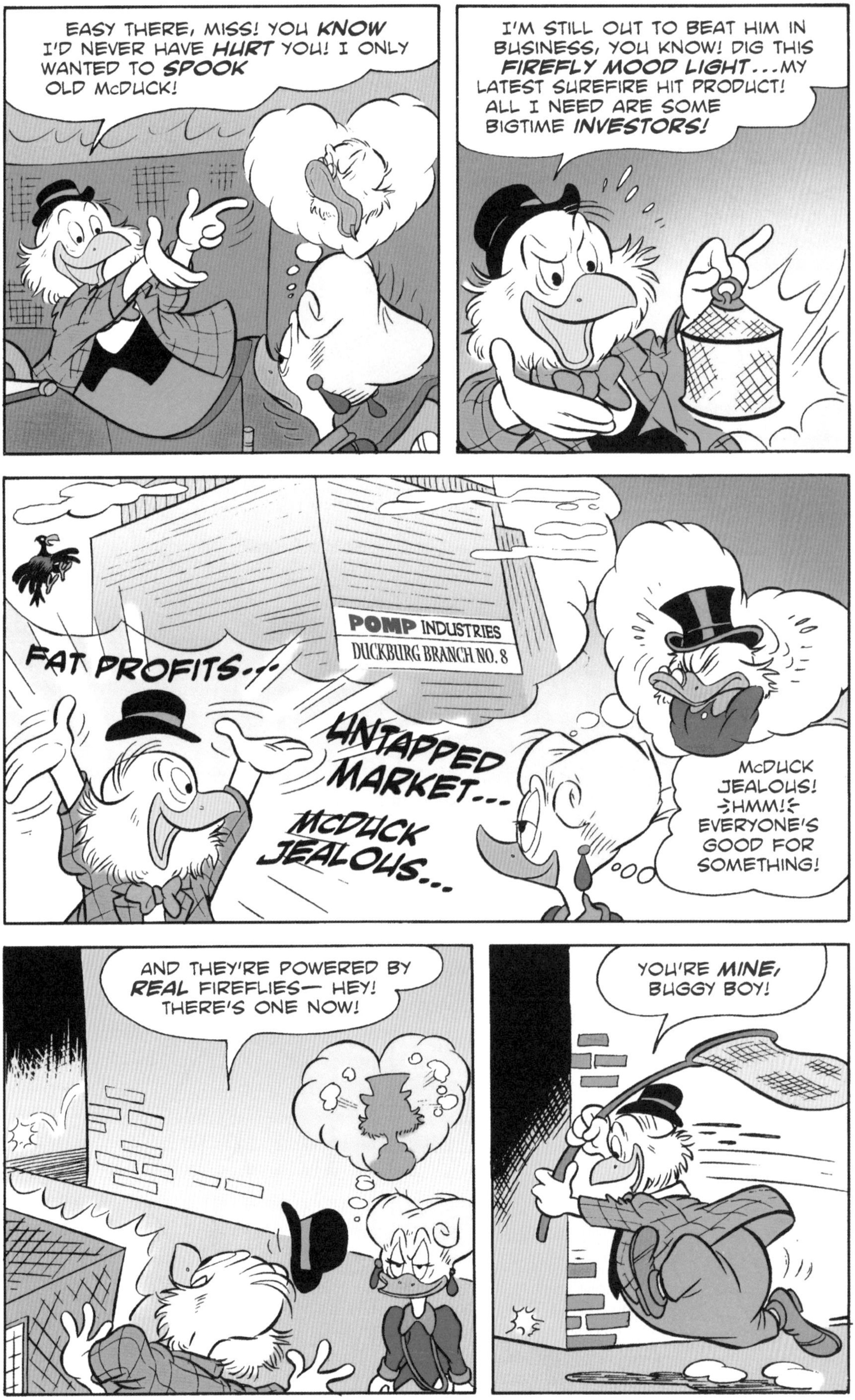

EASY THERE, MISS! YOU KNOW I'D NEVER HAVE HURT YOU! I ONLY WANTED TO SPOOK OLD McDUCK!
I'M STILL OUT TO BEAT HIM IN BUSINESS, YOU KNOW! DIG THIS FIREFLY MOOD LIGHT... MY LATEST SUREFIRE HIT PRODUCT! ALL I NEED ARE SOME BIGTIME INVESTORS!
POMP INDUSTRIES
DUCKBURG BRANCH NO. 8
FAT PROFITS...
UNTAPPED MARKET...
McDUCK JEALOUS...
McDUCK JEALOUS! HMM! EVERYONE'S GOOD FOR SOMETHING!
AND THEY'RE POWERED BY REAL FIREFLIES— HEY! THERE'S ONE NOW!
YOU'RE MINE, BUGGY BOY!

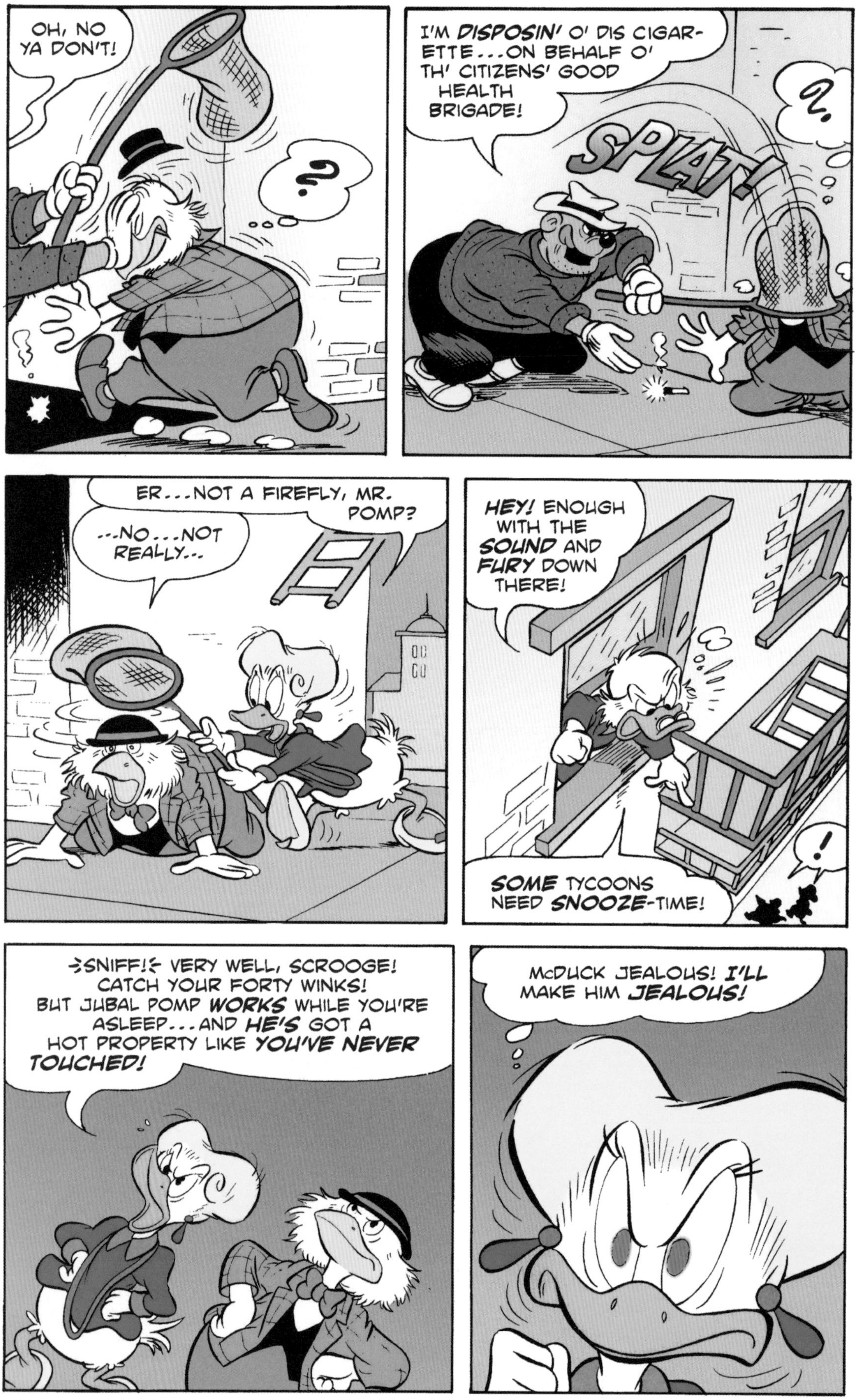

OH, NO YA DON'T!
?
I'M DISPOSIN' O' DIS CIGAR-ETTE...ON BEHALF O' TH' CITIZENS' GOOD HEALTH BRIGADE!
SPLAT!
?
ER...NOT A FIREFLY, MR. POMP?
--NO...NOT REALLY--
HEY! ENOUGH WITH THE SOUND AND FURY DOWN THERE!
SOME TYCOONS NEED SNOOZE-TIME!
!
SNIFF! VERY WELL, SCROOGE! CATCH YOUR FORTY WINKS! BUT JUBAL POMP WORKS WHILE YOU'RE ASLEEP...AND HE'S GOT A HOT PROPERTY LIKE YOU'VE NEVER TOUCHED!
McDUCK JEALOUS! I'LL MAKE HIM JEALOUS!

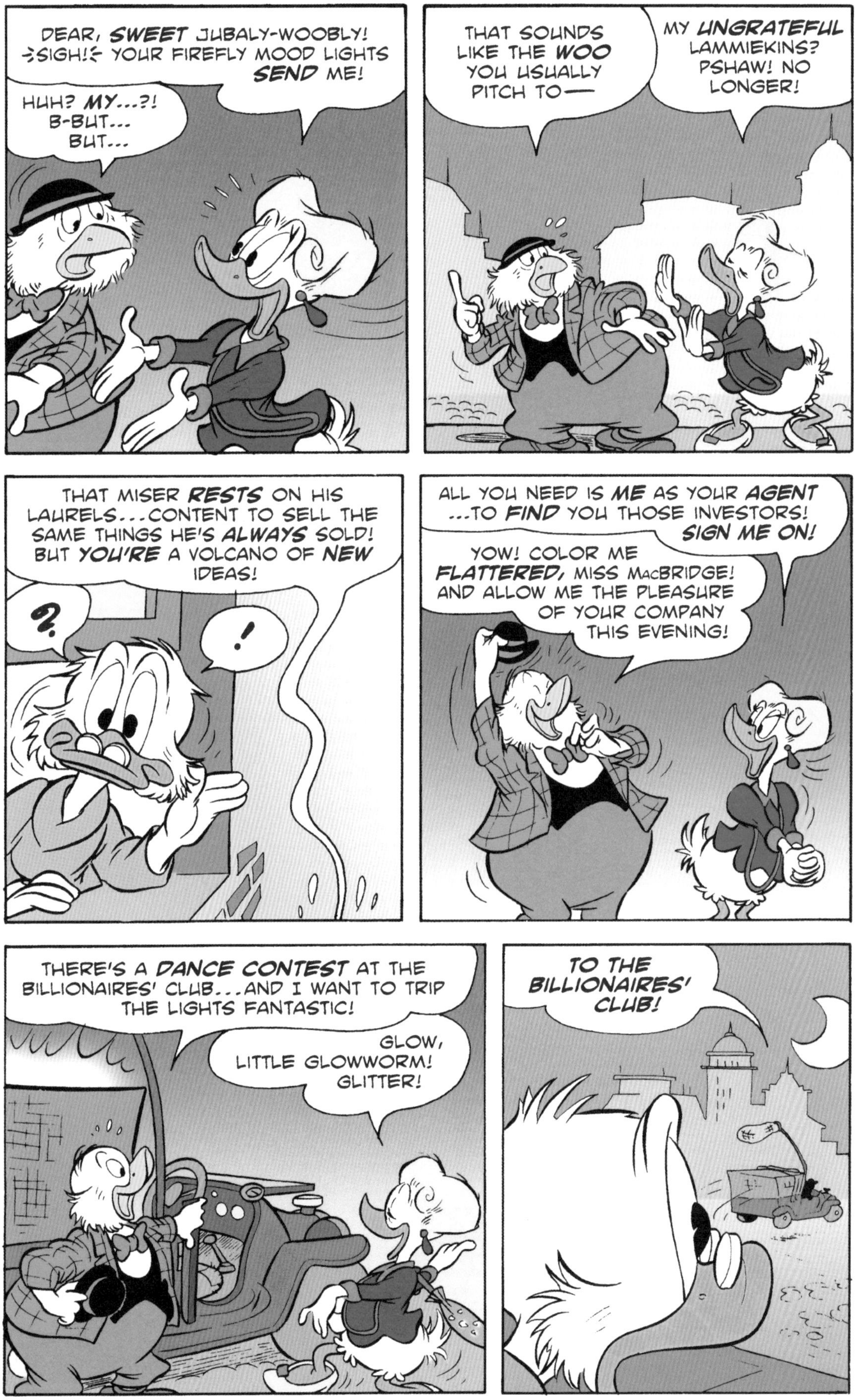
DEAR, SWEET JUBALY-WOOBLY! ⁓SIGH!⁓ YOUR FIREFLY MOOD LIGHTS SEND ME!
HUH? MY...?! B-BUT... BUT...
THAT SOUNDS LIKE THE WOO YOU USUALLY PITCH TO—
MY UNGRATEFUL LAMMIEKINS? PSHAW! NO LONGER!
THAT MISER RESTS ON HIS LAURELS...CONTENT TO SELL THE SAME THINGS HE'S ALWAYS SOLD! BUT YOU'RE A VOLCANO OF NEW IDEAS!
?
!
ALL YOU NEED IS ME AS YOUR AGENT ...TO FIND YOU THOSE INVESTORS! SIGN ME ON!
YOW! COLOR ME FLATTERED, MISS MacBRIDGE! AND ALLOW ME THE PLEASURE OF YOUR COMPANY THIS EVENING!
THERE'S A DANCE CONTEST AT THE BILLIONAIRES' CLUB...AND I WANT TO TRIP THE LIGHTS FANTASTIC!
GLOW, LITTLE GLOWWORM! GLITTER!
TO THE BILLIONAIRES' CLUB!

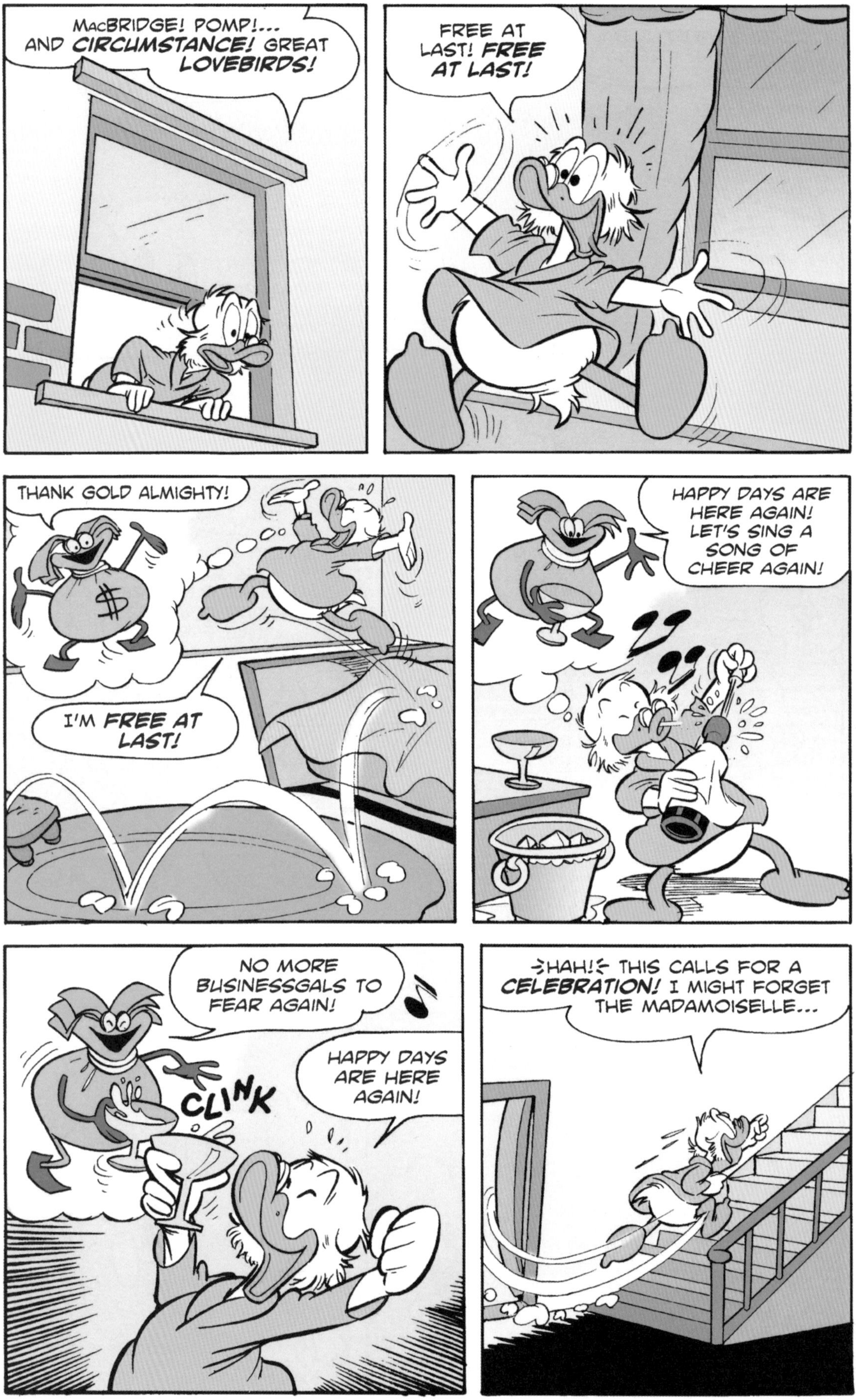
MacBRIDGE! POMP!... AND CIRCUMSTANCE! GREAT LOVEBIRDS!
FREE AT LAST! FREE AT LAST!
THANK GOLD ALMIGHTY!
I'M FREE AT LAST!
HAPPY DAYS ARE HERE AGAIN! LET'S SING A SONG OF CHEER AGAIN!
NO MORE BUSINESSGALS TO FEAR AGAIN!
CLINK
HAPPY DAYS ARE HERE AGAIN!
HAH! THIS CALLS FOR A CELEBRATION! I MIGHT FORGET THE MADAMOISELLE...

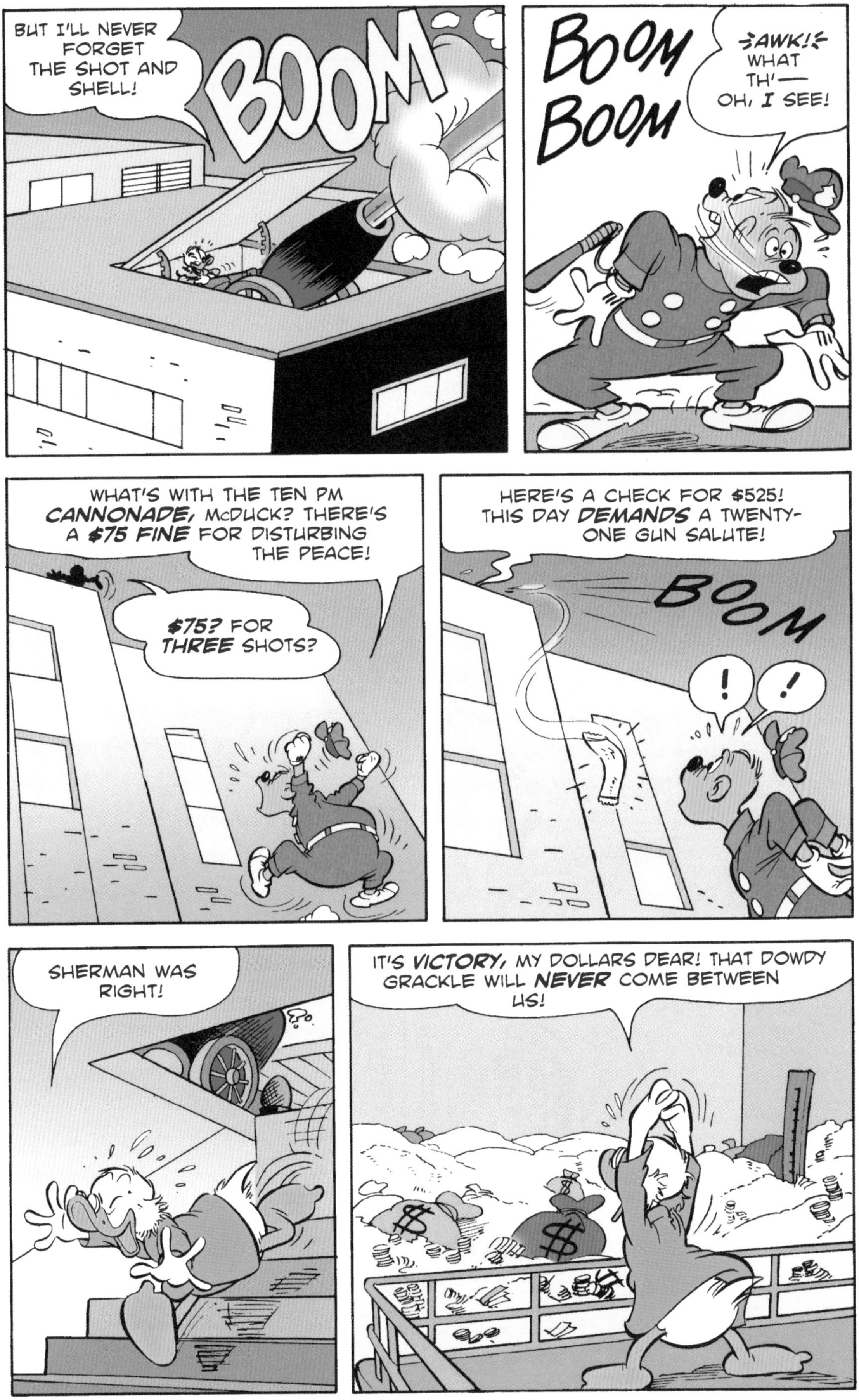
BUT I'LL NEVER FORGET THE SHOT AND SHELL!
BOOM
BOOM BOOM
AWK! WHAT TH'— OH, I SEE!
WHAT'S WITH THE TEN PM CANNONADE, McDUCK? THERE'S A $75 FINE FOR DISTURBING THE PEACE!
$75? FOR THREE SHOTS?
HERE'S A CHECK FOR $525! THIS DAY DEMANDS A TWENTY-ONE GUN SALUTE!
BOOM
!
!
SHERMAN WAS RIGHT!
IT'S VICTORY, MY DOLLARS DEAR! THAT DOWDY GRACKLE WILL NEVER COME BETWEEN US!

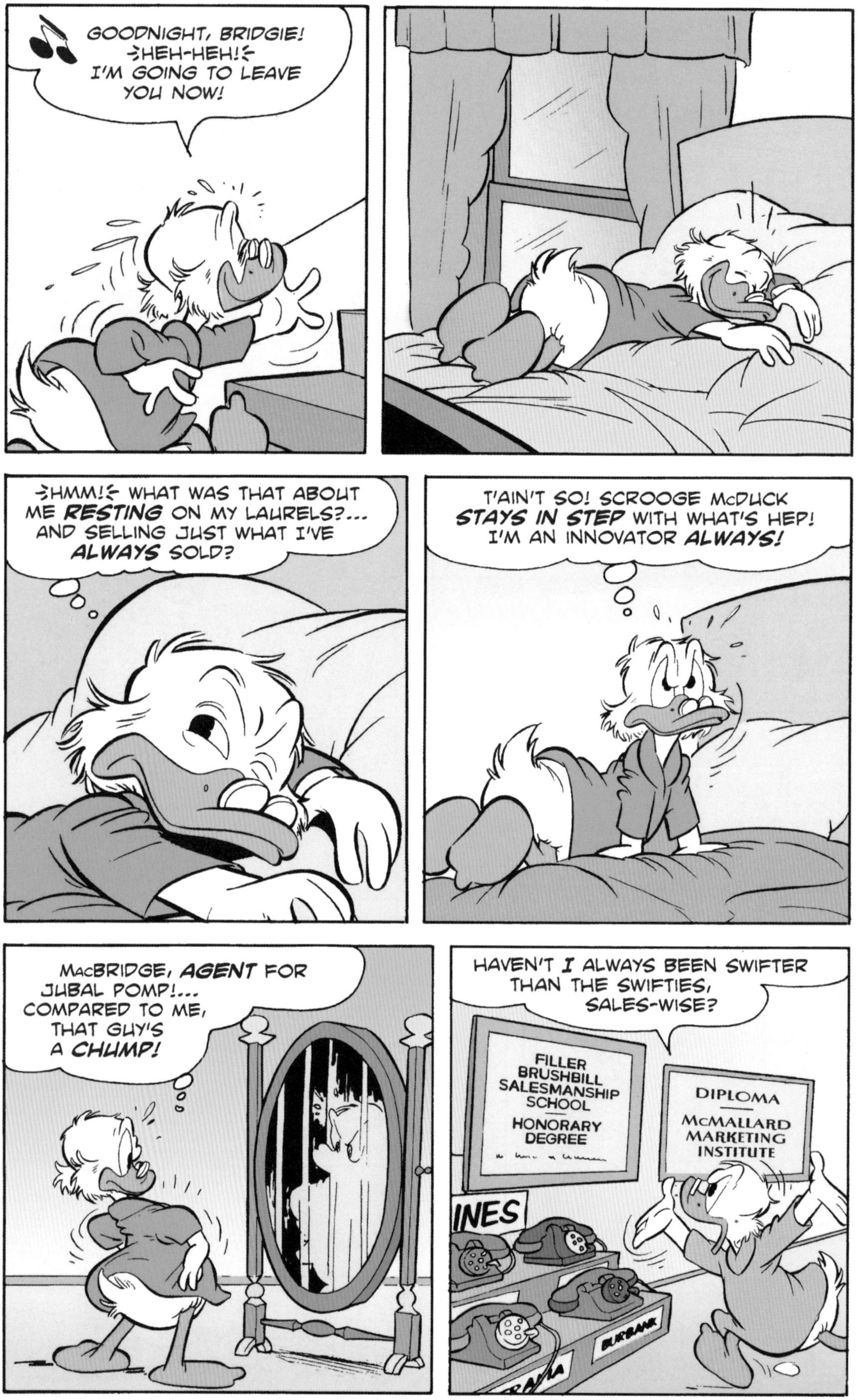
GOODNIGHT, BRIDGIE! HEH-HEH! I'M GOING TO LEAVE YOU NOW!
HMM! WHAT WAS THAT ABOUT ME RESTING ON MY LAURELS?... AND SELLING JUST WHAT I'VE ALWAYS SOLD?
T'AIN'T SO! SCROOGE McDUCK STAYS IN STEP WITH WHAT'S HEP! I'M AN INNOVATOR ALWAYS!
MacBRIDGE, AGENT FOR JUBAL POMP!... COMPARED TO ME, THAT GUY'S A CHUMP!
HAVEN'T I ALWAYS BEEN SWIFTER THAN THE SWIFTIES, SALES-WISE?
FILLER BRUSHBILL SALESMANSHIP SCHOOL HONORARY DEGREE
DIPLOMA McMALLARD MARKETING INSTITUTE
INES
BURBANK

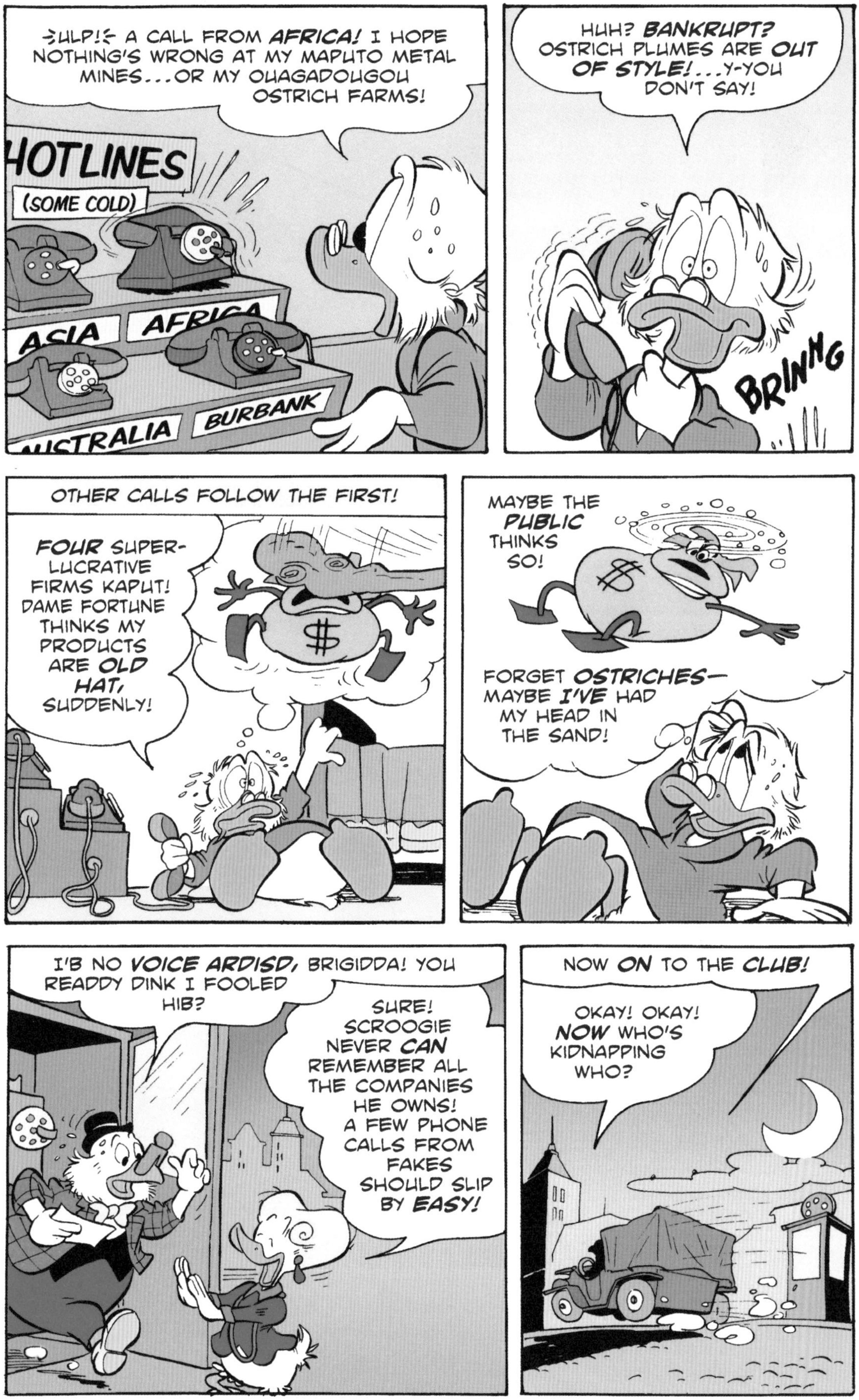

≈ULP!≈ A CALL FROM *AFRICA!* I HOPE NOTHING'S WRONG AT MY MAPUTO METAL MINES...OR MY OUAGADOUGOU OSTRICH FARMS!
HOTLINES
(SOME COLD)
ASIA
AFRICA
AUSTRALIA
BURBANK
HUH? *BANKRUPT?* OSTRICH PLUMES ARE *OUT OF STYLE!*...Y-YOU DON'T SAY!
BRINNG
OTHER CALLS FOLLOW THE FIRST!
FOUR SUPER-LUCRATIVE FIRMS KAPUT! DAME FORTUNE THINKS MY PRODUCTS ARE *OLD HAT,* SUDDENLY!
MAYBE THE *PUBLIC* THINKS SO!
FORGET *OSTRICHES*—MAYBE *I'VE* HAD MY HEAD IN THE SAND!
I'B NO *VOICE ARDISD,* BRIGIDDA! YOU READDY DINK I FOOLED HIB?
SURE! SCROOGIE NEVER *CAN* REMEMBER ALL THE COMPANIES HE OWNS! A FEW PHONE CALLS FROM FAKES SHOULD SLIP BY *EASY!*
NOW *ON* TO THE *CLUB!*
OKAY! OKAY! *NOW* WHO'S KIDNAPPING WHO?

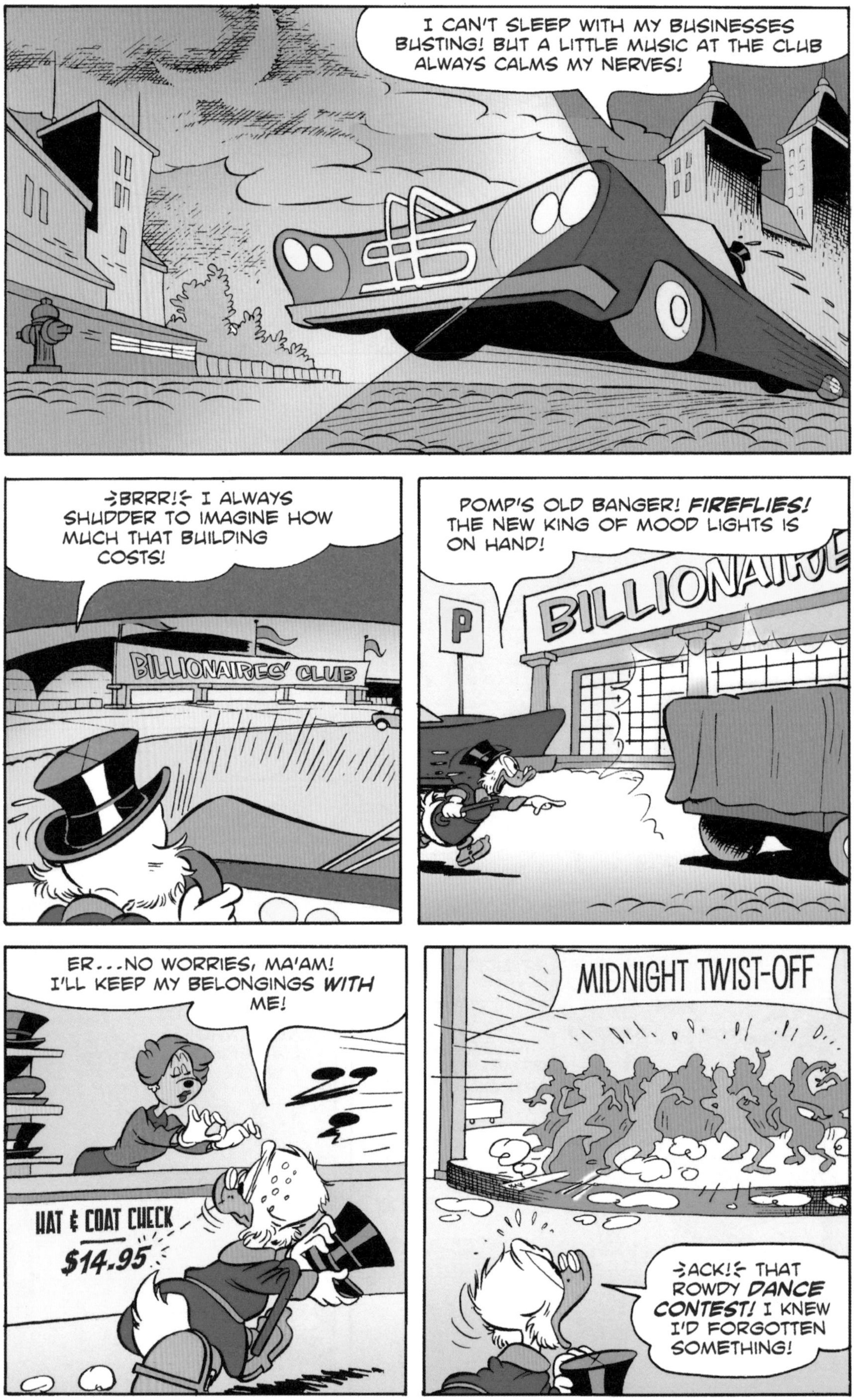
I CAN'T SLEEP WITH MY BUSINESSES BUSTING! BUT A LITTLE MUSIC AT THE CLUB ALWAYS CALMS MY NERVES!
⋾BRRR!⋲ I ALWAYS SHUDDER TO IMAGINE HOW MUCH THAT BUILDING COSTS!
BILLIONAIRES' CLUB
POMP'S OLD BANGER! FIREFLIES! THE NEW KING OF MOOD LIGHTS IS ON HAND!
P
BILLIONAIRE
ER...NO WORRIES, MA'AM! I'LL KEEP MY BELONGINGS WITH ME!
HAT & COAT CHECK
$14.95
MIDNIGHT TWIST-OFF
⋾ACK!⋲ THAT ROWDY DANCE CONTEST! I KNEW I'D FORGOTTEN SOMETHING!

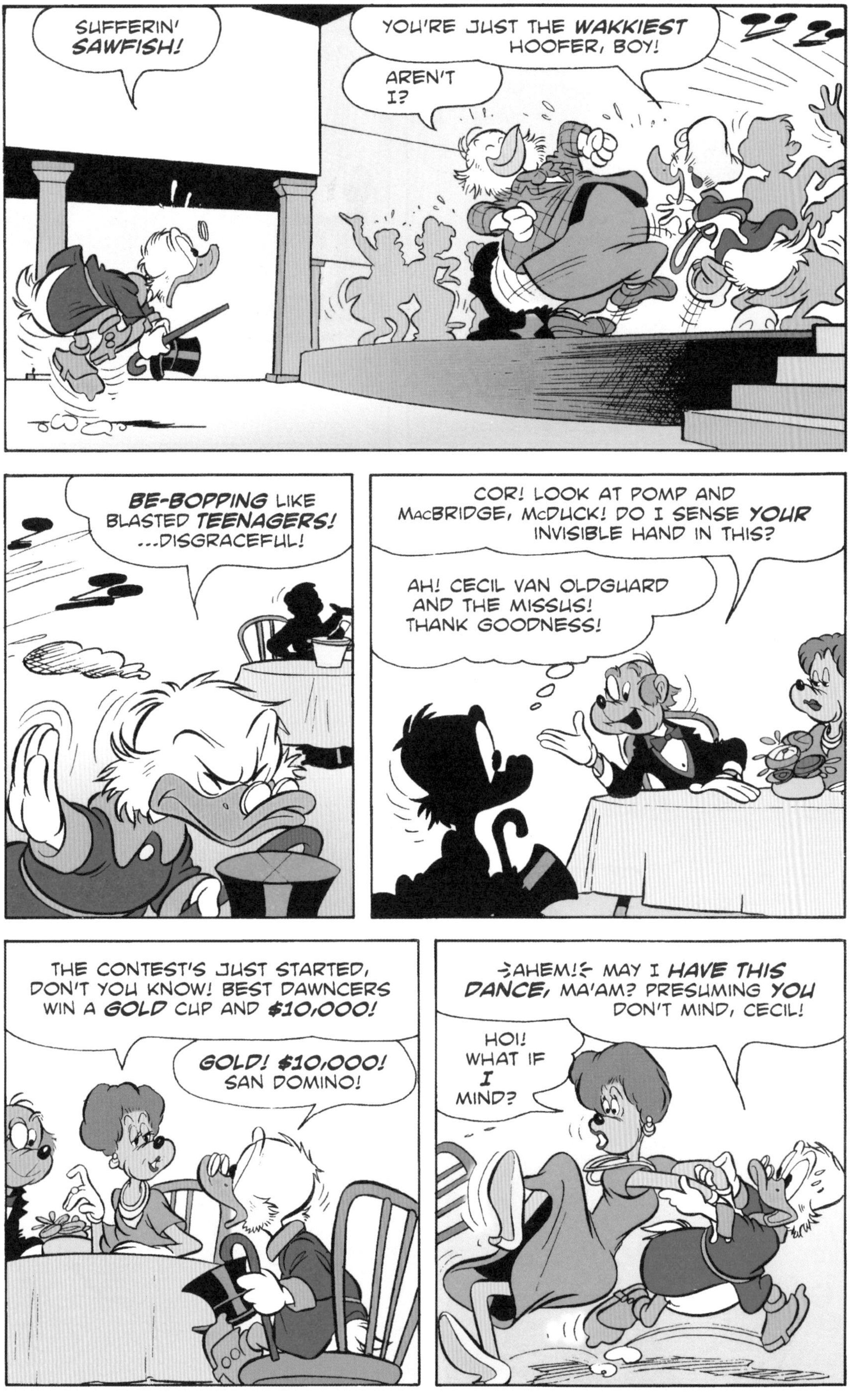
SUFFERIN' SAWFISH!
YOU'RE JUST THE WAKKIEST HOOFER, BOY!
AREN'T I?
BE-BOPPING LIKE BLASTED TEENAGERS! ...DISGRACEFUL!
COR! LOOK AT POMP AND MACBRIDGE, McDUCK! DO I SENSE YOUR INVISIBLE HAND IN THIS?
AH! CECIL VAN OLDGUARD AND THE MISSUS! THANK GOODNESS!
THE CONTEST'S JUST STARTED, DON'T YOU KNOW! BEST DAWNCERS WIN A GOLD CUP AND $10,000!
GOLD! $10,000! SAN DOMINO!
AHEM! MAY I HAVE THIS DANCE, MA'AM? PRESUMING YOU DON'T MIND, CECIL!
HOI! WHAT IF I MIND?

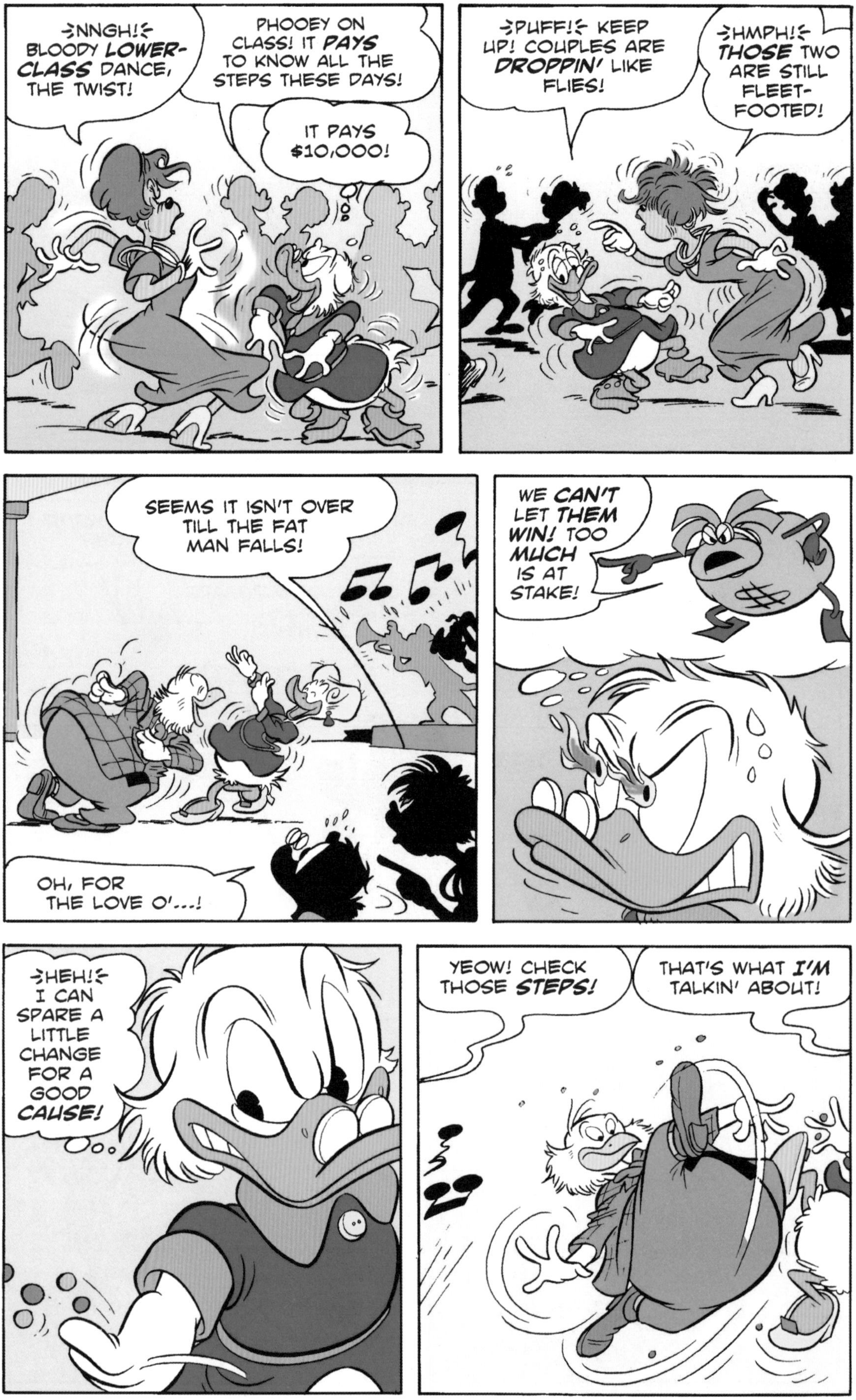

≡NNGH!≡ BLOODY LOWER-CLASS DANCE, THE TWIST!
PHOOEY ON CLASS! IT PAYS TO KNOW ALL THE STEPS THESE DAYS!
IT PAYS $10,000!
≡PUFF!≡ KEEP UP! COUPLES ARE DROPPIN' LIKE FLIES!
≡HMPH!≡ THOSE TWO ARE STILL FLEET-FOOTED!
SEEMS IT ISN'T OVER TILL THE FAT MAN FALLS!
OH, FOR THE LOVE O'...!
WE CAN'T LET THEM WIN! TOO MUCH IS AT STAKE!
≡HEH!≡ I CAN SPARE A LITTLE CHANGE FOR A GOOD CAUSE!
YEOW! CHECK THOSE STEPS!
THAT'S WHAT I'M TALKIN' ABOUT!

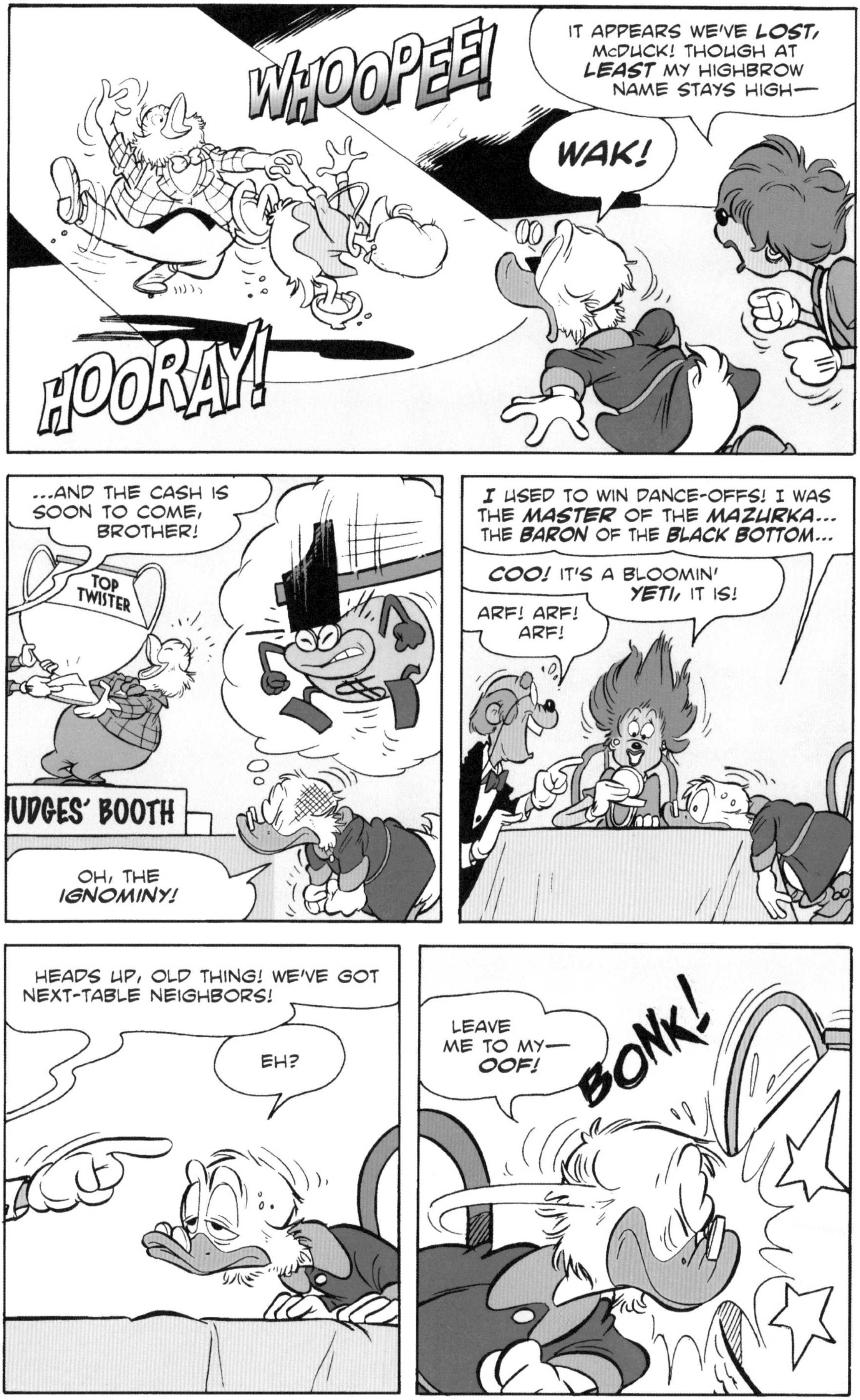
WHOOPEE!
HOORAY!
IT APPEARS WE'VE LOST, McDUCK! THOUGH AT LEAST MY HIGHBROW NAME STAYS HIGH—
WAK!
...AND THE CASH IS SOON TO COME, BROTHER!
TOP TWISTER
JUDGES' BOOTH
OH, THE IGNOMINY!
I USED TO WIN DANCE-OFFS! I WAS THE MASTER OF THE MAZURKA... THE BARON OF THE BLACK BOTTOM...
COO! IT'S A BLOOMIN' YETI, IT IS!
ARF! ARF! ARF!
HEADS UP, OLD THING! WE'VE GOT NEXT-TABLE NEIGHBORS!
EH?
LEAVE ME TO MY— OOF!
BONK!

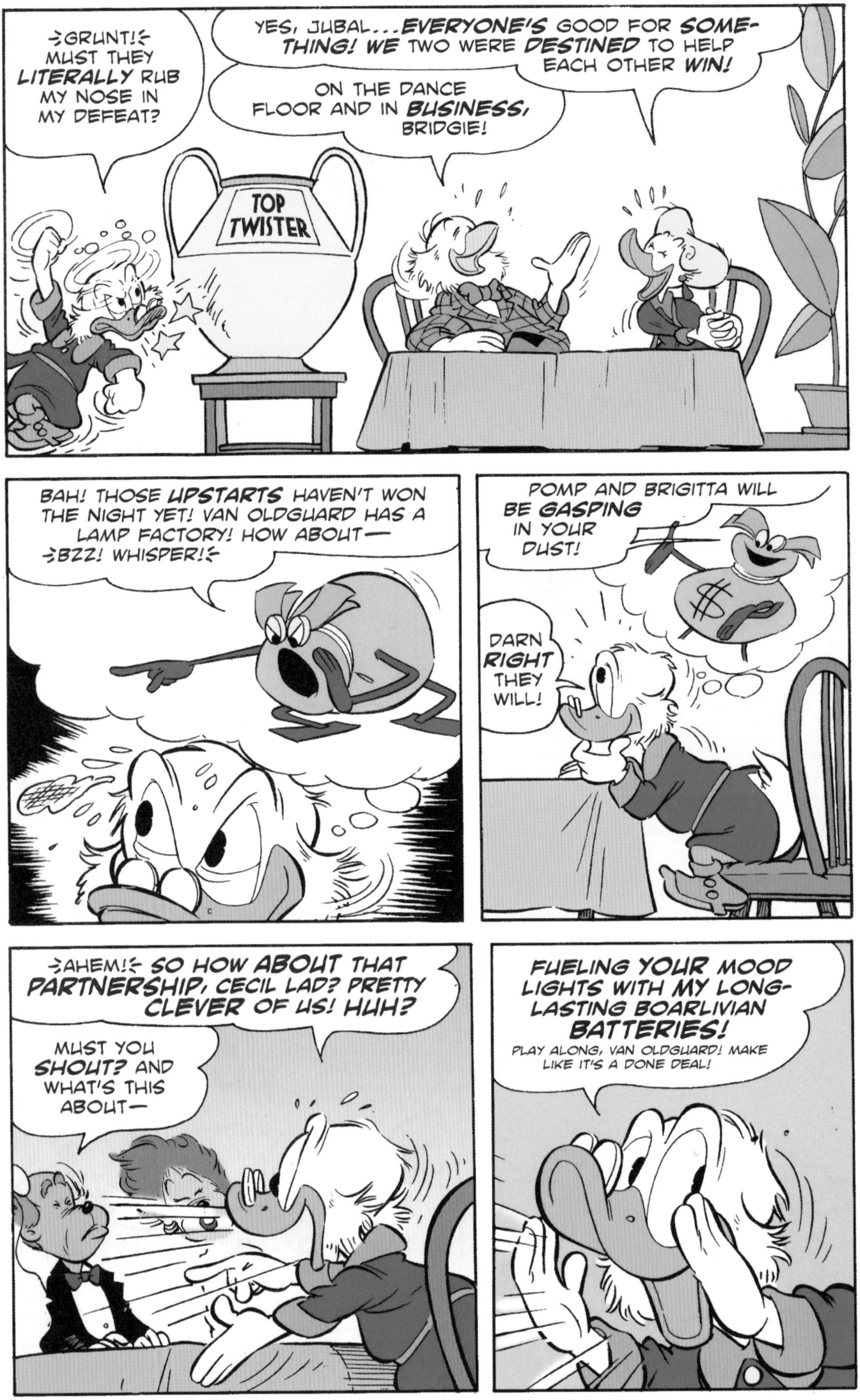

⇉GRUNT!⇇ MUST THEY LITERALLY RUB MY NOSE IN MY DEFEAT?
YES, JUBAL... EVERYONE'S GOOD FOR SOMETHING! WE TWO WERE DESTINED TO HELP EACH OTHER WIN!
ON THE DANCE FLOOR AND IN BUSINESS, BRIDGIE!
TOP TWISTER
BAH! THOSE UPSTARTS HAVEN'T WON THE NIGHT YET! VAN OLDGUARD HAS A LAMP FACTORY! HOW ABOUT— ⇉BZZ! WHISPER!⇇
POMP AND BRIGITTA WILL BE GASPING IN YOUR DUST!
DARN RIGHT THEY WILL!
⇉AHEM!⇇ SO HOW ABOUT THAT PARTNERSHIP, CECIL LAD? PRETTY CLEVER OF US! HUH?
MUST YOU SHOUT? AND WHAT'S THIS ABOUT—
FUELING YOUR MOOD LIGHTS WITH MY LONG-LASTING BOARLIVIAN BATTERIES!
PLAY ALONG, VAN OLDGUARD! MAKE LIKE IT'S A DONE DEAL!

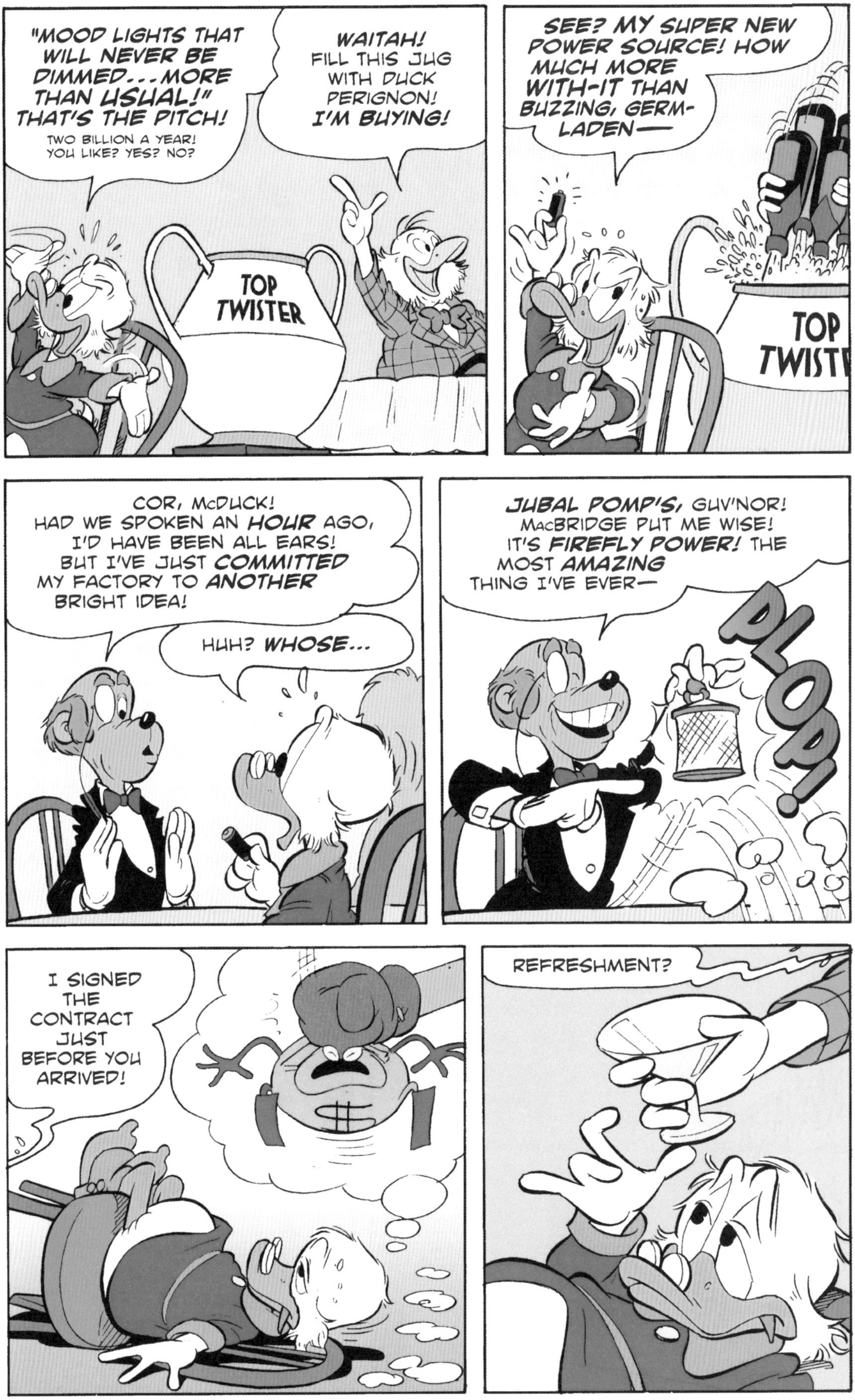
"MOOD LIGHTS THAT WILL NEVER BE DIMMED...MORE THAN USUAL!" THAT'S THE PITCH!
TWO BILLION A YEAR! YOU LIKE? YES? NO?
WAITAH! FILL THIS JUG WITH DUCK PERIGNON! I'M BUYING!
TOP TWISTER
SEE? MY SUPER NEW POWER SOURCE! HOW MUCH MORE WITH-IT THAN BUZZING, GERM-LADEN—
TOP TWIST
COR, McDUCK! HAD WE SPOKEN AN HOUR AGO, I'D HAVE BEEN ALL EARS! BUT I'VE JUST COMMITTED MY FACTORY TO ANOTHER BRIGHT IDEA!
HUH? WHOSE...
JUBAL POMP'S, GUV'NOR! MacBRIDGE PUT ME WISE! IT'S FIREFLY POWER! THE MOST AMAZING THING I'VE EVER—
PLOP!
I SIGNED THE CONTRACT JUST BEFORE YOU ARRIVED!
REFRESHMENT?

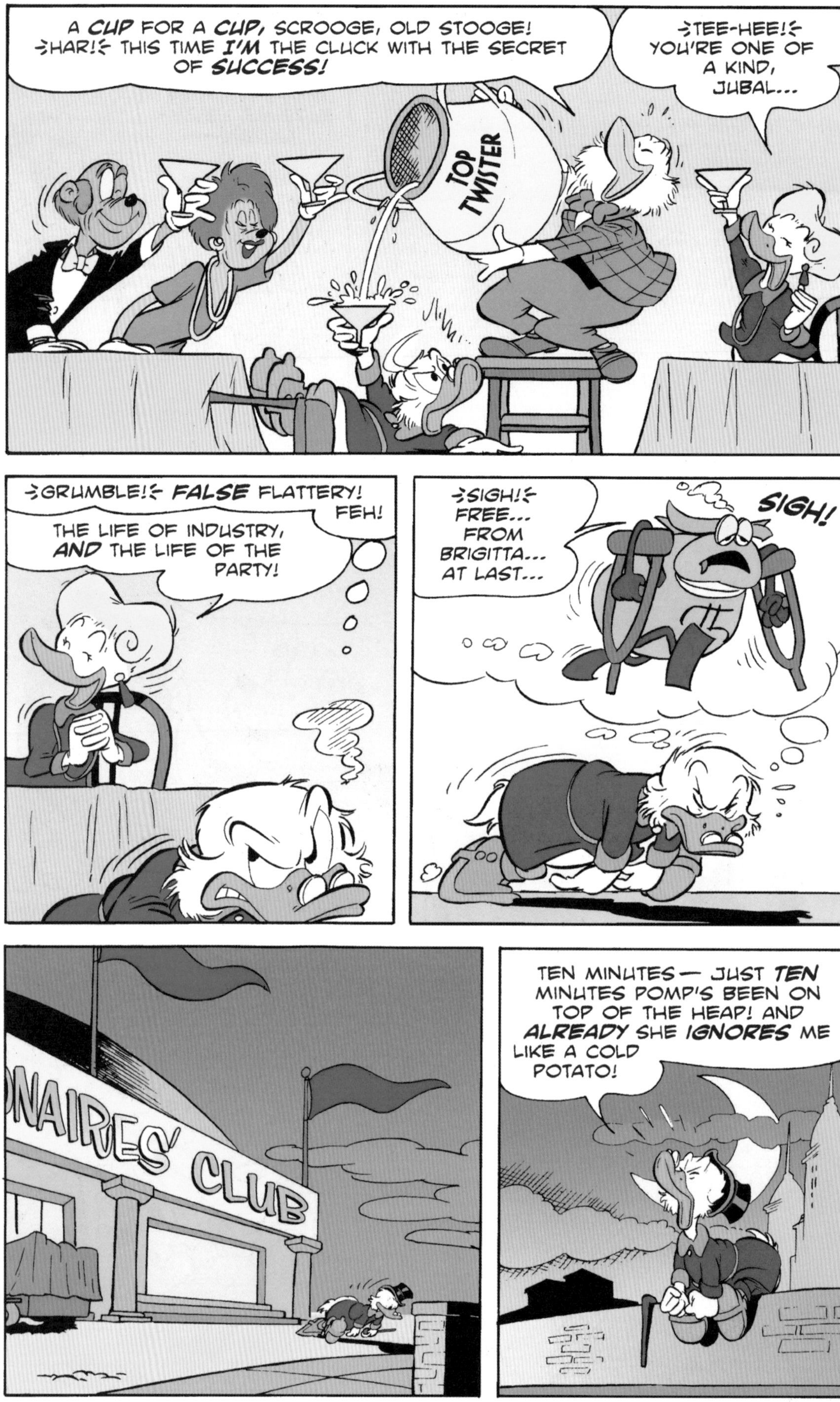
A CUP FOR A CUP, SCROOGE, OLD STOOGE! ⁃HAR!⁃ THIS TIME I'M THE CLUCK WITH THE SECRET OF SUCCESS!
⁃TEE-HEE!⁃ YOU'RE ONE OF A KIND, JUBAL...
TOP TWISTER
⁃GRUMBLE!⁃ FALSE FLATTERY! FEH!
THE LIFE OF INDUSTRY, AND THE LIFE OF THE PARTY!
⁃SIGH!⁃ FREE... FROM BRIGITTA... AT LAST...
SIGH!
ONAIRES' CLUB
TEN MINUTES— JUST TEN MINUTES POMP'S BEEN ON TOP OF THE HEAP! AND ALREADY SHE IGNORES ME LIKE A COLD POTATO!

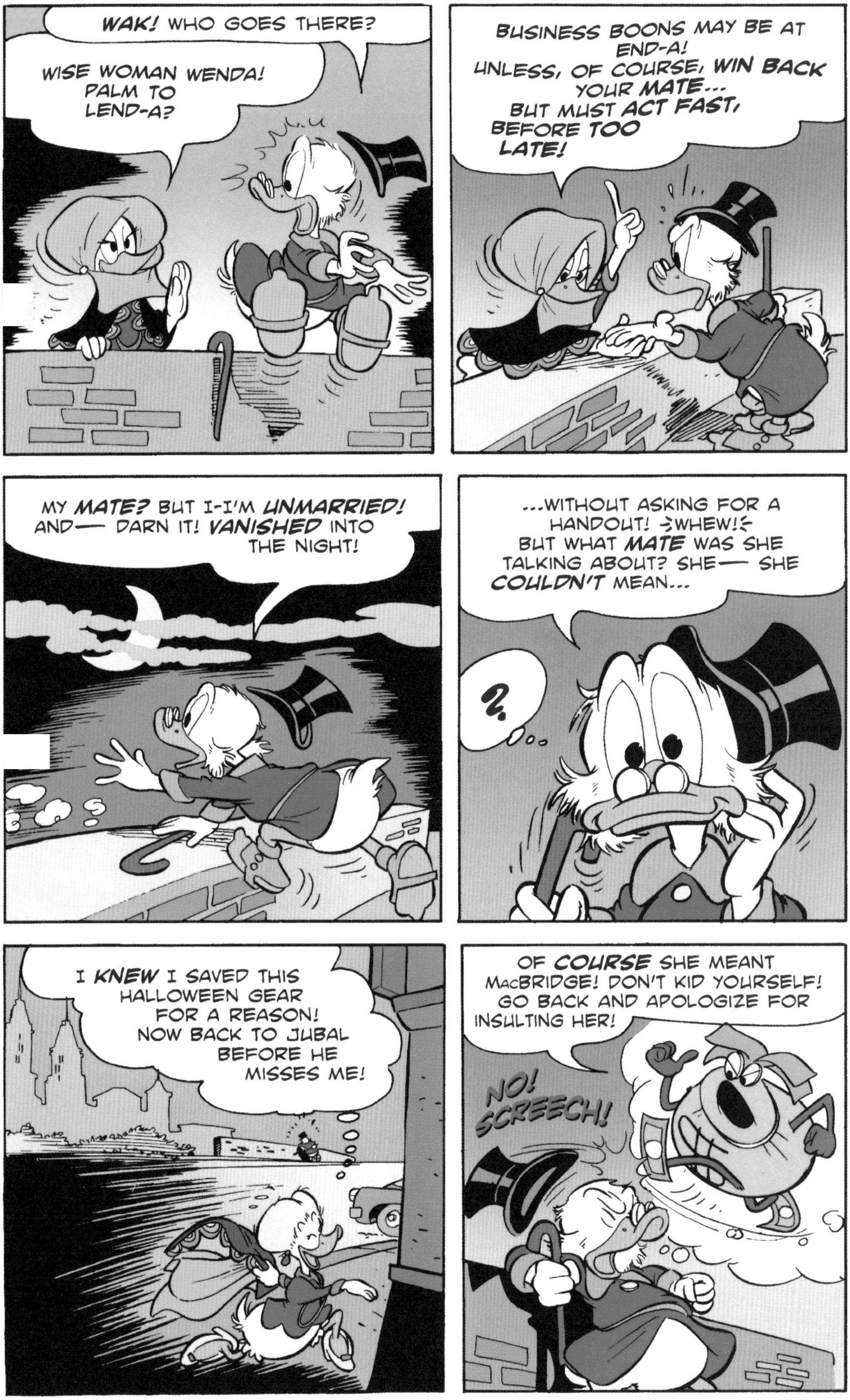
WAK! WHO GOES THERE?
WISE WOMAN WENDA! PALM TO LEND-A?
BUSINESS BOONS MAY BE AT END-A! UNLESS, OF COURSE, WIN BACK YOUR MATE... BUT MUST ACT FAST, BEFORE TOO LATE!
MY MATE? BUT I-I'M UNMARRIED! AND— DARN IT! VANISHED INTO THE NIGHT!
...WITHOUT ASKING FOR A HANDOUT! WHEW! BUT WHAT MATE WAS SHE TALKING ABOUT? SHE— SHE COULDN'T MEAN...
?
I KNEW I SAVED THIS HALLOWEEN GEAR FOR A REASON! NOW BACK TO JUBAL BEFORE HE MISSES ME!
OF COURSE SHE MEANT MacBRIDGE! DON'T KID YOURSELF! GO BACK AND APOLOGIZE FOR INSULTING HER!
NO! SCREECH!

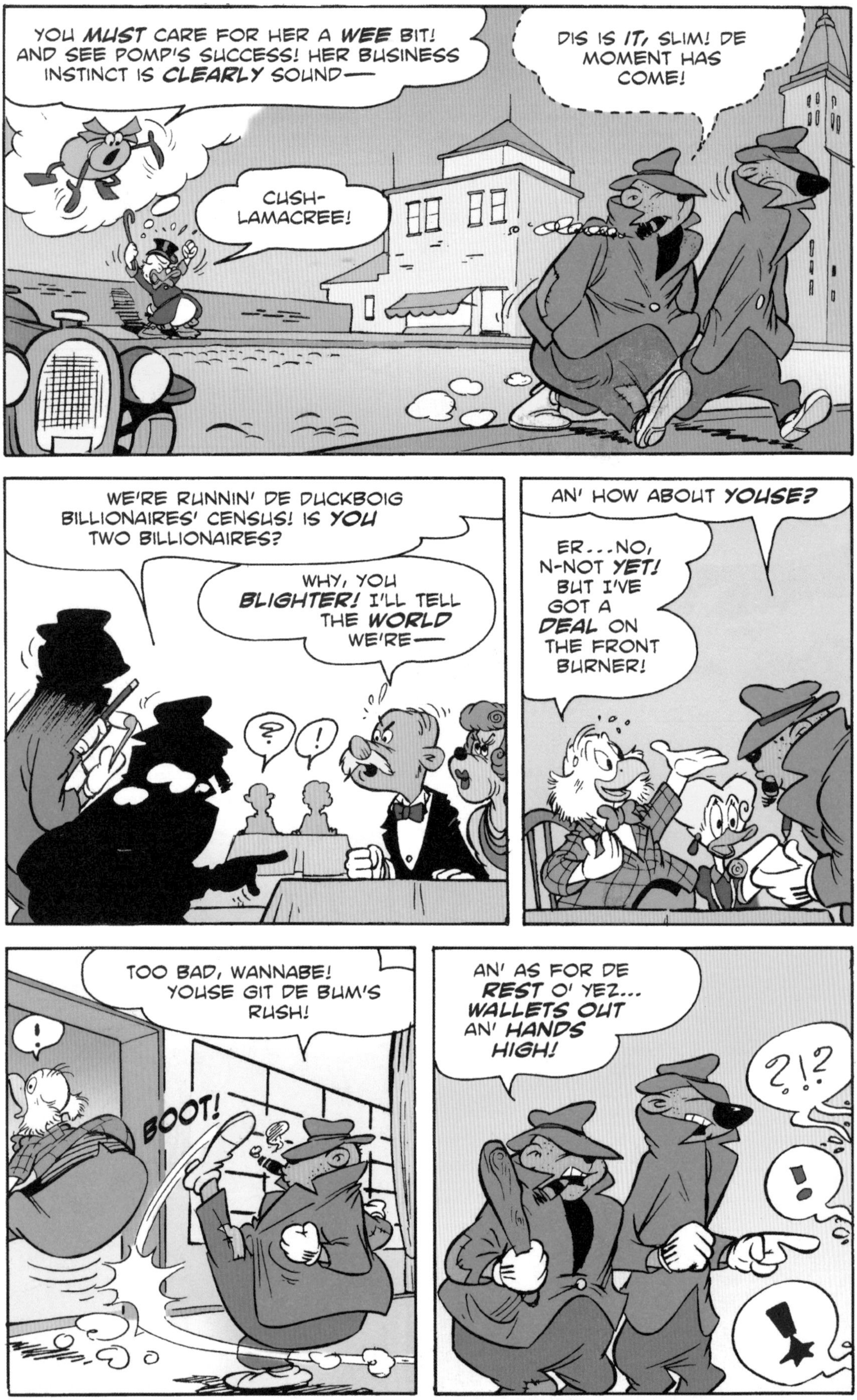
YOU MUST CARE FOR HER A WEE BIT! AND SEE POMP'S SUCCESS! HER BUSINESS INSTINCT IS CLEARLY SOUND—
DIS IS IT, SLIM! DE MOMENT HAS COME!
CUSH-LAMACREE!
WE'RE RUNNIN' DE DUCKBOIG BILLIONAIRES' CENSUS! IS YOU TWO BILLIONAIRES?
WHY, YOU BLIGHTER! I'LL TELL THE WORLD WE'RE—
?
!
AN' HOW ABOUT YOUSE?
ER...NO, N-NOT YET! BUT I'VE GOT A DEAL ON THE FRONT BURNER!
TOO BAD, WANNABE! YOUSE GIT DE BUM'S RUSH!
!
BOOT!
AN' AS FOR DE REST O' YEZ... WALLETS OUT AN' HANDS HIGH!
?!?
!
!

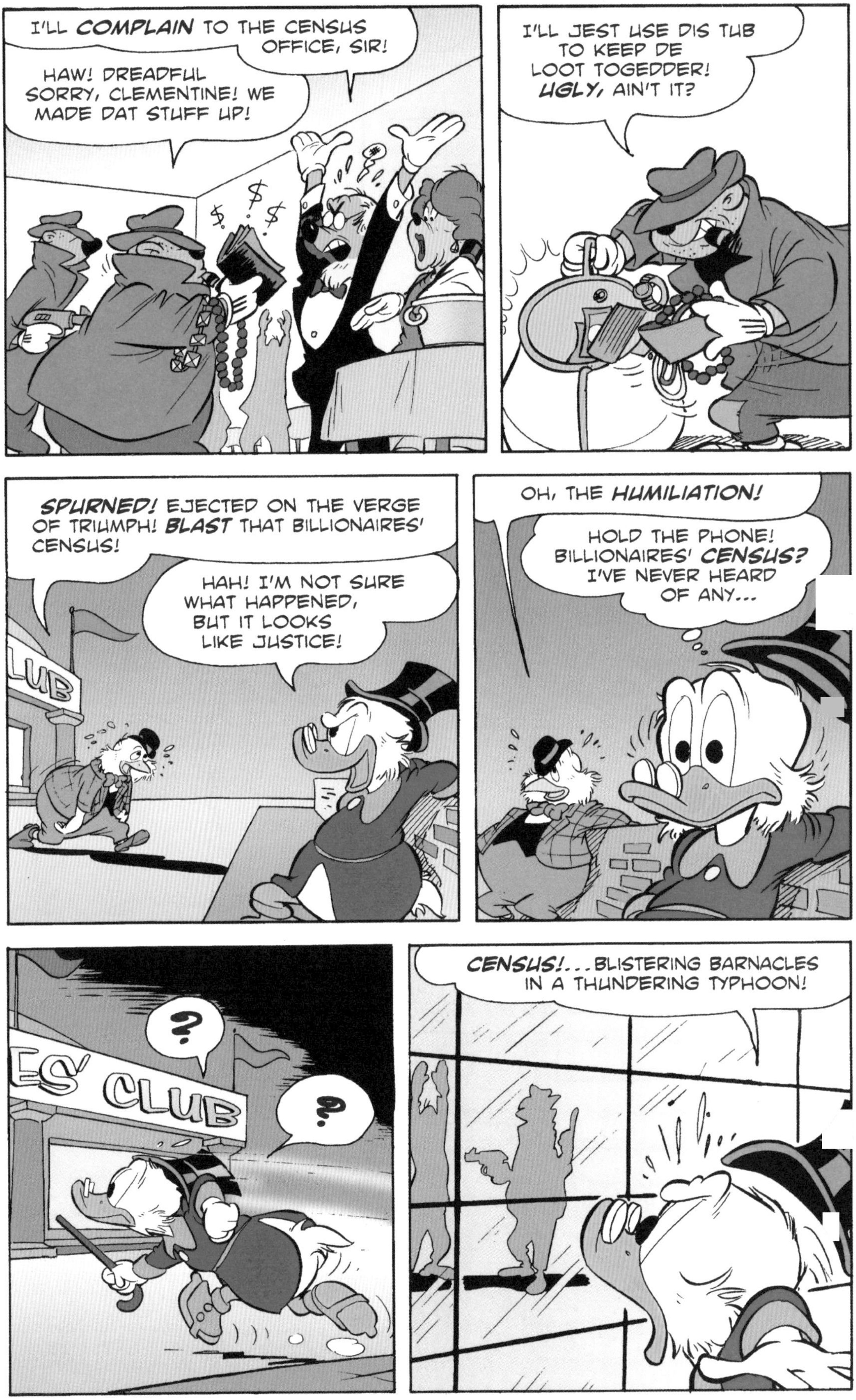
I'LL COMPLAIN TO THE CENSUS OFFICE, SIR!
HAW! DREADFUL SORRY, CLEMENTINE! WE MADE DAT STUFF UP!
I'LL JEST USE DIS TUB TO KEEP DE LOOT TOGEDDER! UGLY, AIN'T IT?
SPURNED! EJECTED ON THE VERGE OF TRIUMPH! BLAST THAT BILLIONAIRES' CENSUS!
HAH! I'M NOT SURE WHAT HAPPENED, BUT IT LOOKS LIKE JUSTICE!
CLUB
OH, THE HUMILIATION!
HOLD THE PHONE! BILLIONAIRES' CENSUS? I'VE NEVER HEARD OF ANY...
?
ES' CLUB
?
CENSUS!...BLISTERING BARNACLES IN A THUNDERING TYPHOON!

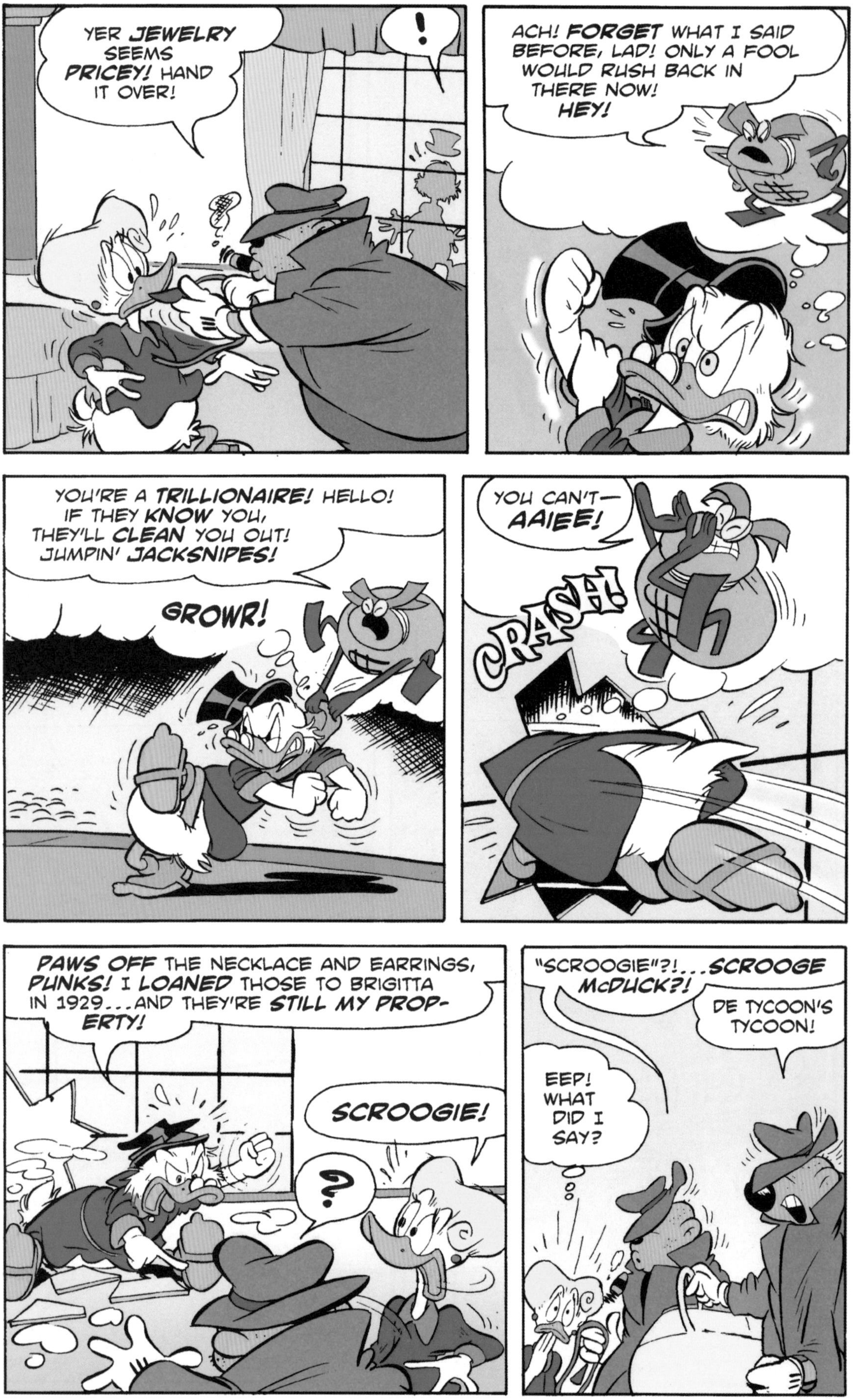
YER JEWELRY SEEMS PRICEY! HAND IT OVER!
!
ACH! FORGET WHAT I SAID BEFORE, LAD! ONLY A FOOL WOULD RUSH BACK IN THERE NOW! HEY!
YOU'RE A TRILLIONAIRE! HELLO! IF THEY KNOW YOU, THEY'LL CLEAN YOU OUT! JUMPIN' JACKSNIPES!
GROWR!
YOU CAN'T— AAIEE!
CRASH!
PAWS OFF THE NECKLACE AND EARRINGS, PUNKS! I LOANED THOSE TO BRIGITTA IN 1929...AND THEY'RE STILL MY PROP-ERTY!
SCROOGIE!
?
"SCROOGIE"?!...SCROOGE McDUCK?!
DE TYCOON'S TYCOON!
EEP! WHAT DID I SAY?

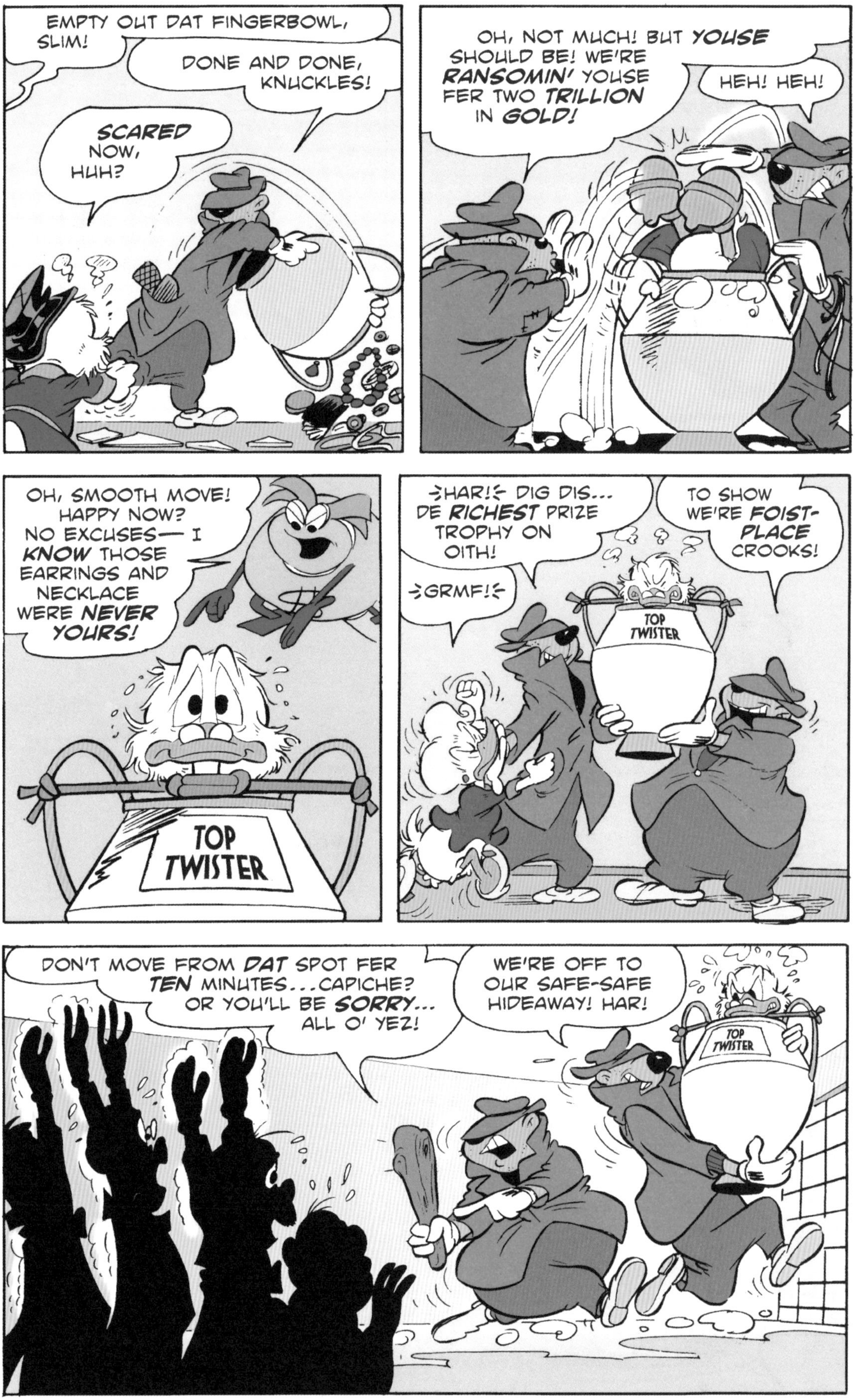
EMPTY OUT DAT FINGERBOWL, SLIM!
DONE AND DONE, KNUCKLES!
SCARED NOW, HUH?
OH, NOT MUCH! BUT YOUSE SHOULD BE! WE'RE RANSOMIN' YOUSE FER TWO TRILLION IN GOLD!
HEH! HEH!
OH, SMOOTH MOVE! HAPPY NOW? NO EXCUSES— I KNOW THOSE EARRINGS AND NECKLACE WERE NEVER YOURS!
TOP TWISTER
HAR! DIG DIS... DE RICHEST PRIZE TROPHY ON OITH!
TO SHOW WE'RE FOIST-PLACE CROOKS!
GRMF!
TOP TWISTER
DON'T MOVE FROM DAT SPOT FER TEN MINUTES...CAPICHE? OR YOU'LL BE SORRY... ALL O' YEZ!
WE'RE OFF TO OUR SAFE-SAFE HIDEAWAY! HAR!
TOP TWISTER

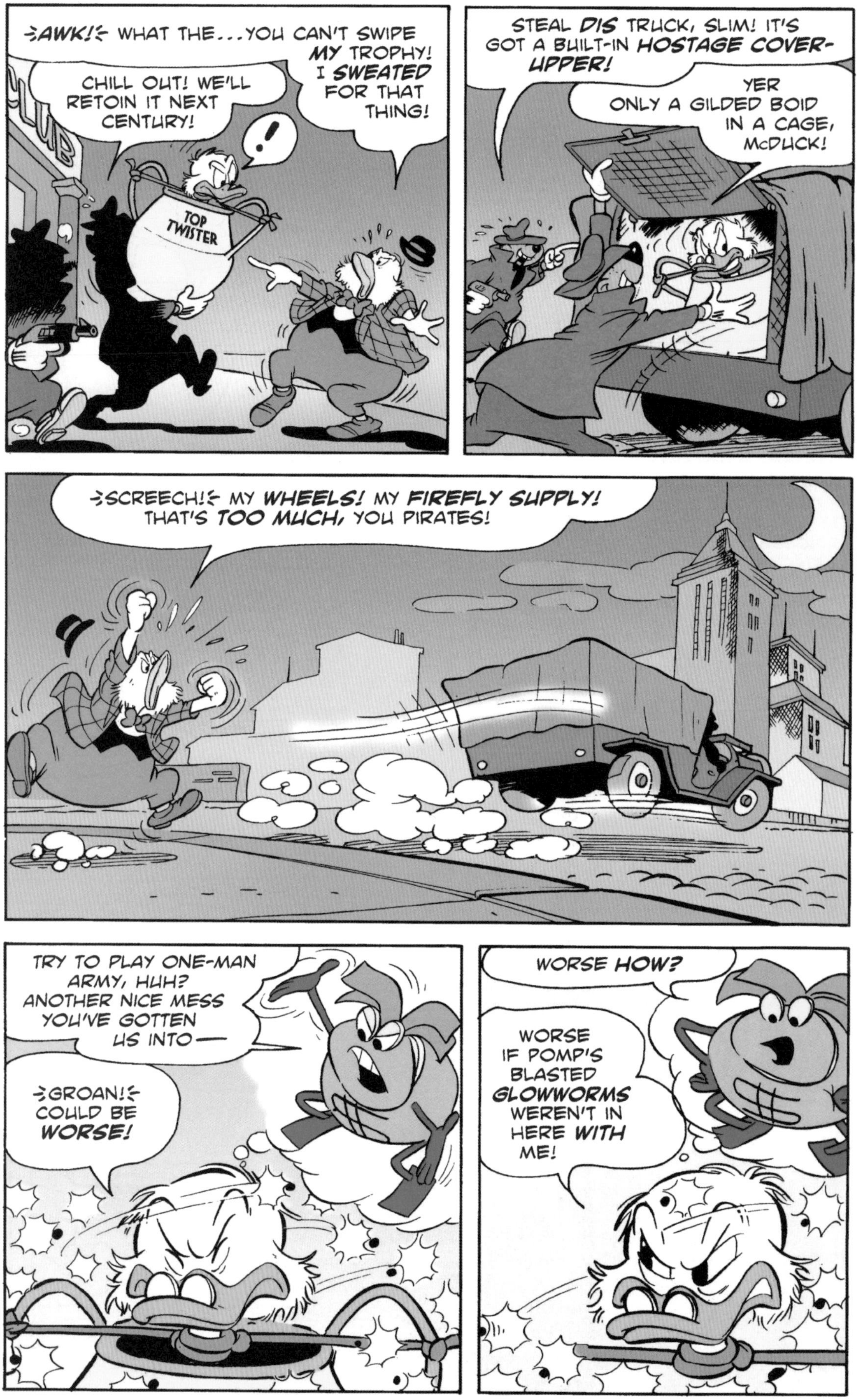
AWK! WHAT THE...YOU CAN'T SWIPE MY TROPHY! I SWEATED FOR THAT THING!
CHILL OUT! WE'LL RETOIN IT NEXT CENTURY!
!
CLUB
TOP TWISTER
STEAL DIS TRUCK, SLIM! IT'S GOT A BUILT-IN HOSTAGE COVER-UPPER!
YER ONLY A GILDED BOID IN A CAGE, McDUCK!
SCREECH! MY WHEELS! MY FIREFLY SUPPLY! THAT'S TOO MUCH, YOU PIRATES!
TRY TO PLAY ONE-MAN ARMY, HUH? ANOTHER NICE MESS YOU'VE GOTTEN US INTO—
GROAN! COULD BE WORSE!
WORSE HOW?
WORSE IF POMP'S BLASTED GLOWWORMS WEREN'T IN HERE WITH ME!

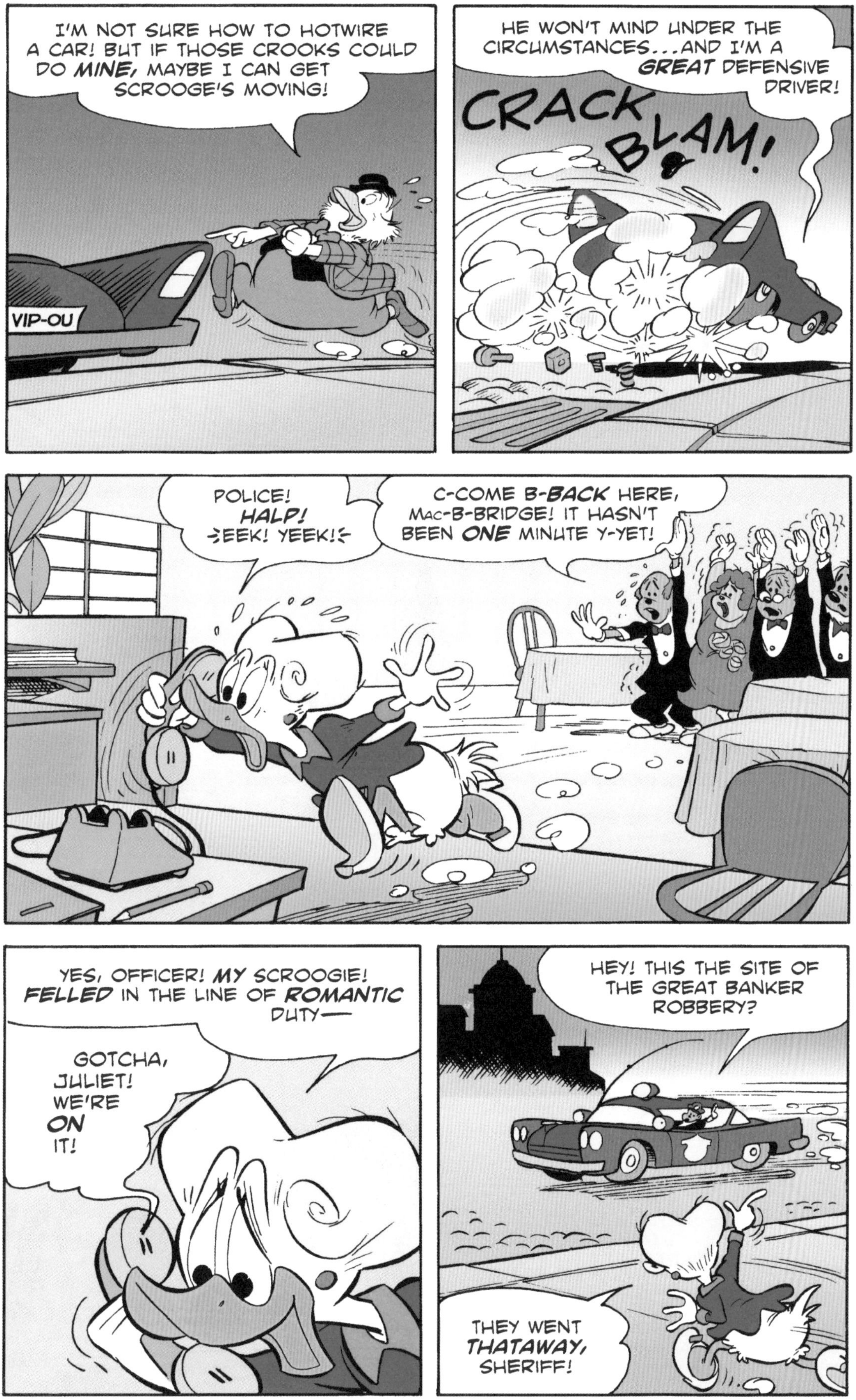
I'M NOT SURE HOW TO HOTWIRE A CAR! BUT IF THOSE CROOKS COULD DO MINE, MAYBE I CAN GET SCROOGE'S MOVING!
VIP-OU
HE WON'T MIND UNDER THE CIRCUMSTANCES...AND I'M A GREAT DEFENSIVE DRIVER!
CRACK
BLAM!
POLICE! HALP! EEK! YEEK!
C-COME B-BACK HERE, MAC-B-BRIDGE! IT HASN'T BEEN ONE MINUTE Y-YET!
YES, OFFICER! MY SCROOGIE! FELLED IN THE LINE OF ROMANTIC DUTY—
GOTCHA, JULIET! WE'RE ON IT!
HEY! THIS THE SITE OF THE GREAT BANKER ROBBERY?
THEY WENT THATAWAY, SHERIFF!

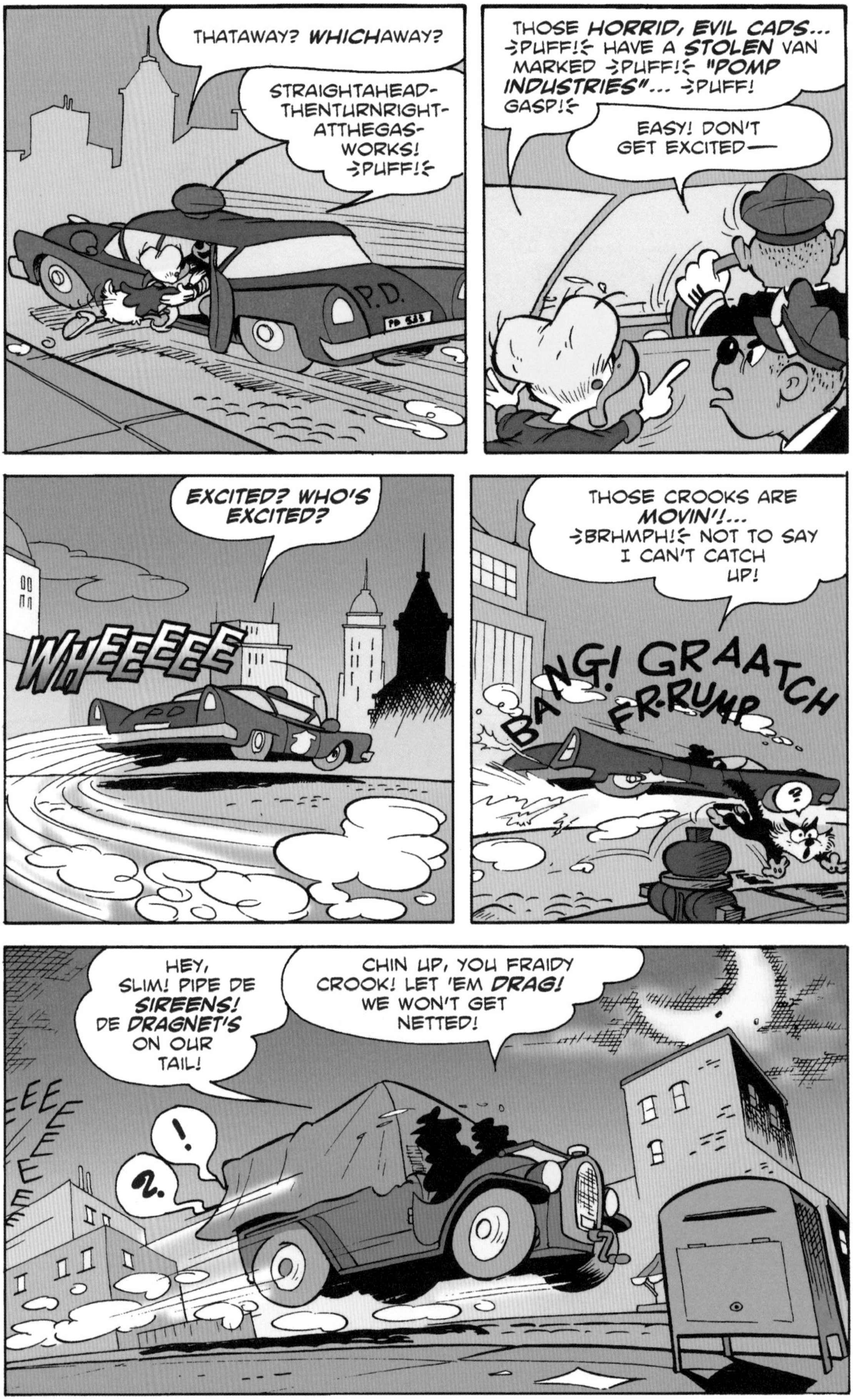

THATAWAY? WHICHAWAY?
STRAIGHTAHEAD-THENTURNRIGHT-ATTHEGAS-WORKS! ⊰PUFF!⊱
THOSE HORRID, EVIL CADS... ⊰PUFF!⊱ HAVE A STOLEN VAN MARKED ⊰PUFF!⊱ "POMP INDUSTRIES"... ⊰PUFF! GASP!⊱
EASY! DON'T GET EXCITED—
P.D.
EXCITED? WHO'S EXCITED?
WHEEEEEE
THOSE CROOKS ARE MOVIN'!... ⊰BRHMPH!⊱ NOT TO SAY I CAN'T CATCH UP!
BANG! GRAATCH
FR-RUMP
HEY, SLIM! PIPE DE SIREENS! DE DRAGNET'S ON OUR TAIL!
CHIN UP, YOU FRAIDY CROOK! LET 'EM DRAG! WE WON'T GET NETTED!

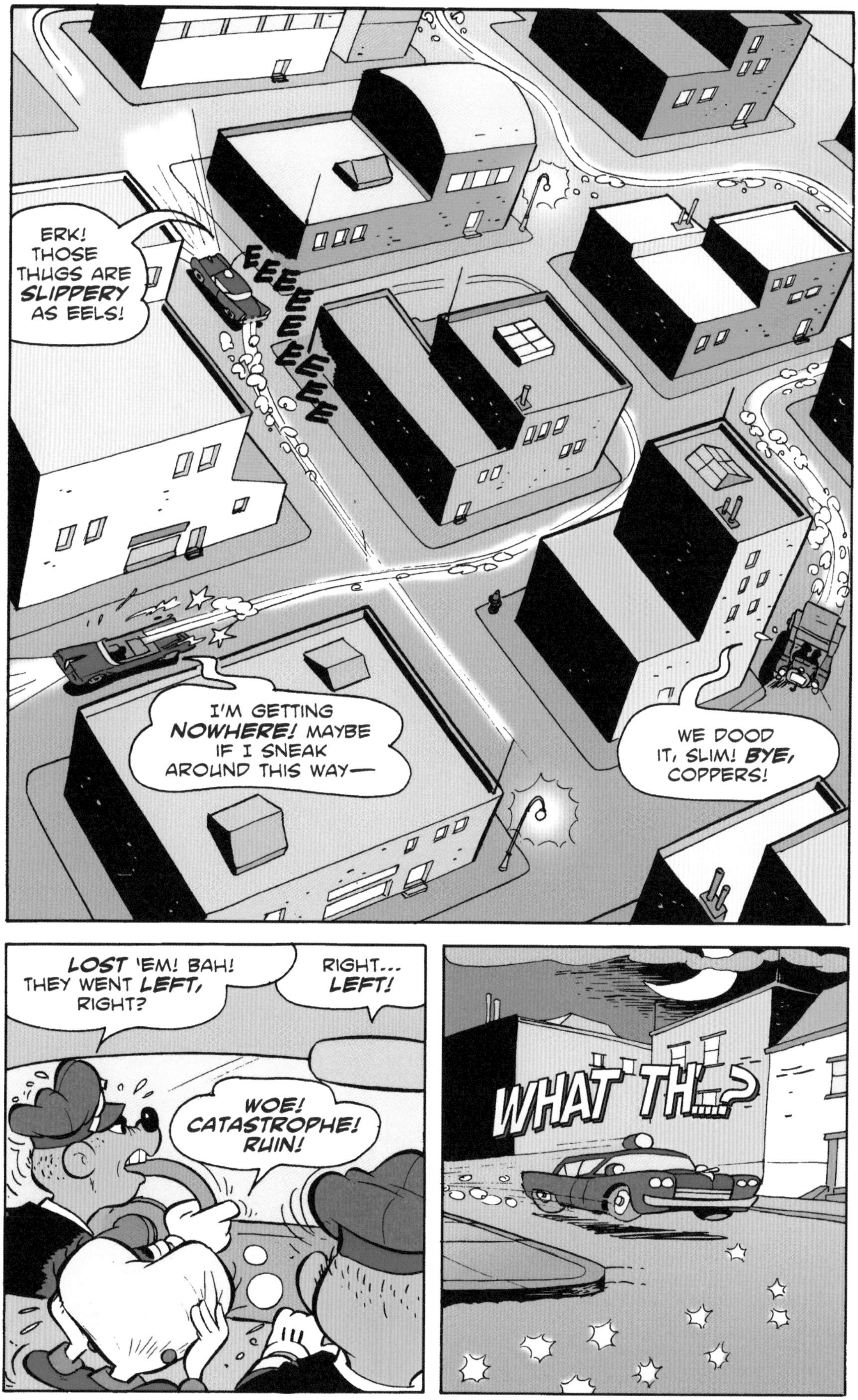

ERK! THOSE THUGS ARE SLIPPERY AS EELS!
EEEEEEEEEE
I'M GETTING NOWHERE! MAYBE IF I SNEAK AROUND THIS WAY—
WE DOOD IT, SLIM! BYE, COPPERS!
LOST 'EM! BAH! THEY WENT LEFT, RIGHT?
RIGHT... LEFT!
WOE! CATASTROPHE! RUIN!
WHAT TH...?

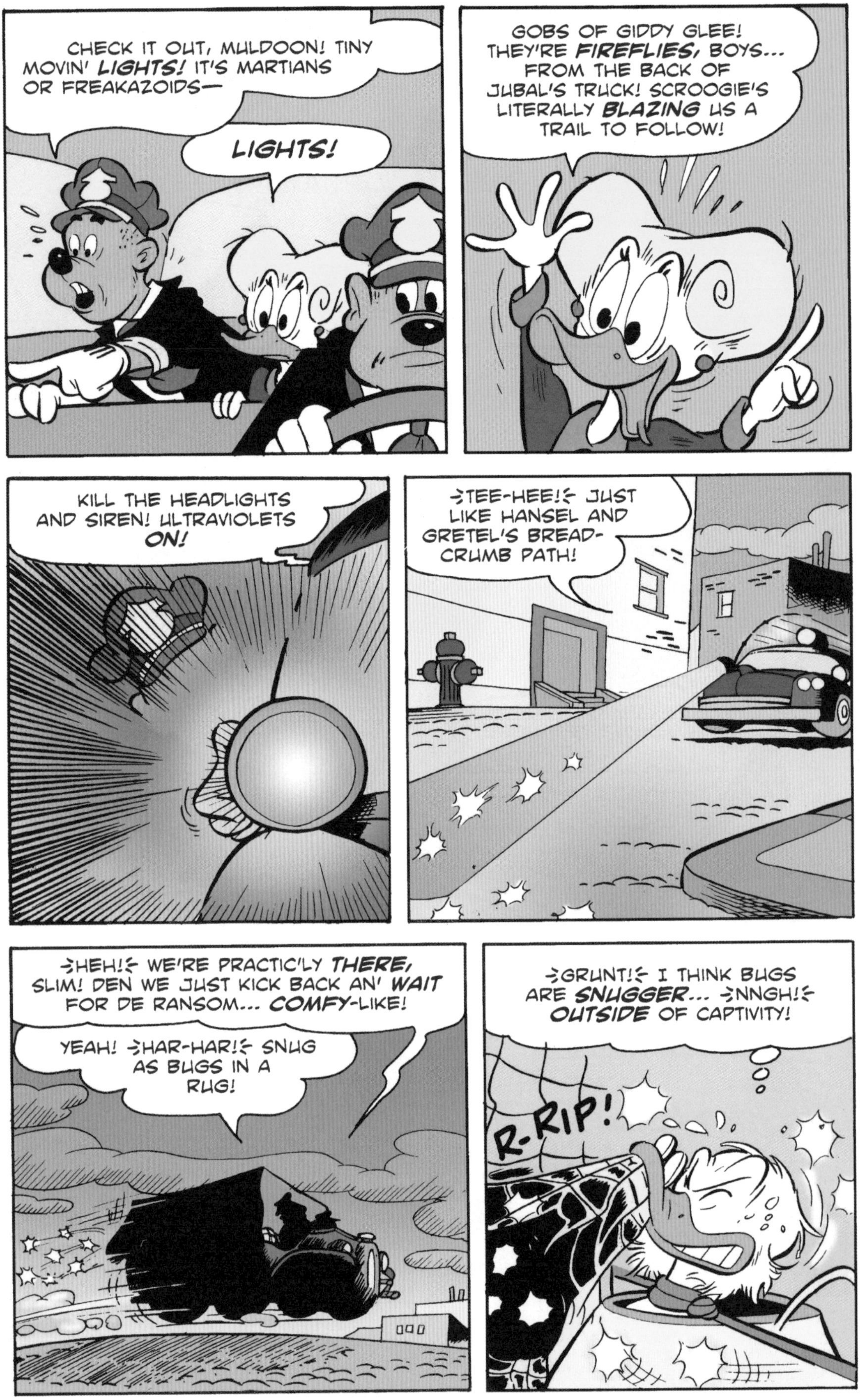
CHECK IT OUT, MULDOON! TINY MOVIN' **LIGHTS!** IT'S MARTIANS OR FREAKAZOIDS—
LIGHTS!
GOBS OF GIDDY GLEE! THEY'RE **FIREFLIES,** BOYS... FROM THE BACK OF JUBAL'S TRUCK! SCROOGIE'S LITERALLY **BLAZING** US A TRAIL TO FOLLOW!
KILL THE HEADLIGHTS AND SIREN! ULTRAVIOLETS **ON!**
⇛TEE-HEE!⇚ JUST LIKE HANSEL AND GRETEL'S BREAD-CRUMB PATH!
⇛HEH!⇚ WE'RE PRACTIC'LY **THERE,** SLIM! DEN WE JUST KICK BACK AN' **WAIT** FOR DE RANSOM... **COMFY**-LIKE!
YEAH! ⇛HAR-HAR!⇚ SNUG AS BUGS IN A RUG!
⇛GRUNT!⇚ I THINK BUGS ARE **SNUGGER**... ⇛NNGH!⇚ **OUTSIDE** OF CAPTIVITY!
R-RIP!

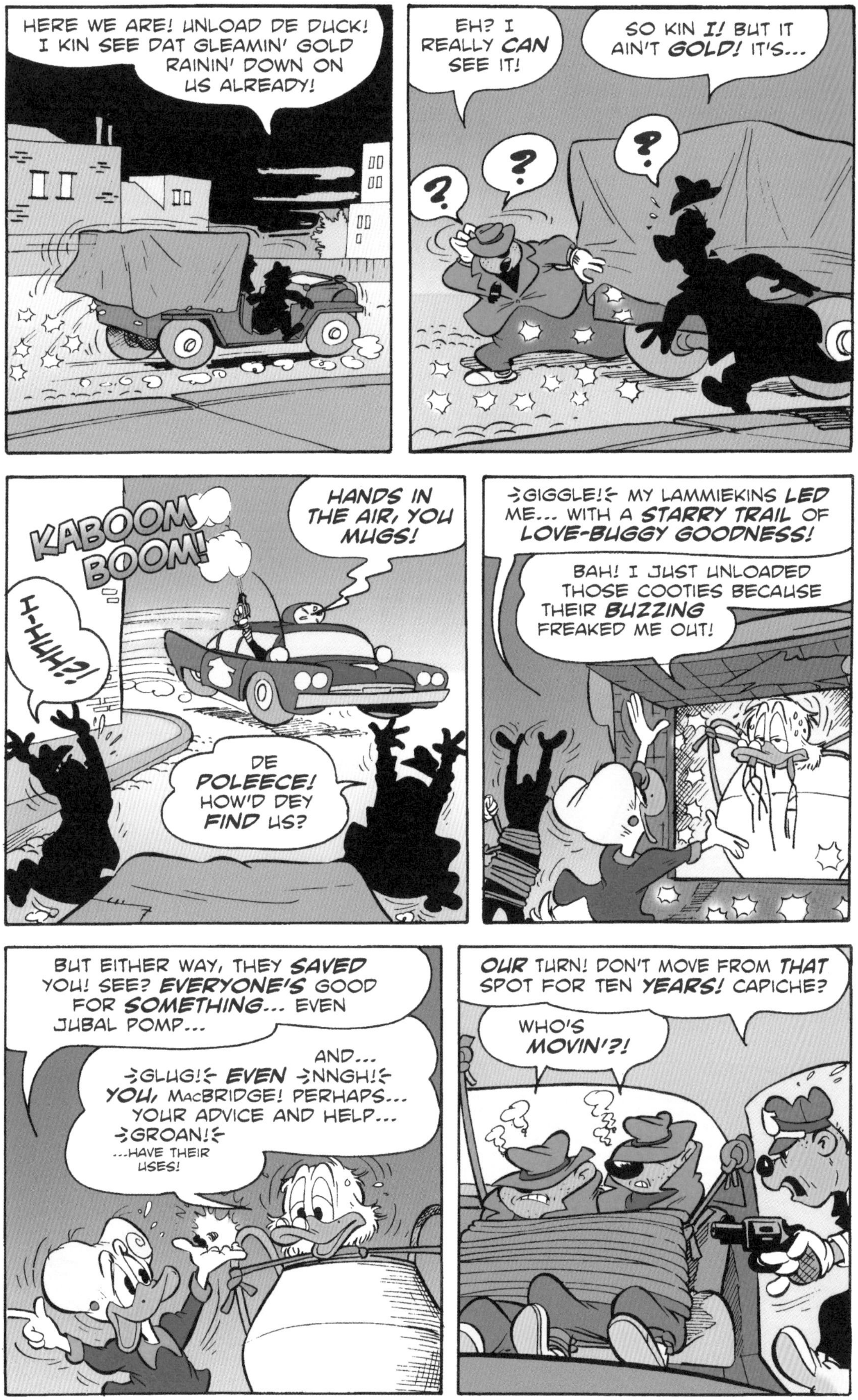
HERE WE ARE! UNLOAD DE DUCK! I KIN SEE DAT GLEAMIN' GOLD RAININ' DOWN ON US ALREADY!
EH? I REALLY CAN SEE IT!
SO KIN I! BUT IT AIN'T GOLD! IT'S...
?
?
?
KABOOM BOOM!
HANDS IN THE AIR, YOU MUGS!
I-HUH?!
DE POLEECE! HOW'D DEY FIND US?
-GIGGLE!- MY LAMMIEKINS LED ME... WITH A STARRY TRAIL OF LOVE-BUGGY GOODNESS!
BAH! I JUST UNLOADED THOSE COOTIES BECAUSE THEIR BUZZING FREAKED ME OUT!
BUT EITHER WAY, THEY SAVED YOU! SEE? EVERYONE'S GOOD FOR SOMETHING... EVEN JUBAL POMP...
AND... -GLUG!- EVEN -NNGH!- YOU, MacBRIDGE! PERHAPS... YOUR ADVICE AND HELP... -GROAN!- ...HAVE THEIR USES!
OUR TURN! DON'T MOVE FROM THAT SPOT FOR TEN YEARS! CAPICHE?
WHO'S MOVIN'?!

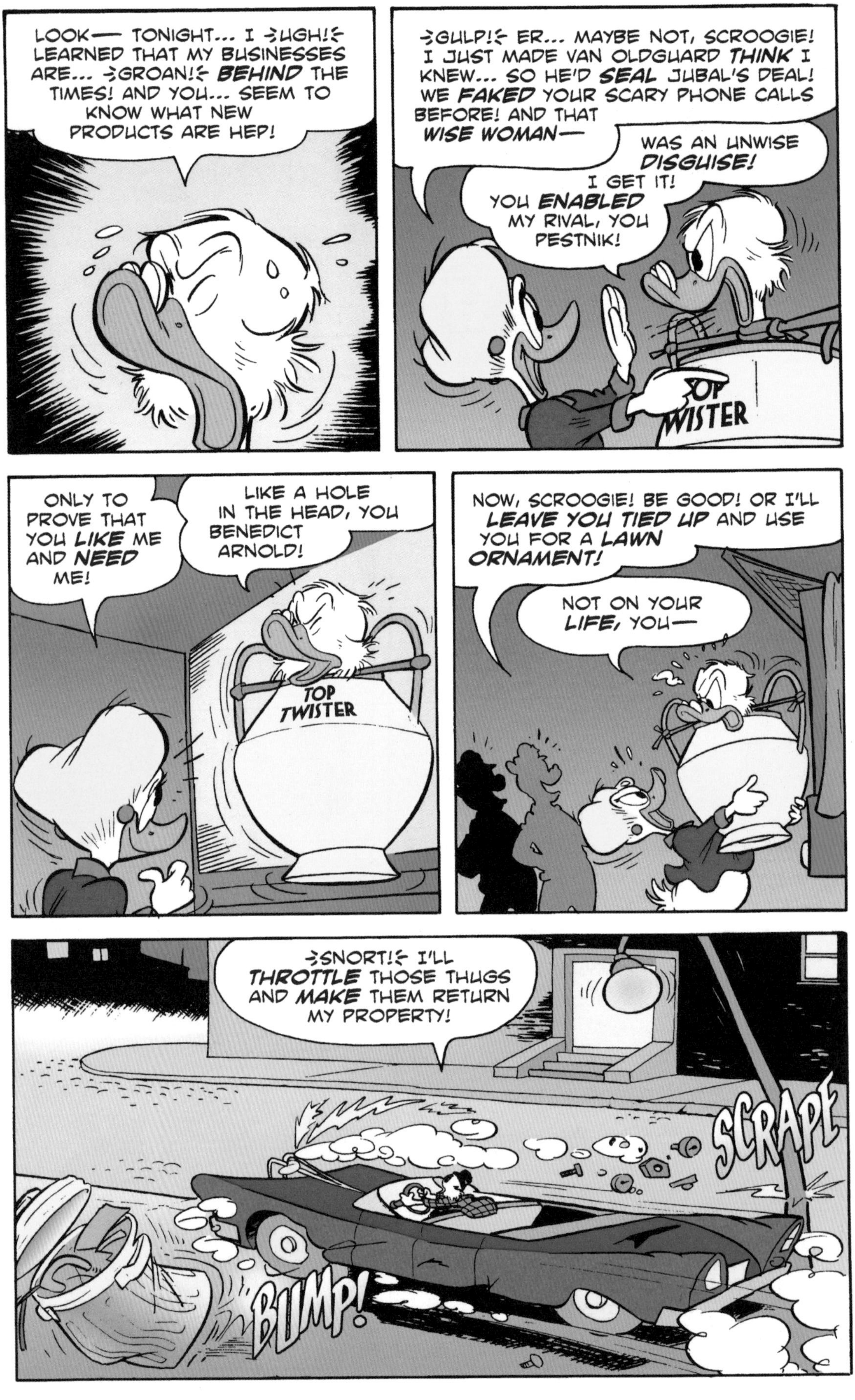
LOOK— TONIGHT... I ⊰UGH!⊱ LEARNED THAT MY BUSINESSES ARE... ⊰GROAN!⊱ BEHIND THE TIMES! AND YOU... SEEM TO KNOW WHAT NEW PRODUCTS ARE HEP!
⊰GULP!⊱ ER... MAYBE NOT, SCROOGIE! I JUST MADE VAN OLDGUARD THINK I KNEW... SO HE'D SEAL JUBAL'S DEAL! WE FAKED YOUR SCARY PHONE CALLS BEFORE! AND THAT WISE WOMAN—
WAS AN UNWISE DISGUISE!
I GET IT! YOU ENABLED MY RIVAL, YOU PESTNIK!
TOP TWISTER
ONLY TO PROVE THAT YOU LIKE ME AND NEED ME!
LIKE A HOLE IN THE HEAD, YOU BENEDICT ARNOLD!
TOP TWISTER
NOW, SCROOGIE! BE GOOD! OR I'LL LEAVE YOU TIED UP AND USE YOU FOR A LAWN ORNAMENT!
NOT ON YOUR LIFE, YOU—
⊰SNORT!⊱ I'LL THROTTLE THOSE THUGS AND MAKE THEM RETURN MY PROPERTY!
SCRAPE
BUMP!

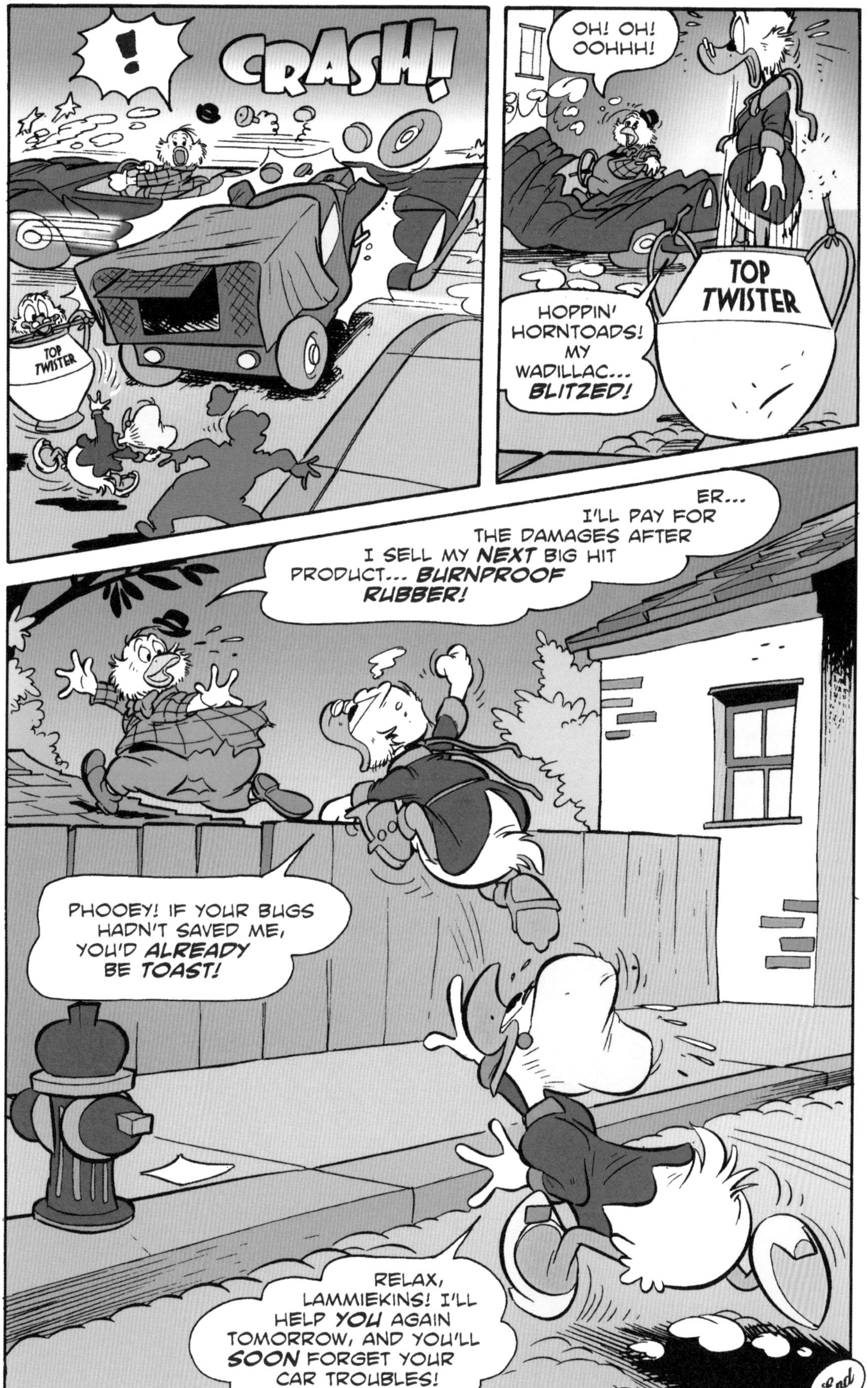
!
CRASH!
OH! OH! OOHHH!
HOPPIN' HORNTOADS! MY WADILLAC... BLITZED!
TOP TWISTER
ER... I'LL PAY FOR THE DAMAGES AFTER I SELL MY NEXT BIG HIT PRODUCT... BURNPROOF RUBBER!
PHOOEY! IF YOUR BUGS HADN'T SAVED ME, YOU'D ALREADY BE TOAST!
RELAX, LAMMIEKINS! I'LL HELP YOU AGAIN TOMORROW, AND YOU'LL SOON FORGET YOUR CAR TROUBLES!
End

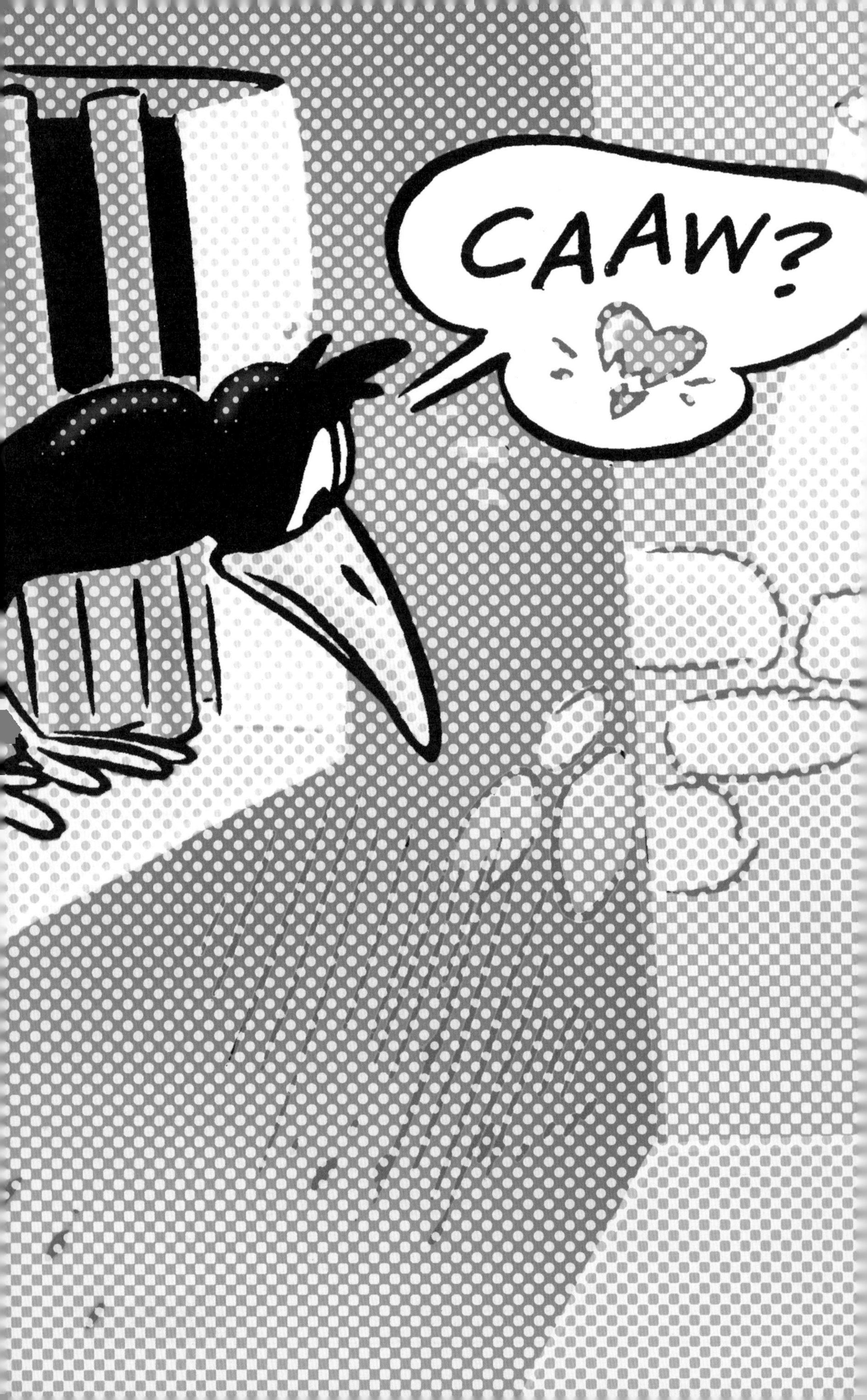
CAAW?

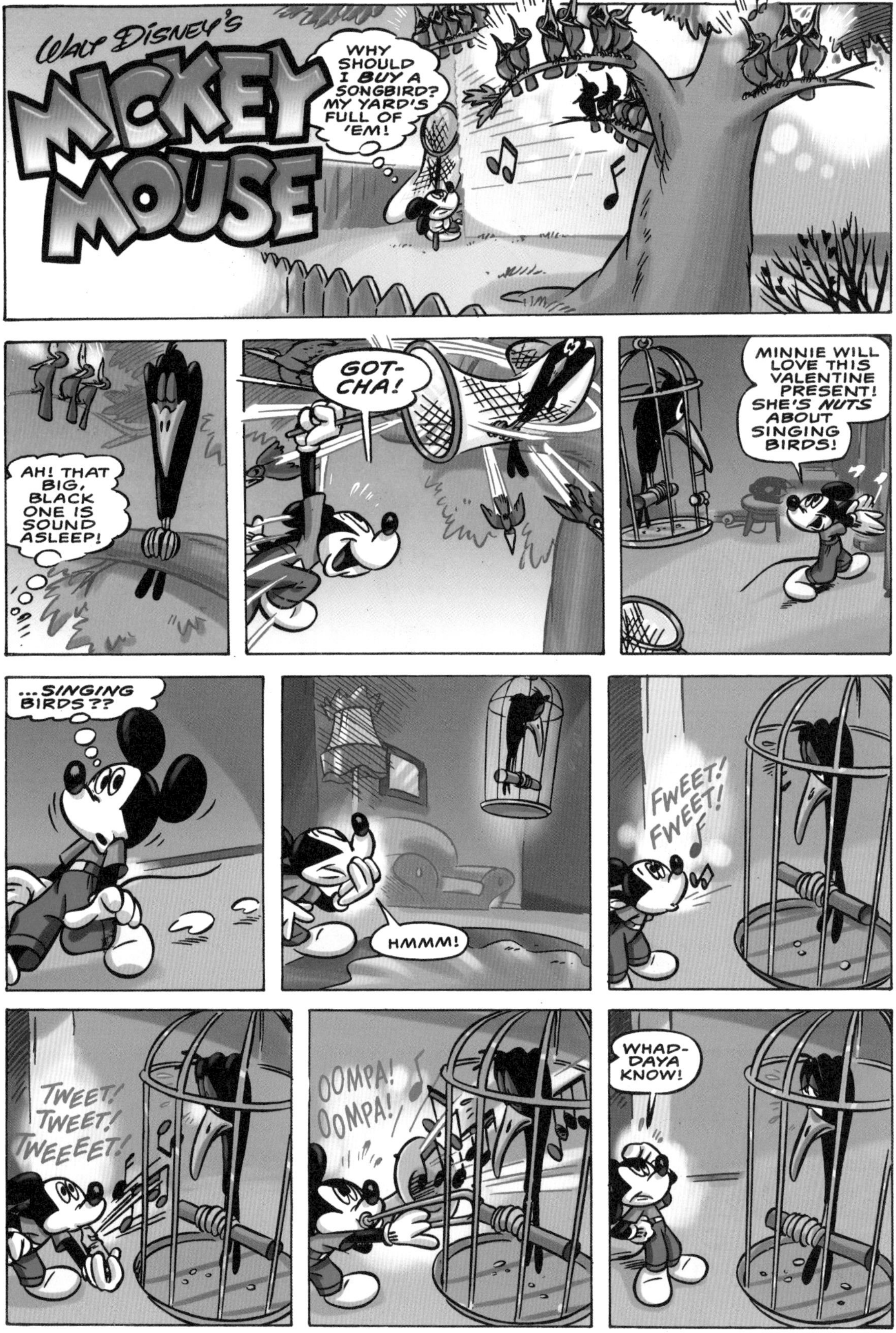
WALT DISNEY'S
MICKEY MOUSE
WHY SHOULD I BUY A SONGBIRD? MY YARD'S FULL OF 'EM!
AH! THAT BIG, BLACK ONE IS SOUND ASLEEP!
GOT-CHA!
MINNIE WILL LOVE THIS VALENTINE PRESENT! SHE'S NUTS ABOUT SINGING BIRDS!
...SINGING BIRDS??
HMMM!
FWEET! FWEET!
TWEET! TWEET! TWEEEET!
OOMPA! OOMPA!
WHAD-DAYA KNOW!

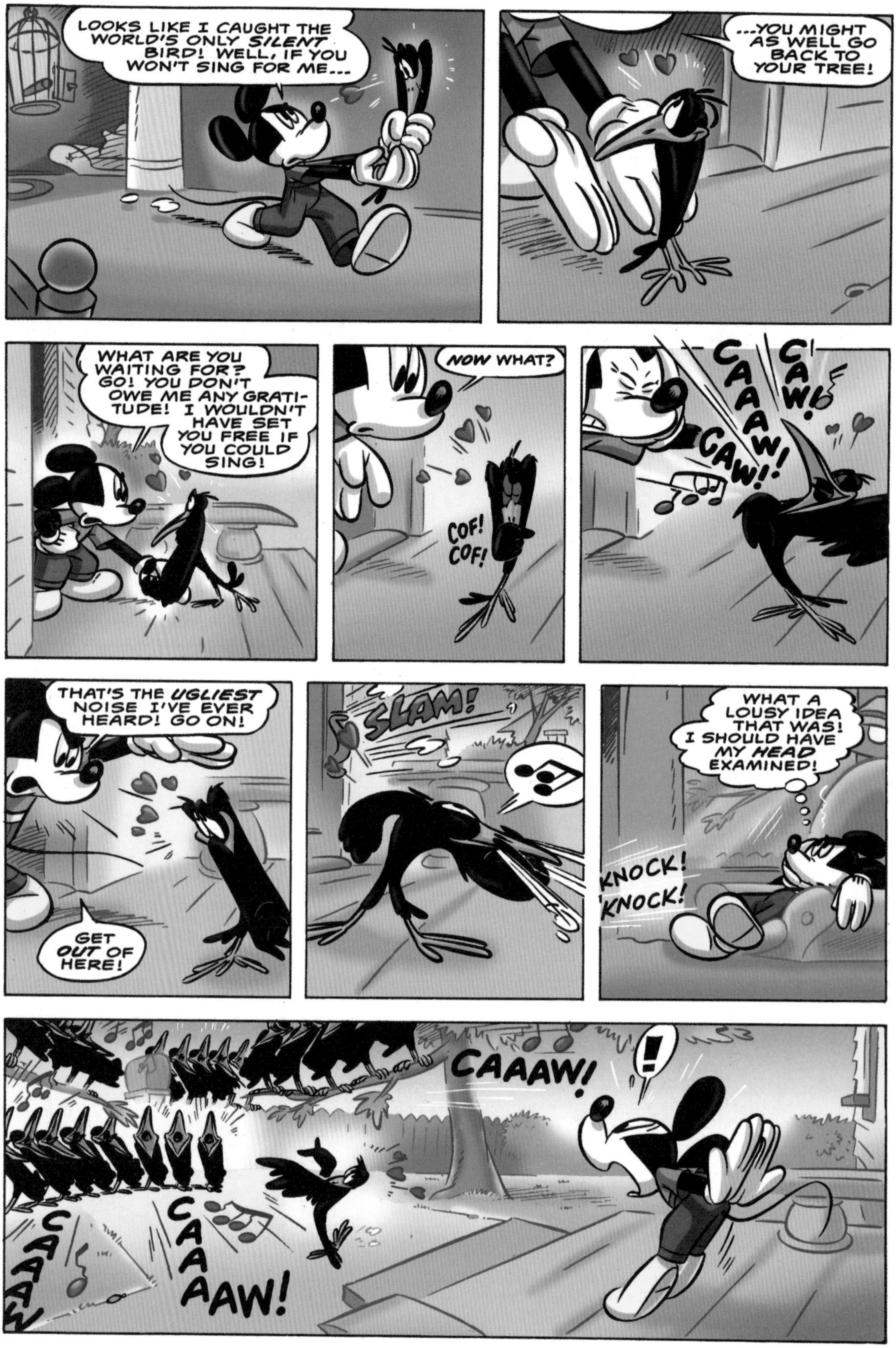
LOOKS LIKE I CAUGHT THE WORLD'S ONLY SILENT BIRD! WELL, IF YOU WON'T SING FOR ME...
...YOU MIGHT AS WELL GO BACK TO YOUR TREE!
WHAT ARE YOU WAITING FOR? GO! YOU DON'T OWE ME ANY GRATITUDE! I WOULDN'T HAVE SET YOU FREE IF YOU COULD SING!
NOW WHAT?
COF! COF!
CAAAAW! CAW! CAW!!
THAT'S THE UGLIEST NOISE I'VE EVER HEARD! GO ON!
GET OUT OF HERE!
SLAM!
WHAT A LOUSY IDEA THAT WAS! I SHOULD HAVE MY HEAD EXAMINED!
KNOCK! KNOCK!
CAAAW!
!
CAAAAW!
CAAAAW

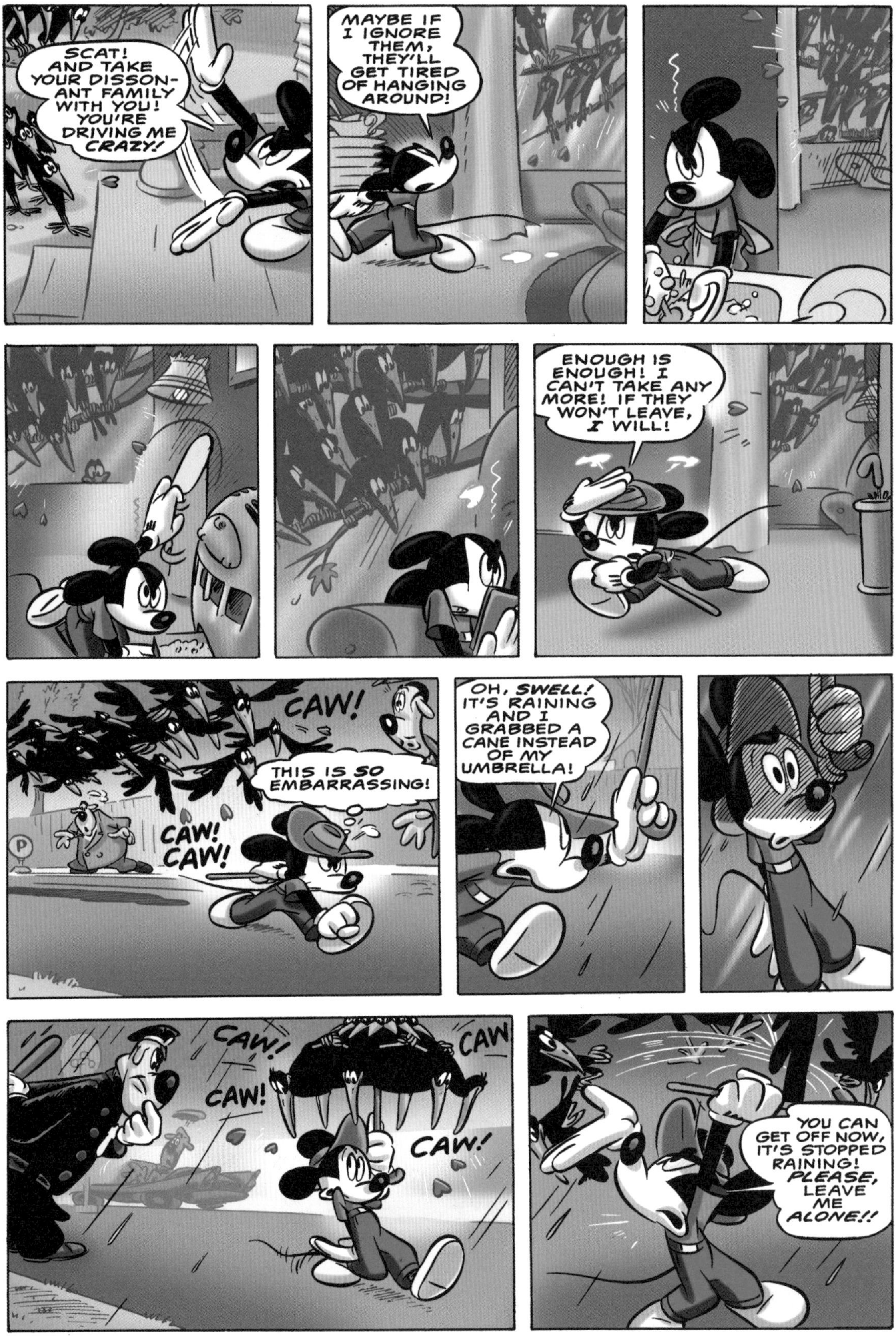
SCAT! AND TAKE YOUR DISSON-ANT FAMILY WITH YOU! YOU'RE DRIVING ME CRAZY!
MAYBE IF I IGNORE THEM, THEY'LL GET TIRED OF HANGING AROUND!
ENOUGH IS ENOUGH! I CAN'T TAKE ANY MORE! IF THEY WON'T LEAVE, I WILL!
CAW!
THIS IS SO EMBARRASSING!
CAW! CAW!
OH, SWELL! IT'S RAINING AND I GRABBED A CANE INSTEAD OF MY UMBRELLA!
CAW!
CAW
CAW!
CAW!
YOU CAN GET OFF NOW, IT'S STOPPED RAINING! PLEASE, LEAVE ME ALONE!!

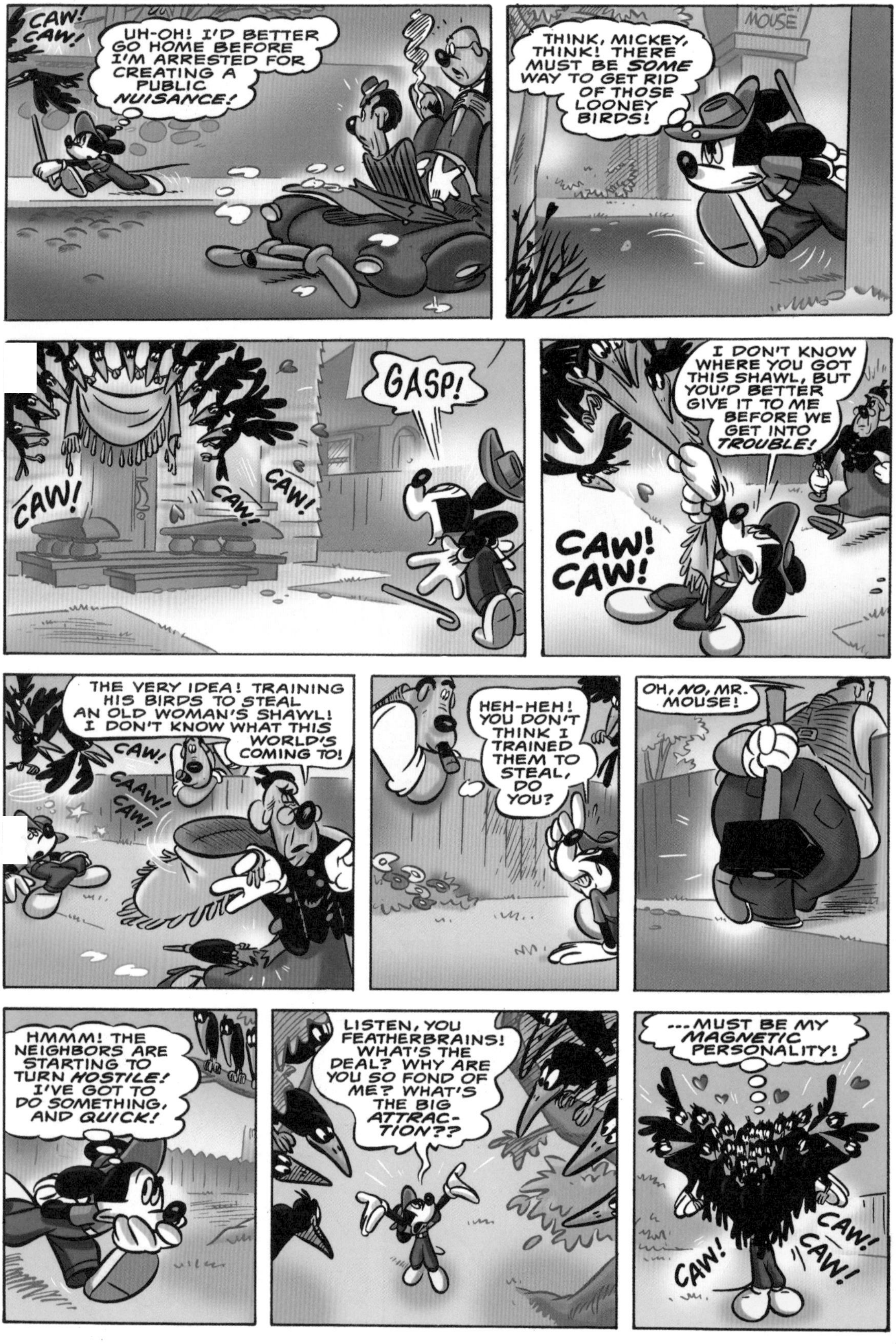
CAW! CAW!
UH-OH! I'D BETTER GO HOME BEFORE I'M ARRESTED FOR CREATING A PUBLIC NUISANCE!
THINK, MICKEY, THINK! THERE MUST BE SOME WAY TO GET RID OF THOSE LOONEY BIRDS!
MOUSE
CAW!
CAW!
CAW!
GASP!
I DON'T KNOW WHERE YOU GOT THIS SHAWL, BUT YOU'D BETTER GIVE IT TO ME BEFORE WE GET INTO TROUBLE!
CAW! CAW!
THE VERY IDEA! TRAINING HIS BIRDS TO STEAL AN OLD WOMAN'S SHAWL! I DON'T KNOW WHAT THIS WORLD'S COMING TO!
CAW!
CAAW!
CAW!
HEH-HEH! YOU DON'T THINK I TRAINED THEM TO STEAL, DO YOU?
OH, NO, MR. MOUSE!
HMMM! THE NEIGHBORS ARE STARTING TO TURN HOSTILE! I'VE GOT TO DO SOMETHING, AND QUICK!
LISTEN, YOU FEATHERBRAINS! WHAT'S THE DEAL? WHY ARE YOU SO FOND OF ME? WHAT'S THE BIG ATTRACTION??
...MUST BE MY MAGNETIC PERSONALITY!
CAW!
CAW!
CAW!

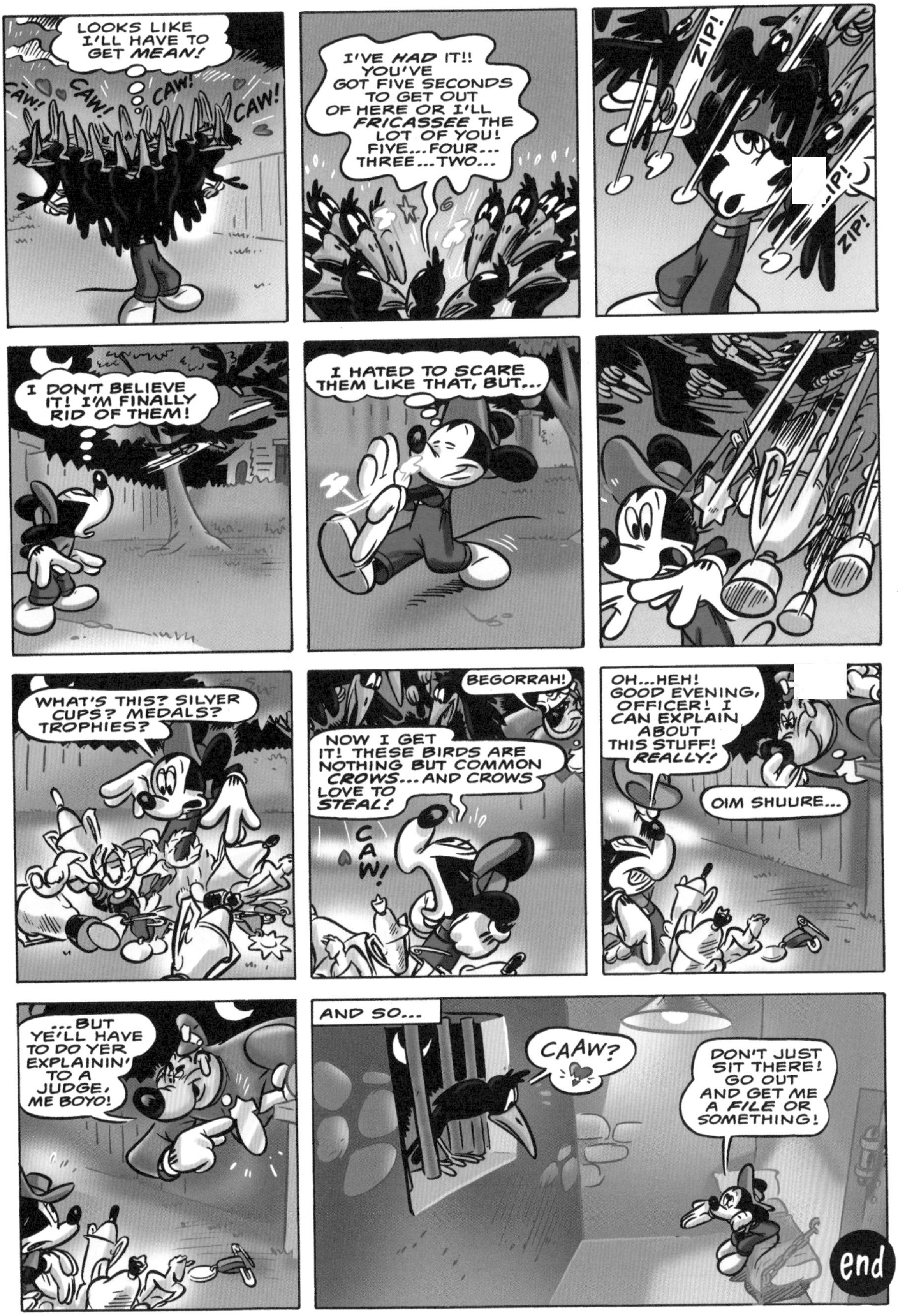
LOOKS LIKE I'LL HAVE TO GET MEAN!
CAW!
CAW!
CAW!
CAW!
I'VE HAD IT!! YOU'VE GOT FIVE SECONDS TO GET OUT OF HERE OR I'LL FRICASSEE THE LOT OF YOU! FIVE... FOUR... THREE... TWO...
ZIP!
...IP!
ZIP!
I DON'T BELIEVE IT! I'M FINALLY RID OF THEM!
I HATED TO SCARE THEM LIKE THAT, BUT...
WHAT'S THIS? SILVER CUPS? MEDALS? TROPHIES?
BEGORRAH!
NOW I GET IT! THESE BIRDS ARE NOTHING BUT COMMON CROWS... AND CROWS LOVE TO STEAL!
CAW!
OH... HEH! GOOD EVENING, OFFICER! I CAN EXPLAIN ABOUT THIS STUFF! REALLY!
OIM SHUURE...
...BUT YE'LL HAVE TO DO YER EXPLAININ' TO A JUDGE, ME BOYO!
AND SO...
CAAW?
DON'T JUST SIT THERE! GO OUT AND GET ME A FILE OR SOMETHING!
end

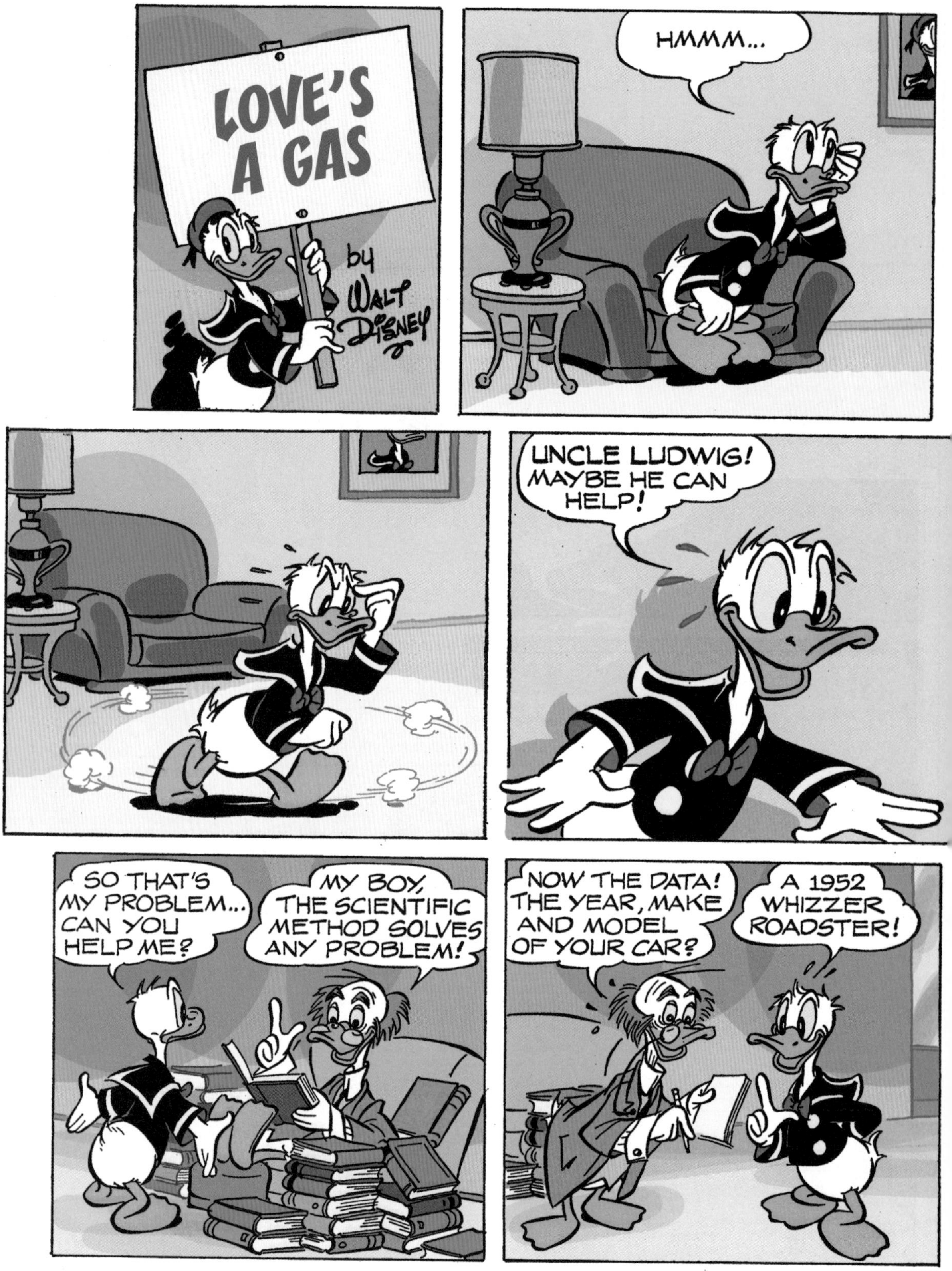
LOVE'S A GAS
by WALT DISNEY
HMMM...
UNCLE LUDWIG! MAYBE HE CAN HELP!
SO THAT'S MY PROBLEM... CAN YOU HELP ME?
MY BOY, THE SCIENTIFIC METHOD SOLVES ANY PROBLEM!
NOW THE DATA! THE YEAR, MAKE AND MODEL OF YOUR CAR?
A 1952 WHIZZER ROADSTER!

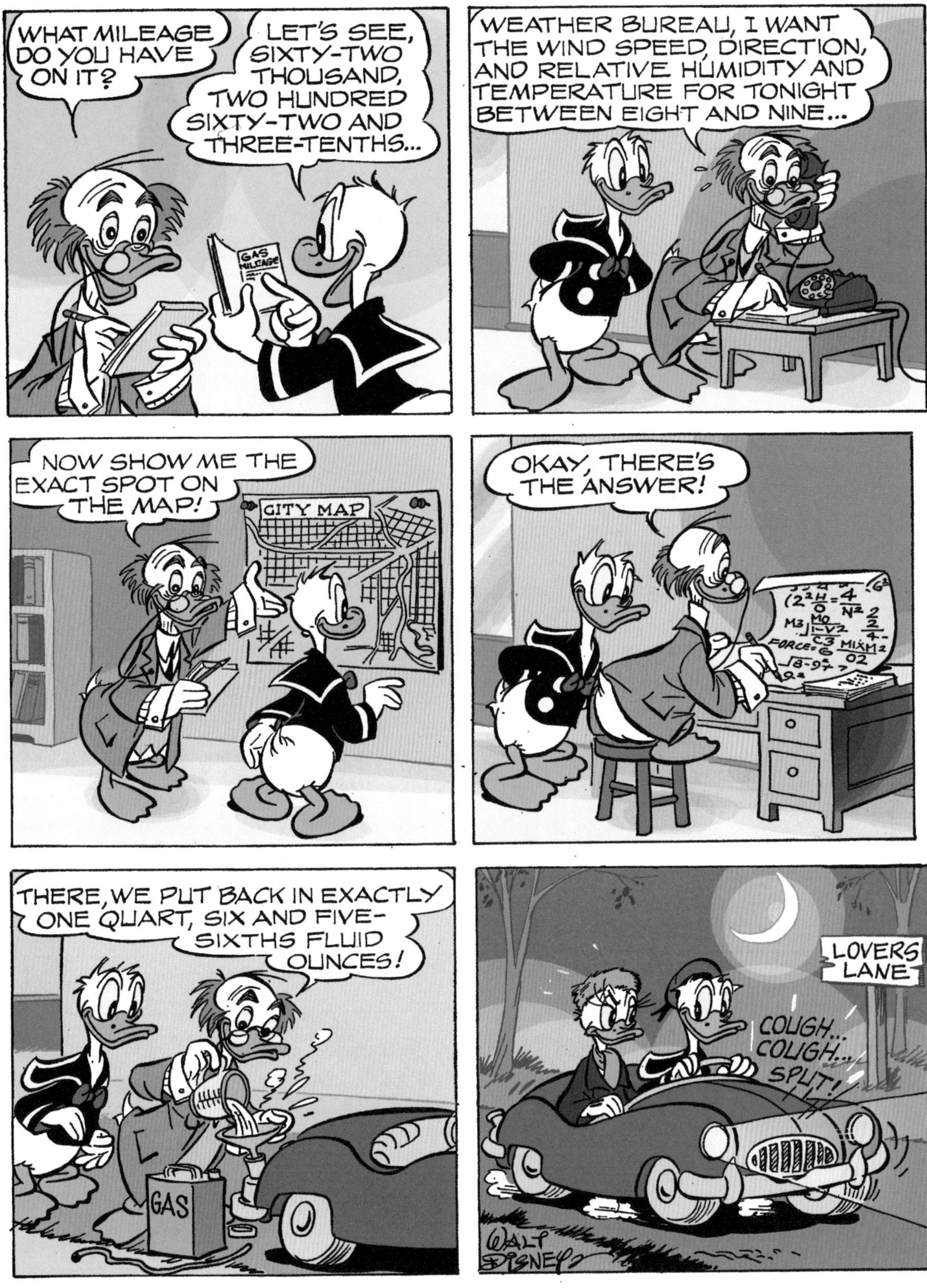
WHAT MILEAGE DO YOU HAVE ON IT?
LET'S SEE, SIXTY-TWO THOUSAND, TWO HUNDRED SIXTY-TWO AND THREE-TENTHS...
GAS MILEAGE
WEATHER BUREAU, I WANT THE WIND SPEED, DIRECTION, AND RELATIVE HUMIDITY AND TEMPERATURE FOR TONIGHT BETWEEN EIGHT AND NINE...
NOW SHOW ME THE EXACT SPOT ON THE MAP!
CITY MAP
OKAY, THERE'S THE ANSWER!
THERE, WE PUT BACK IN EXACTLY ONE QUART, SIX AND FIVE-SIXTHS FLUID OUNCES!
GAS
LOVERS LANE
COUGH... COUGH... SPUT!
WALT DISNEY

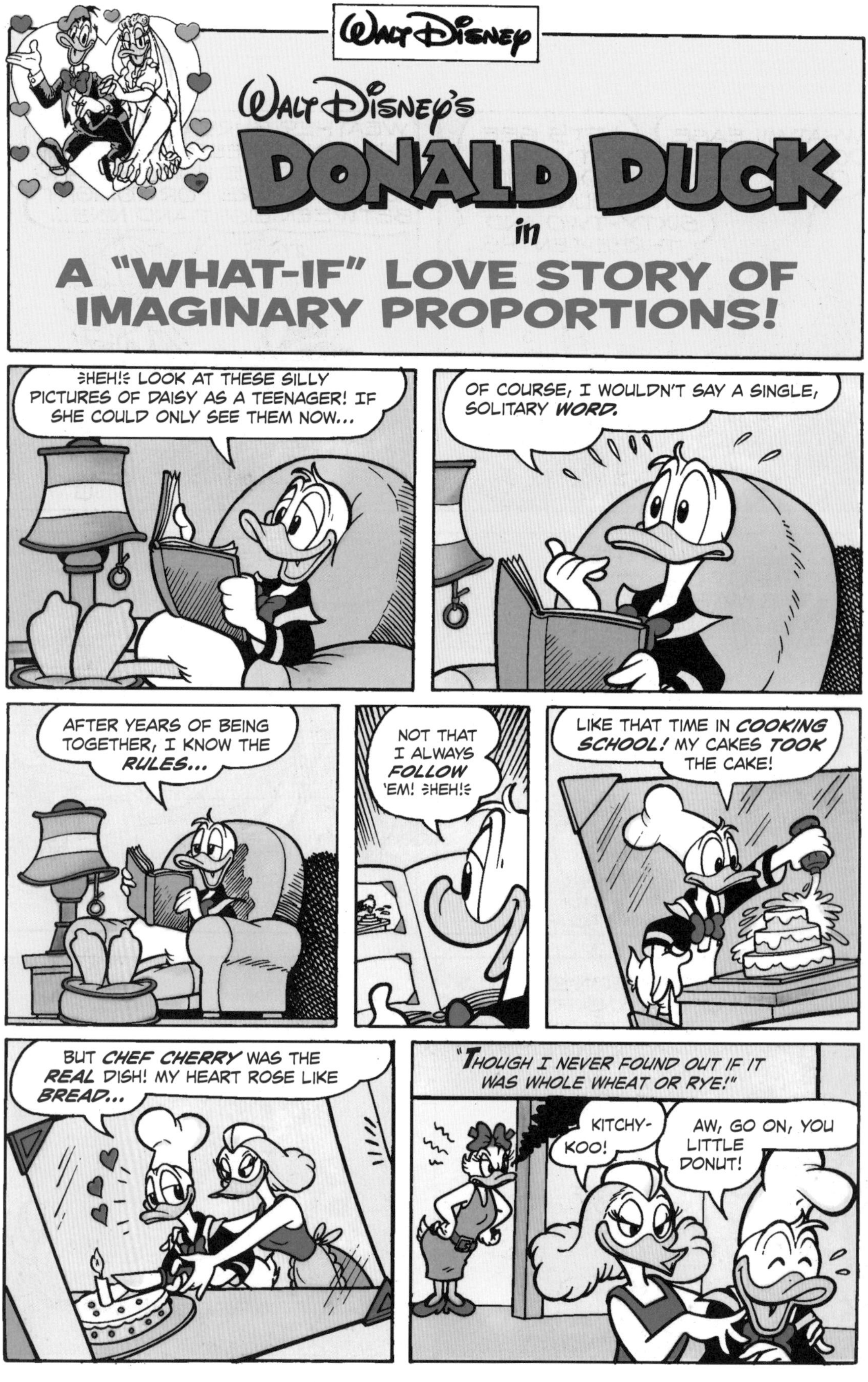
WALT DISNEY
WALT DISNEY'S
DONALD DUCK
in
A "WHAT-IF" LOVE STORY OF IMAGINARY PROPORTIONS!
≡HEH!≡ LOOK AT THESE SILLY PICTURES OF DAISY AS A TEENAGER! IF SHE COULD ONLY SEE THEM NOW...
OF COURSE, I WOULDN'T SAY A SINGLE, SOLITARY WORD.
AFTER YEARS OF BEING TOGETHER, I KNOW THE RULES...
NOT THAT I ALWAYS FOLLOW 'EM! ≡HEH!≡
LIKE THAT TIME IN COOKING SCHOOL! MY CAKES TOOK THE CAKE!
BUT CHEF CHERRY WAS THE REAL DISH! MY HEART ROSE LIKE BREAD...
"THOUGH I NEVER FOUND OUT IF IT WAS WHOLE WHEAT OR RYE!"
KITCHY-KOO!
AW, GO ON, YOU LITTLE DONUT!

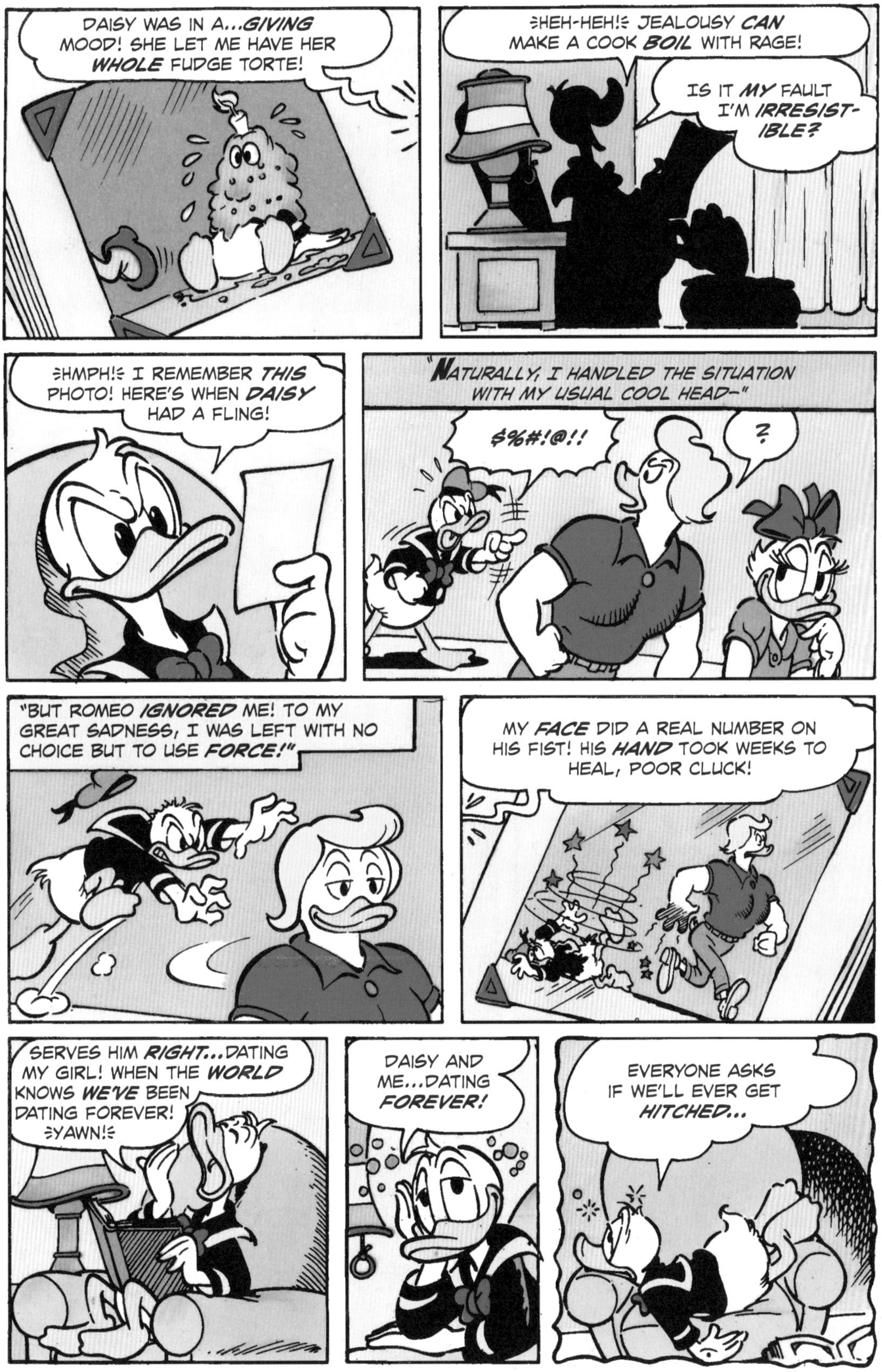

DAISY WAS IN A...GIVING MOOD! SHE LET ME HAVE HER WHOLE FUDGE TORTE!
⪢HEH-HEH!⪡ JEALOUSY CAN MAKE A COOK BOIL WITH RAGE!
IS IT MY FAULT I'M IRRESIST-IBLE?
⪢HMPH!⪡ I REMEMBER THIS PHOTO! HERE'S WHEN DAISY HAD A FLING!
"NATURALLY, I HANDLED THE SITUATION WITH MY USUAL COOL HEAD—"
$%#!@!!
?
"BUT ROMEO IGNORED ME! TO MY GREAT SADNESS, I WAS LEFT WITH NO CHOICE BUT TO USE FORCE!"
MY FACE DID A REAL NUMBER ON HIS FIST! HIS HAND TOOK WEEKS TO HEAL, POOR CLUCK!
SERVES HIM RIGHT...DATING MY GIRL! WHEN THE WORLD KNOWS WE'VE BEEN DATING FOREVER! ⪢YAWN!⪡
DAISY AND ME...DATING FOREVER!
EVERYONE ASKS IF WE'LL EVER GET HITCHED...

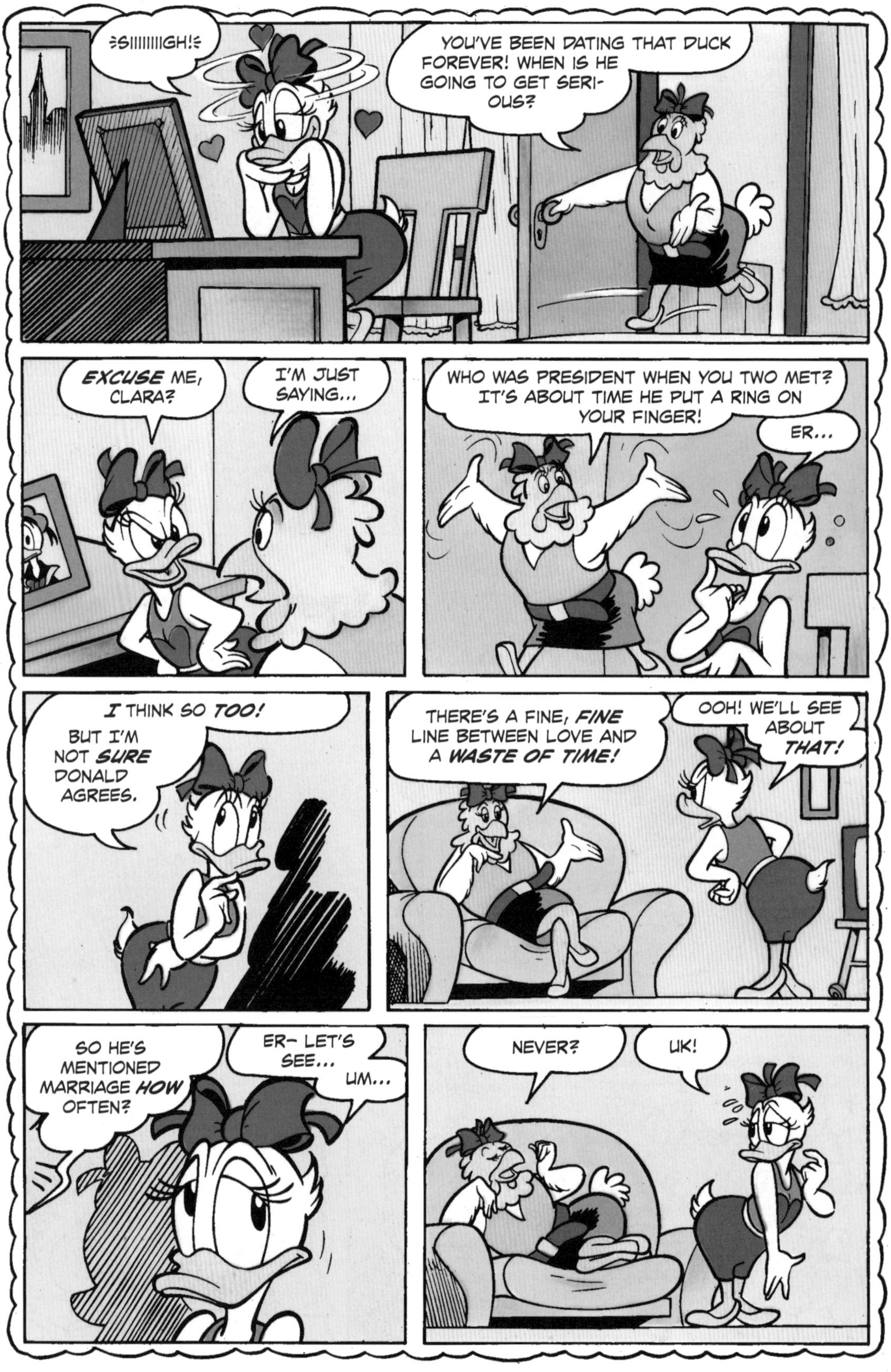

SIIIIIIIGH!
YOU'VE BEEN DATING THAT DUCK FOREVER! WHEN IS HE GOING TO GET SERI-OUS?
EXCUSE ME, CLARA?
I'M JUST SAYING...
WHO WAS PRESIDENT WHEN YOU TWO MET? IT'S ABOUT TIME HE PUT A RING ON YOUR FINGER!
ER...
I THINK SO TOO!
BUT I'M NOT SURE DONALD AGREES.
THERE'S A FINE, FINE LINE BETWEEN LOVE AND A WASTE OF TIME!
OOH! WE'LL SEE ABOUT THAT!
SO HE'S MENTIONED MARRIAGE HOW OFTEN?
ER— LET'S SEE... UM...
NEVER?
UK!

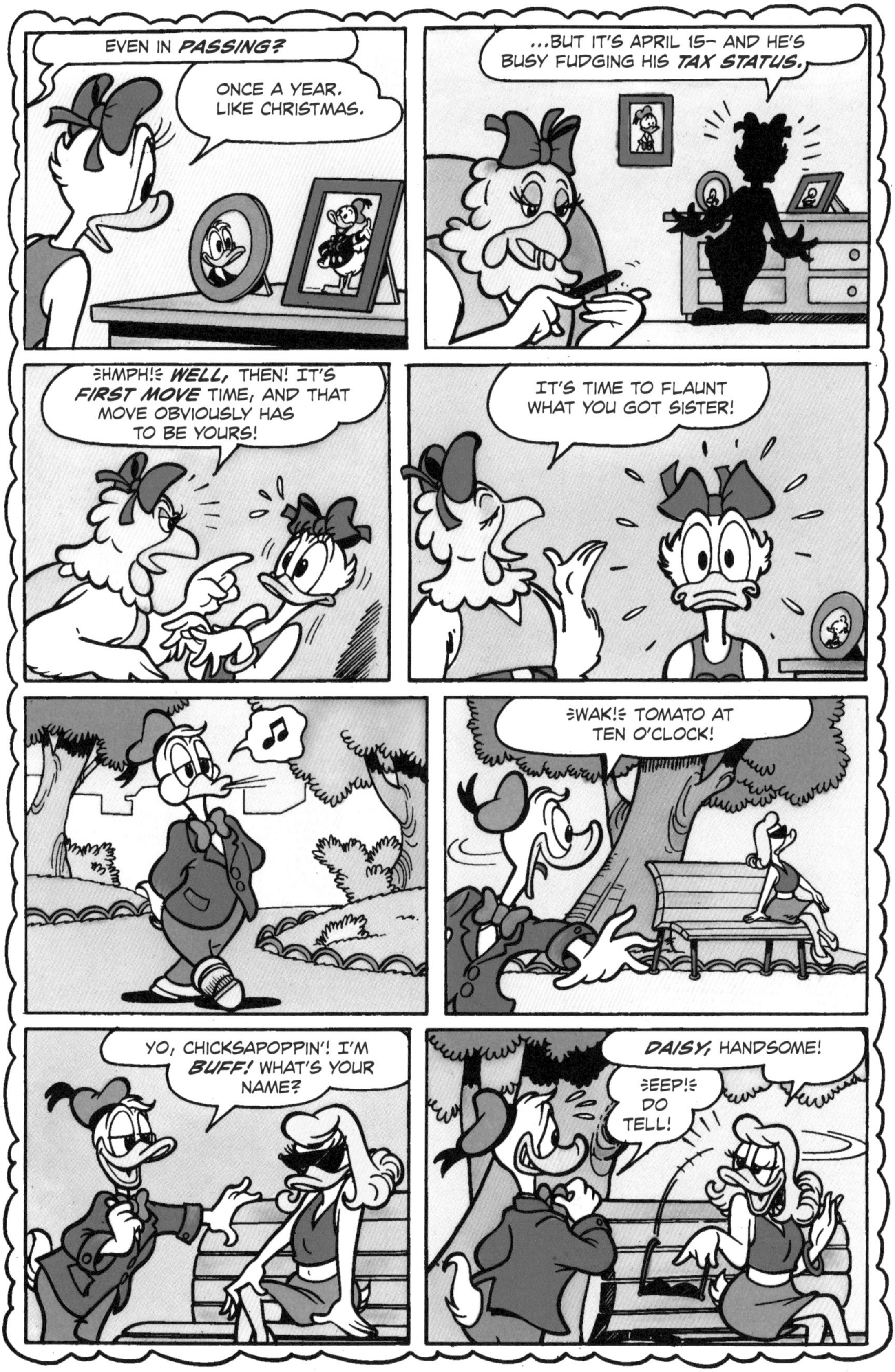
EVEN IN PASSING?
ONCE A YEAR. LIKE CHRISTMAS.
...BUT IT'S APRIL 15– AND HE'S BUSY FUDGING HIS TAX STATUS.
HMPH! WELL, THEN! IT'S FIRST MOVE TIME, AND THAT MOVE OBVIOUSLY HAS TO BE YOURS!
IT'S TIME TO FLAUNT WHAT YOU GOT SISTER!
WAK! TOMATO AT TEN O'CLOCK!
YO, CHICKSAPOPPIN'! I'M BUFF! WHAT'S YOUR NAME?
DAISY, HANDSOME!
EEP! DO TELL!

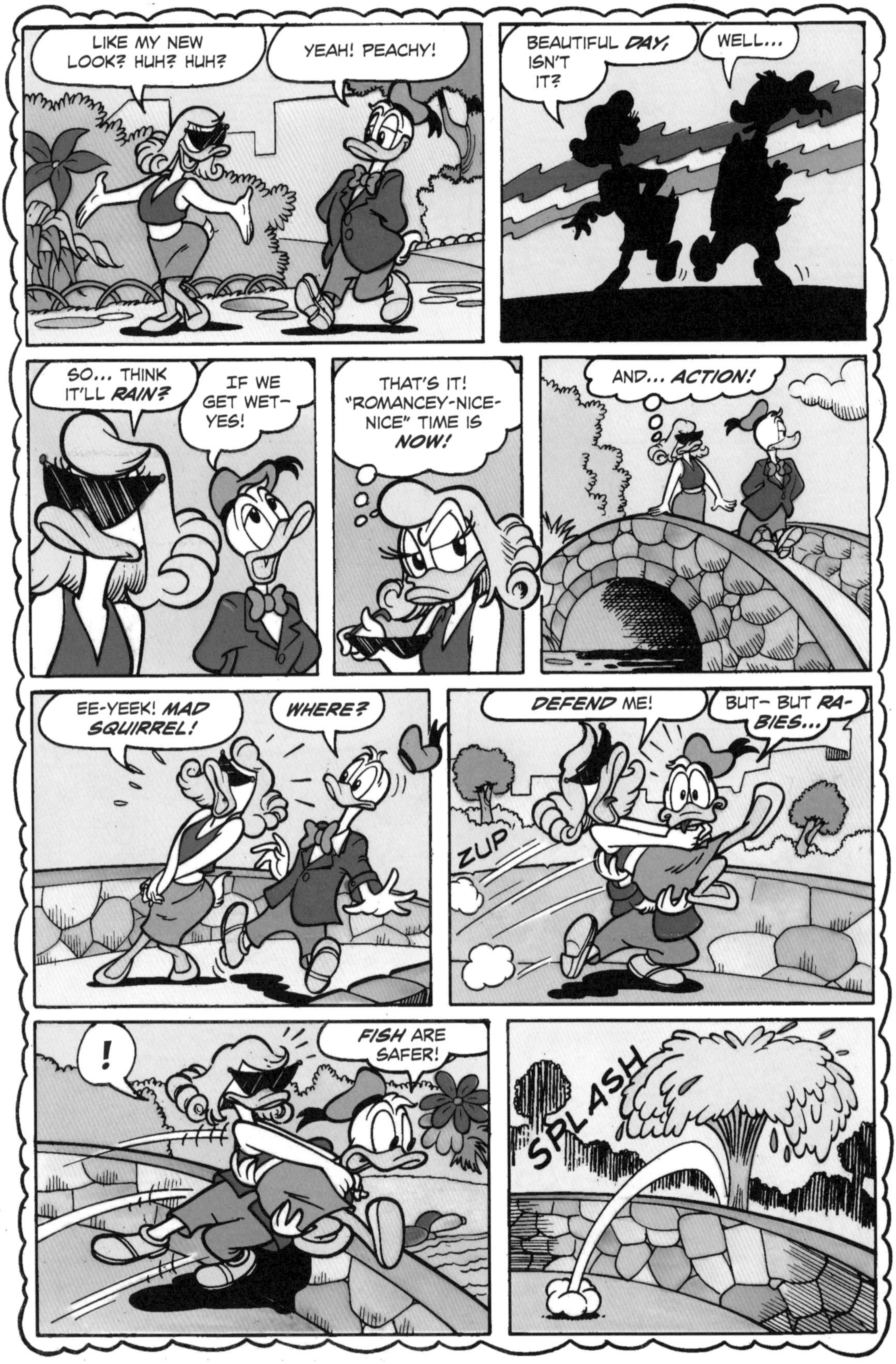
LIKE MY NEW LOOK? HUH? HUH?
YEAH! PEACHY!
BEAUTIFUL DAY, ISN'T IT?
WELL...
SO... THINK IT'LL RAIN?
IF WE GET WET- YES!
THAT'S IT! "ROMANCEY-NICE-NICE" TIME IS NOW!
AND... ACTION!
EE-YEEK! MAD SQUIRREL!
WHERE?
DEFEND ME!
BUT- BUT RA-BIES...
ZUP
!
FISH ARE SAFER!
SPLASH

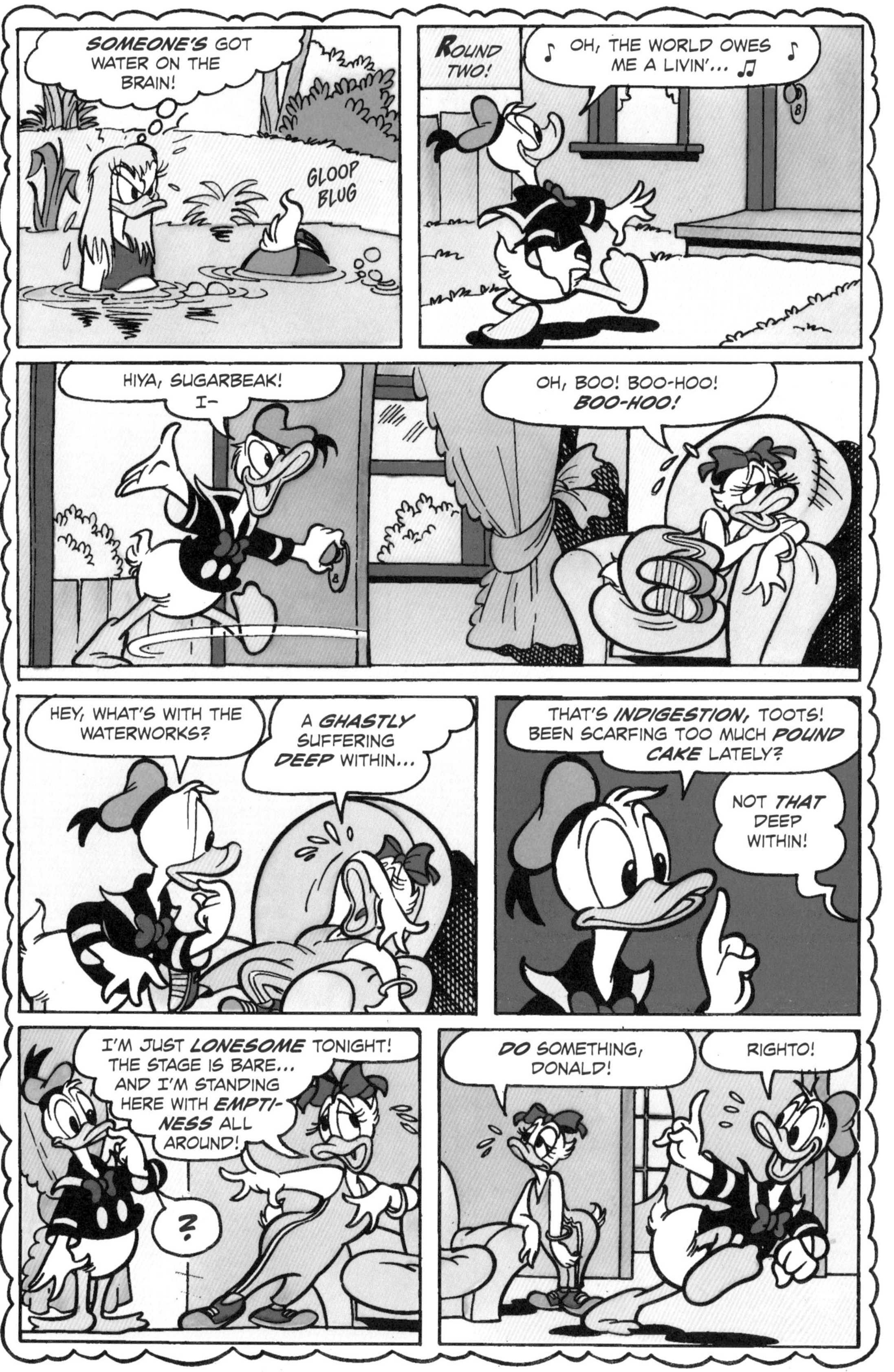
SOMEONE'S GOT WATER ON THE BRAIN!
GLOOP BLUG
ROUND TWO!
♪ OH, THE WORLD OWES ME A LIVIN'... ♫
HIYA, SUGARBEAK! I–
OH, BOO! BOO-HOO! BOO-HOO!
HEY, WHAT'S WITH THE WATERWORKS?
A GHASTLY SUFFERING DEEP WITHIN...
THAT'S INDIGESTION, TOOTS! BEEN SCARFING TOO MUCH POUND CAKE LATELY?
NOT THAT DEEP WITHIN!
I'M JUST LONESOME TONIGHT! THE STAGE IS BARE... AND I'M STANDING HERE WITH EMPTI-NESS ALL AROUND!
?
DO SOMETHING, DONALD!
RIGHTO!

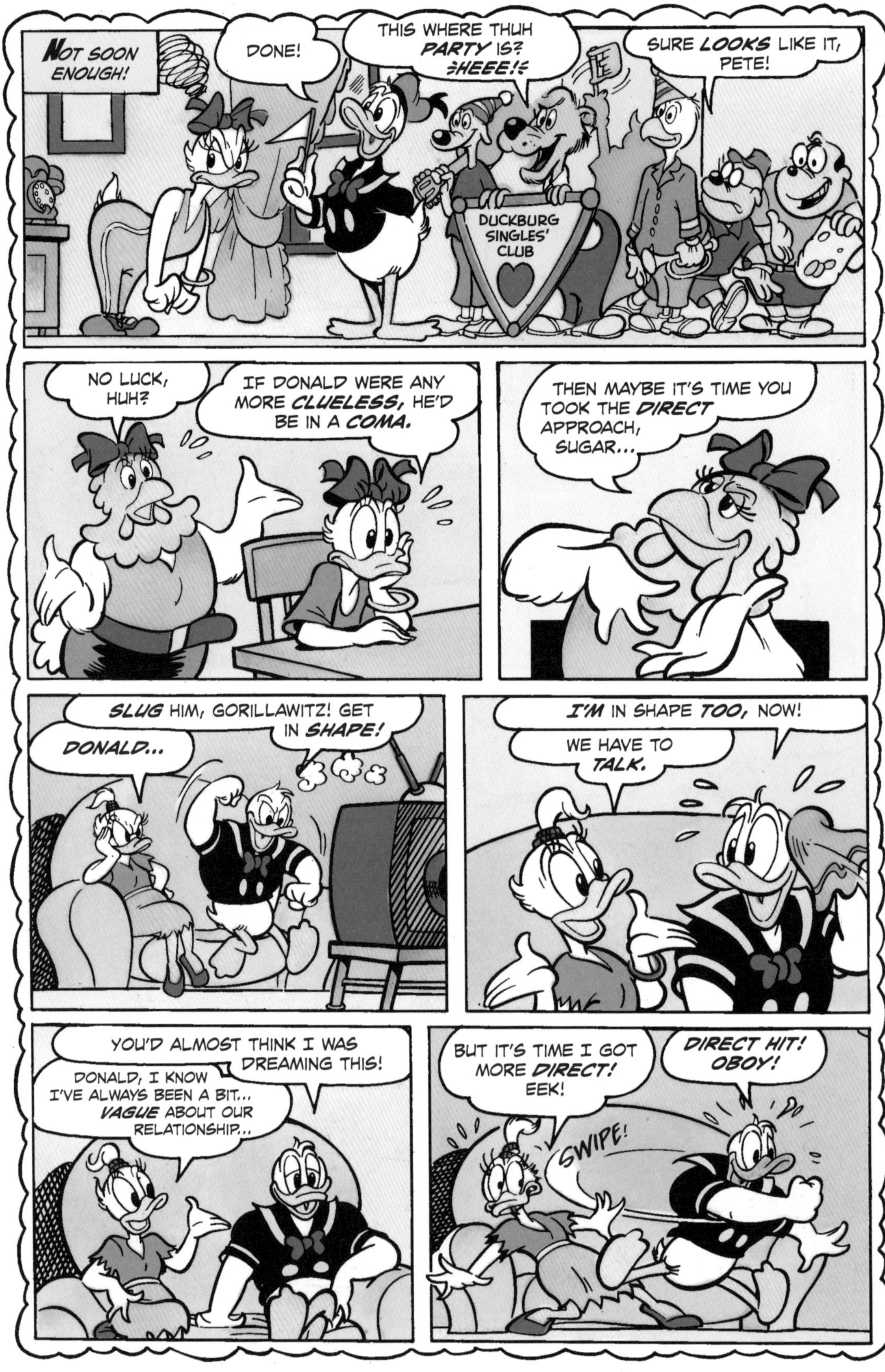
NOT SOON ENOUGH!
DONE!
THIS WHERE THUH PARTY IS? HEEE!
SURE LOOKS LIKE IT, PETE!
DUCKBURG SINGLES' CLUB
NO LUCK, HUH?
IF DONALD WERE ANY MORE CLUELESS, HE'D BE IN A COMA.
THEN MAYBE IT'S TIME YOU TOOK THE DIRECT APPROACH, SUGAR...
SLUG HIM, GORILLAWITZ! GET IN SHAPE!
DONALD...
I'M IN SHAPE TOO, NOW!
WE HAVE TO TALK.
YOU'D ALMOST THINK I WAS DREAMING THIS!
DONALD, I KNOW I'VE ALWAYS BEEN A BIT... VAGUE ABOUT OUR RELATIONSHIP...
BUT IT'S TIME I GOT MORE DIRECT! EEK!
DIRECT HIT! OBOY!
SWIPE!

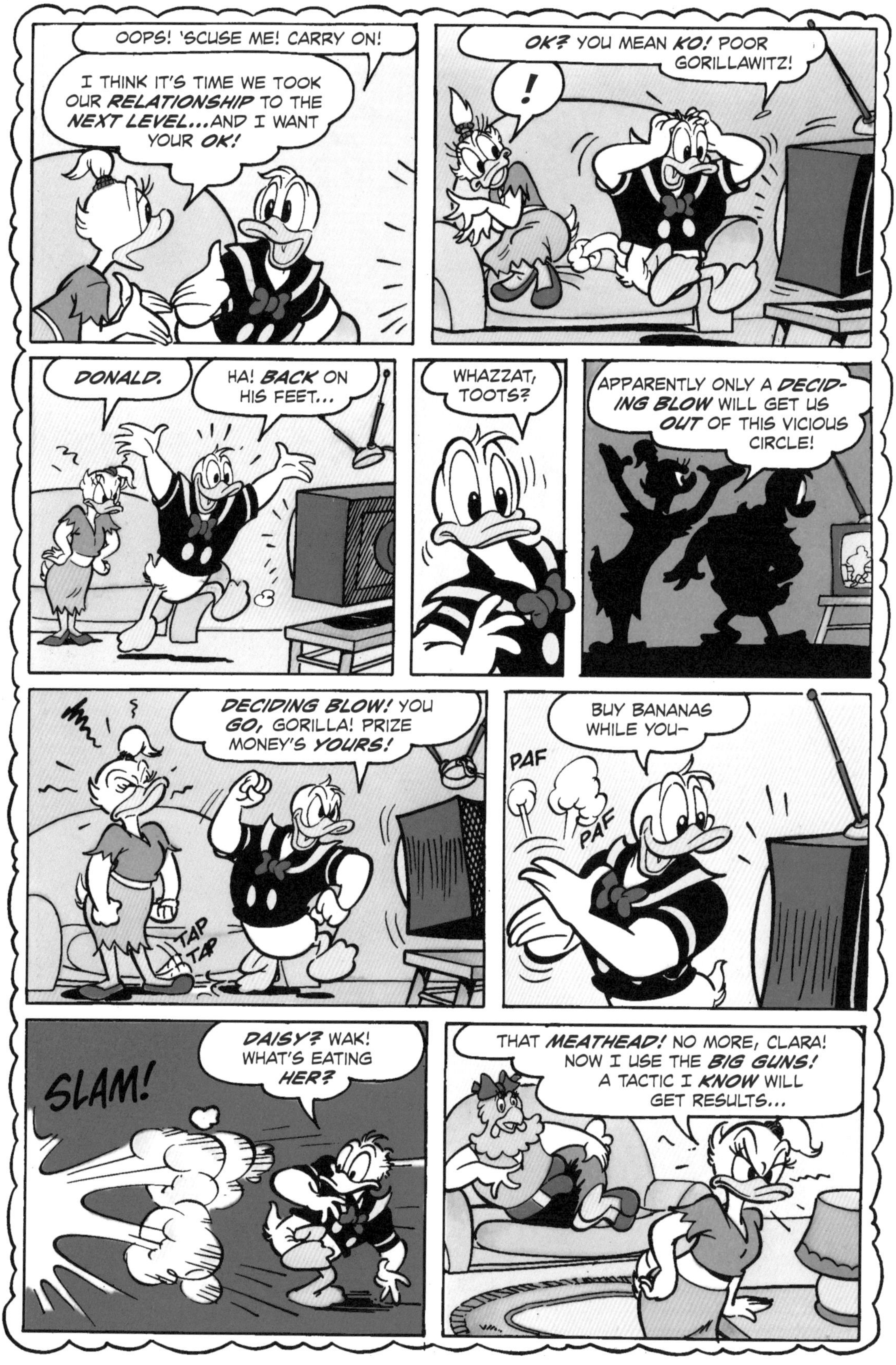
OOPS! 'SCUSE ME! CARRY ON!
I THINK IT'S TIME WE TOOK OUR RELATIONSHIP TO THE NEXT LEVEL...AND I WANT YOUR OK!
OK? YOU MEAN KO! POOR GORILLAWITZ!
!
DONALD.
HA! BACK ON HIS FEET...
WHAZZAT, TOOTS?
APPARENTLY ONLY A DECIDING BLOW WILL GET US OUT OF THIS VICIOUS CIRCLE!
DECIDING BLOW! YOU GO, GORILLA! PRIZE MONEY'S YOURS!
TAP TAP
BUY BANANAS WHILE YOU–
PAF
PAF
SLAM!
DAISY? WAK! WHAT'S EATING HER?
THAT MEATHEAD! NO MORE, CLARA! NOW I USE THE BIG GUNS! A TACTIC I KNOW WILL GET RESULTS...

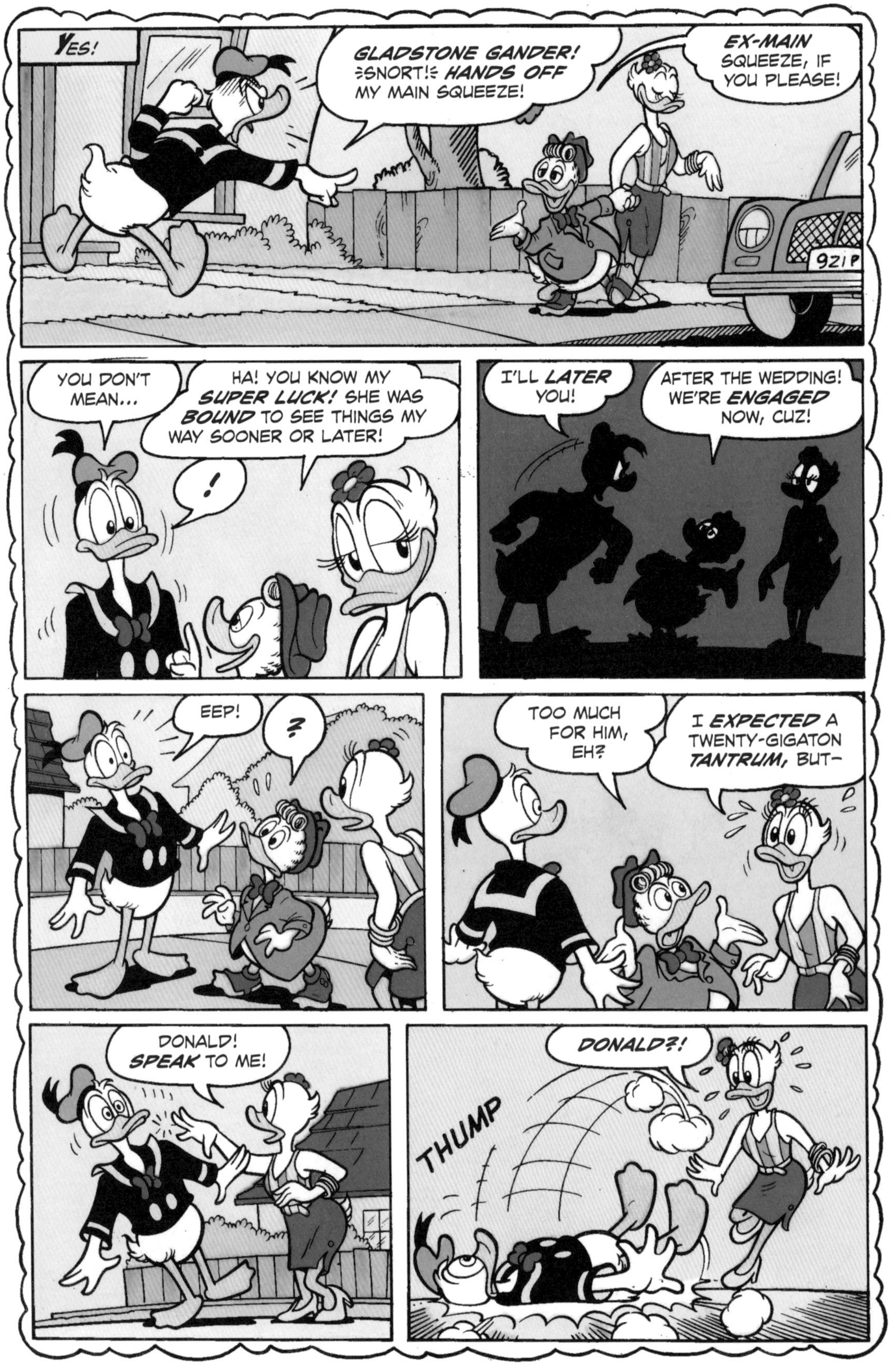

YES!
GLADSTONE GANDER! *SNORT!* HANDS OFF MY MAIN SQUEEZE!
EX-MAIN SQUEEZE, IF YOU PLEASE!
921P
YOU DON'T MEAN...
HA! YOU KNOW MY SUPER LUCK! SHE WAS BOUND TO SEE THINGS MY WAY SOONER OR LATER!
!
I'LL LATER YOU!
AFTER THE WEDDING! WE'RE ENGAGED NOW, CUZ!
EEP!
?
TOO MUCH FOR HIM, EH?
I EXPECTED A TWENTY-GIGATON TANTRUM, BUT–
DONALD! SPEAK TO ME!
DONALD?!
THUMP

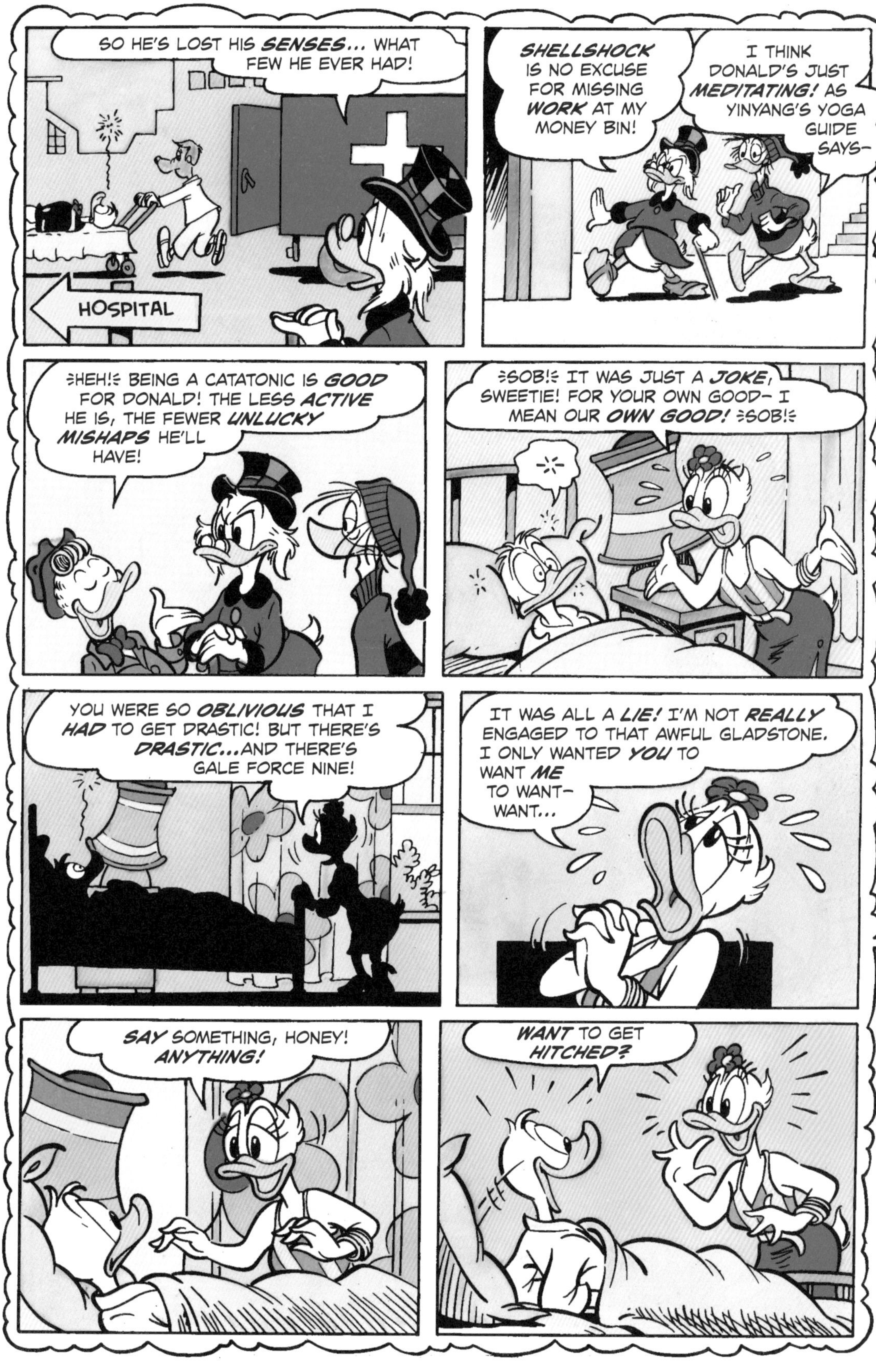
SO HE'S LOST HIS SENSES... WHAT FEW HE EVER HAD!
HOSPITAL
SHELLSHOCK IS NO EXCUSE FOR MISSING WORK AT MY MONEY BIN!
I THINK DONALD'S JUST MEDITATING! AS YINYANG'S YOGA GUIDE SAYS–
HEH! BEING A CATATONIC IS GOOD FOR DONALD! THE LESS ACTIVE HE IS, THE FEWER UNLUCKY MISHAPS HE'LL HAVE!
SOB! IT WAS JUST A JOKE, SWEETIE! FOR YOUR OWN GOOD– I MEAN OUR OWN GOOD! SOB!
YOU WERE SO OBLIVIOUS THAT I HAD TO GET DRASTIC! BUT THERE'S DRASTIC...AND THERE'S GALE FORCE NINE!
IT WAS ALL A LIE! I'M NOT REALLY ENGAGED TO THAT AWFUL GLADSTONE. I ONLY WANTED YOU TO WANT ME TO WANT– WANT...
SAY SOMETHING, HONEY! ANYTHING!
WANT TO GET HITCHED?

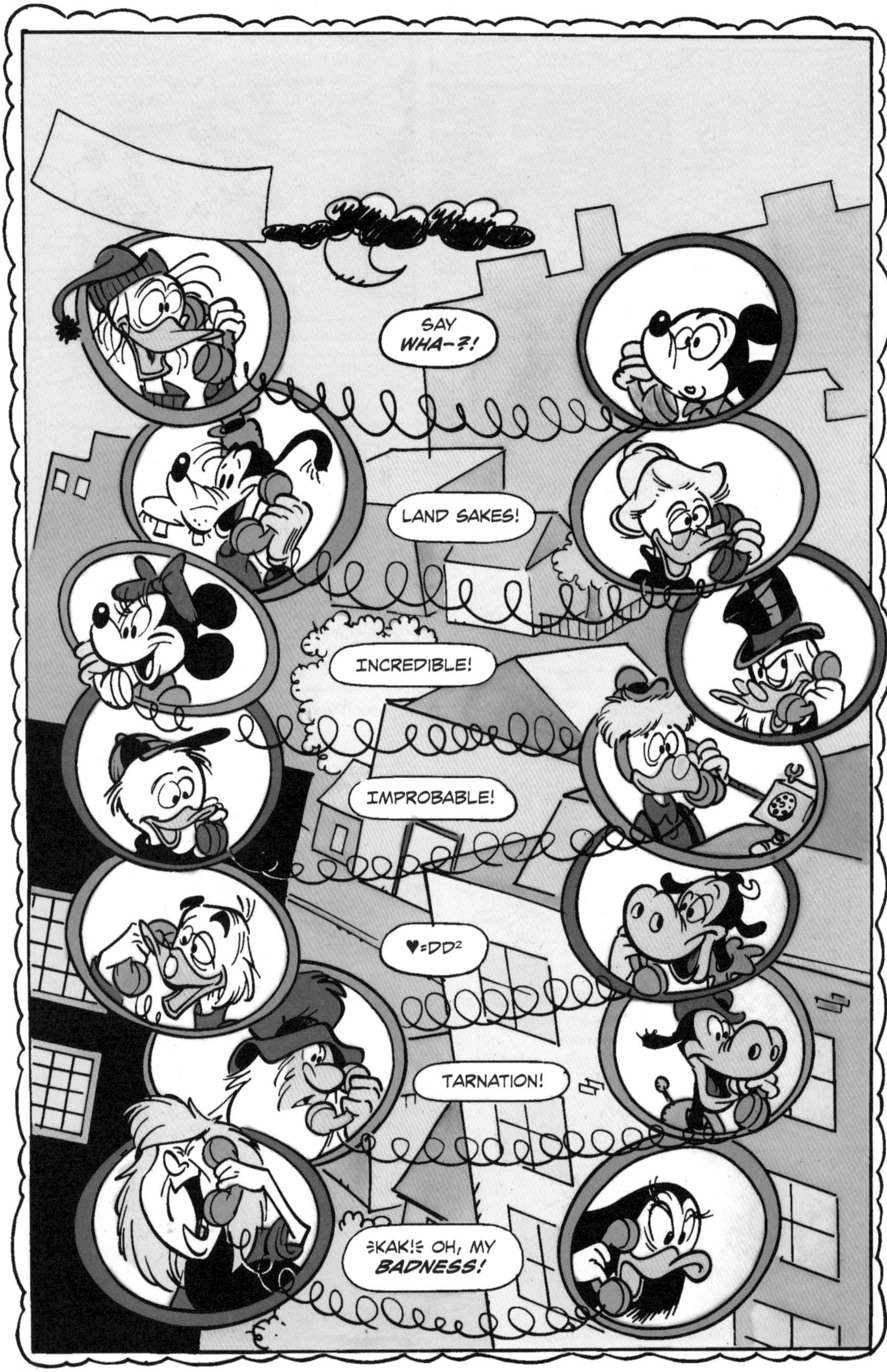
SAY WHA-?!
LAND SAKES!
INCREDIBLE!
IMPROBABLE!
♥=DD²
TARNATION!
KAK! OH, MY BADNESS!

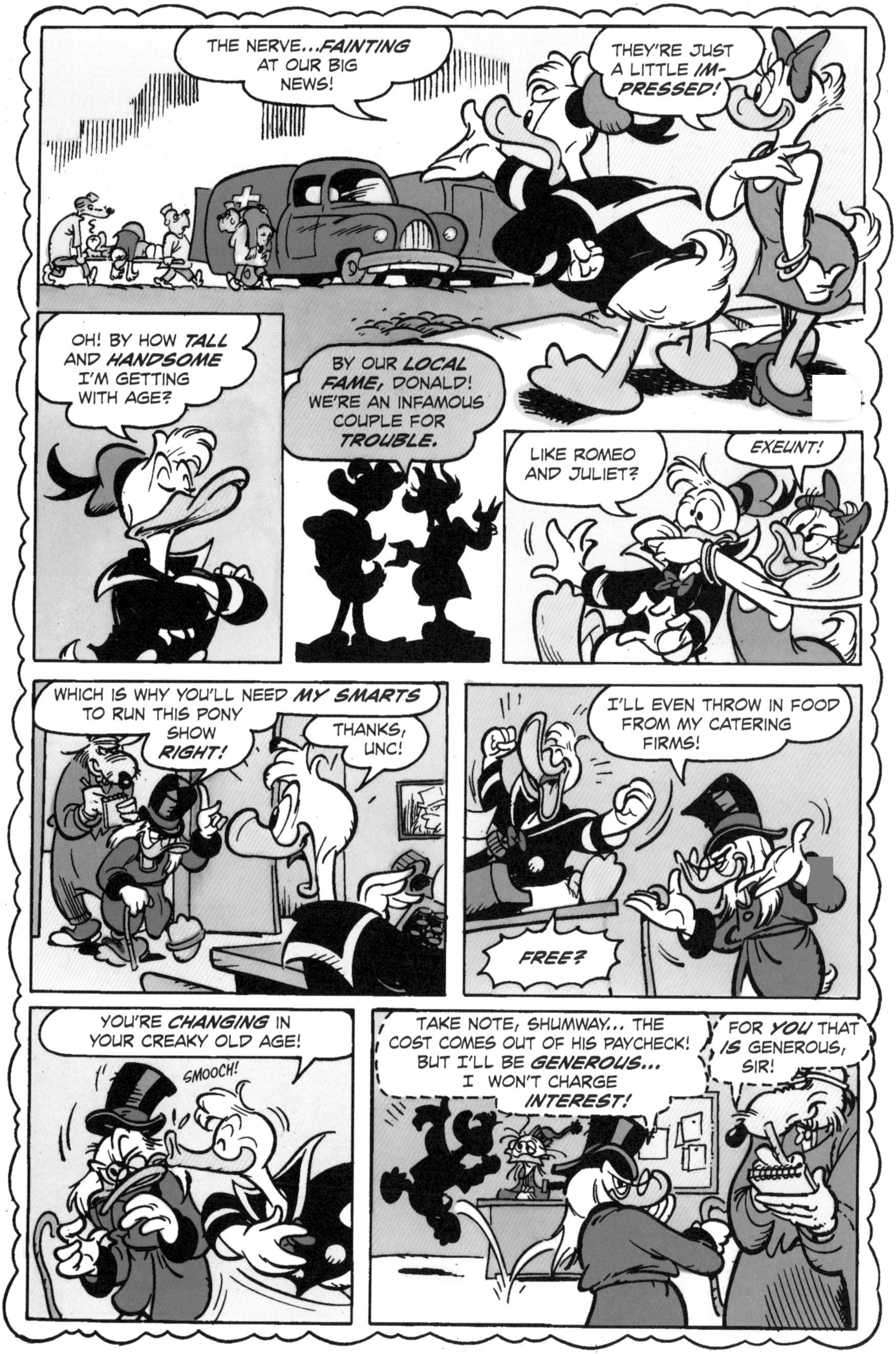

THE NERVE...FAINTING AT OUR BIG NEWS!
THEY'RE JUST A LITTLE IM-PRESSED!
OH! BY HOW TALL AND HANDSOME I'M GETTING WITH AGE?
BY OUR LOCAL FAME, DONALD! WE'RE AN INFAMOUS COUPLE FOR TROUBLE.
LIKE ROMEO AND JULIET?
EXEUNT!
WHICH IS WHY YOU'LL NEED MY SMARTS TO RUN THIS PONY SHOW RIGHT!
THANKS, UNC!
I'LL EVEN THROW IN FOOD FROM MY CATERING FIRMS!
FREE?
YOU'RE CHANGING IN YOUR CREAKY OLD AGE!
SMOOCH!
TAKE NOTE, SHUMWAY... THE COST COMES OUT OF HIS PAYCHECK! BUT I'LL BE GENEROUS... I WON'T CHARGE INTEREST!
FOR YOU THAT IS GENEROUS, SIR!

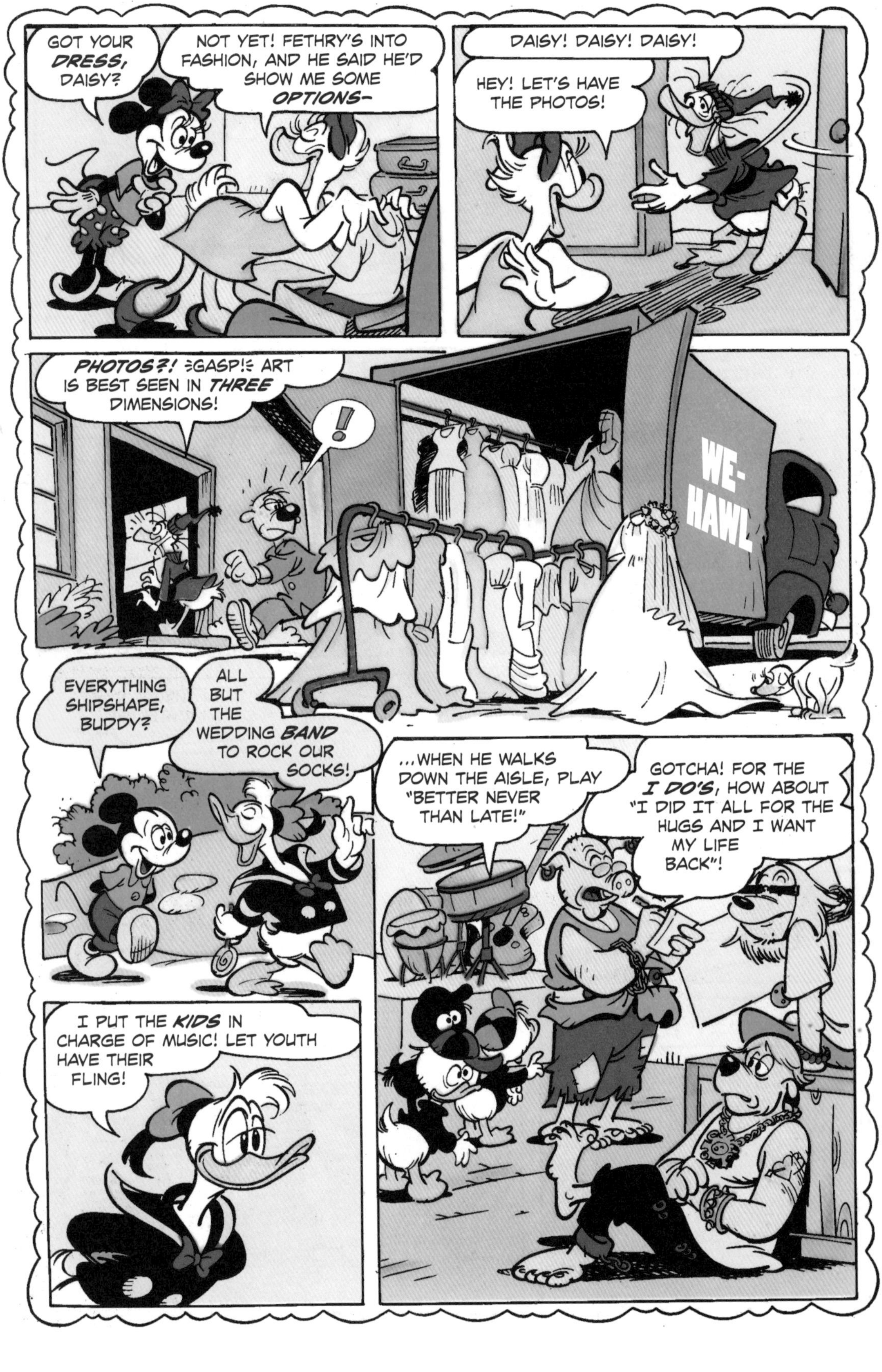
GOT YOUR DRESS, DAISY?
NOT YET! FETHRY'S INTO FASHION, AND HE SAID HE'D SHOW ME SOME OPTIONS–
DAISY! DAISY! DAISY!
HEY! LET'S HAVE THE PHOTOS!
PHOTOS?! ≡GASP!≡ ART IS BEST SEEN IN THREE DIMENSIONS!
!
WE-HAWL
EVERYTHING SHIPSHAPE, BUDDY?
ALL BUT THE WEDDING BAND TO ROCK OUR SOCKS!
...WHEN HE WALKS DOWN THE AISLE, PLAY "BETTER NEVER THAN LATE!"
GOTCHA! FOR THE I DO'S, HOW ABOUT "I DID IT ALL FOR THE HUGS AND I WANT MY LIFE BACK"!
I PUT THE KIDS IN CHARGE OF MUSIC! LET YOUTH HAVE THEIR FLING!

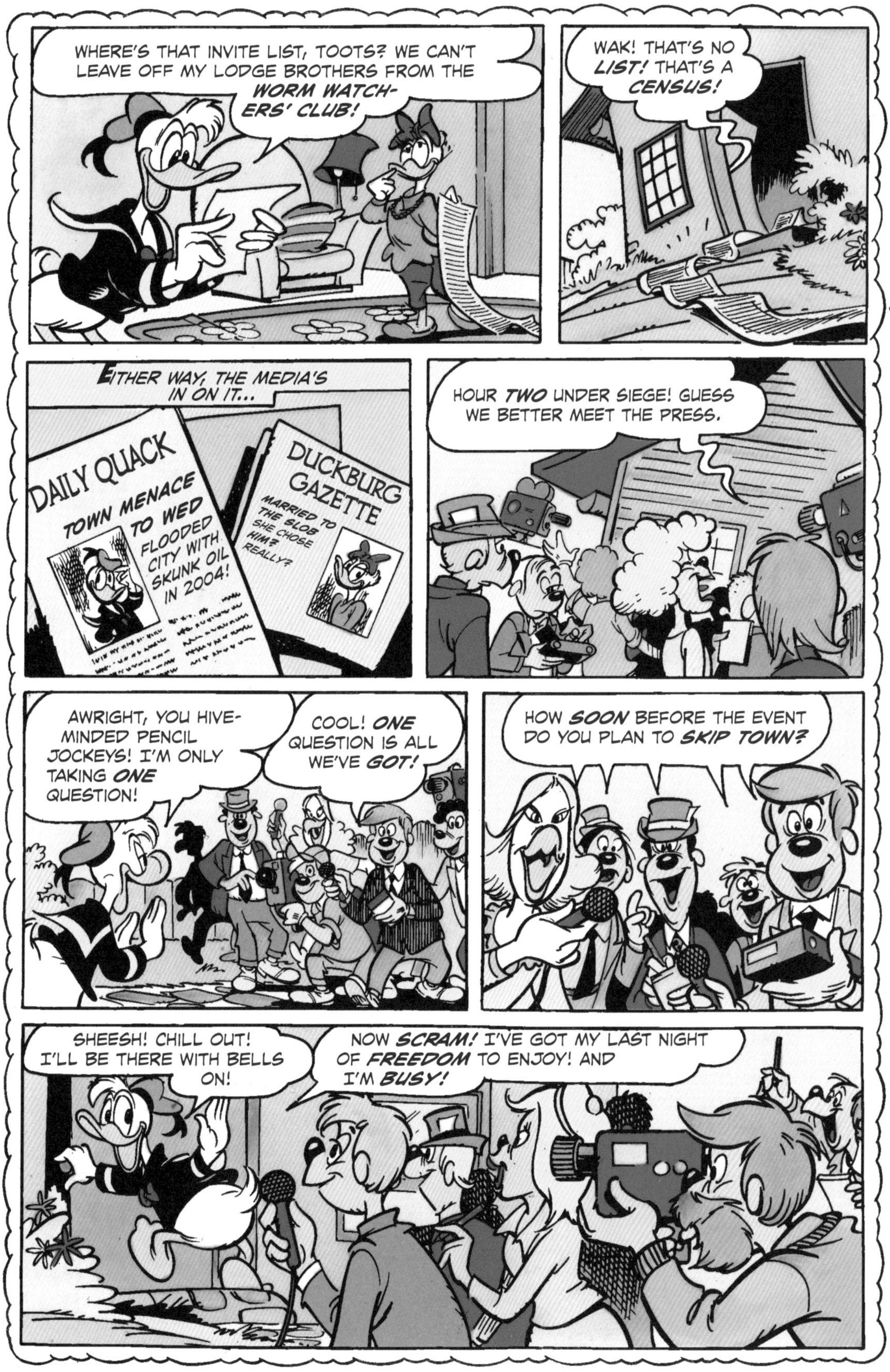
WHERE'S THAT INVITE LIST, TOOTS? WE CAN'T LEAVE OFF MY LODGE BROTHERS FROM THE WORM WATCHERS' CLUB!
WAK! THAT'S NO LIST! THAT'S A CENSUS!
EITHER WAY, THE MEDIA'S IN ON IT...
DAILY QUACK
TOWN MENACE TO WED
FLOODED CITY WITH SKUNK OIL IN 2004!
DUCKBURG GAZETTE
MARRIED TO THE SLOB SHE CHOSE HIM? REALLY?
HOUR TWO UNDER SIEGE! GUESS WE BETTER MEET THE PRESS.
AWRIGHT, YOU HIVE-MINDED PENCIL JOCKEYS! I'M ONLY TAKING ONE QUESTION!
COOL! ONE QUESTION IS ALL WE'VE GOT!
HOW SOON BEFORE THE EVENT DO YOU PLAN TO SKIP TOWN?
SHEESH! CHILL OUT! I'LL BE THERE WITH BELLS ON!
NOW SCRAM! I'VE GOT MY LAST NIGHT OF FREEDOM TO ENJOY! AND I'M BUSY!

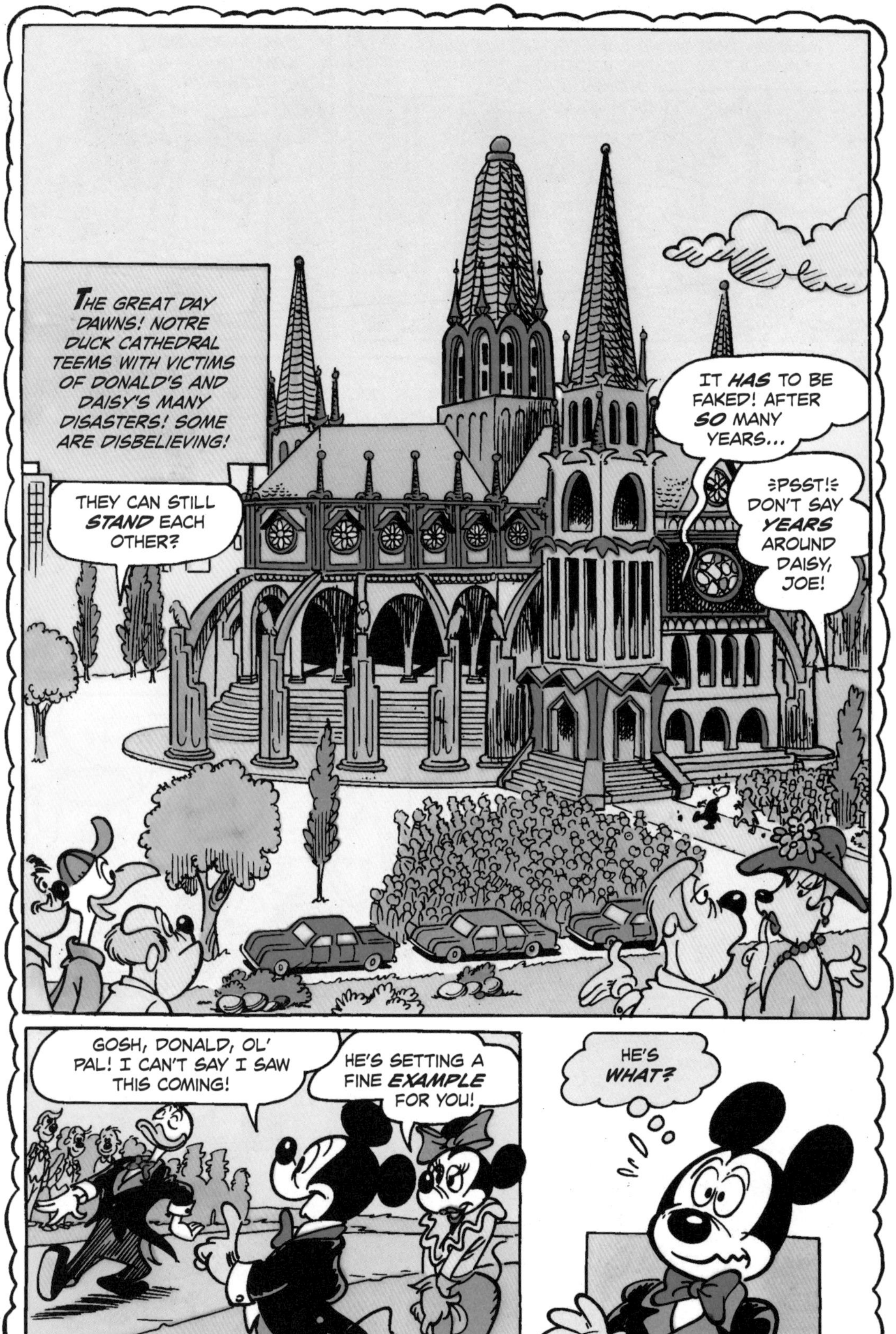
THE GREAT DAY DAWNS! NOTRE DUCK CATHEDRAL TEEMS WITH VICTIMS OF DONALD'S AND DAISY'S MANY DISASTERS! SOME ARE DISBELIEVING!
THEY CAN STILL STAND EACH OTHER?
IT HAS TO BE FAKED! AFTER SO MANY YEARS...
PSST! DON'T SAY YEARS AROUND DAISY, JOE!
GOSH, DONALD, OL' PAL! I CAN'T SAY I SAW THIS COMING!
HE'S SETTING A FINE EXAMPLE FOR YOU!
HE'S WHAT?

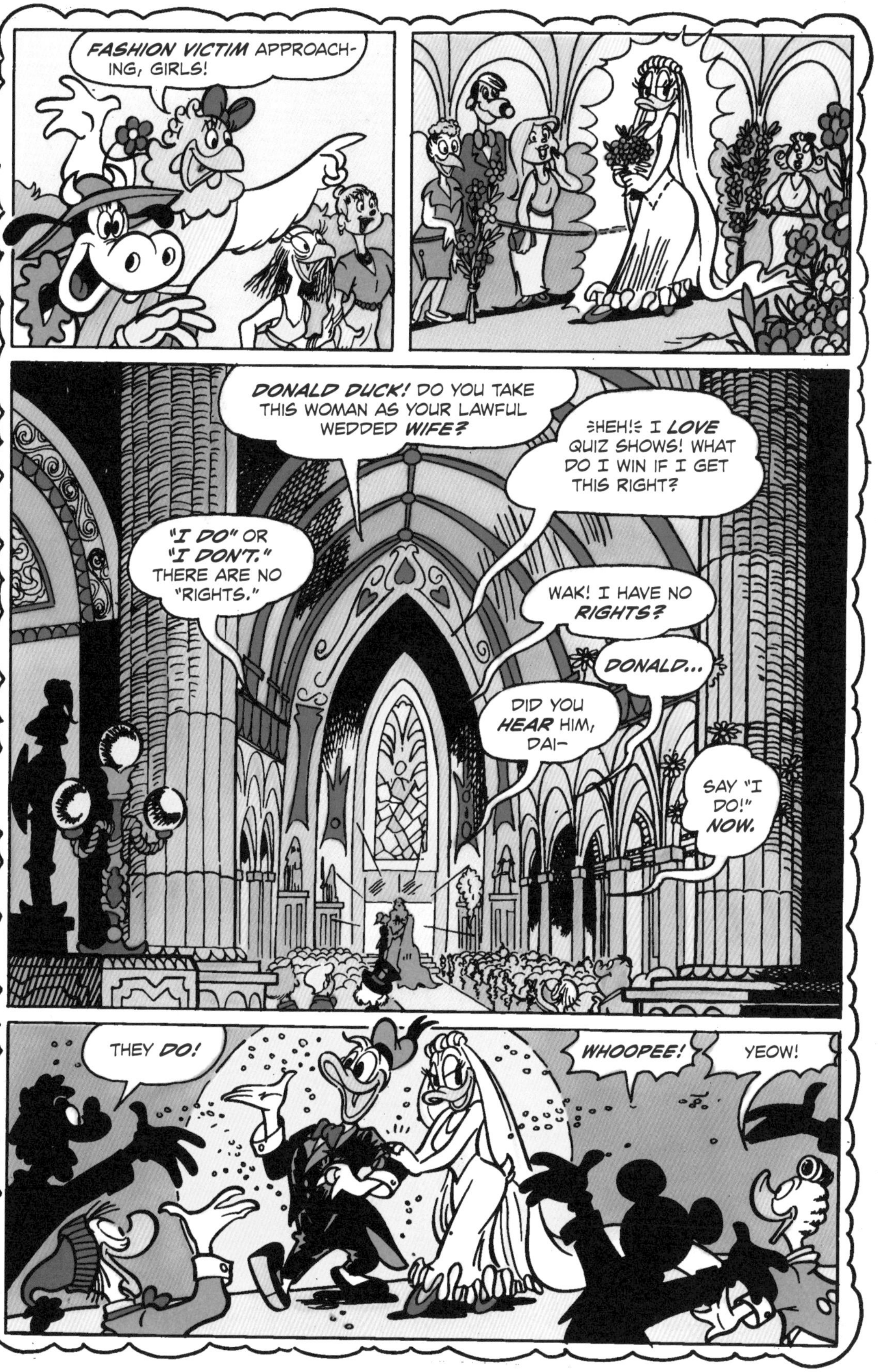
FASHION VICTIM APPROACHING, GIRLS!
DONALD DUCK! DO YOU TAKE THIS WOMAN AS YOUR LAWFUL WEDDED WIFE?
HEH! I LOVE QUIZ SHOWS! WHAT DO I WIN IF I GET THIS RIGHT?
"I DO" OR "I DON'T." THERE ARE NO "RIGHTS."
WAK! I HAVE NO RIGHTS?
DONALD...
DID YOU HEAR HIM, DAI–
SAY "I DO!" NOW.
THEY DO!
WHOOPEE!
YEOW!

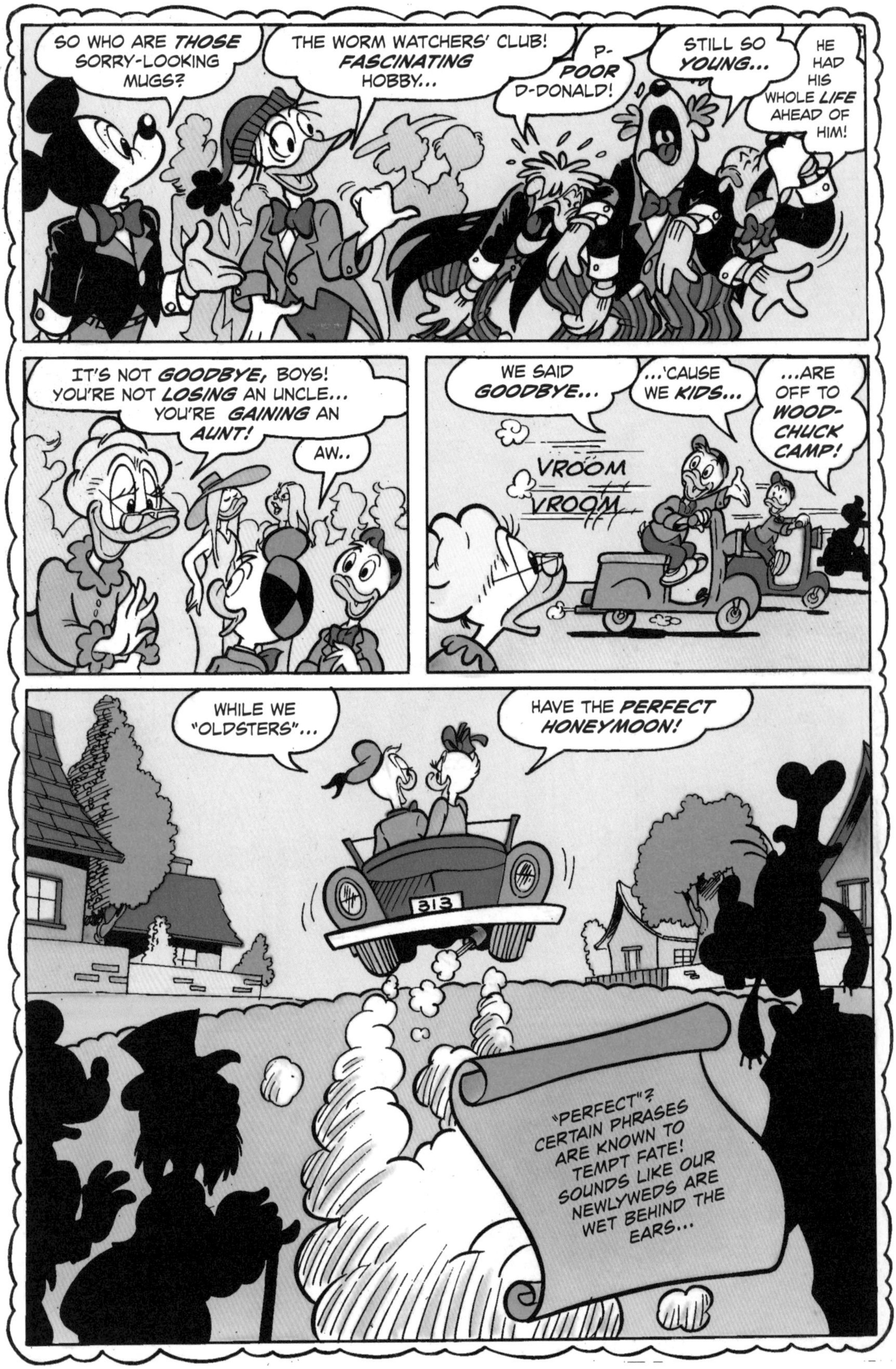
SO WHO ARE THOSE SORRY-LOOKING MUGS?
THE WORM WATCHERS' CLUB! FASCINATING HOBBY...
P-POOR D-DONALD!
STILL SO YOUNG...
HE HAD HIS WHOLE LIFE AHEAD OF HIM!
IT'S NOT GOODBYE, BOYS! YOU'RE NOT LOSING AN UNCLE... YOU'RE GAINING AN AUNT!
AW..
WE SAID GOODBYE...
...'CAUSE WE KIDS...
...ARE OFF TO WOOD-CHUCK CAMP!
VROOM
VROOM
WHILE WE "OLDSTERS"...
HAVE THE PERFECT HONEYMOON!
313
"PERFECT"? CERTAIN PHRASES ARE KNOWN TO TEMPT FATE! SOUNDS LIKE OUR NEWLYWEDS ARE WET BEHIND THE EARS...

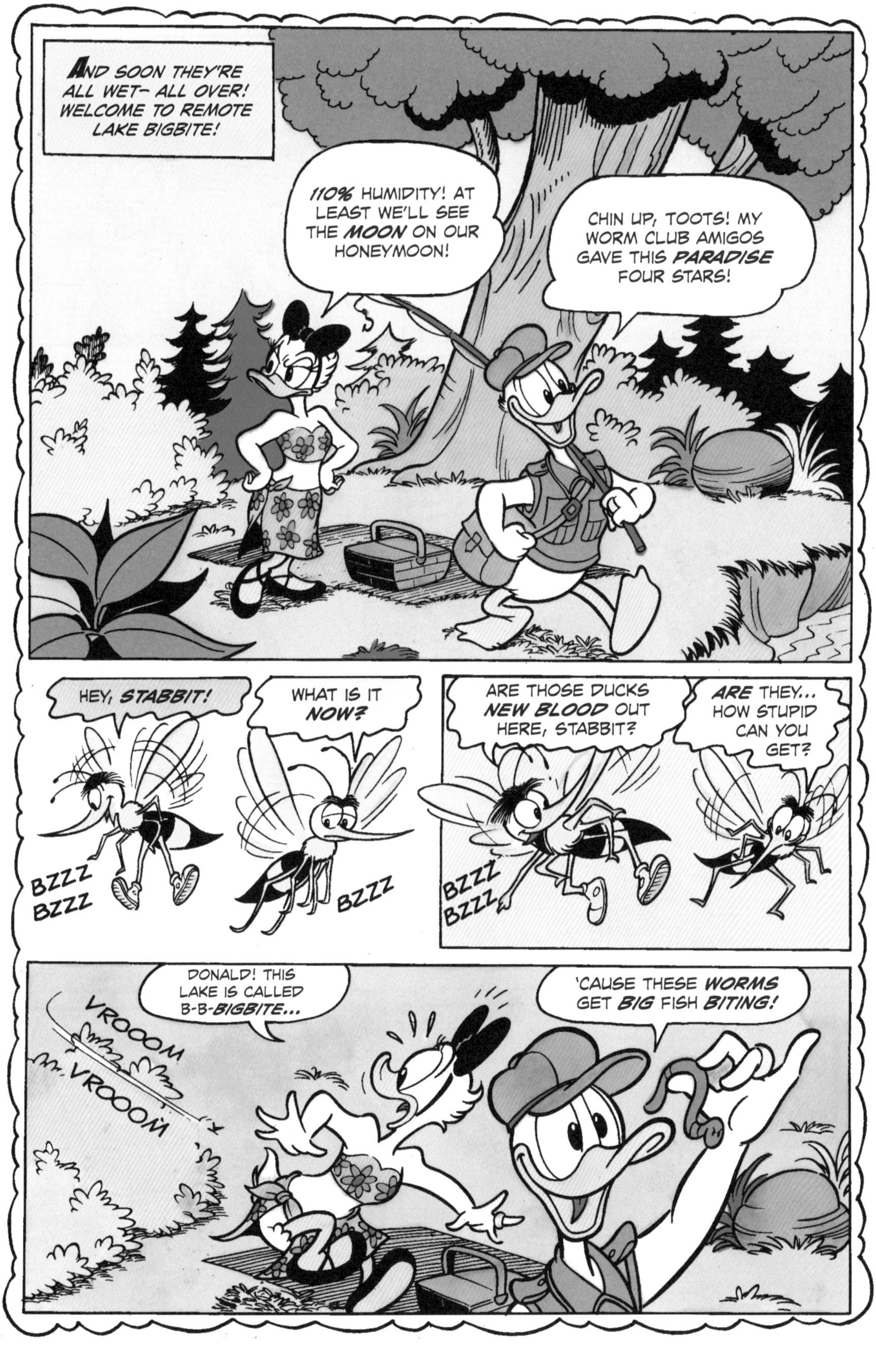
AND SOON THEY'RE ALL WET– ALL OVER! WELCOME TO REMOTE LAKE BIGBITE!
110% HUMIDITY! AT LEAST WE'LL SEE THE MOON ON OUR HONEYMOON!
CHIN UP, TOOTS! MY WORM CLUB AMIGOS GAVE THIS PARADISE FOUR STARS!
HEY, STABBIT!
BZZZ BZZZ
WHAT IS IT NOW?
BZZZ
ARE THOSE DUCKS NEW BLOOD OUT HERE, STABBIT?
ARE THEY... HOW STUPID CAN YOU GET?
BZZZ BZZZ
DONALD! THIS LAKE IS CALLED B-B-BIGBITE...
'CAUSE THESE WORMS GET BIG FISH BITING!
VROOOM
VROOOM

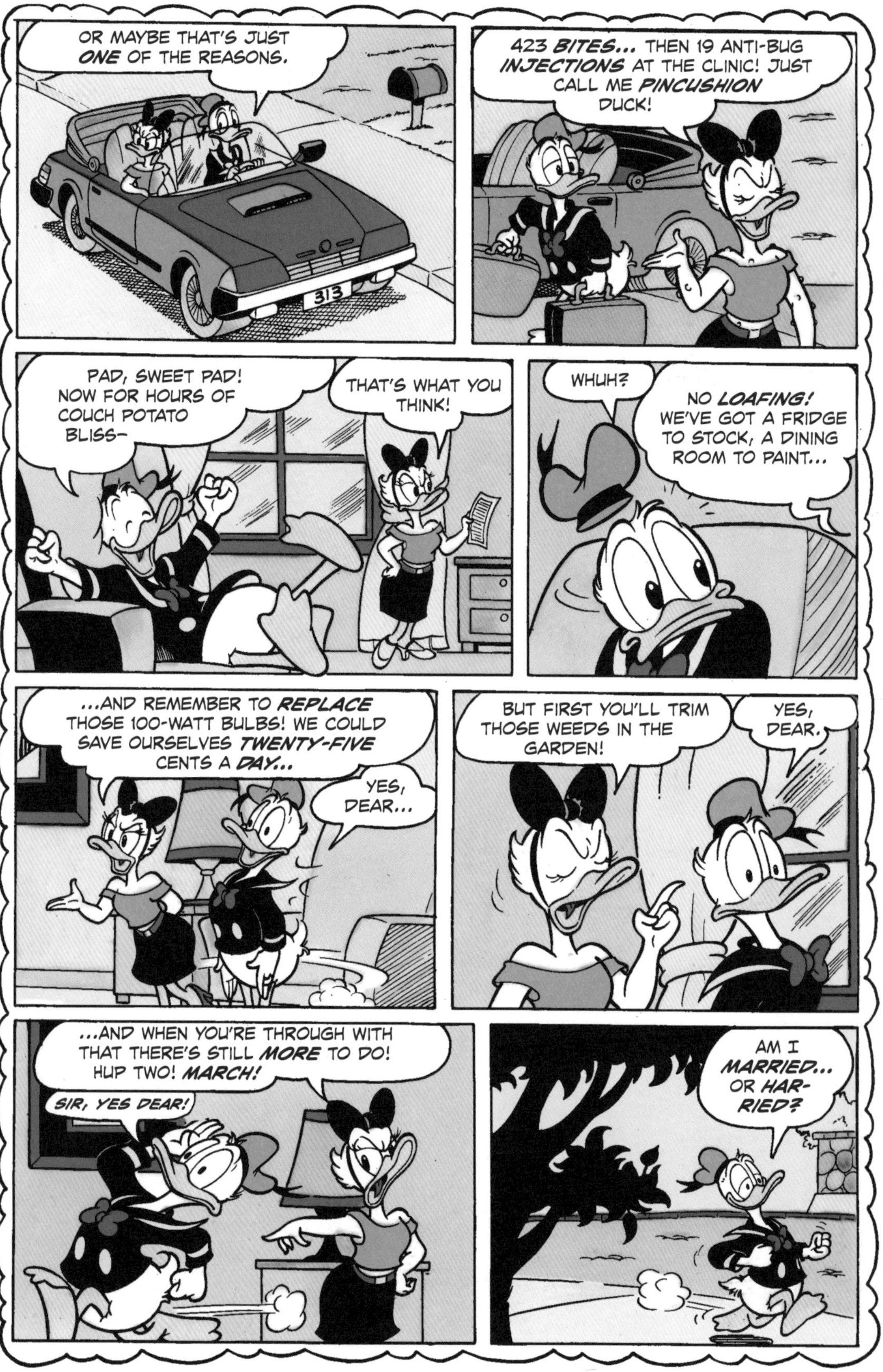
OR MAYBE THAT'S JUST ONE OF THE REASONS.
313
423 BITES... THEN 19 ANTI-BUG INJECTIONS AT THE CLINIC! JUST CALL ME PINCUSHION DUCK!
PAD, SWEET PAD! NOW FOR HOURS OF COUCH POTATO BLISS–
THAT'S WHAT YOU THINK!
WHUH?
NO LOAFING! WE'VE GOT A FRIDGE TO STOCK, A DINING ROOM TO PAINT...
...AND REMEMBER TO REPLACE THOSE 100-WATT BULBS! WE COULD SAVE OURSELVES TWENTY-FIVE CENTS A DAY...
YES, DEAR...
BUT FIRST YOU'LL TRIM THOSE WEEDS IN THE GARDEN!
YES, DEAR.
...AND WHEN YOU'RE THROUGH WITH THAT THERE'S STILL MORE TO DO! HUP TWO! MARCH!
SIR, YES DEAR!
AM I MARRIED... OR HAR-RIED?

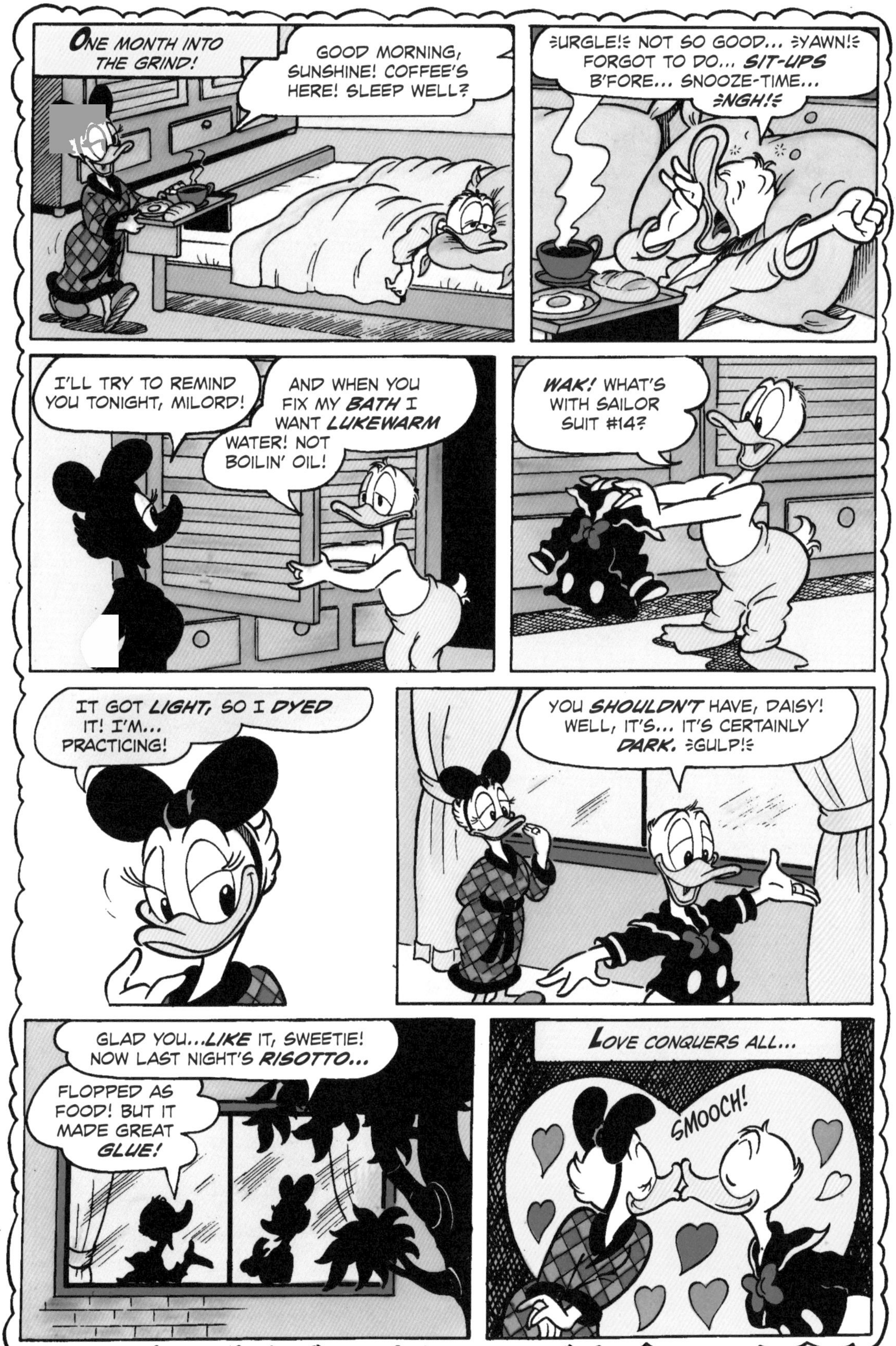
ONE MONTH INTO THE GRIND!
GOOD MORNING, SUNSHINE! COFFEE'S HERE! SLEEP WELL?
URGLE! NOT SO GOOD... YAWN! FORGOT TO DO... SIT-UPS B'FORE... SNOOZE-TIME... NGH!
I'LL TRY TO REMIND YOU TONIGHT, MILORD!
AND WHEN YOU FIX MY BATH I WANT LUKEWARM WATER! NOT BOILIN' OIL!
WAK! WHAT'S WITH SAILOR SUIT #14?
IT GOT LIGHT, SO I DYED IT! I'M... PRACTICING!
YOU SHOULDN'T HAVE, DAISY! WELL, IT'S... IT'S CERTAINLY DARK. GULP!
GLAD YOU...LIKE IT, SWEETIE! NOW LAST NIGHT'S RISOTTO...
FLOPPED AS FOOD! BUT IT MADE GREAT GLUE!
LOVE CONQUERS ALL...
SMOOCH!

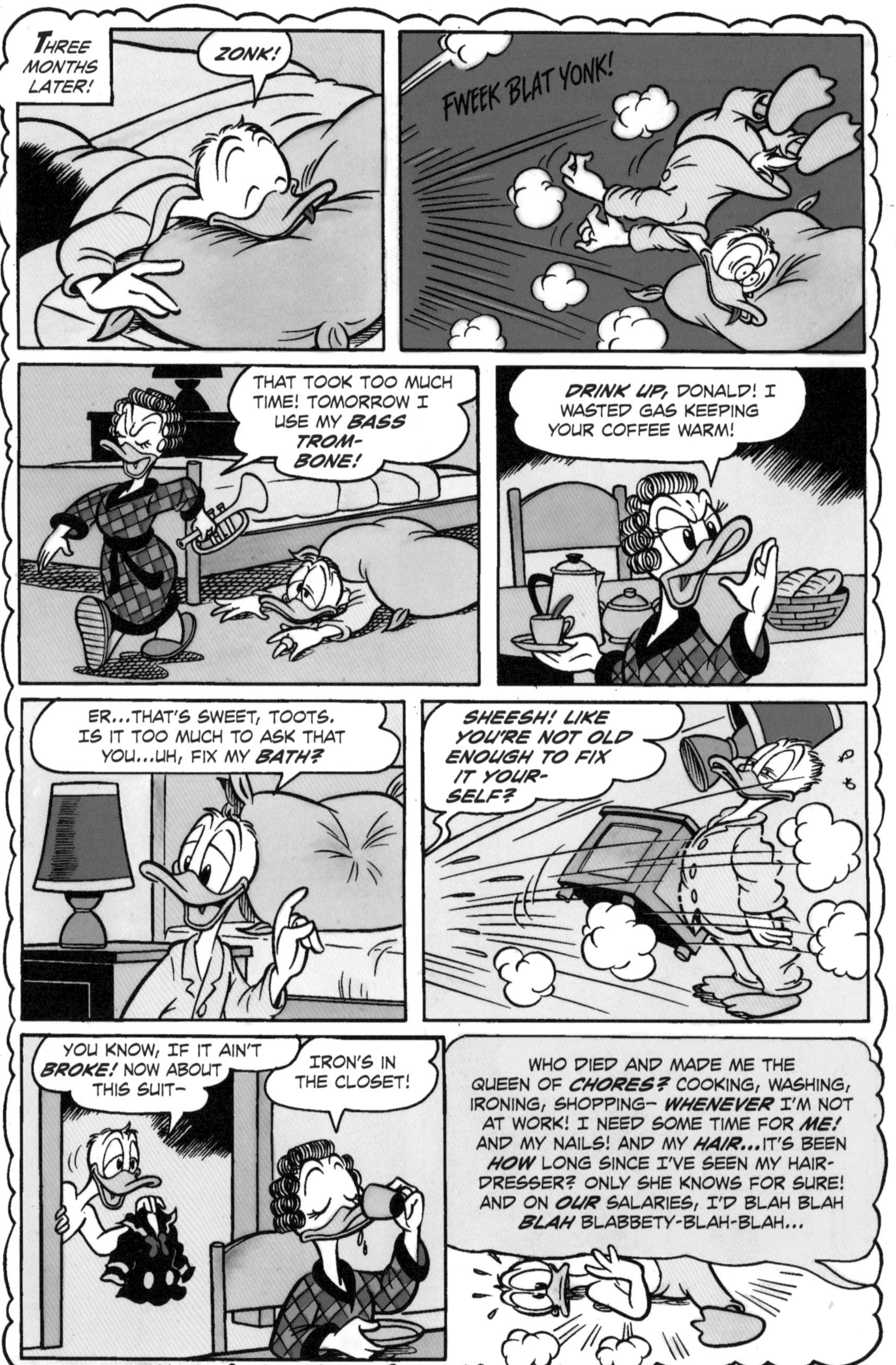
THREE MONTHS LATER!
ZONK!
FWEEK BLAT YONK!
THAT TOOK TOO MUCH TIME! TOMORROW I USE MY BASS TROM-BONE!
DRINK UP, DONALD! I WASTED GAS KEEPING YOUR COFFEE WARM!
ER...THAT'S SWEET, TOOTS. IS IT TOO MUCH TO ASK THAT YOU...UH, FIX MY BATH?
SHEESH! LIKE YOU'RE NOT OLD ENOUGH TO FIX IT YOUR-SELF?
YOU KNOW, IF IT AIN'T BROKE! NOW ABOUT THIS SUIT–
IRON'S IN THE CLOSET!
WHO DIED AND MADE ME THE QUEEN OF CHORES? COOKING, WASHING, IRONING, SHOPPING– WHENEVER I'M NOT AT WORK! I NEED SOME TIME FOR ME! AND MY NAILS! AND MY HAIR...IT'S BEEN HOW LONG SINCE I'VE SEEN MY HAIR-DRESSER? ONLY SHE KNOWS FOR SURE! AND ON OUR SALARIES, I'D BLAH BLAH BLAH BLABBETY-BLAH-BLAH...

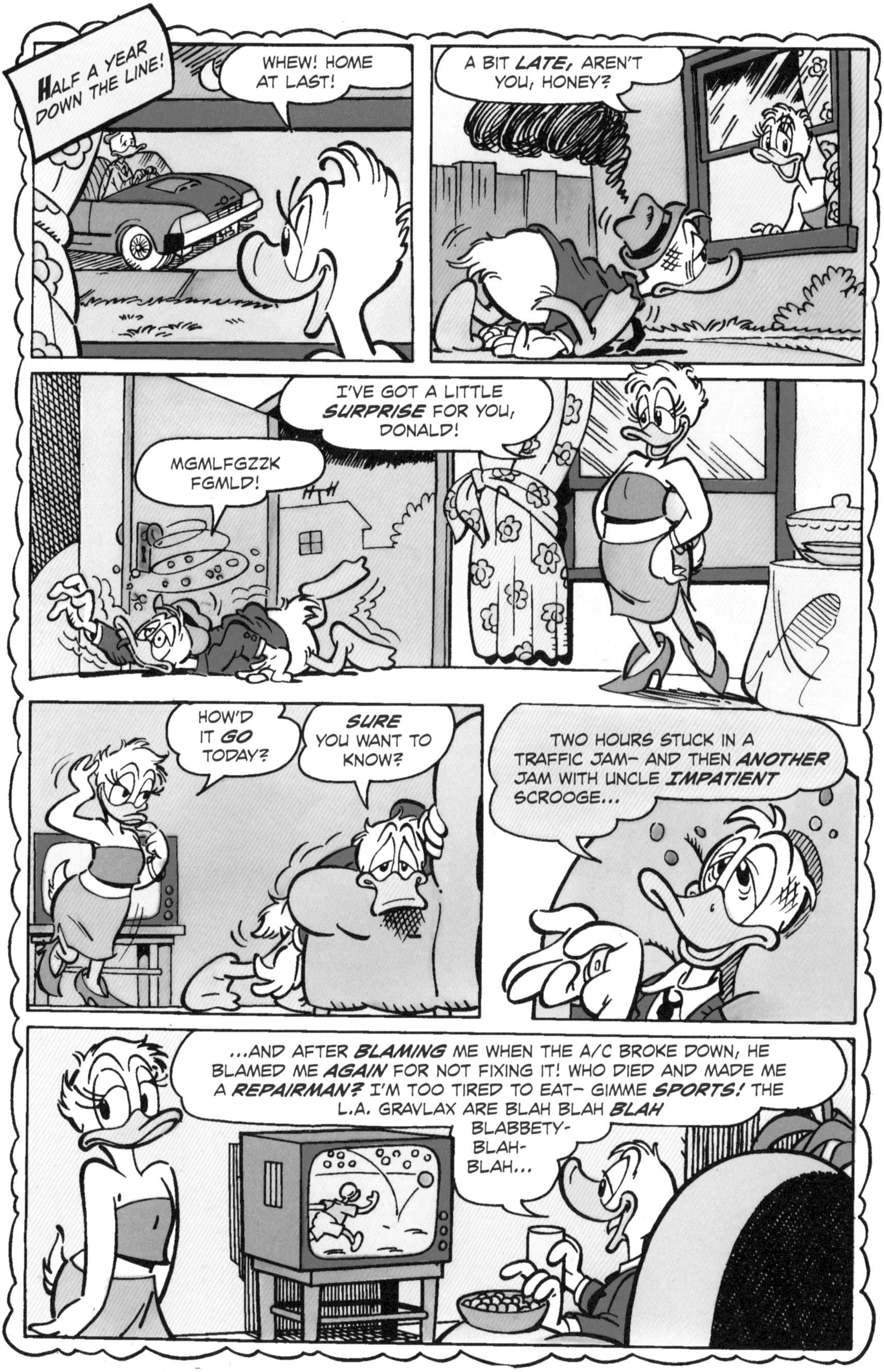
HALF A YEAR DOWN THE LINE!
WHEW! HOME AT LAST!
A BIT LATE, AREN'T YOU, HONEY?
I'VE GOT A LITTLE SURPRISE FOR YOU, DONALD!
MGMLFGZZK FGMLD!
HOW'D IT GO TODAY?
SURE YOU WANT TO KNOW?
TWO HOURS STUCK IN A TRAFFIC JAM– AND THEN ANOTHER JAM WITH UNCLE IMPATIENT SCROOGE...
...AND AFTER BLAMING ME WHEN THE A/C BROKE DOWN, HE BLAMED ME AGAIN FOR NOT FIXING IT! WHO DIED AND MADE ME A REPAIRMAN? I'M TOO TIRED TO EAT– GIMME SPORTS! THE L.A. GRAVLAX ARE BLAH BLAH BLAH BLABBETY-BLAH-BLAH...

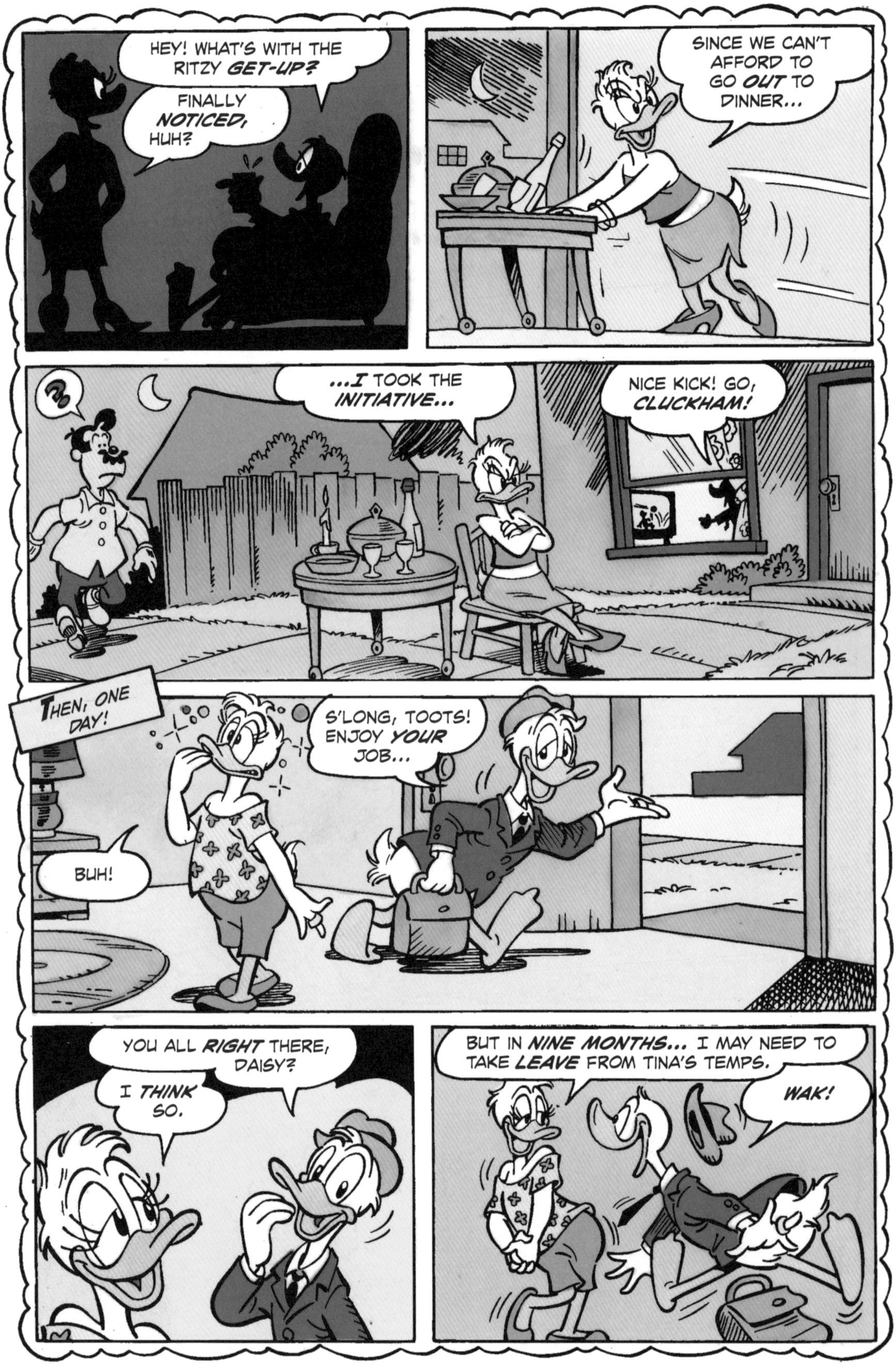
HEY! WHAT'S WITH THE RITZY GET-UP?
FINALLY NOTICED, HUH?
SINCE WE CAN'T AFFORD TO GO OUT TO DINNER...
...I TOOK THE INITIATIVE...
NICE KICK! GO, CLUCKHAM!
THEN, ONE DAY!
S'LONG, TOOTS! ENJOY YOUR JOB...
BUH!
YOU ALL RIGHT THERE, DAISY?
I THINK SO.
BUT IN NINE MONTHS... I MAY NEED TO TAKE LEAVE FROM TINA'S TEMPS.
WAK!

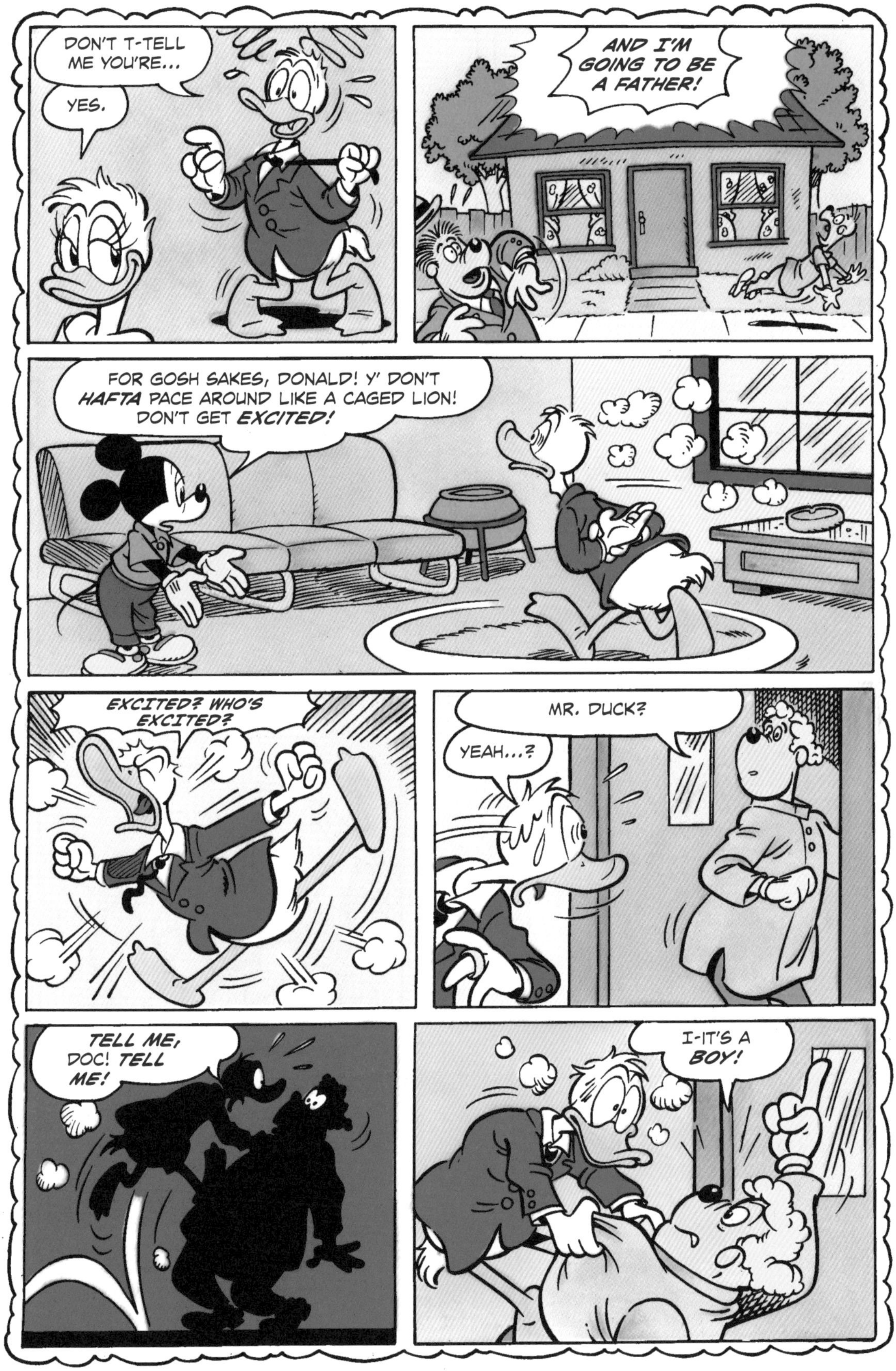

DON'T T-TELL ME YOU'RE...
YES.
AND I'M GOING TO BE A FATHER!
FOR GOSH SAKES, DONALD! Y' DON'T HAFTA PACE AROUND LIKE A CAGED LION! DON'T GET EXCITED!
EXCITED? WHO'S EXCITED?
MR. DUCK?
YEAH...?
TELL ME, DOC! TELL ME!
I-IT'S A BOY!

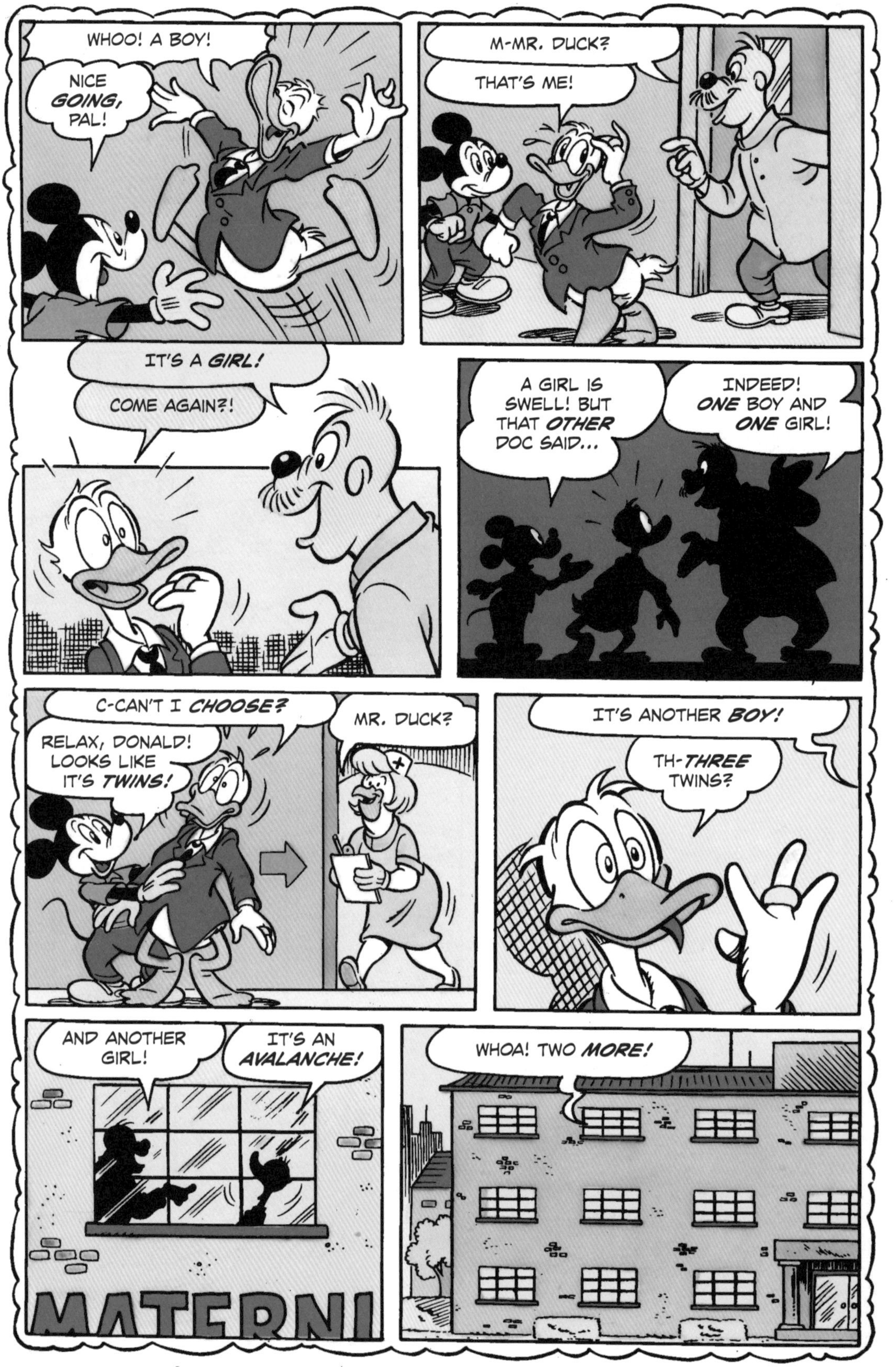
WHOO! A BOY!
NICE GOING, PAL!
M-MR. DUCK?
THAT'S ME!
IT'S A GIRL!
COME AGAIN?!
A GIRL IS SWELL! BUT THAT OTHER DOC SAID...
INDEED! ONE BOY AND ONE GIRL!
C-CAN'T I CHOOSE?
RELAX, DONALD! LOOKS LIKE IT'S TWINS!
MR. DUCK?
IT'S ANOTHER BOY!
TH-THREE TWINS?
AND ANOTHER GIRL!
IT'S AN AVALANCHE!
MATERNI
WHOA! TWO MORE!

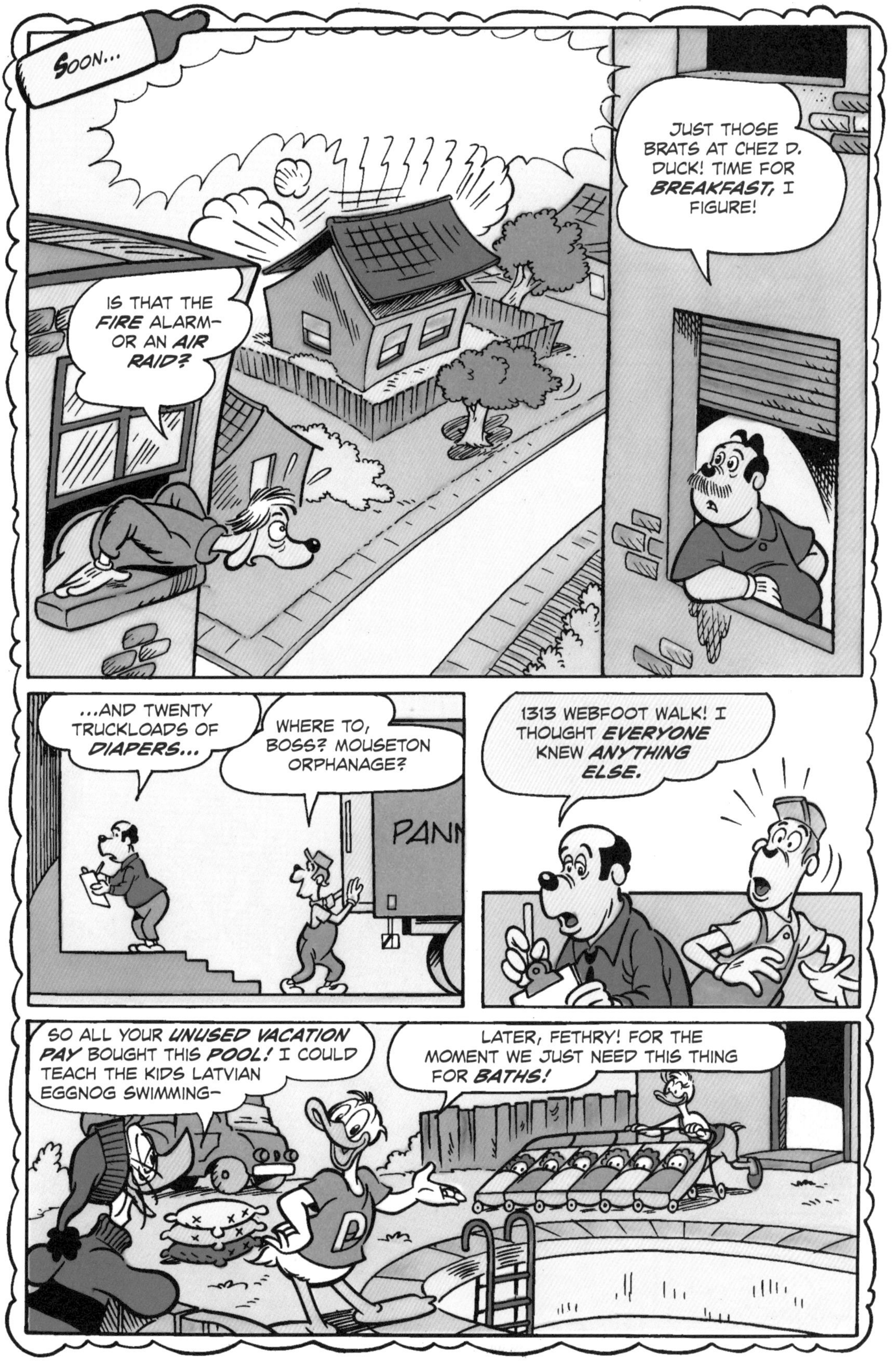
SOON...
IS THAT THE FIRE ALARM— OR AN AIR RAID?
JUST THOSE BRATS AT CHEZ D. DUCK! TIME FOR BREAKFAST, I FIGURE!
...AND TWENTY TRUCKLOADS OF DIAPERS...
WHERE TO, BOSS? MOUSETON ORPHANAGE?
PANN
1313 WEBFOOT WALK! I THOUGHT EVERYONE KNEW ANYTHING ELSE.
SO ALL YOUR UNUSED VACATION PAY BOUGHT THIS POOL! I COULD TEACH THE KIDS LATVIAN EGGNOG SWIMMING—
LATER, FETHRY! FOR THE MOMENT WE JUST NEED THIS THING FOR BATHS!

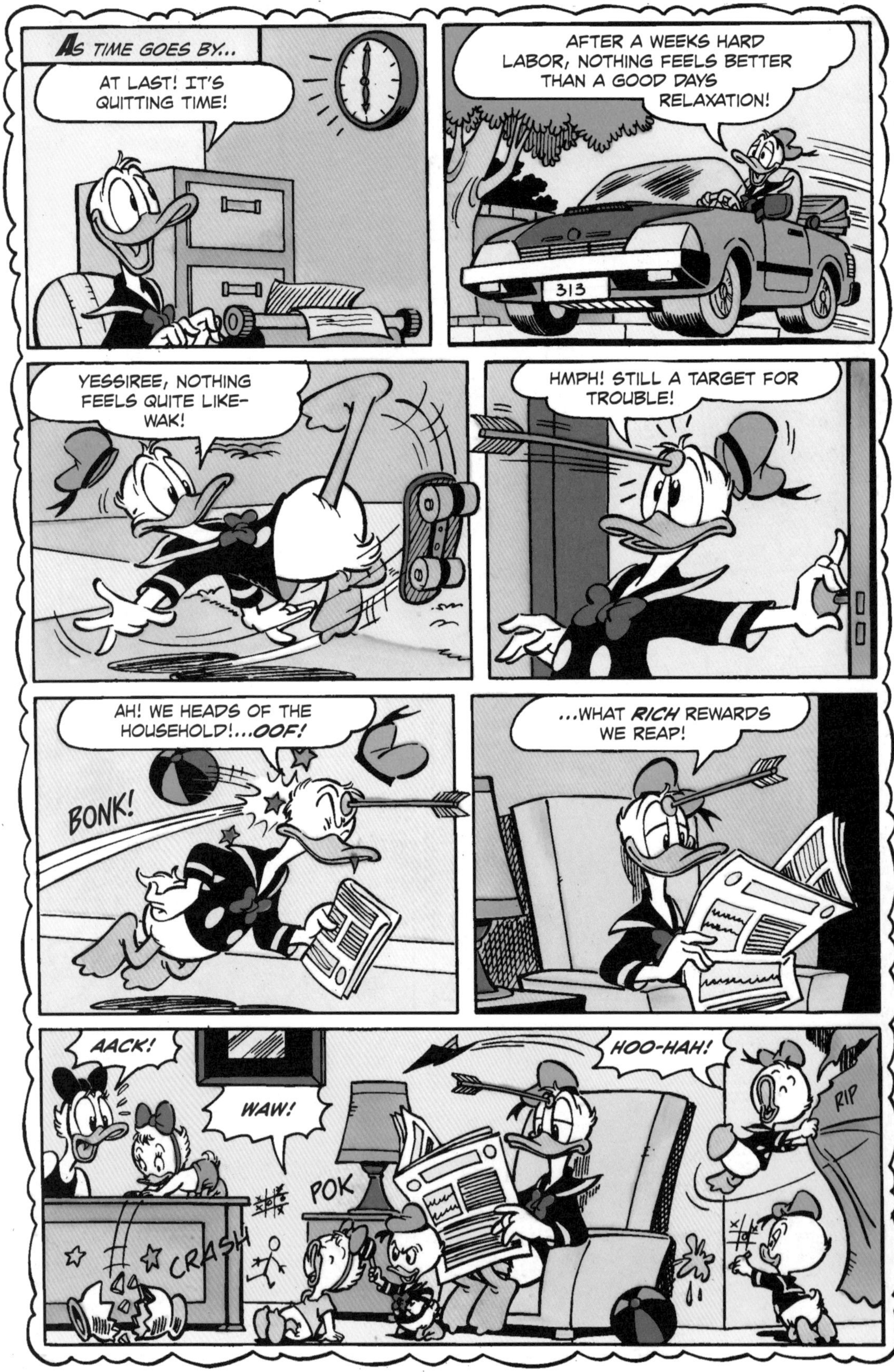
AS TIME GOES BY...
AT LAST! IT'S QUITTING TIME!
AFTER A WEEKS HARD LABOR, NOTHING FEELS BETTER THAN A GOOD DAYS RELAXATION!
313
YESSIREE, NOTHING FEELS QUITE LIKE-WAK!
HMPH! STILL A TARGET FOR TROUBLE!
AH! WE HEADS OF THE HOUSEHOLD!...OOF!
BONK!
...WHAT RICH REWARDS WE REAP!
AACK!
WAW!
HOO-HAH!
RIP
POK
CRASH

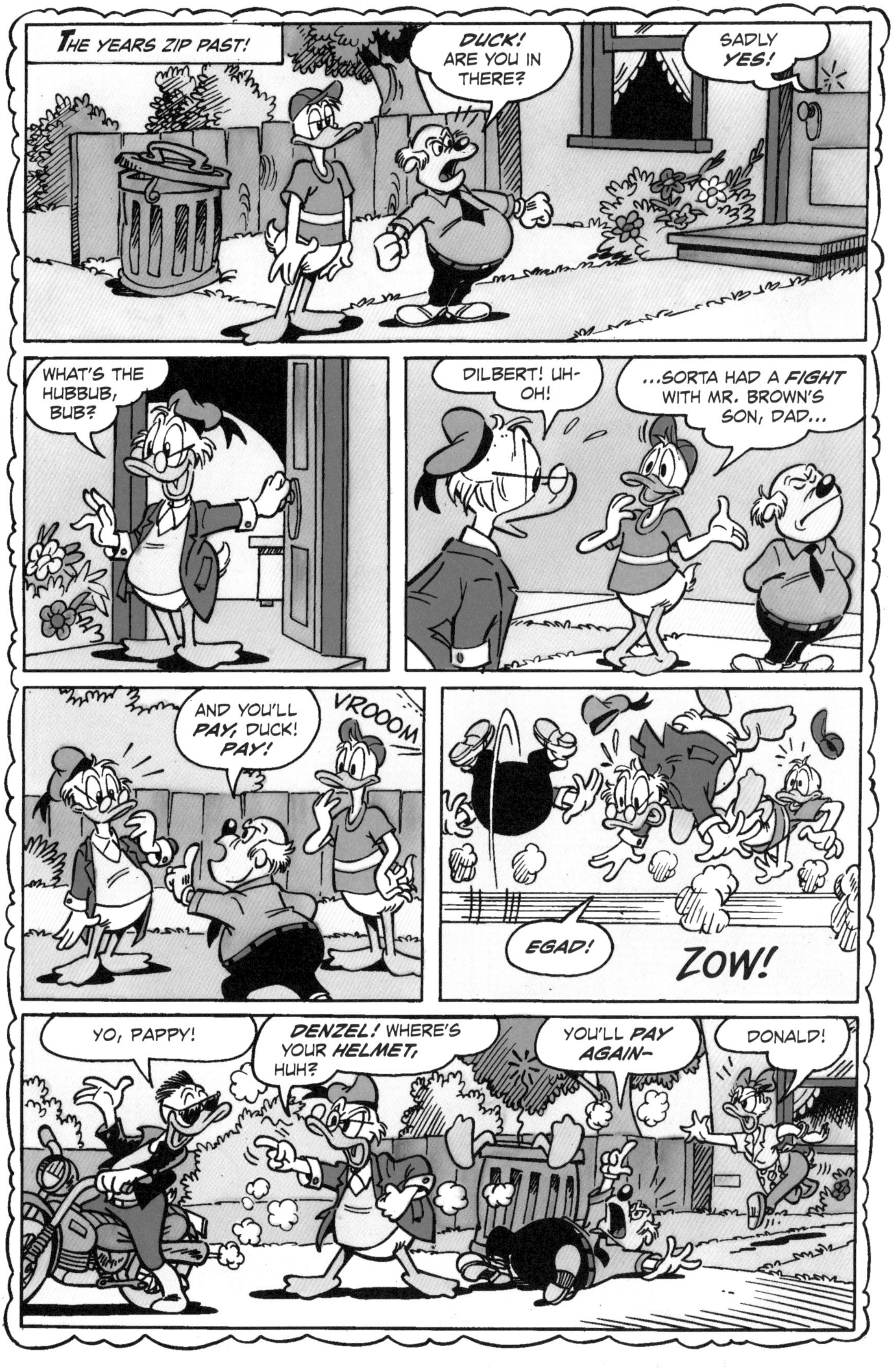
THE YEARS ZIP PAST!
DUCK! ARE YOU IN THERE?
SADLY YES!
WHAT'S THE HUBBUB, BUB?
DILBERT! UH-OH!
...SORTA HAD A FIGHT WITH MR. BROWN'S SON, DAD...
AND YOU'LL PAY, DUCK! PAY!
VROOOM
EGAD!
ZOW!
YO, PAPPY!
DENZEL! WHERE'S YOUR HELMET, HUH?
YOU'LL PAY AGAIN-
DONALD!

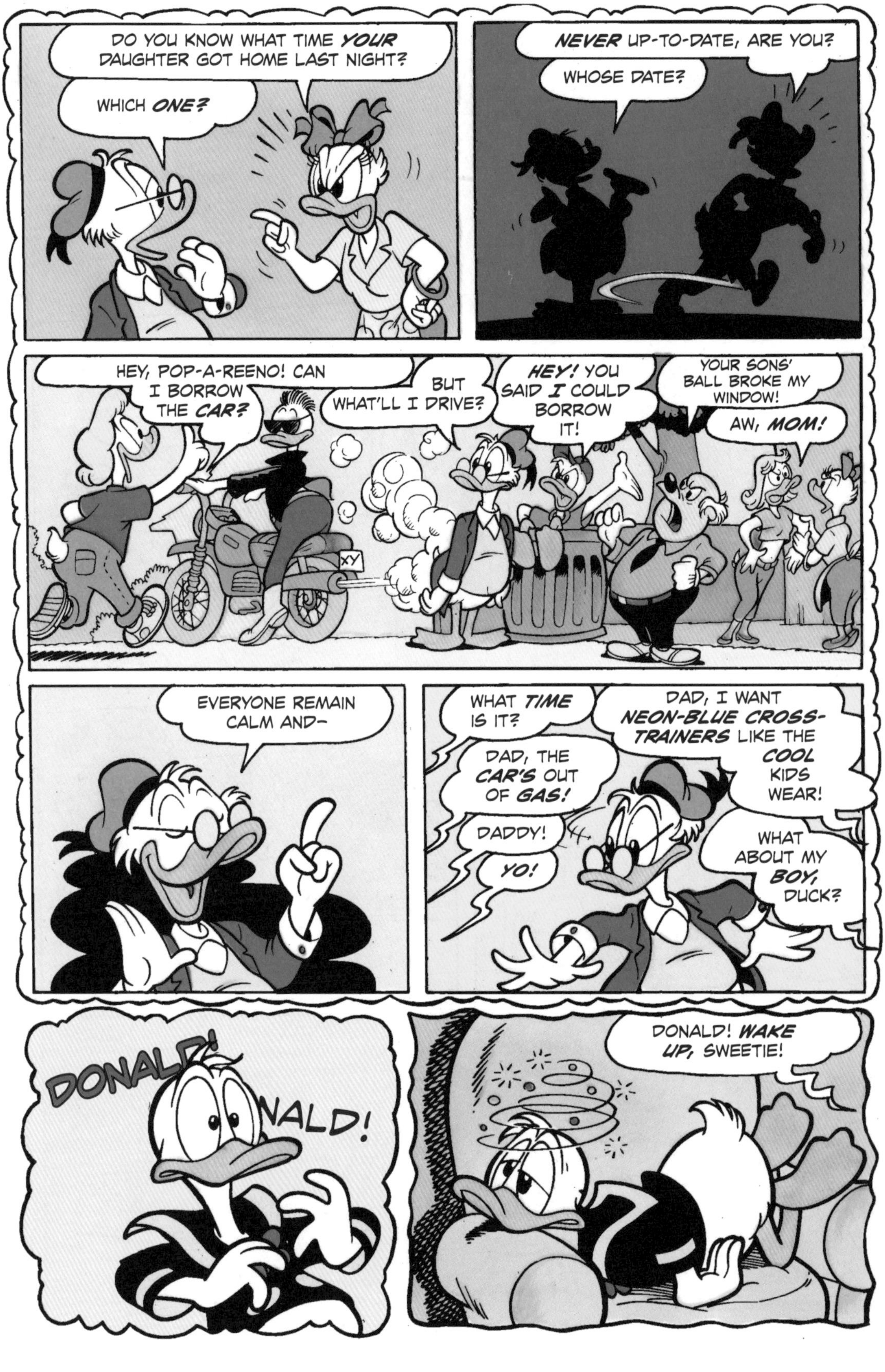
DO YOU KNOW WHAT TIME YOUR DAUGHTER GOT HOME LAST NIGHT?
WHICH ONE?
NEVER UP-TO-DATE, ARE YOU?
WHOSE DATE?
HEY, POP-A-REENO! CAN I BORROW THE CAR?
BUT WHAT'LL I DRIVE?
HEY! YOU SAID I COULD BORROW IT!
YOUR SONS' BALL BROKE MY WINDOW!
AW, MOM!
XY
EVERYONE REMAIN CALM AND–
WHAT TIME IS IT?
DAD, I WANT NEON-BLUE CROSS-TRAINERS LIKE THE COOL KIDS WEAR!
DAD, THE CAR'S OUT OF GAS!
DADDY!
YO!
WHAT ABOUT MY BOY, DUCK?
DONALD!
NALD!
DONALD! WAKE UP, SWEETIE!

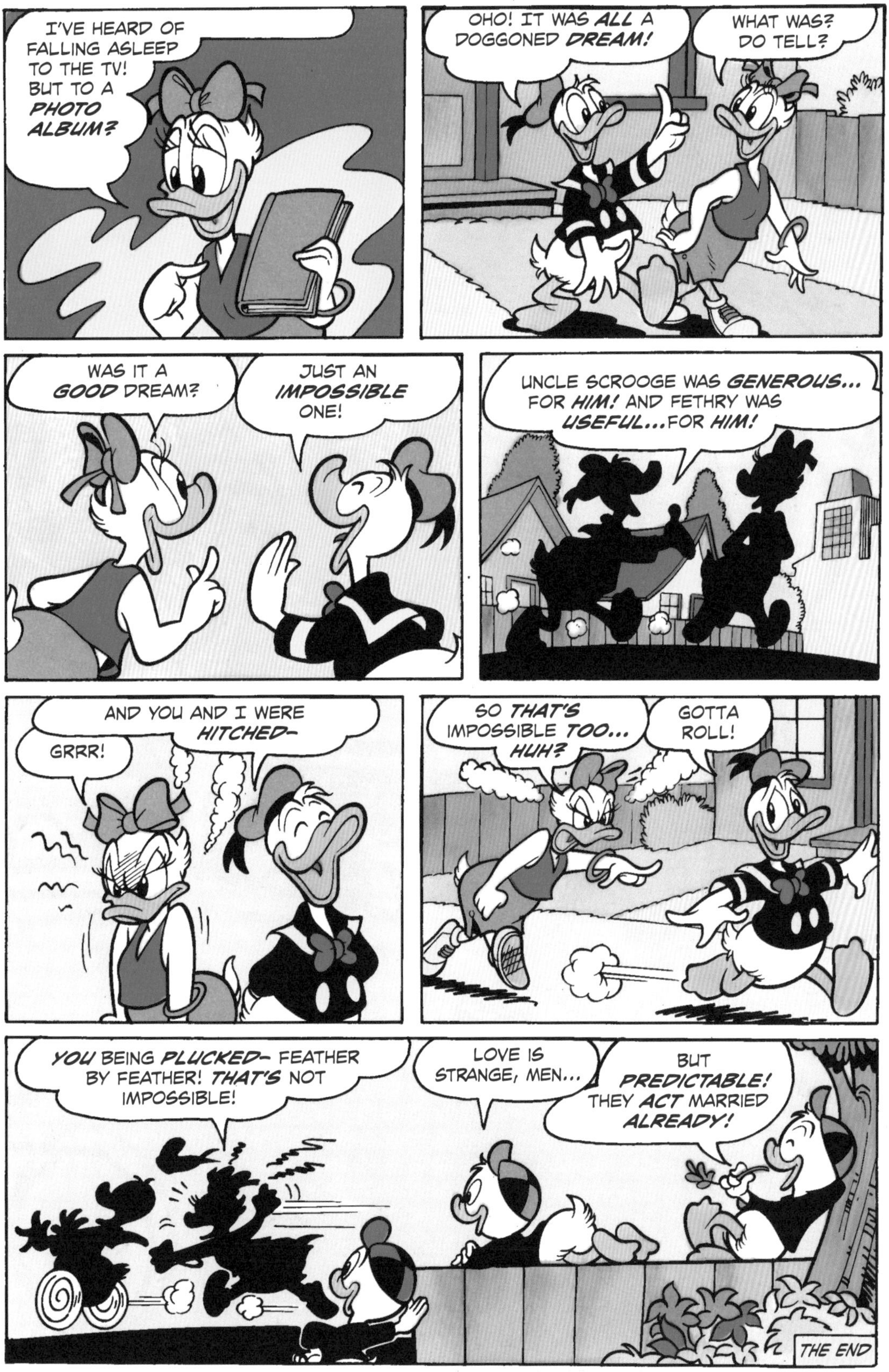
I'VE HEARD OF FALLING ASLEEP TO THE TV! BUT TO A PHOTO ALBUM?
OHO! IT WAS ALL A DOGGONED DREAM!
WHAT WAS? DO TELL?
WAS IT A GOOD DREAM?
JUST AN IMPOSSIBLE ONE!
UNCLE SCROOGE WAS GENEROUS... FOR HIM! AND FETHRY WAS USEFUL...FOR HIM!
AND YOU AND I WERE HITCHED–
GRRR!
SO THAT'S IMPOSSIBLE TOO... HUH?
GOTTA ROLL!
YOU BEING PLUCKED– FEATHER BY FEATHER! THAT'S NOT IMPOSSIBLE!
LOVE IS STRANGE, MEN...
BUT PREDICTABLE! THEY ACT MARRIED ALREADY!
THE END

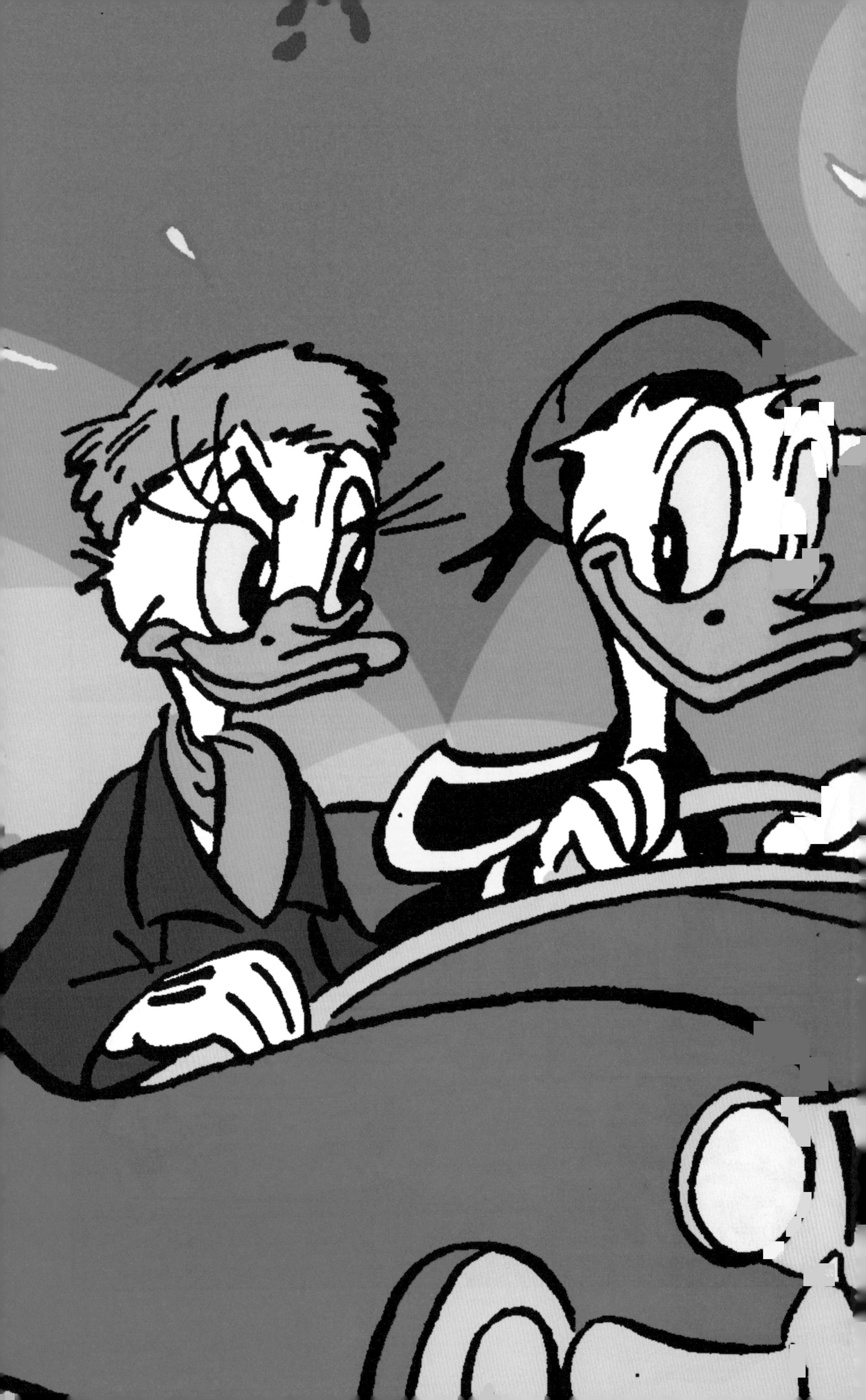

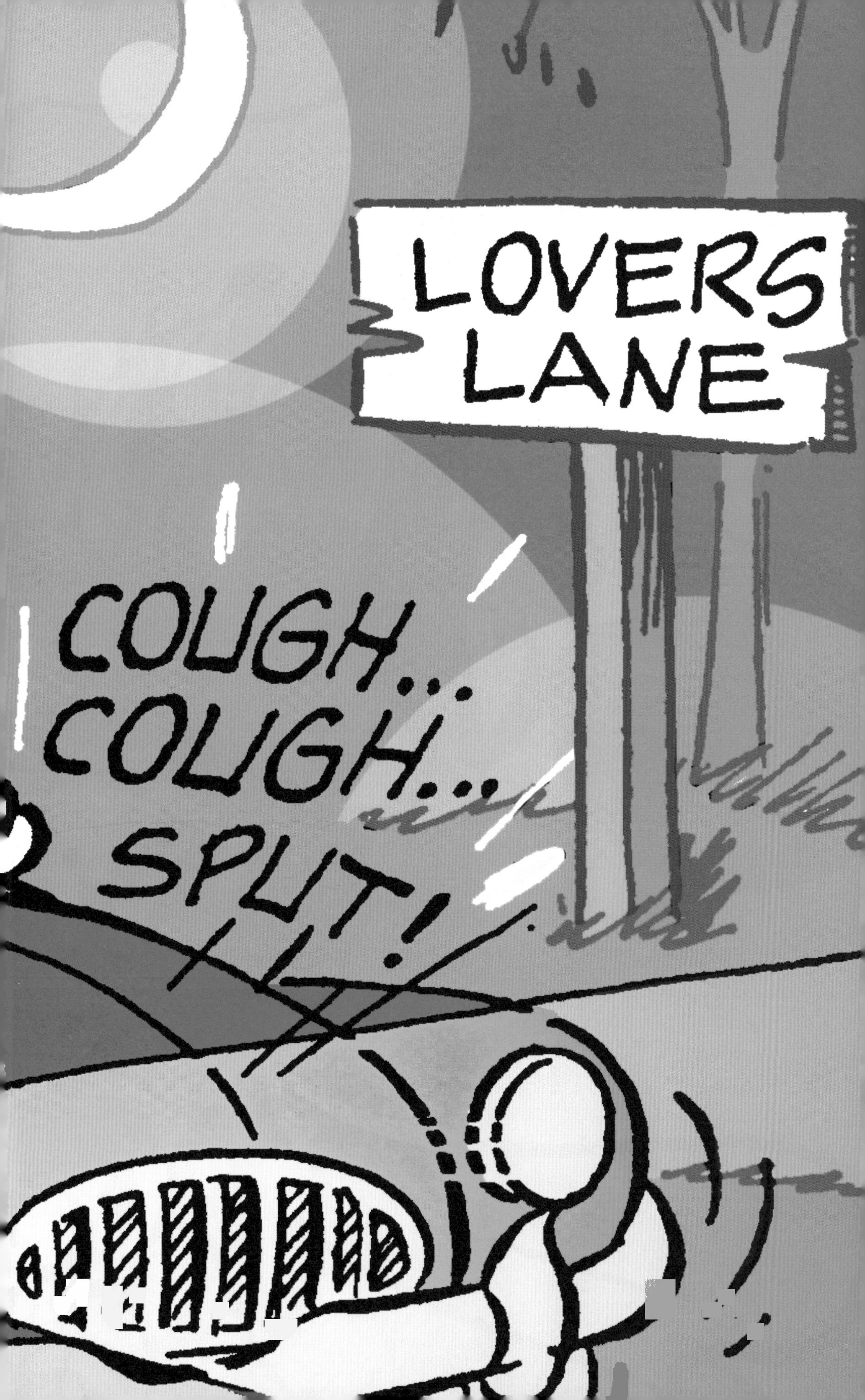
LOVERS LANE
COUGH... COUGH... SPUT!

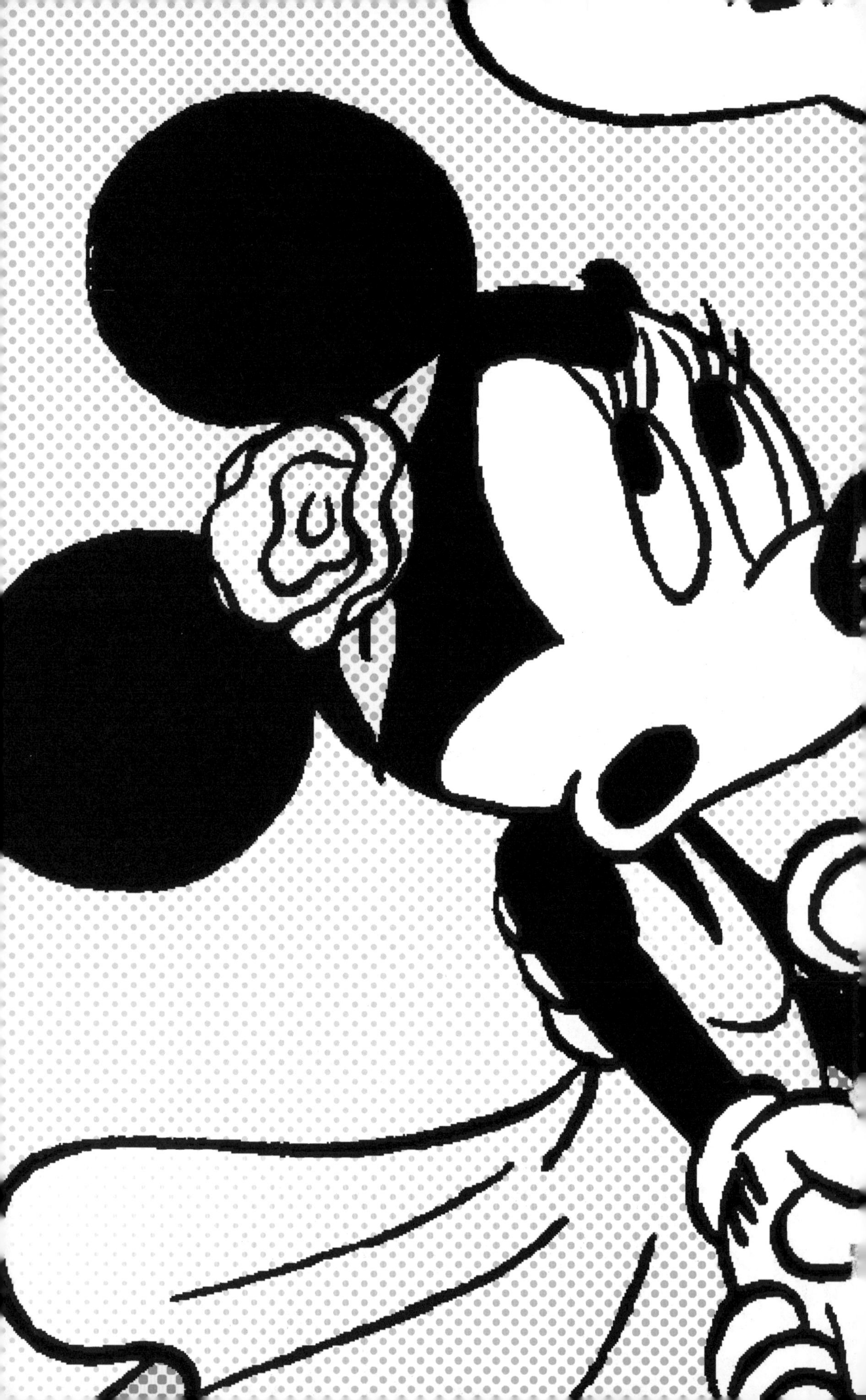

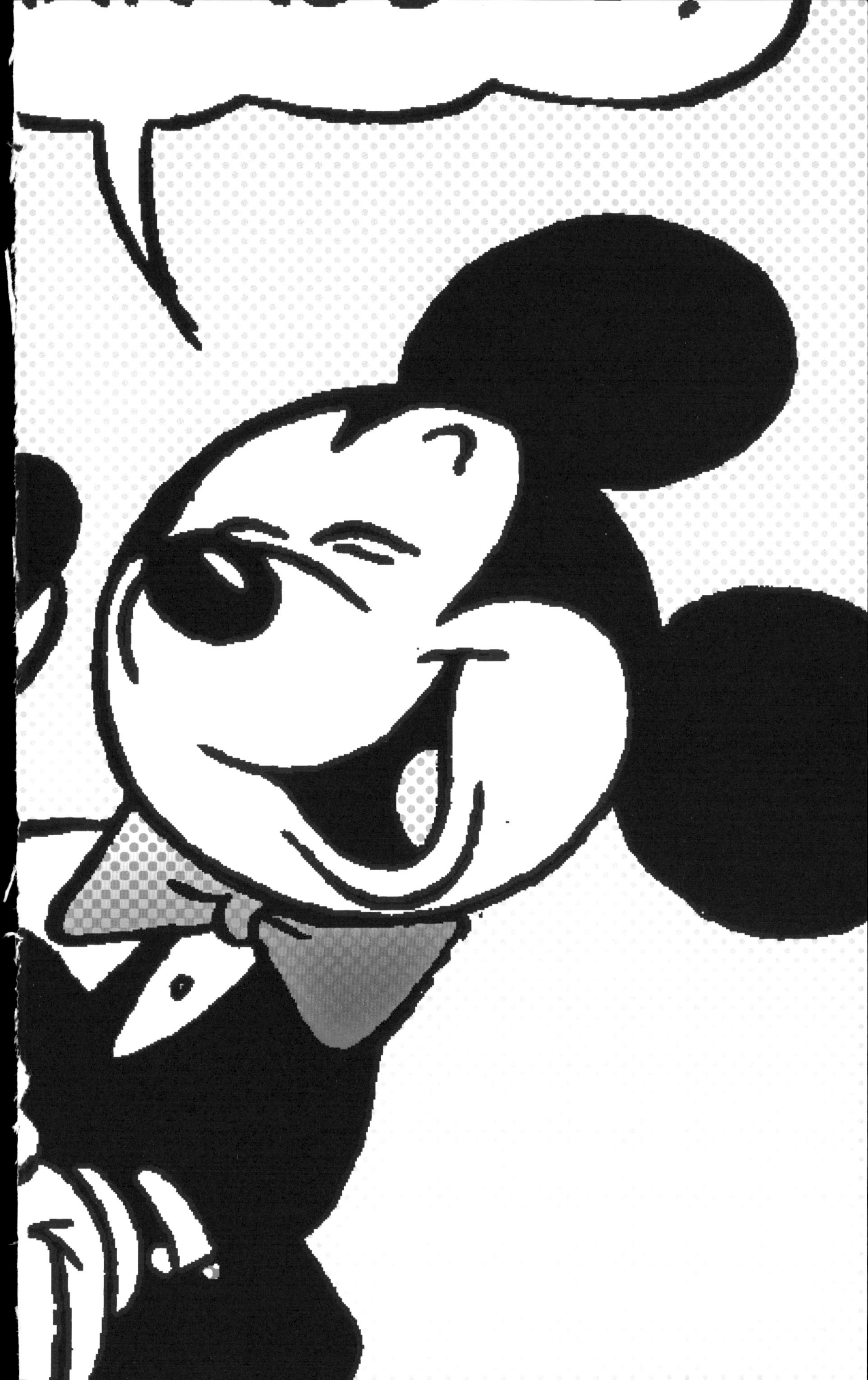

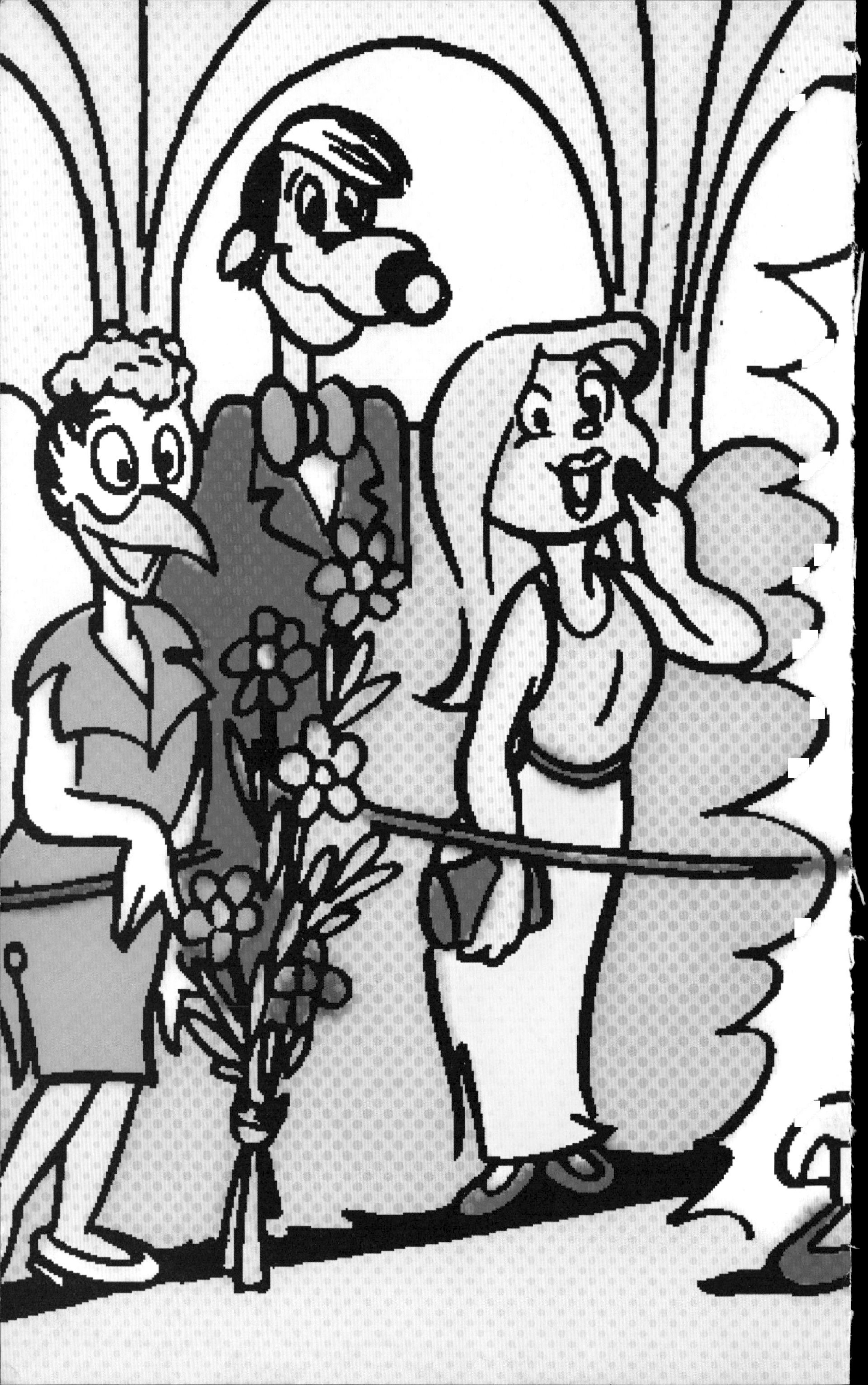